T0348176

ABOUT TRICIA STRINGER

Tricia Stringer is the bestselling author of the rural romances *Queen of the Road*, *Right as Rain*, *Riverboat Point* and *Between the Vines*, and two historical sagas in the Flinders Ranges series, *Heart of the Country* and *Dust on the Horizon*.

Queen of the Road won the Romance Writers of Australia Romantic Book of the Year award in 2013 and *Riverboat Point* was shortlisted for the same award in 2015.

Tricia grew up on a farm in country South Australia and has spent most of her life in rural communities, as owner of a post office and bookshop, as a teacher and librarian, and now as a full-time writer. She now lives in the beautiful Copper Coast region with her husband Daryl. From here she travels and explores Australia's diverse communities and landscapes, and shares this passion for the country and its people through her stories.

For further information go to triciastringer.com or connect with Tricia on Facebook or Twitter @tricia_stringer

A Chance *of*
Stormy Weather

Also by Tricia Stringer

Queen of the Road
Right as Rain
Riverboat Point
Between the Vines

THE FLINDERS RANGES SERIES
Heart of the Country
Dust on the Horizon

A Chance *of* Stormy Weather

TRICIA STRINGER

mira

First Published 2016
Second Australian Paperback Edition 2017
ISBN 978 1 489 24250 1

A Chance of Stormy Weather
© 2016 by Tricia Stringer
Australian Copyright 2016
New Zealand Copyright 2016

Except for use in any review, the reproduction or utilisation of this work in whole or in part in any form by any electronic, mechanical or other means, now known or hereafter invented, including xerography, photocopying and recording, or in any information storage or retrieval system, is forbidden without the permission of the publisher.

This book is sold subject to the condition that it shall not, by way of trade or otherwise, be lent, resold, hired out or otherwise circulated without the prior consent of the publisher in any form of binding or cover other than that in which it is published and without a similar condition including this condition being imposed on the subsequent purchaser.

All rights reserved including the right of reproduction in whole or in part in any form.

This is a work of fiction. Names, characters, places, and incidents are either the product of the author's imagination or are used fictitiously, and any resemblance to actual persons, living or dead, business establishments, events, or locales is entirely coincidental.

Published by
Harlequin Mira
An imprint of Harlequin Enterprises (Australia) Pty Ltd.
Level 13, 201 Elizabeth St
SYDNEY NSW 2000
AUSTRALIA

® and TM are trademarks of Harlequin Enterprises Limited or its corporate affiliates. Trademarks indicated with ® are registered in Australia, New Zealand and in other countries.

Cataloguing-in-Publication details are available from the National Library of Australia www.librariesaustralia.nla.gov.au

Printed and bound in Australia by McPherson's Printing Group

In memory of my much loved mum, Pat,
who was the quintessential country woman.

CHAPTER

1

Paula stretched lazily under the fluffy quilt. Her feet reached the chill at the bottom of the bed and at the same moment her hands found the empty space beside her. It too was cold. She opened her eyes. He was gone. She curled herself into a ball, savouring the memory of their lovemaking, and with the tip of her finger traced the dent in the pillow where his head had been.

A grey blur shot across her hand.

"Arrrgggh!" Paula's scream echoed around her in the empty room. She lurched back, flinging out her arm and knocking the bedside table. The old lamp teetered for a moment. She grabbed at it but it was too late. It toppled over the edge and crashed to the floor, shattering.

"Ohh!" She hoped it wasn't a family heirloom.

Clutching the quilt, she rolled back and scanned the bed. Had she really seen something or was it just her imagination?

The phone rang, interrupting her inspection. She reached out and pulled the handset to her ear.

"Hello darling." Her mother's voice sounded so close even though she was half the country away in Sydney.

"Hello Mum." Paula gave Dan's pillow one more wary glance.

"Did I wake you? You sound tired. I suppose Daniel is at work already."

"I'm awake, and yes," Paula hated the way her mother called him Daniel, "Dan is at work."

"How was the trip? We're all missing you. Is everything okay there?" Paula didn't bother to reply. Her mother had a habit of firing questions and not really listening to the answers. "I've got wonderful news, darling." The excitement in her mother's voice rang a little alarm bell in Paula's head. She didn't always share her mother's view of what was wonderful. Like the time four days before the wedding when Dan had just arrived in Sydney. They hadn't seen each other for a month and besides wanting him all to herself they had a long list of wedding jobs to discuss. Her mother had organised a large surprise welcome party with extended family and close friends. There was no escape given that the evening event was at her parents' home.

"Yes, Mum?" Paula didn't feel confident.

"Your father is taking some time off." Her mother's voice rose. "And we're coming to visit you."

Paula sat straight up in the bed. Her father was a company director who rarely took holidays. "When?" The question came out in a high-pitched squeak.

"I told Dad you'd be excited. We'll be there in two weeks. We're going to hire one of those four-wheel drives. He's always wanted one but I can't see the need for it in Mosman. Anyway, we're getting a trailer and loading up all the things you wanted sent over as well as the wedding presents. It will save organising a removalist and we'll get to see your new home."

Paula flopped back onto the pillows. She wasn't ready for this. She was looking forward to finally having Dan to herself. She didn't want her parents coming to take over and pass judgement on her new life, at least not until she understood it better herself.

Something moved on the window ledge. Paula blinked. She sat up again and pulled the quilt around her. The room was freezing and the cold nipped at her nakedness. She looked carefully at the ledge. Nothing.

"Paula? Are you still there, darling?"

"Mum, it's kind of you both, but there's not that much to freight over." She tried madly to think of a way to deter her parents. "Dan will still be working long hours and I'm not organised for visitors yet."

"We're not visitors, darling, we're family. You don't have to make a fuss for us, and your father knows Daniel will be busy but he wants to get a feel for what that new husband of yours gets up to on the farm. He likes to understand what you girls are involved in."

Yes, thought Paula, but he had a habit of getting too involved and trying to take over.

"What kind of food are you eating? Is there something you'd like me to bring? I hope you're taking care of yourself. You've got a man to feed now, you know."

"Mum, we've only just arrived. I don't know what we're going to eat but I am quite capable of cooking."

"Of course you are. But you know how you can be forgetful about food." Paula cringed at her mother's reference to the dark days after her breakup with Marco when her appetite had left her. That was all behind her now. She'd met Dan and well and truly laid the ghost of her previous relationship to rest.

"I'm fine, Mum. I can manage…"

"Of course you can." Her mother cut in. "Anyway, darling, I must fly. Susan is picking up your photos today and Alison and the children are coming over. We're going to look at all the pictures and the DVD and repack all your wedding gifts. Dad and I should be able to bring most of them with us."

Paula had a momentary pang of jealousy as she imagined her mother and her two older sisters poring over her wedding photos and looking again at the gifts that she and Dan had seen so briefly.

"Are the photos ready? That was quick."

"Friends can always pull strings. I wish you weren't so far away, darling." Her mother's tone was more regret than complaint. "Never mind, your father and I will be with you in two weeks. Now, I really must go and prepare a nice little lunch for the girls. Best love, darling."

The phone clicked and Paula hung up with a mixture of relief and dread. One of the bonuses of marrying Dan was that they now lived in rural South Australia, a long way from Paula's previous life.

Images of their wonderful wedding in Sydney replayed in her head. Everything had gone so well, despite her mother's fears that it couldn't possibly be arranged so quickly. To Paula, it had all been magical. She and Dan had spent three beautiful nights at a Darling Harbour hotel, which would have extended to four or five if it hadn't been for the urgent call from Dan's aunt, Rowena. The rain had come, their working man was injured and Dan was needed on the farm.

From the first time the date had been suggested Paula had the impression that Rowena Woodcroft hadn't thought April a good time for a wedding, but Dan had been reassuring and they'd gone ahead. He had warned Paula several times that farming was unpredictable and plans often had to change. If Tom hadn't been injured they would have stayed two more nights before flying back to South

Australia. She'd been disappointed, of course, but at the same time excited to check out her new home and officially start married life on the farm.

She rolled over and looked at the room. Their bedroom, Dan and Paula's, Mr and Mrs Woodcroft. It was her wedding present from Dan. The rest of the house needed lots of work, but he had renovated this room ready for her arrival. He had chosen a sky blue for the walls and painted the door and the skirtings white. The curtains were a blue-and-white damask print. Paula would have liked soft filmy scrim behind, instead of the plain pull-down blind. Perhaps she could add that later.

Last night they had arrived home well after the late autumn sun had set. Dan had given her a quick tour of the house but it was cold, dark and sparsely furnished, and most rooms needed work. Quickly they had retreated to the haven of their bedroom.

Paula had been impressed at the effort Dan had put into making the room habitable, but was easily distracted by the joys of having him to herself, in their very own home, in their brand-new bed. She trailed her fingers slowly down the fabric of the bedhead. Goosebumps tingled across her skin and she smiled to herself.

Bother her mother for wanting to come so soon. This old house was not ready for visitors. Dan had lived with his Aunt Rowena in his parents' house before the wedding. The house he and Paula had moved into once belonged to his grandparents, but it hadn't been lived in for years. It would take a lot of work but they were looking forward to making it their own.

Paula looked over the clothes they had left scattered on the floor to their cases, still standing just inside the door where they'd dumped them last night. Hers had developed a fluff ball on the handle. She looked again. The fluff ball moved. It zoomed down the case and zipped across the floor where it disappeared from her sight under the bed. She jumped up in the middle of the bed, pulling the quilt with her.

"Aggh!" she screeched to the empty room. "A mouse."

She pressed her lips together and looked around. There was no one to hear her. Dan had told her on the drive to the farm that he would be off first thing on the tractor and in a paddock some distance from the house. Goodness knows when she would see him next.

She looked at her case. No more fluff balls. Paula told herself she wasn't actually scared of the mouse – after all it was only one small creature – but she didn't like the idea of it climbing over her things.

She got off the bed, dragging the quilt with her, and reached for her case. She took a firm grip on the handle, snatched it up, swung around and flung it onto the bed. At the same time a small, grey fluff ball whizzed across the sheets. The case landed, smack, right on top.

Paula's hand flew to her mouth and she shuddered. Now there would be squashed mouse all over the lovely new sheets. She stood in the cold room, still draped in the quilt, and glared at the case.

"Welcome to life down on the farm, Mrs Woodcroft," she muttered. "Lesson number one. How to get rid of any mice you accidentally kill, while unpacking your jeans and knickers."

Carefully, she lifted one end of the case and peered underneath. Nothing. She grabbed hold of the other end and slowly began to lift. The mouse shot out across the bed. Paula screamed and jumped back, tangled herself in the quilt and landed in a heap on the floor. Thankfully the quilt and the mat protected her bare behind from the cold polished floorboards. She looked around for the mouse. Then she heard the voice. It was male and was coming from somewhere inside her house.

Paula forgot about fresh clothes and grabbed the things she had worn yesterday. A quick shake ensured they harboured no feral surprises before she hurried to pull them on. Who could be here? She'd thought she was alone.

She looked around frantically for something to protect herself. Behind the door was a broom. She picked it up and, holding the brush end in front of her like a shield, she moved into the passage. The floorboards creaked under her feet and she froze. The male voice spoke again from the other end of the house.

Despite squeaking with every step, and keeping a wary eye out for more mice, Paula attempted to tiptoe along the passage to the door that separated the bedrooms from the back of the house. It was a heavy swinging door and it groaned softly as she slowly pushed it open. There was no one ahead of her in the passage that continued to the back door and no one to her right where the passage narrowed and led to the bathroom and laundry.

"I'm here, Dan, I'll check it out." A female voice crackled from the kitchen. With a thumping heart Paula turned left and stepped into the room. There was an old wooden table and six assorted chairs, but no people.

"Okay, I'll be home for lunch."

Paula recognised Dan's voice. She looked behind the door at the gleaming new fridge and then her gaze lifted higher to the small black box with a handpiece attached by a cord and the number eighteen illuminated on its green screen, which perched on top of the fridge.

"The bloody two-way radio." Paula gritted her teeth, reached up and snapped it off. Relieved that she wasn't about to be attacked, she turned to peruse the kitchen.

It was a long room. The floor was covered in grimy linoleum that curled at the edges and the walls were yellowed from years of smoke from the wood oven. With her back to the passage door she'd entered by, she realised there were two more doors along the wall to her left. One led into the lounge and at the other end was another door with a stained glass inlay at the top that looked like it would open to the outside. The wall at the opposite end to where she stood was nearly all bay window, with a tattered curtain which failed to block out the weak morning light. The other long wall was taken up with cupboards, sink, an old stove and an even older wood stove. Paula could see an assortment of dishes where Dan must have made himself some breakfast. In the corner, between the stove and the fridge, was the door to the large pantry.

Paula reached forward and pushed the pantry door open. A grey blur shot out between her feet. She yelped, jumped backwards and spun around swinging the broom in search of the mouse.

"Paula? Are you all right?" Dan's Aunt Rowena barged through the passage door and walked straight into the end of Paula's broom. She staggered backwards into the wall.

"Rowena! I'm sorry." Paula directed the older woman to a chair. "I was chasing a mouse. There seem to be a few of them in the house."

"You'd have to be a damn good shot to get one with a broom," Rowena muttered.

Paula propped the offending weapon behind the door. Her brief meetings with Rowena had left her with the feeling that Dan's aunt didn't really approve of her. She was a tall woman with a sharp pointy noise and arched eyebrows that gave the impression she was always asking a question. Her fading fair hair was streaked with hints of grey and was neatly cut at chin length. Today, she was classically dressed in denim jeans, a chambray shirt and sleeveless navy jacket.

Both Dan's parents were dead and Rowena had taken on the role of his mother. Not that she fussed over him, but she was his only living relative that Paula knew of and was clearly an influence. Now here was the dishevelled new bride attacking her with a broom.

"I told Dan this place wasn't habitable." Rowena had regained her breath and glared around the kitchen. "You could still come and live at the new house with me until this place is ready. I wouldn't get in your way."

Paula had stayed at the 'new' house when she had first visited the farm several months earlier. She recalled feeling that it very much belonged to another woman, even though Rowena had been away in Adelaide that weekend. Paula knew she wouldn't feel comfortable there.

"We'll be fine, really, Rowena. There just seem to be a few mice."

"A few!" Rowena snorted. "I wouldn't be surprised if we ended up with a plague. In the few days Dan and I were away from the place the mice have multiplied considerably. They're around everywhere, in the sheds, on the roads. My house is pretty well mouse-proof, but I don't know how you'll keep them out of here."

Paula looked around nervously. She thought of the Black Death when she heard the word 'plague'. Surely Rowena was exaggerating.

Rowena stood up. "The two-way is off." She turned it back on. "Dan has been trying to call you. He'll be here for lunch around midday."

"Oh, food." Paula glanced at her bare wrist. In her rush to dress she hadn't put on her watch. She had no idea what the time was but her stomach felt empty. She hadn't eaten since they'd stopped for a quick meal at a fuel station on the way from the city the night before.

"I've brought some things with me to help out till you can get into town, but I'm not bringing them in until we see about getting rid of these mice and keeping them out. They'll ruin the food in a flash." Rowena headed into the pantry. "We'll start in here."

Paula followed and wrinkled her nose at the smell. There was evidence of mice everywhere. Anything in glass or tin was okay, but some of the plastic containers bore chew marks and mouse droppings trailed everywhere. Packets of biscuits were partly destroyed and flour mingled with sugar in pools dotted with mouse turds that gave the impression of chocolate sprinkles. They took everything out and threw away the damaged packets and their contents.

"What a terrible waste." Paula tossed the last of the packets into the almost full garbage bag and brushed her hands together.

"Stinking little rodents, shit and pee everywhere." Rowena muttered. "Dan should have known better than to bother stocking up without mouse-proofing before he left."

Paula looked at Rowena in surprise. Dan's aunt had always appeared to be a proper, well-spoken woman. Where had that language come from? And how dare she criticise Dan? He had been so busy before the wedding, preparing for seeding and trying to make the house habitable. Where had Rowena been then?

"I suppose he ran out of time."

"Hmph!" Rowena turned back to the pantry door and bent down to inspect it. "I could probably find something in the shed. We need something to put across the bottom of this. The walls and floor are in good condition but there's a gap underneath the door. If we can close that off your food will be safe – as long as you keep the door shut."

Rowena straightened and looked from the pantry to Paula who knew how the poor door felt, not measuring up to the job.

"I think I can manage that." Paula snatched up the brush, turned back to the shelves and scrubbed harder. The scent of the pine disinfectant filled her nostrils until she could smell nothing else. She decided it had to be better than the sickening pong of mice.

Rowena returned from her search with a long rubber fitting for the bottom of the door and proceeded to attach it while Paula restacked the now sparkling shelves with the items that had not been contaminated. Finally the older woman was satisfied that the door would seal properly and they brought in the fresh food from the car.

Paula was dirty and tired and everything smelled of disinfectant. After dealing with the mouse-riddled pantry she had gone off the idea of food.

Rowena looked at her watch. "It's after twelve. I'll wash up and organise some lunch. Why don't you go and have a shower?"

It was more of a command than a question but Paula didn't argue. She dug out some clean clothes from the case, which lay where she'd left it in the middle of the unmade bed. She looked at the clock. Had it really only been three hours since she'd dreamily opened her eyes to the new day?

After an extensive search Paula deemed the bathroom to be mouse free. She studied the decor as she stripped off her clothes. Large black and white tiles covered the floor and smaller white tiles, crazed with age and sandwiched between greying mortar, went halfway up the wall where they met peeling white paint.

To Paula's delight there was an old pink bath with a shower over it. The bath was big and deep and apart from a few rust stains it looked to be in good condition. They didn't make them like this any more.

She stood in the bath and let the water pound down, washing the mouse grime from her skin. She imagined sharing the lovely deep bath with Dan. Then she remembered Rowena out in the kitchen. She would probably stay for lunch and Dan would eat and be off again. Paula wouldn't have him to herself till whenever he came home tonight.

At least she felt refreshed and her hunger had returned as she stepped lightly back to the kitchen. Lunch with Rowena wouldn't be so bad. She was a bit of a dragon but she was Dan's aunt, almost his mother really. Paula wondered how her own mother would get on with Rowena. The two women were both in their mid-fifties but had only met briefly at the wedding. Rowena had flown back to the farm the next day.

Paula smiled and opened the kitchen door to reveal the table set with a cloth, plates, cutlery and a small vase of flowers but there was no sign of Rowena. The sink was clean and a chopping board and some cutlery drained alongside. The smell of disinfectant still lingered in the air.

The outside door banged followed by two thumps. Paula turned as Dan poked his head into the kitchen.

"Hello, Sweet Pea." His smile lit up his face and Paula was ready to jump into his arms. He held his dirty brown hands up. "I'll just wash up."

She stood warmed in the afterglow of his presence. She loved it when he called her Sweet Pea. Normally she hated those cutesy names people called each other but Dan had called her 'P' instead of Paula right from the start. When they became lovers he had changed it to his 'Sweet Pea'.

His head appeared around the door again. "Rowena was just heading off. She said to say she'd talk to you later about mouse-proofing the house. Sounds like you've had a busy morning." He looked closely at her then at the table. "Are you going to daydream or get my lunch? Rowena said there was plenty in the fridge."

Paula opened the fridge and discovered a plate of sandwiches and a small bowl of freshly cut fruit salad. Rowena had been busy while Paula had been de-mousing in the shower. Perhaps she had been hasty with her uncharitable thoughts about Dan's aunt. The mice were being dealt with, Dan was home and they were alone. She felt refreshed and now here was lunch already prepared.

Paula hummed to herself. Married life down on the farm was wonderful.

*   *   *

Rowena Woodcroft brushed a wisp of hair from her eyes. The car slid sideways and she eased back on the accelerator to edge it around a large muddy puddle that had spread across the track. She knew every inch of the way along the race, a dirt track fenced on either side that ran through the property connecting the two houses. She'd lived on this piece of land all her life with the exception of a few years away at boarding school and some time at business college. Now it was her entire life.

She'd lived with her parents in the old house and stayed on there alone after they retired to a nearby seaside town. Then, when Dan's mother, Amanda, had died, Rowena had given up her job in town and moved into the new house to care for her dear brother, Daniel, and young Dan. Now she was on her own again. She sighed. That puddle was getting worse and would be difficult to pass if they had more rain. It needed filling. She made a mental note to tell Dan. Not that he would have time to do it at present. He would be working flat out and would also have to do without Tom's help for a few more days.

Trust young Tom to injure himself at this critical time of the year. Blasted football. Rowena loved the sport but injuries meant time and money on the land. Dan used to play too but had stopped after a knee reconstruction had kept him from farm work half of the winter four years back. That's when they'd first employed Tom.

He had been just sixteen and most unhappy at school. His parents were decent people who barely scratched a living doing odd jobs in the district. They were pleased for Tom to get regular paid work. He'd turned out to be a hard worker with an intuitive feel for the tasks Dan gave him. He had developed good practical skills, useful on a farm, and Rowena had grown to like the lad.

With Dan lovesick over Paula, Rowena had recently come to rely on Tom more to do some of the tasks about the place she couldn't tackle. The car bounced over a rut as she took the corner into her yard without slowing. Rowena cursed as she heard her shopping spill from one of those dratted plastic bags in the back seat. She'd left in such a hurry her sturdy hessian carry bags were at home on the bench. She longed for the old days when you brought your shopping home in boxes and brown paper bags supplied by the shop. Plastic shopping bags were the bane of modern life.

She had planned to be home much earlier. By the time she unpacked the shopping and grabbed a bite to eat she'd be late for the Children's Hospital Auxiliary meeting. She hated lateness in others and was always on time herself. If she hadn't stopped to help Paula clean up the kitchen she'd have had plenty of time. It really was too bad of Dan to take his new bride to live in that old house before he'd had a chance to make it liveable. Paula was a city girl and used to all the comforts and excitement of life in Sydney.

Rowena frowned and flicked at the wayward piece of hair again. This wedding had all happened far too quickly. Dan had hardly been out with a woman in more than a year and suddenly he'd come home from a holiday in Sydney saying he'd found the girl he wanted to marry.

Rowena sighed again as she pulled the car in under the carport. She hoped it was not going to be history repeating itself. Paula was a wispy little thing. Certainly pretty, her straight fair hair bounced to a stop just under her chin and her hazel eyes sparkled. Rowena could see why Dan had been attracted, but she had a nervous quality that was a concern.

Rowena didn't think she had what it took to be a farmer's wife. Then there were a few loose ends Dan really should have sorted out before he committed to another relationship. But he had made his decision without consulting Rowena. She just prayed it wouldn't cause him grief. Heaven knew they'd had enough of that in this family.

The two-way radio crackled and she paused to listen as a male voice spluttered into the car. It wasn't Dan or a close neighbour so she tuned out and opened the car door. *Look at the time, nearly one o'clock.* She'd have to rush or she'd be very late for the meeting.

* * *

Paula turned on the light in the bedroom to hang the last of her clothes in the wardrobe. It had been late afternoon before she'd made it back to the bedroom to tidy up and now the day was grey and the air chilly. She paused. Had she heard a vehicle? She listened but all was quiet. A world without constant background sound would take some getting used to. She closed the wardrobe door and shoved her case under the bed, keeping a cautious eye out for mice.

She stopped again. There was definitely a vehicle nearby. This time she hadn't imagined the sound. It was probably Rowena returning to show Paula how to mouse-proof the house. She said she'd call back after she'd been to her meeting.

Paula left the bedroom and crossed to the lounge, casting a quick eye over the sparse furnishings. Rowena was so officious. Paula wanted to make sure everything was in its place before Dan's aunt returned.

She pushed open the door into the kitchen.

"Aggghh!" She clutched at her chest. There was an old man standing in her kitchen.

He turned towards her. "What did you do that for?" he squawked in an offended voice. "Are you trying to give me a heart attack?"

Paula's heart rate slowed slightly and she looked at the old man. He was thin and frail and looked to be at least ninety. He was dressed in brown pinstriped trousers held up by suspenders over a white shirt. Somehow she didn't think he was likely to be a deranged murderer.

The door from the passage flew open and Rowena walked in with an armload of gear.

Doesn't anybody knock in the country? Paula thought.

"Hello, Uncle Gerald. Have you come to meet Paula?" Rowena put her bags on the kitchen table.

"What?"

"Have you met Paula?" Rowena repeated in a louder voice.

"Is that her name? Orla? She screamed at me. Gave me quite a start."

He glared at Paula and she glared back. He was the one standing uninvited in her house.

"Paula." Rowena shouted and turned to Paula. "This is Uncle Gerald. Perhaps you could put the kettle on." She began to unpack her supplies.

Paula switched on the kettle, wishing she had her coffee machine and wondering if Dan had any more weird relatives tucked away.

Uncle Gerald settled himself at the table and stared out the window. "Chance of stormy weather."

"Do you think?" Rowena cast a gaze towards the glass, shook her head and stepped back to survey the kitchen table. It was partly covered with steel wool, bits of wood, gap filler, mouse traps and bacon.

Paula picked up the bacon.

"Bacon rind is one of the best things I know for catching mice." Rowena selected one of the boxes of mouse traps and began to open it. "Mice love it and it's difficult to get off the trap without setting it off."

"Peanut paste."

Both women looked at Uncle Gerald.

"Peanut paste is all I use. Gets the little buggers every time."

Paula shuddered and dropped the bacon packet back onto the table. She made a cup of tea for Uncle Gerald. After a bit of shouting she worked out he had a lot of sugar and no milk in his tea.

Rowena declined Paula's offer of a cup. "We'd better get this done. I've got other jobs I should be doing."

Paula felt every bit the nuisance she so obviously was and fell into step behind Rowena. They went over every room in the main part of the house closely followed by Uncle Gerald, who made all kinds of comments that had nothing to do with the job in hand.

Paula was amazed at the tiny gaps Rowena pointed out.

"Surely that's too small a hole for a mouse." Paula bent closer as Rowena used steel wool to plug a spot at the end of a piece of skirting that was the size of her little finger.

"Mice can squeeze through the smallest space. We'll have to plug up everything we can find." Rowena continued to give instructions and Paula followed them. She was alarmed to think how easily the little rodents could infiltrate her home. In the case of keeping out mice she had to concede that the country woman knew her stuff.

At least Paula now knew every inch of her new home and she was already conjuring up decorating ideas. There were three bedrooms, a laundry and bathroom down one side of a long passage and the large lounge and kitchen/dining down the other. The passage was divided from the back rooms of the house by a large wooden swing door. Paula loved the way it gave a soft groan as it opened then swung back into place with a gentle whoosh behind her. It felt solid beneath her fingers and she hoped one day to strip the white paint from it to reveal the wood underneath, which she was sure would gleam with a varnish.

A verandah ran from the front door around the lounge and met the kitchen door on the other side. The verandah across the back of the house was enclosed. It housed the toilet at one end and a sleep-out at the other.

"You won't be able to keep the mice out of here as easily." Rowena peered at the offending back room. "But if you don't keep anything out here to attract them you should be all right."

Paula wasn't listening. She had been distracted by a collection of old furniture stacked in a corner of the sleep-out. There were a few possibilities there for her to explore. Uncle Gerald walked past and peered closely at the bric-a-brac.

"Whose things are these?" Paula asked.

Rowena glanced through the doorway. "Just cast-offs that no one wants. Dan should have cleared it out."

"Can I use them?" Paula watched Uncle Gerald drag out an old wicker chair.

"I can't imagine there'd be anything the slightest bit useful there, but help yourself." Rowena dismissed the room and then Paula. "Now I really must get home. I've been out all day, what with one thing and another. I'll leave you to get Dan's evening meal." She turned to the old man who was inspecting the chair closely. "Come on, Uncle Gerald, time you went home too."

He left the furniture and followed Rowena, pausing in front of Paula to hand her his empty cup. "Thanks, Orla."

"Hurry along, Uncle Gerald," Rowena commanded from outside.

Paula watched the old man shuffle towards the back door where he turned and gave her a wink before he set off along the cement path towards the old green car pulled up by the gate. Rowena was already crossing to her own car.

Paula said a feeble goodbye then stood to attention and saluted Rowena's departing back. She stifled a giggle. It was getting dark, perhaps it was time to investigate what she could whip up for dinner.

*   *   *

The pasta carbonara was gluggy and Paula was restlessly flicking television channels in front of a roaring fire when she heard the sound of Dan's ute. Her first day on the farm had been a long one and she was desperate to talk to Dan and feel his arms around her.

Living here was a total change from her previous life but she was excited by her new world and determined to embrace it. Even though she was twenty-eight, Paula was the baby and had always felt smothered and stifled by her family. She had met Dan at a time when her life was crowding in on her. Work had become a string of temp jobs and she hadn't been interested in relationships after the breakup with Marco. Dan had been a tall, rugged breath of fresh air and so different from the manipulative, smooth Marco.

She shook her head, physically trying to erase the memories of the past, and slipped into her jacket. The cold night air chilled her face as she walked across the yard towards the big shed. She could see Dan silhouetted by the interior lights of his ute parked just outside the huge doors. She hugged the jacket tightly to her body and wished she'd put on some trackpants as well.

She had nearly reached him when movement on the ground in front of the ute stopped her. A mass of little grey bodies swarmed around, caught in the glare of the headlights.

She clamped both hands over her mouth to strangle the scream of revulsion that erupted as a groan around her fingers. For a moment she stood, mesmerised by the sight. Then reality forced her to move. She was only wearing a skirt and slip-on shoes. The thought of the repulsive little creatures running up her bare legs propelled her into the ute beside Dan.

He looked up from the notebook he was writing in. "Hello, Sweet Pea. Where did you spring from?"

She flung her arms around him and buried her head in his shoulder, too breathless to speak. His clothes smelled earthy and there was another oily type of odour.

"Well this is a nice homecoming." He slipped his hands under her jacket. "We should have got married years ago."

"Mice," she mumbled into his shoulder.

He sat back a little and studied her in the dim light of the interior. "That wasn't the response I expected."

"They're everywhere, in the headlights, I could see them." She shuddered again. He put one arm around her and she nestled into his shoulder.

"They are certainly reaching nuisance proportions. Not a good sign for the season."

"Can't you get rid of them?"

"If only it was that easy." He hugged her again and smiled that wonderful smile that made her heart flutter. "Bit of a rough start to farm life for you, Sweet Pea."

"There was one in our bed this morning."

"Only one? I hope you dealt with it severely." He smiled and she relaxed. With Dan beside her she felt much braver.

"I don't mind sharing my bed with you, farm boy, but I draw the line at having to share with your critters as well. And who the heck is Uncle Gerald? You didn't warn me about him."

"Has he been here?"

"Walked straight into the kitchen without even a hello. I could have been naked."

Dan smiled rakishly, pulled her close and kissed her, a long slow kiss that sent shivers over her body.

"Come on," he whispered in her ear. "Let's go inside. I think I'm the only one who should see you naked."

"I don't want to walk. I've got bare legs," she wailed.

Dan laughed and drove the ute into the shed. He opened her door, bowed low and held out his arms. "Your servant, ma'am."

Paula's giggles turned to laughter punctuated with shrieks of alarm as he carried her back across the yard, sometimes threatening to drop her. The lights shone brightly from the house and in spite of his teasing she felt safe in his arms. She forgot all about mice and concentrated on the joy of having Dan to herself.

CHAPTER

2

"Dan, you've got to come home now!" Paula spoke into the two-way handset in an urgent whisper. "They're everywhere."

"I'll be there in about an hour. You'll have to manage until then."

"But, Dan..."

The two-way buzzed and went silent. Paula shoved the handset back on the fridge. She crept down the kitchen and checked the door leading to the outside. The seal was still firmly in place.

In the bay window her worried face was reflected back at her. She shivered and pulled the old curtain across. She told herself it was to keep out the chill but she knew she was also trying to hide the emptiness outside.

After only a few days in her new home she already loved the daylight view from this window, out across the long gradual slope of the valley. But she had not yet got used to the total blackness of the nights on the farm. It was so different from the constant light of Sydney.

The two-way crackled and she jumped. Another disembodied male voice gave orders to an unseen partner. This had been the first time she'd used the two-way radio. Dan had shown her how it worked and explained his call sign was 'Woodie'. Everyone needed a call sign so they knew whether to pay attention or not. He'd said they'd need to think of one for her but Paula didn't pursue it. She didn't like the two-way. Give her the privacy of her mobile phone any day. Just a pity it was useless here. She would have to change it to another carrier. Right now there were more important things to deal with.

She made herself a cup of tea and climbed onto the kitchen table. From this position she watched the room around her. She knew there were mice in here somewhere. So much for mouse-proofing the house. She was under siege.

She had been sitting in the lounge by the fire when the first clack from behind the wood basket had startled her. A mouse was still twitching, caught with the metal trap across its back. Paula had left it, hoping it would die quickly. She couldn't bear to touch the trap while the mouse was still moving.

Then there was a distant clack from the kitchen. She had traps set by the fridge, the stove and the outer door. To her horror they all had mice in them. She'd checked them after she'd prepared the evening meal only an hour ago. There had been no mice in the traps then. She wrapped the little bodies in newspaper, reset the traps and hurried to the bathroom to scrub her hands.

The flick of the light switch in the passage revealed several mice scattering along the passage floor from under the back door.

Paula clamped her lips together. She stretched up onto her toes and pressed against the wall, too frightened to move. The mice scurried in all directions and disappeared from sight. Now what would she do?

The back door didn't actually lead directly outside. It opened into the enclosed back verandah and the toilet was there. She would have to go out eventually. Cautiously she stepped forward on her toes, ready to run at the first sign of a mouse. There was a rubber seal along the bottom of the inner back door. She leaned down warily. It had little holes along the bottom of it. Chewed holes. And poking out from underneath she could see several little grey tails.

That's when she'd made a desperate dash back to the kitchen and called Dan on the two-way. Now she sat on the table awaiting his return. She didn't know what else to do.

There had been some difficult customers in her last job but she'd been able to manage them. She'd worked to impossible deadlines and coordinated huge events but this tide of little grey bodies had her beaten. She felt a twinge of panic.

A bang at the back door startled her and she slopped her tea.

"Paula!" Rowena called.

"Damn."

Rowena was through the kitchen door before Paula could get off the table.

"Are you all right?" Rowena watched Paula step gingerly to the floor. "What's the matter?"

"I'm fine, Rowena." Embarrassment replaced panic. Why couldn't it be Dan who had come to her rescue?

"I heard your call on the two-way. You have to realise Dan can't dash home for nothing. Tom was eating tea at the house when we heard your call. We thought something must have happened."

Paula looked beyond Rowena to see a young man grinning shyly behind her. He had roughly brushed dark curls and large brown eyes that he lowered under Paula's gaze. Great, someone else to witness her inability to cope.

"This is Tom March."

Tom said "G'day", then looked back at his feet.

Paula studied the gangly young man who was the reason for their honeymoon ending so abruptly. He'd injured himself at footy practice or something, Dan had said, and couldn't drive the tractor. He looked hardly more than a boy despite his height. He'd be taller than Dan. Rowena moved forward and revealed the rest of Tom. He wore a dark windcheater and blue jeans and Paula noticed his right foot was covered only in a footy sock.

"Should you be walking on that? I thought Dan said it was broken." She pulled out a chair for him.

"It's only a bit mangled…"

"It's not broken." Rowena cut him off and pushed the chair back under the table. "He'll be back helping Dan tomorrow. Now what was so urgent we've left our meal for it?"

Paula seethed. She hadn't asked Rowena to leave her meal. She hadn't asked her to come at all. Rowena had eavesdropped on her conversation with Dan. Silently, Paula made a vow not to use the two-way again, then she looked squarely at her visitor.

"I can't keep the mice out."

"Really, Paula, is this what the fuss is about? You will have to learn to deal with them. They're everywhere and this house is old. If it bothers you that much you know you can come and stay with me." Rowena glared at Paula, who was speechless.

The clack of another trap from beside the fridge punctuated the chilly air between them. They both turned to look.

Paula flung up her hands. "You see what I mean."

"You'll have to keep setting the traps."

"There's too many."

Another trap clacked.

"Your outer back door is the problem." Tom spoke quietly. He was still standing just inside the kitchen door. Both women looked at him. "It's old timber and the floor is rough cement, too many gaps. There are mice everywhere outside and once they get into that back porch they can get into the rest of the house through open doors or under them or any other little spot they can find. I've even seen them use each other to climb over."

Paula shuddered and he continued. "We had the same trouble at our place a few years back. My mum was terrified of mice, but the last plague we had made her real mad. My brother and I came home one day and she was in Dad's overalls and rubber boots with a piece of poly pipe whacking them on the head as they came under the back door. There was blood and guts everywhere. We had to replace the door quick smart and fix up the floor or she would have taken the poly pipe to us." He grinned.

Paula smiled back at him. He wasn't a particularly good-looking fellow. His grin revealed crooked teeth and his nose looked like it may also have met with an accident on the footy field sometime but there was something about the gentle way he spoke that made her feel as if he at least understood a little of how she felt.

"Well we can't do anything much about it at this hour," Rowena snapped.

"I could block off the back door for now," Tom said. "It would mean you would have to go outside through another door till we can fix this one. If your other doors are all sealed you should be okay."

"Could you?" Paula glanced down at the footy sock. "What about your foot?"

"Don't need that to hammer in a few nails."

"All right, Tom, what do you need?" Rowena suddenly accepted that something needed to be done and they might as well get on with it.

"There's some timber and bits up at the shed I can use."

"Come on then, I'll drive you. We don't want you wearing that foot out before you can get back to work." Rowena sailed out.

"Don't worry, if you can organise a new door and a bag of cement I'll fix it up for you." Tom gave a lopsided smile.

"Thank you, but Dan's so busy I don't know when that will be." Paula thought nervously of her parents' arrival in just over a week's time. Her mother was terrified of mice. Paula had always thought it a joke but she was beginning to understand how her mother felt.

"There's a big rain on the way. That could hold up seeding for a while." He smiled shyly again and Paula watched as he hobbled away. She shook her head. There had been no sign of rain when she had been outside before dark. She couldn't imagine it raining enough to keep Dan off the tractor.

Back in the kitchen, she emptied the traps again. The two-way crackled and she heard Rowena telling Dan to come in the front door as Tom was boarding up the back door, due to the mice.

Once again Paula seethed. Surely she could have told her own husband about the house. She smiled grimly to herself as she dropped another little body into the bin. Let Rowena tell him, at least that meant that Paula could avoid using that bloody two-way radio.

They were back from the shed in no time at all. Rowena waited in the car and Paula shivered inside the back verandah as Tom hammered some wood in place from the outside. It was cold in the unlined room.

Tom finished the job and called goodnight. Paula listened as he shuffled away and the sound of the vehicle faded into the distance. The house settled into silence. But not for long. A faint scratching sound came from outside.

She sprinted to the toilet. It was a shabby little room with no inner lining on the walls. She lifted her feet and watched the floor carefully for movement. Then from the distance came a long, low rumbling and the light flickered. What if the power went off? She would be alone in a dark house with who knows how many mice still running free. She made a frantic dash into the house to look for the torch.

She found one on the shelf in the laundry next to the bathroom. The new washing machine sat on the grey cement floor, a single monument to the twenty-first century. Surrounded by authentically distressed green-painted wooden cupboards and cement wash troughs, it looked out of place. The first time she'd come in to do a load of washing Paula had been relieved to find a working hot-water tap. There was still a space in the corner where Dan said there had been a copper for heating the water in his grandma's day. Paula flicked the switch on the torch and was relieved to see a strong beam of light. At least it worked.

A flash lit the dark sky beyond the old bubbled glass of the laundry window. Paula shut the laundry door.

The phone rang, the shrill sound echoing loudly from the kitchen. Surely it wouldn't be her mother again so soon.

"Hello?"

"Hello, Paula."

"Alison." Paula was relieved to hear her oldest sister's voice. Alison always understood how she was feeling without needing to pry. Susan was their middle sister and more like their mother, firing off lots of questions but never really listening to the answers.

"How are you, baby sister? Have you and Dan left the bedroom yet?" Alison's teasing was a welcome diversion from the mouse-infested house.

"He's a farmer, Alison. Even if I was the sex goddess herself I couldn't keep him from his tractor for that long."

"You'll have lots of time to tackle the redecorating then. What's the house like?"

Paula sat on a chair, tucked her legs up and hugged her arms in. "I love it. Dan has done the bedroom already but the rest will need some work." She decided not to mention the mice.

"He is capable of getting some priorities right then."

"Stop, Alison, you'll have me blushing."

"You! No way." There was a wailing sound in the background. "Oh, Oscar is awake again. He's got a cold, poor baby. Julian's still at the shop so I'll have to go." Alison and her husband, Julian, ran a successful import business, owned a beautiful home on Sydney's North Shore near their parents and had produced a girl and a boy, Isabelle and Oscar.

"Thanks for ringing, Alison." Paula tried not to let the disappointment sound in her voice. It was good to be talking to another human being, even if they were thousands of kilometres away.

"I've sent you an email."

Paula sank further into her chair. "My mobile and tablet don't work out here and Dan doesn't have a computer."

"That explains the message on your mobile when I try to ring. Anyway, doesn't matter. I wanted to let you know I did try to deter the parents from their trip." Alison was the mediator of the family, always trying to smooth the way. She knew Paula wanted time to adjust to her new life without her parents interfering. "At least you'll get your presents soon and Susan and I have included some extras." Oscar's cries were louder.

"Sounds intriguing. I hope Oscar is okay."

"He's had a temp so I'd better go. Just wanted to touch base before the parents arrived. Stand firm, won't you. I think Dad has some idea you'll want to come back to Sydney…" Thunder rumbled and the line crackled.

"What do you mean?" Paula raised her voice to counter the poor line and Oscar's screaming.

"Have to go. Love you, bye."

Paula wondered what her sister meant. She was married to Dan, for goodness sake. Surely her father wasn't thinking it was some little fling and she would wake up one day and decide country life wasn't for her.

She shivered and looked down at the handset she still clutched tightly in her hand. She wondered how many other calls and emails she was missing. Her carrier had no service here and even Dan's phone didn't work well in the house. She'd have to change her phone and they needed some kind of internet connection. Another thing to add to her list, which kept getting longer.

Paula closed her eyes. Time to test out that nice deep bath. It would be warm and relaxing and she could forget about her parents, the mice and having no mobile phone service.

The thunder rumbled closer as she set the taps running. She took the torch for security and went to the bedroom where she dug out two sweet-smelling candles she'd brought with her from Sydney.

The fire was burning low in the lounge so she added more wood then returned to the bathroom where the steam was already filling the room.

The candles were a deep purple and contained sandalwood, patchouli and ylang-ylang. Paula grinned ironically to herself. The message on the back said the combination of these three aromas was known to enhance passion and sensuality. Not a lot of use to a farming couple during seeding.

She placed one candle on the side of the washbasin and one at the end of the bath, then lit them. The water pressure was good and the bath was filling quickly. She stripped off her clothes, tested the water with her foot then climbed in and slid gratefully into the warmth. Just as she stretched out, there was a bright flash of light from outside and a huge clap of thunder boomed overhead.

The bathroom light flickered then went out. From the front of the house, Paula heard a bang.

She sat up. Once again her heart raced. There was another loud thump. What could it be? Surely Uncle Gerald wouldn't be cruising around at this late hour.

"Paula?"

She let out her breath at Dan's call and sank back into the water. "I'm in the bathroom."

There were more thumps and scuffles as Dan fumbled his way from the front of the house then stuck his head around the door.

"This looks like the place to be."

Paula could see the sparkle in his eyes by the soft glow of the candles.

"I thought I had the place to myself. I wasn't expecting you yet." She watched him remove his clothes. She still had to remind herself that this gorgeous man was all hers.

"You shouldn't have worried with all that fuss about mice. If I'd known this was why you wanted me home, I would have been here in a flash."

Right on cue, as he said the word, thunder rumbled and lightning once again flashed through the room, illuminating Dan's naked body.

In spite of the warm water, goosebumps prickled Paula's skin. She made room for him in the bath. "I can just imagine the flapping ears if I'd called you over the two-way radio to come home for a bath."

"You might have got a few extras." He grinned and moved in closer, straddling her with his legs.

Paula sprinkled water on his head. Dan splashed her face then wrapped her in his arms and kissed her. She felt the strength of his embrace, the softness of his skin against hers. The purple candles gave off a sweet aroma in the steamy bathroom and overhead rain crashed down onto the old tin roof.

Dan released her from his embrace. She opened her eyes, not wanting to lose the feel of him pressed tight against her. A lock of his fair hair had fallen across one eye and his lips were turned up in a cheeky grin giving him a rakish look.

"So tell me, mistress of the bath. Do your services run to back scrubs?"

"They might." She smiled as he scrunched his long legs up and turned around in the bath.

Paula reached for the soap and face washer just as the room was illuminated by another flash of lightning. The accompanying clap of thunder drowned her scream as a little grey body whizzed out from underneath the cloth and slipped into the bath.

CHAPTER
3

The next morning rain continued to fall.

Dan turned back from the kitchen window where he'd been watching the weather for the last five minutes. "Looks like I get to take you to town. No way we can get into the paddocks for a day or so if this keeps up. We'd better try to fix this door and see what else needs doing before your folks get here. We don't want them having any surprises in the bath."

Paula laughed and hugged him. The mouse in the bath seemed funny now but last night had been a nightmare. She'd jumped from the bath and it had taken Dan some time to work out what had driven his wife screaming from his arms. Eventually he'd managed to calm her down, wrap her in a towel and sit her by the fire while he dealt with the mouse.

Much later, she had lain awake listening to Dan's gentle breathing and the rain beating down overhead. It had seemed as if they were alone in the world, in their own little cocoon, safe and warm from the storm outside, but it had taken her a long time to go to sleep. There were still mice roaming freely in her house.

Now in the light of day, with Dan beside her, it didn't seem so bad.

Paula kissed him and stepped back. "I'll tidy myself up a bit."

"You look fine to me." He reached for her but she slipped away. "Won't be long."

★ ★ ★

Dan watched her disappear through the door. Her fair hair swished around her face as she walked. She might look small but she was no pushover. He sensed a deeper resilience in Paula. He'd seen it in her eyes the day he'd asked her to be sure she could accept his way of life before she said yes to being his wife. Some might say she had an air of aloofness but beneath that Dan had discovered a loving warmth along with feisty determination. She was just what he needed.

He still found it hard to believe that he'd been fortunate enough to find her. He'd never had much luck with women in the past. Rowena accused him of not trying hard enough to make a commitment. As if she could talk. She had male friends but no close relationships, as far as Dan knew.

He switched on the kettle for a cuppa and smiled to himself. Rowena was a very determined woman. He wasn't sure if there was a man who would be strong enough to take her on.

Dan had been only three when his mother was killed in a car accident and Rowena had moved in to look after him and his father. His father, Daniel, had been a quiet, reserved man who never got over the loss of his wife. Rowena had stepped into the breach and cared for both of them. She had been the one to insist that Dan be sent to boarding school to broaden his outlook.

Each holiday he had returned home to a father who was visibly fading. After his time away there had only been a few more years working together, back on the farm, before his father became too weak to work and finally died at fifty.

Rowena had continued to manage the house and encouraged Dan to keep up with his friends, especially the girls who lived locally. Girls had been an enigma to him, perhaps because he had no sisters or because he had spent four years in an all-male boarding school. He didn't really know why, he just didn't know the right moves to make back then.

There hadn't been anyone he liked well enough to romance from his point of view, although his mate Bruce always teased him that the girls fancied him. There were a couple of local girls he'd had some fun with but they had gone off to uni and he only caught up with them at Christmas and parties and, gradually, they'd lost touch.

There had been one other woman, who he'd thought could have been the one, but he didn't want to remind himself of that relationship now. He frowned. Rowena had said he was a fool to marry Paula when he had unfinished business. It would be terrible if he jeopardised his future by not being honest but there was no need. He could sort things out.

"That's a serious face." Paula had returned.

He loved that she wore only scant makeup, a splash of lipstick and a hint of mascara. She was beautiful and looking huggable in snug jeans and a brown leather jacket.

She picked up the notepad from the kitchen table and waved it under his nose playfully. "I've made a list of food we need. Your aunt has been very kind but I really should find out how to take myself to the shops and back. There are other things we need as well."

Dan took it and read the list. "This won't be enough food." He laughed. "You might not get a chance to go back into town for a while. We don't have a corner store out here."

"I know." Paula snatched back the note. "I am capable of shopping."

Dan wrapped her in his arms. "I'm just worried that you'll dish up some of that cement or paint on the list if we run out of real food." She struggled but he wouldn't let her go. She relaxed against him. The top of her head only reached his shoulder but she nestled against him in a perfect fit. This was how life was meant to be. With Paula in his arms he felt like the luckiest bloke alive. His body began to respond to hers. Sadly there was no time to follow up on that right now. He kissed her head. "Time to go."

★   ★   ★

Outside the air was chilly and Paula was grateful for the new jacket she'd bought before she left Sydney.

Dan smiled at her across the top of the ute roof. It was a battered old vehicle that had seen better days. When they had flown in to Adelaide they had collected it from Dan's friend Rob. Rob had commented on how clean it looked at the time. Now it was covered in mud. Paula struggled with the door handle and Dan pushed some oily rags off the seat before she sat down.

"I have a surprise for you when we get to town."

Paula looked into his mischievous blue eyes. "What is it?" She wasn't really fond of surprises.

"If I told you it wouldn't be a surprise."

"Oh, come on, Dan." She poked him but he wouldn't be drawn.

He chuckled, started the motor then picked up the two-way handpiece. "Woodie, calling Croft. Are you on channel, Rowena?"

Paula watched him in silence. It was like an old American truckie movie.

"This is Woodie calling Croft. Rowena, are you there?"

Dan looked at Paula. She raised an eyebrow.

"We had to come up with a new call sign now that we're in two houses," he explained. "I kept the Woodie and Rowena took on Croft, get it?"

"Yes Dan, I'm here." Rowena's reply saved Paula from having to answer.

"Paula and I are off to town, do you need anything?"

"No, thanks. I'll be in over the weekend." There was a crackle and the two-way went silent.

Dan revved the engine. "Well, here we go. Mr and Mrs Woodcroft are off to town." His face lit in a secretive smile as he manoeuvred the ute over the ramp and out onto the track that led to the road. Paula felt like she was no longer watching the movie, but had become a part of it.

Rain fell intermittently on their trip to town. She wanted to talk to Dan about some of the things on her shopping list but she was trying to concentrate on the road. The surroundings all looked the same to her. They turned right from their property onto a dirt road, which crossed several other similar roads before Dan took a series of twists, turns and corners until they reached the bitumen, where he turned right again. All around them the land flowed for as far as the trees and the grey day would let her see. She glanced at her watch. She knew it took about thirty minutes to reach the town from Rowena's so she assumed it was a similar distance from their place.

"Don't look so worried, Sweet Pea, we'll find our way home again."

"I know you can, but this country all looks the same to me." She waved a hand towards the brown and grey paddocks, hemmed in by fences and straggling tree lines whizzing past her window.

"Won't be long and you'll know your way as well as I do."

Paula studied her surroundings as Dan slowed to make another right turn. She couldn't imagine how she would find her way home. At least the bitumen road had signposts directing them to town. The last sign had said fifteen kilometres. Now they were this close she could relax a little.

"I thought I'd paint the small third bedroom for Mum and Dad," she said.

"I'm sorry I won't be much help. I'll get Tom to give me a hand to fix the back door then I've got some machinery repairs to do and as soon as the paddocks have dried out enough, I'll be back on the tractor."

"That's okay. I don't mind. I've helped some friends redecorate before. The painting will give me a project and take my mind off Mum and Dad's impending visit."

Dan reached across and put his hand on her knee. "Will it really be that bad? I thought you'd enjoy the company. You haven't had a chance to meet anyone yet."

"I'm not lonely, Dan." She squeezed his hand. "I know the mice rattled me a bit. I didn't mean to cause a fuss but I couldn't stop them."

"Rowena's already given me a lecture about how inconsiderate I've been. You know she's offered for us to move in with her until seeding's finished and I can get some more work done on the place?"

"I'm okay, Dan, really."

"Are you sure? At least you would have company at Rowena's and there's plenty of room for your mum and dad to stay there as well."

"I love our home." Paula spoke firmly. She didn't want to move in with Rowena. "My parents will have to take us as we are. I did warn them the house wasn't ready for visitors. If I can paint the room and put in a few basics before they come, I'll be happy and they will be fine."

"I love our home, too." Dan leaned across and kissed her cheek then put on a phoney American accent. "And I love my little woman."

"Keep your eyes on the road." She laughed, looked across at this wonderful man she had married and wanted to pinch herself. Side on he had angular features but they added character to his rugged good looks. He was so tall, a whole head higher than her. They were the long and the short of it, he'd joked early in their relationship.

They'd never talked much about their lives before they met. There had always been more important things to talk about. It didn't matter but she wondered briefly why he hadn't been snapped up. Perhaps he'd been unlucky in love like her. Before she had met Dan she'd been in a long-term relationship with Marco who had also happened to be her boss. She'd been so happy at first, both in her job and her relationship, but the two had merged until she realised that their private life had become an extension of her day job. To Marco she was just another possession to be used as he pleased. After ending it with Marco she'd also left her job and had been caught up in the clutches of a deep-seated tiredness — she just wasn't interested in meeting people. That was in the past now. Paula shifted in her seat and glanced at Dan concentrating on the road. It was incredible to think they could so easily have never met.

She had nearly stayed home from the friend's wedding that had brought them together, but her mother had insisted she go. For once she could be grateful for her mother's interference. Dan was a good friend of the groom and his smile had been like a light switching on in her life. After meeting over the pre-reception drinks they had stayed together. She had found his jokes funny and his honesty refreshing. He had been quiet but not shy and before the day was over Paula knew she was in love with him.

Dan had stayed a week in Sydney and they had spent as much of that time together as they could. In spite of her deep feelings for him she'd kept from falling into his bed until the last night before he left. That night, when they'd finally come together as lovers, had sealed their commitment. Two weeks later she'd flown to Adelaide to spend the weekend with him and before she returned to Sydney Dan had asked her to marry him. She would have said 'yes' immediately but he wanted her to come back again and visit his farm before she committed. She recalled his quiet, serious voice urging her to think carefully.

She had made the trip. That's when she'd stayed in Rowena's house. Paula had been comfortable with the land. Dan had driven her around the property but she really didn't care where they lived, as long as they were together. She recalled the mingled look of doubt and relief that had crossed his face when she'd told him.

Their short engagement had caused problems for her mother who had wanted to plan the lavish style of wedding she had for Alison. Susan had avoided the fuss a year earlier by inviting close family and friends to Bali and holding her wedding there. Paula had stuck to her timeline despite her mother's protests and the wedding had gone ahead in a small chapel with refreshments afterwards in her parents' beautiful garden overlooking the harbour.

"Ready for your surprise?" Dan's question brought her back to the present. She smiled at him. There was no point in asking him again what it was. She could see it would get her nowhere. The outskirts of town appeared through the windscreen wipers. The heavy rain had eased but misting showers accompanied their journey. She shivered. The heater in the old ute didn't work and it had become quite cold.

She had seen the town in daylight once on her first visit to the farm. Dan said there were about three thousand people living here and another thousand in the nearest little towns and extended rural area. The community served the surrounding agricultural industry and catered for all basic needs. If you wanted more you had to travel to Adelaide several hours away. The main street was lined with assorted shops and businesses and one Foodland supermarket. On the other edge of town was a large car yard and it was here that Dan pulled in.

"This old ute has had its day. I've bought us a new vehicle." Dan beamed at her and Paula could see he was expecting a big reaction.

"That's wonderful, Dan." She smiled back.

"I've got some papers to sign and it's all ours. Come and meet Jim."

Paula got out of the ute and followed him into the yard. She looked at the rows of cars lined up and wondered which one was going to be theirs. She'd left her sleek little Mazda hatch in Sydney and planned to get her father to sell it for her, not really thinking she'd need it here, although she had briefly wondered how she would manage with things like shopping with only the old ute.

A short, plump man looking overdressed in a shirt and tie with a checked jacket came to meet them.

"Hello, Jim." Dan shook his hand then turned to Paula. "This is my wife, Paula. Jim McInerney is the best car man in the district."

"Hello, Paula. It helps when you are the only car dealer in town."

"You're too modest, Jim. People can easily go elsewhere," Dan said.

Jim smiled and shook Paula's hand firmly. "It's nice to meet you." The moustache over his top lip flopped as he spoke and his hair looked as if it had been plastered down with a layer of grease, but he had a warm sparkle in his voice and a genuine smile. Paula liked him straight away.

"Come into my office. We can have a cuppa and finish the paper-work. I suppose you'll be glad to have a decent vehicle. I told Dan he couldn't expect his new bride to have the same love for that old ute that he has."

"It's been a good vehicle." Dan defended his ute. "It's done a few kays, that's all."

"Not much good for weekly shopping trips or offering rides to the neighbours though." Jim winked at Paula. "You've got other priorities now, Dan. Please, help yourself to a cuppa, Paula. We shouldn't take long here." He indicated a table and Paula noticed a filter coffee pot and cups. Jim already had a cup on his side of the desk so Paula made a cup for Dan and herself and left them to it.

The window in front of her looked over the sparkling vehicles in the showroom. They were arranged with strips of carpet between them and some lush plants carefully placed at intervals. In the back of the showroom, proudly raised on a dais, was a vintage car and the wall behind it was decorated with parts and accessories of early motoring days. She breathed in the fresh coffee aroma and decided Jim had style.

"That's it then. She's out the back ready to go." Paula turned to see Jim shaking Dan's hand. They both grinned at her. "I'm sure you'll be much happier with this vehicle. Come through and you can drive her away."

Their enthusiasm was infectious and Paula felt a little tingle of anticipation as she followed the two men through the office door and out into a huge garage. Jim led them past mechanics working on cars, finally stopping beside a large vehicle.

"This is it." Dan flung his arm out with a flourish. "Our new car."

Paula stared at the metallic grey vehicle, which looked like an overgrown cross between a four-wheel drive and a ute. It had a four-door cabin with a long back tray enclosed in a solid canopy.

"Dual cabs are the way to go." Jim opened the door for Paula. "A work vehicle but a family car when needed. Hop in, take a look."

Dan hovered beside her. "What do you think?"

The new smell of the interior was very strong. She glanced back at the two of them beaming like they'd won the lottery and knew she had to appear delighted.

"It's great." She glanced around madly for something to be excited about. "The seats are comfortable."

Dan got into the driver's seat beside her and started the engine.

"It was nice to meet you, Paula." Jim shook her hand again. His eyes crinkled into a gentle smile and he lowered his voice. "I've known this lad all his life. He's honest and hardworking. I think you've both made a good choice." Paula didn't know what to say. Did he mean their marriage or the car? "Oh Dan, we put the new two-way in this morning, so you're all set." Jim shut the door and waved.

Dan drove out of the garage with a smile from ear to ear. Paula stared at the black box installed between them in the dash. A slightly smaller version than the one that perched on top of their fridge at home but it was a two-way radio none the less. At least there was a phone plug. She could play music. Which reminded her.

"I really need to change my phone, Dan. Can we do that while we're here?"

"Sorry, Sweet Pea. No time today. I'll get Rowena to bring you in next week. You can do it then."

Paula opened her mouth to say she didn't need Rowena's help but Dan spoke first.

"Okay if I drop you at the supermarket? I've got some things to do across town. I shouldn't be long."

"Sure." Paula smiled. Suddenly she felt nervous. There were quite a few people in the streets now. Would everyone be staring at her and inspecting Dan's new wife?

As it turned out no one took much notice of her in the super-market. The aisles were busy with women pushing overflowing trolleys and towing squabbling children. The checkout girl was polite but not interested in Paula, just like any operator in any Sydney supermarket.

Paula pushed her trolley out onto the verandah. Women smiled and dodged around her, pushing stacks of full shopping bags in their trolleys. They must have big families to feed. She looked at her own bags and wondered if she should have bought a few more things. She worried about the ice-cream. It was a cold day but it would be sloppy by the time they reached the farm. She wondered how other people got their frozen goods safely home.

She peered out at every passing vehicle looking for Dan. Cars came and went but there was no sign of him. It was a funny feeling to have complete strangers smile and nod at her as they passed. It was as if she was someone they knew. Paula felt very conspicuous and wished Dan would hurry up. She looked at her watch. It had taken about half an hour to complete her shopping and she had been waiting nearly that long again. Occasional puffs of wind drove the misty showers under the verandah and she was getting cold.

Perhaps she'd misunderstood Dan. Just as she was wondering what she should do, he pulled up beside her and jumped out to help her load the shopping into the back seat.

"Sorry, Paula. Every man and his dog's in town today. I kept running into people who wanted to know how seeding was going and how the new vehicle was sizing up. Oh, and how my new woman was settling in." He grinned.

Paula was cold and damp but she couldn't be cross when he smiled at her like that.

"Damn I forgot to bring an esky."

Paula frowned at him.

"For the milk and ice cream." He waved one of the shopping bags full of dairy items at her. "Still, it's a cold day. They should be okay till we get them home."

"I did wonder about —"

"Hello, Dan."

They both turned to take in the tall woman of about their age who stood behind them on the footpath. She was dressed immaculately in an expensive tan suit, stockings and neat ankle boots. Her straight blonde hair was pulled back into a low loose ponytail, held in place by a bow.

"Hello, Katherine. I didn't know you were back." Dan stepped stiffly up onto the path.

"It's a busy time of year." She smiled at Dan. "And you've been even busier." Her sharp gaze took in Paula who was still standing in the gutter feeling like a midget.

"Paula, this is Katherine Melton, our local solicitor. Katherine, my wife." He underlined the last two words and Paula could feel the tension in his body as she accepted his hand and stepped up onto the path between them.

"Pleased to meet you, Katherine." Paula shook hands and imagined she understood how a mouse felt under the stare of a cat. Katherine's gaze was piercing, summing her up. She was glad she'd decided to pull on her new leather jacket and her designer jeans.

A car tooted behind and a male voice teased Dan about taking up all the space with his flash new car.

"We should get going, Paula." Dan nodded at Katherine and turned and waved to the car behind.

"Dan, we must catch up." Katherine put a hand on his arm. "There are some decisions to be made."

"After seeding." Dan tugged his arm back and Paula watched as he walked stiffly around the car.

"We should get together over a coffee, Paula." Katherine had stepped closer. "We have a few things in common." Her gaze flicked towards Dan, who was getting into the car. Paula thought she looked almost predatory. "Sydney, for instance. My mother lives there now and I've spent a bit of time there." Her gaze flicked in Dan's direction again. "Farmers get so caught up in their work they can neglect their wives. You'll probably find life here terribly dull at times."

Dan started the engine.

"Thanks for the offer, Katherine," Paula said, glancing in Dan's direction then smiling meaningfully back at Katherine, "but I haven't found it dull here yet."

Paula could feel Katherine's eyes follow her as she got into the car beside Dan. His mood had become serious and he kept his eyes on the road. There was definitely a history between Dan and Katherine, and Paula wondered what Katherine had meant by 'decisions to be made' but she didn't feel inclined to ask Dan. Somehow she didn't think friendship with Katherine was on the cards.

CHAPTER

4

The sound of a car outside her window woke Paula from a deep sleep. She looked at her clock and sat up with a jolt. It was nearly ten o'clock. She felt thick-headed and disoriented. Dan had left at six to go back on the tractor and Paula had lain in bed planning her day.

It had been very cold when Dan got up and she'd only meant to stay in bed for a few more minutes. Today she was planning to paint the bedroom in readiness for her parents' arrival.

But instead of getting up and getting stuck into the painting she'd drifted back into a restless sleep. She'd dreamed she was with Marco who was guiding her away from something she was trying desperately to see. The something turned out to be Dan kissing Katherine, who looked at her with a smug possessive smile. Paula had woken feeling disturbed by the dream but she must have drifted off to sleep again. Now the morning was half gone.

She peeped through the curtain to see a woman leaning into the back of a car, a little boy standing beside her. Quickly Paula threw on some clothes and brushed her hair. She shut the bedroom door just as the sound of voices reached her with a knock on the front door. The passage was quite dark with only leadlight windows either side of the door so Paula switched on the light before she opened the door.

There was a woman of about Paula's age loaded up with a baby and a basket. Beside her the little boy was carrying a small Batman bag. He turned his head shyly and clung to her leg.

"Paula?"

"Yes."

"I'm Jane Freeman. My husband, Bruce, and I live nearest you, over that way." She nodded her head over her shoulder. "I'm sorry I haven't come to see you earlier. Andrew and James have both been sick and with Bruce seeding it's been a pig of a week." She laughed. "Bruce says I must stop using that description as a derogatory term. Considering we're now pig farmers, he says it's always going to be a pig of a week."

"Please come in." Paula stepped back. Dan had often mentioned Bruce.

"Sorry, I should have rung first." The baby in Jane's arms squirmed and she struggled with the basket.

"Can I carry that for you?"

Jane gave up the basket, which Paula discovered was quite heavy, and manoeuvred into the passage with the little boy still attached to her leg.

"Andrew, let go of my leg now. This is Paula, our new neighbour."

"Hello, Andrew." Paula spoke without going any closer. She could see he was not sure of her. "Let's go to the kitchen. I've got a heater in there."

Paula's initial discomfort was soon overcome by Jane's friendly banter and Andrew quickly got over his shyness. He was an independent three year old and was soon making engine noises with his trucks on the floor.

Baby James was five months old and very sweet. Jane breastfed him while they chatted over a cuppa and a delicious homemade cake she had produced from the basket. Paula had held the baby while Jane took Andrew to the toilet. Awkward at first, Paula was soon taken in by his big brown eyes gazing sleepily back at her. She'd never felt very maternal, even with her sister Alison's babies, but this one was certainly cute.

Children were something she and Dan had never discussed. She had a pang of anxiety. Did he expect her to stay home and breed like Jane, who had come to the area as a young teacher, married Bruce and straight away produced Andrew? Paula wasn't ready for that. She loved and adored Dan but she didn't think she could feel the same about his children just yet.

Jane had lived in the area for five years and had known Dan for most of that time. Dan and Bruce had been friends since school, so when Jane and Bruce had started seeing each other, Dan had often gone along.

"I was beginning to wonder if he would move in with us when we married." Jane laughed. "He's a lovely guy, Paula. I'm so glad he's found you. He deserves someone special."

Paula was pleased but embarrassed by Jane's words. She had been tempted to ask Jane about Katherine Melton but that would be snooping into Dan's past and she didn't want to do that.

"I'm sorry we couldn't come to your wedding. Bruce was very sick. The doctor threatened to put him in hospital if he didn't stay in bed. Do you have photos?"

"Not yet. My parents will be here next week. They're bringing the photos and our presents."

"That's good, you'll have company. I'm an Adelaide girl. I don't miss living there; it's close enough for me to visit if I need and my family come here from time to time. I love country life but it can get a bit lonely. What did you do before you married Dan?"

"I'm an accountant by trade but I've done all sorts, mainly in big business."

"Gosh that kind of work is thin on the ground here. I used to do some relief teaching in between having Andrew and James but now that we have the pigs there's usually something Bruce needs help with every day so I haven't gone back to it. Tractor season is a special challenge." Jane's eyes twinkled with mischief. "Although sometimes I'm glad of it now we have kids. Bruce and I are both too tired at the same time." She laughed. "But newlyweds don't worry about that."

"Dan does work long hours but I don't think we are quite up to having children yet."

"Oh, no. Enjoy your time together. Kids change the dynamics. Although, Bruce and I wouldn't give them back." She cuddled James in close. "You'll have to get used to the questions though. The whole district likes to organise your life. When you're going out it's 'how long till you marry?' When you get married it's 'when are you going to have kids?' You and I are what the locals call 'new blood'."

"What's that?"

"Our men have brought outsiders into the district. It broadens the gene pool." Jane laughed again and looked at her watch. "Speaking of men, I'd better get mine his lunch."

It was nearly twelve o'clock and Paula, still full of Jane's delicious chocolate cake, hadn't given food a thought.

"Will Dan come home for lunch now they've started on Harvey's place?"

Paula looked at Jane as if she was speaking another language. Where was Harvey's place and why wouldn't Dan come home for lunch?

"I take Bruce's lunch to the paddock when he's not close to home. Sometimes he takes it with him but he prefers something warm if I have time. I'd better fly."

Paula waved Jane off and went back to the kitchen. It was suddenly empty without Jane's happy laugh and Andrew's engine noises. She had no idea where Harvey's place was or why Dan would be working there. She only had vague recollections of the property from her first visit. She knew the house yard and the sheds but other than their trip to town, she had not been anywhere. Everything revolved around this house and Dan returning to it. She frowned at the brief thought that she had simply swapped one master for another. Marco had dominated her world when she was with him but at least she'd had some independence with transport and friends. Here Paula realised she relied on Dan for everything. When he was gone she didn't even have a car.

The phone rang, startling her.

"Hello, Paula?" Rowena's voice boomed down the line.

"Yes." Paula grimaced. Who else was going to answer this phone?

"I'm taking Dan out some lunch. He asked me to ring you rather than use the two-way. He's started on Harvey's place and doesn't want to stop for long while conditions are good. I can pick you up and you can come for a ride." Rowena's command annoyed Paula.

"Thanks, Rowena but I've got to get the painting finished. Tell Dan I'll have dinner waiting for him when he gets home." She hung up and went to look at paint tins. Why was Rowena organising Dan's lunch? Didn't they think Paula was up to it?

The passage door swung closed behind her with its strong swoosh and she stopped dead. How could she take Dan lunch even if she had thought of it? She didn't know where he was and she didn't have a vehicle of any description. She would need to sort that out with Dan once he came home. She didn't really have anywhere to go but she felt suddenly isolated without a means of transport.

Paula pushed her disquiet away. There was nothing she could do about it right now and she had a room to paint. She marched into the spare bedroom where everything was set out, ready for her to begin. She had an old shirt of Dan's to cover her clothes and brought in a lamp for extra light. It was a grey day outside and the ceiling light struggled to illuminate the room.

The one mouse trap had done its job. It was flipped over in the corner and the legs and tail of a mouse were protruding from underneath. Dan and Tom had replaced the back door and fixed the floor but there were still a few mice in the house.

She wrapped the pathetic little body in newspaper and dropped it in the bin, then she took out a chicken from the freezer. Paula decided a roast would be their evening meal. She'd hardly ever cooked one before. Stir fries and grills were more her thing when she ate at home but she knew Dan enjoyed a roast. He'd made a fuss of her mother's roast beef when they'd eaten there on one of his visits. A chicken wouldn't take long to cook. She'd get the first coat of paint on then see to it.

Back in the bedroom she prised the lid off the first tin. She'd chosen a soft white with just a hint of pink for the ceiling. It rolled on easily and even though she had to drag ladders around it didn't take long to get the first coat on. It looked plain white but it was probably just the dull day. Once she had the Coffee Rose on the walls it would be okay.

Paula made herself a quick sandwich. The chicken was still rock solid so she put it in the microwave to defrost while she went back to tackle the walls. Lifting the lid off the next tin she stopped in dismay. The colour she'd chosen for the walls was meant to have pink hues but it looked too muddy. Stirring the paint furiously she hoped it would change with the mixing but the colour remained brown rather than the deep pink she had chosen.

That bloody man at the hardware store. What was his name? Carl. He'd been so busy talking to Paula about the finer points of painting he'd mixed the wrong colours. Dan had taken her to the hardware store, introduced her to Carl, explained he wanted everything charged to the farm account then he'd been distracted by a power-tool display. Carl was a lively character. He wanted to know all about her project and what she thought she might do.

She checked her colour sheets again. The contents of the tin were nothing like the colour she had chosen. A name was scrawled on the side.

"Coffee Time! Damn!" It was meant to be Coffee Rose. Paula glanced at the grey day beyond the window. There was no car to drive back into town. "Even if I knew the way." Her voice made a hollow echo around her.

The microwave beeped insistently. Paula left the offending paint and went back to the kitchen. There was a sizzling, popping sound coming from the microwave. She flung open the door to reveal a shrivelled chicken.

"Ohh!" She dragged the miserable lump of meat out to the sink. The microwave was new and she'd never used it before. "I mustn't have selected defrost." She looked around the empty kitchen. "This is what you've come to, Paula, no one to talk to but a dead bird." She left the chicken and went back to her paint.

There was nothing for it but to go with the colour Carl had mixed for her. She topped up the tin with some of the pale ceiling colour but it made little impact on the depth of the colour. Fuelled by her anger at Carl, Paula rolled on the paint.

By the time she had done one wall she was beginning to calm down and at the end of the second she stood back to look at her work. The colour was beginning to grow on her. Even though the light wasn't good, the fresh paint lifted the room. She threw herself into covering the remaining walls and finally sat down in the middle of the room smiling at the walls around her.

"Well, well, Carl. I take it all back." It looked okay. She wondered whether the old devil had mixed the colour on purpose.

It was dark outside by the time she'd cleaned up. She wondered about the colour she'd chosen for the skirting boards. It was called China Silk but Carl may have changed that too. She was too tired to bother with it tonight. Tomorrow she would see if Carl had mixed her any more surprises.

Paula lit the fire in the lounge, put on the television for some background noise and went to the kitchen to try to do something with the poor wretched chicken.

Dan didn't come home till after eleven. Paula had been listening anxiously for his dual cab since about nine. He looked exhausted. She served up the reheated remains of the chicken and tried to make conversation while he ate. She probably could have served mouse stew and he wouldn't have noticed.

"There's enough meat left for sandwiches. I can make some for your lunch tomorrow."

"Thanks." Dan's reply was more of a croak. His eyes were red and his usually soft wavy hair was a greasy mat plastered to his head.

Paula brushed her hands over the tablecloth, flattening imaginary ripples. "Rowena said she was taking you lunch today."

"Yes."

"I am capable of making you lunch."

"I can do my own but there wasn't anything in the fridge this morning and Rowena offered. Now that we're out at Harvey's place it's too far to come home."

Dan pushed the food around his plate and Paula realised she hadn't thought enough about meals and planning ahead. She watched her bleary-eyed husband poke at the remnants of the rubbery chicken. Finally he picked up the almost empty plate and carried it to the sink.

"I'm bushed, Sweet Pea. Thanks for tea."

"It was terrible." Paula jumped up to hug him. "I'm sorry, I'm just not used to this kind of cooking."

Dan trudged out to the shower and Paula cleaned up and followed him to bed. There was no point sitting in the empty kitchen. She cuddled up to him and remembered her earlier thoughts about lack of transport.

"Dan, do we have another vehicle anywhere?"

His hand patted her back. "Sure, Sweet Pea, sheds full of them."

Paula's spirits rose.

"There're two tractors, a ride-on mower, a harvester and a truck. Which one would you like?"

Paula stiffened in his arms. "Don't make fun of me, Dan. You use the dual cab every day and I've no way of getting around."

"Where do you want to go?"

"I don't know but it would be nice to take myself to town or to see Jane or just drive if I want to. Couldn't you take the truck?"

"We're using it in the paddock at the moment...I'm sorry," he murmured into her hair. "I hadn't thought about it. We'll have to work something out..."

His voice faded and Paula could feel his arms going slack. She thought he was asleep then he surprised her when he said they could sleep in tomorrow.

"I'm going to church with Rowena in the morning." His voice was barely audible. "You're welcome to join us."

She thought about his offer, which had sounded very casual. She didn't know whether he wanted her to go or not and the thought of sitting with Rowena on a hard church pew didn't excite her.

Paula didn't think about God much. She thought she believed he existed but had not explored beyond that for years. Her mother was Anglican and had taken Paula and her sisters to church when they were young. Alison was still a regular attendee but Susan and Paula were not.

Dan's gentle snores told Paula there would be no more cuddles or anything else tonight. She felt tired – painting was strenuous work – but sleep eluded her. Once again she lay awake for a long time while her husband slept the deep sleep of exhaustion beside her.

CHAPTER
5

"You're a bit of a drawcard," Dan whispered. "I haven't seen this many here since Christmas."

Paula smiled nervously back at him. She was sitting with Dan and Rowena at the back of the little Uniting Church building. She glanced around and estimated there were about twenty people seated on the hard wooden pews. The only ones she recognised were Jane and her children sitting a few rows in front. A nuggety guy with dark wavy hair sat beside Jane holding baby James. Paula assumed he was Bruce.

Over breakfast Dan had been more encouraging. The church had been built over a hundred years ago at a crossroads when a much bigger local community existed. He was anxious to be back on the tractor but there was only a service in the local church once a month and the small congregation liked to go to ensure its continued existence. Tom was driving the tractor in his absence but Dan didn't want to leave him for long. Paula did wonder why he had

Tom in the first place if he couldn't leave him to do a job for a few hours, but she didn't say anything. She sensed an underlying tension in Dan which she didn't understand.

By the time she had dithered over what she should wear and they'd picked up Rowena, who had been waiting impatiently at her front gate, there were several cars at the front of the church and nearly every pew was full. The stone church with its tin roof, small porch and arched windows was perched alone near a junction where five roads met. There were a few straggly gums behind it but otherwise the ground around in all directions was devoid of any growth.

Paula felt as nervous as she had when Dan had dropped her at the supermarket. There no one had taken much notice of her, but here she didn't think she could escape so easily. She glanced around at the congregation again. They were mostly women, children and older men. Dan and Bruce seemed to be the only two men under forty.

Never having been to a Uniting Church service she didn't know what to expect but the words of praise washed over her and gave her a chance to reflect. So much had happened in the last few months. She had changed her life completely to come and live with this wonderful man who sat beside her. That she loved him she had no doubt and she liked what she'd seen of country life, except the mice.

She slipped her hand into his. He smiled down at her and gave her hand a squeeze. Dan was all that mattered. She could live anywhere if she was with him. Looking past him she caught the flash of a frown on Rowena's face as she glanced down at their joined hands. Paula edged closer to Dan.

At the end of the service Rowena was quickly ahead of them and after a shake of the minister's hand, moved over to speak to a smartly dressed woman waiting outside. Dan introduced Paula to the minister, who welcomed her warmly.

Jane took her arm and introduced her to Bruce. He was the same height as his wife and had a daredevil twinkle in his eye. His dark brown hair curled into a boyish wave on top.

"I can see why you've swept this beauty away to your country lair," he teased. "You've certainly tamed him, Paula. He used to be quite a wild man."

"Not me, I'm the quiet one. You used to lead me astray until Jane taught you some manners." Dan grinned.

"Come on you two, that's enough. You're giving Paula the totally wrong impression," Jane said. "They both think they've got some kind of past reputation, Paula, but they'd run a mile if anyone took up the challenge."

Other people came to be introduced. Paula had no hope of remembering all the names and working out where they lived but everyone was so friendly. An older grey-haired woman, with a limp that made her rock wildly from side to side as she walked, asked Paula if she liked to cook and without waiting for a reply produced a dozen eggs. A shy woman, even shorter than Paula but twice as wide, brought over a foam tray covered with a serviette and a generous number of carefully arranged homemade biscuits.

Dan and Bruce were talking earnestly about some problem Bruce was having with machinery so Paula deposited her gifts in the dual cab and went to help Jane load the children in the car. James was beginning to grizzle and Andrew was jumping up and down in the back seat.

"I want Daddy's truck," he yelled.

"Where did you leave it, Andrew?" Jane's reply was patient as she tried to strap the squirming baby into the car seat.

Andrew kicked his legs. "I want Daddy's truck."

Jane turned to Paula. "He must have left it in the church, I'll get Bruce to look."

"I'll go," Paula said. "You'll have to tell me what I'm looking for though. I don't remember any big trucks in church."

"It's only a small toy but it looks like Bruce's truck. Andrew won't go anywhere without it." Jane gave Paula a grateful smile then turned back to the two noisy children.

Paula stepped through the door of the church. The lights had been turned off and it was dim inside. She started down the aisle but as her eyes adjusted she realised she wasn't alone. Two women were up at the front of the church clearing away the flowers. They both had their backs to Paula.

"She's only a little thing," one was saying.

"Height's not important," the other replied.

"I'm sure it helps."

"No, it's all in the hips."

Paula didn't like to interrupt their conversation. She reached the pew where the Freemans had been sitting and bent down to pick up the little truck, which had been partly hidden by the leg.

"Well, the other one certainly had the hips."

"You mean Katherine?"

"Yes. They made a striking couple."

Paula froze. Were they talking about Dan and Katherine Melton?

"But she wasn't right for him."

"I don't know, there definitely was some chemistry between them for a time. Makes you wonder how it can disappear so easily. Although I have heard they still have a 'connection', you might say, and Katherine has spent quite a bit of time away."

"Yes, well, we don't know if the rumours are true."

"I just hope he hasn't rushed into this new affair too quickly."

"Well, it's hardly what you'd call an affair. Dan's married her, and child-bearing hips or not, there's bound to be children soon. Rowena is concerned." The women picked up a vase each. Paula was trapped, aghast at their conversation and terrified that they might turn and find her standing there.

"Give the poor love a chance to see if she likes country life."

"Rowena's point exactly. She doesn't want a baby to complicate things and keep the new wife bound to Dan if she doesn't like it."

"It would be a case of history repeating itself."

"A terrible shame." They went off to the side and disappeared through a door into another room without looking in Paula's direction.

The little truck cut into Paula's palm. She opened her hand and looked at the red imprint it had left. Her life was not private. These women knew more about it than she did. Dan had never mentioned wanting children, and what did they mean by history repeating itself? What had happened with Katherine? Was there still something between her and Dan? Paula's head spun with questions.

"Paula?"

She turned, startled at Dan's call.

"There you are. Did you find the truck? Andrew won't go home without it."

Confused about the conversation she had overheard, she mumbled a 'yes' and hurried past Dan to Jane's car.

The drive home was torturous. Rowena was relating a story to Dan about the minister and how he hadn't visited some woman Paula had never heard of, called Betty, when she was sick in hospital. More gossip, Paula thought angrily to herself, and she tuned out.

It seemed Rowena must have had plenty to say about Paula. If the two women in church were anything to go by, the whole

community would know her business. She and Dan had not discussed their past and they had not really discussed a future. Not
things like children anyway. Had they done the wrong thing? What
was in Dan's past that was a terrible shame? She felt sure he loved
her but the Katherine factor was a mystery she wasn't sure how to
deal with.

Anyway, their marriage and children were Paula and Dan's business. She fumed again at the thought of Rowena discussing these
things with other people. How dare she!

★   ★   ★

Rowena watched the dual cab drive away then went into her house.
She flicked the kettle on and went to the bedroom to change into
casual clothes. She wanted a cup of tea and something to eat before
she made a phone call to the minister's wife.

Pam Mason was a sensible woman. She was a good support to her
husband who often got so caught up in the parish responsibilities
he didn't always have time for the little touches. Pam would know
how to help her husband patch things up with Betty. Not that he
could possibly have known the woman was in hospital. She'd had a
fall and was only in for observation, for goodness sake. Betty didn't
attend church often but was happy to tell anyone who would listen
how the minister had visited others in hospital but not her.

Rowena made a pot of tea, took a couple of homemade biscuits
from the tin and carried it all on a tray into her little sunroom.
Originally it had been a small verandah off the kitchen and she'd
had a door knocked through and the verandah enclosed with timber and glass. It was a cheery, warm spot in the colder months.

She poured her tea and ate one of the biscuits while she waited
for it to cool. Paula had been very quiet on the way home. Seeding
was a lonely time for farm wives and even tougher for new wives

from the city. She was glad Paula had become friendly with Jane. She was such a sensible down-to-earth girl. Even though she wasn't a local she would be a good influence on Paula.

While she sipped her tea, Rowena made a list of some of the other younger women in the district who might help Paula to settle in. A luncheon would be the thing. She stopped, pen poised over the paper.

"Blast," she muttered. She had several meetings and appointments that week, then Paula's parents would be here. The luncheon would have to wait.

She finished her tea and tidied up. There was the call to make to Pam and then she had Dan's lunch to prepare and deliver. If she didn't do it the poor boy would only have cold sandwiches. That was another thing Paula would have to learn. He needed good hot food to keep him going through the long hours of seeding.

So much depended on a decent return this year. Rowena had been quietly confident they could continue to pay their share of the loan for Harvey's place providing they had at least average returns. Dan's personal life had thrown a spanner in the works. Katherine was back and would have to be dealt with, and Dan's marriage had created expenses they hadn't factored in. He'd spent money on the wedding, furnishings, updating the plumbing for the old place and a new vehicle.

Which reminded her, he hadn't passed on the paperwork for some of those things yet. Rowena flicked a piece of hair from her face, looked over at the pile of papers in the basket waiting for her to tackle the quarterly tax statement and shook her head. She'd always done the farm books and enjoyed it. They'd progressed from the cashbook and shoe box full of cheque butts and statements to the computer years ago, and then had followed the new tax system and the enjoyment of keeping the books had gradually withered away.

She'd been to several financial and bookkeeping training days when it first came in. BAS, as they called it, had not been an easy task to learn. Even now, it still took hours of work and she'd grown to hate it. She shook her head again. The government had a lot to answer for, lumping the extra paperwork burden on them. Rowena turned her back on it. The paperwork could wait. She wasn't going to spoil her Sunday with it.

If she could get the BAS done in the coming week and Paula settled in, perhaps Rowena would go to Adelaide next weekend. The Crows were playing a home game and if Austin was in town they could go together. It was several weeks since she'd seen him. Even though he was travelling less now she hadn't been able to make the trip to the city. With a wedding, seeding, the new city girl and paperwork, she'd been too busy.

Austin was a wonderful man. He was kind and thoughtful and romantic. A few years ago she'd given up any thought of a relationship, let alone a physical one. Then they'd met at drinks after the football through a mutual friend. She closed her eyes and imagined his lips on hers. Warmth spread through her then her eyes snapped open. No point daydreaming.

Rowena gave a fleeting thought to his suggestion on their last weekend together that she give up the country life and move in with him permanently. She had to admit it was lonely now that Dan was married. If everything worked out and the finances were arranged maybe it was time for Rowena to make the move.

Still, that was in the future. The sun went behind the clouds, turning the day grey. A chill ran down her back. The temperature had dropped. She did up the buttons on her cardigan and flicked on the gas heater.

Rowena was glad Dan had finally found someone to share his life with. He'd had some tough times and he slipped easily into solemn and reclusive habits. Paula did seem to make him happy, but the house was barely habitable and the girl's poor parents were bound to get a shock. Maybe there was something more Rowena could do to help. Perhaps she'd go and visit Paula today. There was someone in town who might be useful with the redecorating. That was another call she'd have to make.

Rowena ran her fingers through her hair and headed for the phone. Once again she lamented Dan's decision to marry at this time of year and move a city bride into a rundown country house.

CHAPTER

6

"It looks great, Paula. You've done a wonderful job." Dan's strong arms wrapped around her as they stood in the doorway of the spare room and admired the paintwork. It was early morning but Paula was determined to spend a few minutes with her husband before he disappeared to that wretched tractor again.

He'd come home so late last night she hadn't even heard him come to bed. After several restless nights tossing and turning in the blackness, bereft of sound bar the breathing of Dan beside her, she had at last had a deep refreshing sleep.

"I am rather pleased with it." She nestled back against him, enjoying the closeness of his embrace.

"The coffee looks great against the paler colour of the woodwork."

"That was the colour Carl mixed..." She started to explain about the muddle up but Dan cut her off.

"I reckon that must be the kind of thing he suggested for the lounge. I brought him out here to give me some ideas before I started on the bedroom. He's got a good eye for colour."

Paula was stunned. So Carl had visited the house. Maybe he had intended she have that colour all along. Had Dan known Carl would mix his own version of colours? Paula turned in Dan's arms.

"You didn't say anything about selecting colours when you took me to Carl's." She studied him closely. He gazed steadily back at her, his look serious. She could detect no sign of duplicity.

"I'm sorry, I had other things on my mind that day and I knew Carl would have a better idea than me. I wish I could have done more of the painting before you arrived. I had planned to do the kitchen and lounge but —"

"It doesn't matter, Dan." Paula put her fingers to his lips. "Maybe we can tackle another room when you've got more time." She kissed him, and their closeness quickly turned into a passionate embrace.

"I'd better go." He broke away and held her at arms-length. "If we keep this up I won't get to the tractor."

"Would that be so bad?"

His face was serious again. "I'm sorry, Paula. I have to go." He kissed her on the cheek and left to put on his boots. Paula felt cold after the warmth of their bodies together. She glanced around the room one more time and sighed. Turning her back on her handiwork, she headed off to make the bed. There was a whole morning to kill before Rowena came.

She smoothed over the sheets and tried to work out what to make of Dan's aunt. She couldn't decide whether the woman liked her or not and she certainly hadn't forgotten the conversation she'd overheard in the church. Then, yesterday afternoon Rowena had called in on Paula with a casserole for their dinner. Which was just as well, she thought as she fluffed up the quilt. *I wouldn't be winning country woman of the year on my attempts at meals so far.*

Rowena had admired the spare room and they'd talked about how Paula was going to furnish it for her parents' visit. Rowena had some of the old curtains that had fitted the windows and she promised to bring them back with her the next day. She'd told Paula she would take her to drop off Dan's lunch and then they would go into town to meet someone who could help with the decorating.

That was the problem really, Paula thought. Rowena had told her what she would do. Paula gave the pillow she was holding an extra thump. She didn't like being told what to do. Some of the people she had worked with had made the mistake of thinking her size meant she was someone who could be pushed about. Paula had soon set them straight.

She smiled to think little more than a year ago she'd been executive assistant to the boss. It sounded fancy but was just another name for Marco's gofer. In one day she could end up covering anything from overseeing the reception, phones and meetings to casting her eye over a financial report. Then she might have an evening PR event to organise and finally end up in Marco's bed. How could she have been such a fool?

She pulled the quilt tight. Forget it. Sydney was another world now, another lifetime. Once again, she was thankful for Dan.

She checked the trap under the bed. No mice. She was still getting the odd one in the living areas. They were fairly thick outside but Dan was hopeful his baiting program would stop them reaching the plague proportions he'd experienced in the past. Paula just hoped she could keep her mother from seeing any. Mrs Crawford could get a bit hysterical over a picture of a mouse let alone the real thing.

Only a few more days and her parents would be here. Dan was probably right. It would be nice to have a bit of company and she knew her father wouldn't stay long. He never left his work for an extended time. She sighed and glanced at her watch. Time to tackle another project before Rowena came. The middle bedroom had to be swept out ready to stack the boxes her parents were bringing.

Paula pushed open the door. A rotten smell stopped her and her hand flew to cover her mouth and nose. She edged into the all-but-empty room wondering what could make such a stink. A fly buzzed in the corner and she remembered the trap. When had she checked it last? It must be a couple of days. Keeping her hand to her face she moved closer, bent towards it, then quickly stepped back as warm bile rose in her throat. A mouse lay caught by the trap and maggots writhed in its rotting body. She rushed from the room, gasped a deep breath of fresh air and steadied herself against the passage wall.

"How will I clean that up?" she moaned. Just recalling the sight made her stomach churn.

In the laundry she gathered rubber gloves, disinfectant, air freshener, hot water, and picking up a newspaper and a small broom she went back to the bedroom. Before she went in she tied one of Dan's clean hankies around her face, pushed the door open a little and squirted air freshener into the room; then with gloved hands raised she took a deep breath and pushed the door with her shoulder. She rushed to the old window and shoved it up as far as it would go.

Back at the door she armed herself with the broom and newspaper and turned to approach the mouse with the same stealth as a bomb defuser. She turned away quickly as the sight of the squirming maggots made the bile rise in her throat again. Reaching blindly she swept at the body. A quick peek showed she had it on the paper. She wrapped it tightly, trap and all, and rushed the bundle out.

Outside she took several gulps of fresh air before returning to the bedroom where she discovered several maggots still writhing in the spot where the mouse had been, looking for their dinner. Paula scrubbed at the floor with the hot water and large dollops of disinfectant until the only thing she could smell was the odour of pine. Her skin and hair reeked of it but it was better than the alternative.

By the time she could hear Rowena's car approaching along the race Paula was showered, changed and sitting on the side verandah in one of the wicker chairs she'd rescued. The old chairs and table had been stacked in the sleep-out among other old bits of furniture. She was sad to see most of it was beyond repair but she had dragged the chairs out and cleaned them. They had a few holes and straggly bits of wicker but were still usable. Some new cushions would make them quite comfortable. Tucked along the wall just outside the door where the verandah ran along to meet the kitchen, it would be a cosy spot to sit with a cuppa.

Paula shuddered as a vision of the maggoty mouse returned, along with the smell of pine disinfectant. She would have to remember to check every trap every day.

She distracted herself by focusing on the view across the gently sloping valley. It really was picturesque and one she didn't think she'd ever get tired of looking at. The deep earthy browns of the recently ploughed land showed up in sharp contrast to the patchwork grey and green shades of paddocks not touched yet. The darker shades of fences crisscrossed in straight lines, marking the boundaries dotted with trees.

Paula stood up as Rowena roared past and around to the back of the house. She was looking forward to going to town. Now that the bedroom was painted she did need a few things to go with the furniture that her parents would be bringing in the trailer. And she might be able to find some cushions and throw rugs to cover the old furniture. She wasn't sure where Rowena was taking her so she'd dressed in a beige cable-knit wool sweater and a chocolate brown long-line skirt with her flat boots. Even though the sun was shining there was a chill in the air and she'd thrown a soft woollen scarf in a blend of browns and soft yellows around her neck.

"Paula?" Rowena's call came from the kitchen. Paula drew in a deep breath and took one more look across the peaceful view before she went inside to find out what Rowena had in store for her today.

Rowena drove at breakneck speed across the dirt roads, only slowing down once they reached the track that led them to the paddock where Dan was working. She pulled up abruptly between Dan's vehicle and a truck with a huge container on the back. Paula was relieved to get out of the car and watch as the tractor Dan was driving worked its way around the paddock towing a huge machine spread out behind like a winged monster.

Tom climbed out of the truck to meet them as Rowena unpacked a basket of homemade pasties.

"Hello, Paula." Tom lowered his gaze as she smiled back at him.

"Come on, Tom," Rowena called. "Eat these while they are still warm. Dan will soon be here and you can take over while he eats his lunch."

Paula watched as Tom went back to the truck and poured water from a container over his hands before wiping them on an old towel. He still limped slightly but she was relieved to see he had boots on both feet.

"How's your foot, Tom?" she asked as he took a pastie from Rowena.

"Well and truly on the mend." Rowena's raised voice cut in. "Eat up, Tom. He's nearly here."

Paula looked from Rowena to Tom. Did she mean to be so rude?

"It's okay, thanks." His voice was barely audible over the noise of the approaching tractor. He gave Paula another of his lopsided smiles.

Rowena was already waving Dan out of the cabin as he stopped the huge tractor a few metres across the paddock from them. Tom set off towards it clutching his pastie. Dan climbed down from the cabin and talked to Tom before walking over the ploughed dirt to join Paula and Rowena.

"A picnic, ladies, how nice." Dan grinned and kissed Paula, then went to wash his hands. The tractor revved and then jerked before it moved away on its repetitive journey once more.

Dan sat on a drum and Rowena leaned on the car as they ate their pasties.

"How many acres have you done today?" Rowena asked as they all watched the distant tractor progressing around the paddock.

"Not many. The motor on the seed and super unit wouldn't start. It got moisture in it overnight so that set us back an hour or so."

"How is Tom going?"

"He's fine. No need to worry about him. It's the weather that bothers me." Dan nodded towards the western horizon at a low bank of dark clouds. "We've already had a hold-up today and I don't want rain again for a while. At least until we get this paddock finished."

Paula listened enviously to their conversation and wished she knew enough to be more involved. She wanted to be the one Dan shared his concerns with. She watched the distant cloud bank and then breathed in the freshness of the newly turned soil around her. Bathed in sunshine it was hard to imagine rain could be close.

"Have some tea, Paula. There's cake as well." Paula accepted the steaming cup but not the cake.

"I'm still eating the pastie." She watched as Rowena and Dan took slices of cake. They certainly ate fast. The pastie was large but she was enjoying the spicy taste of peppery vegetables encased in the thin crispy pastry. Had she eaten breakfast? She'd had coffee while Dan had eaten his but she couldn't remember eating anything herself. And she hadn't felt hungry after discovering the dead mouse.

"What are you getting up to in town?" Dan's question drew her back to the conversation.

"Rowena's taking me to meet someone."

"I thought Paula should go to Dara's new shop," Rowena said.

"It's been there over a year."

"That's new," Rowena countered. "Anyway, I think she may have some things Paula will like for the house."

"Uh-oh! I hear the sound of shopping." Dan grinned.

"Paula has to get out and meet people. I think she will enjoy a trip to Dara's." Rowena bustled about, packing up the lunch things and loading them into the boot. Dan rolled his eyes in Paula's direction and she gave him a nod. He had been put in his box.

"We will get to go out more once seeding is finished," he said quietly.

"I know. I'm fine, really, but Rowena offered to take me to town."

"Told you, more likely."

Paula giggled. "I'm looking forward to it anyway."

"And I'll give some thought to getting you a vehicle."

"It's okay, Dan. I know you're busy. I should have organised it myself."

Rowena shut the boot with a boisterous bang and got into the car.

"Get Dara to book the purchases to me," Dan said as Paula went to follow.

"I've got my card."

"She's an independent woman." Rowena started the car and backed away. Paula gave Dan a weak smile and a wave before she gripped the armrest. She didn't know whether to be more worried about Rowena's brusque tongue or her wild driving.

★   ★   ★

Dan watched as Rowena's vehicle roared off down the track and shook his head slowly. He had long ago given up worrying about her driving but now that she had Paula with her he felt some concern. He couldn't imagine how unbearable life would be if anything happened to Paula.

He thought briefly of his own parents and what a sad man his father had been. Dan couldn't remember his father any other way. Thank goodness for Rowena, who had made sure she brought some happy times into his young life. He was indebted to her. She had been the mother he never knew and she had tried hard to give him a normal childhood in spite of the sad shadow of his father never far away.

The sound of the tractor coming closer reminded him they still didn't have the replacement set of ploughshares he'd ordered weeks ago.

Bugger it. He'd forgotten to ask Rowena to call in at the agent while she was in town. It would save him a trip. The shares hadn't arrived when he'd been in town last week and the agent promised he'd have them by today. Blunt shares were a hold-up he didn't want to waste time on. Dan strode over to the truck. He'd have to try to catch Rowena on the two-way.

* * *

Paula tried hard to concentrate on the first part of the drive so she could remember the way, but it was useless. They were travelling from another direction and none of it looked familiar to her. She could find her way to most locations in Sydney with only a little help from her phone. Out here it was just endless paddocks, trees and fence lines punctuated with the occasional farm gate.

Dan's voice crackled at them from the two-way and Paula kept her eyes glued to the road as Rowena answered him and continued to drive at the same speed.

Rowena replaced the handpiece. "One thing you find out about trips to town, you can never go without having to bring something back for the men. Even when you think you've escaped without a list, they can still get you on the two-way. I've been thinking we should update our mobile phones and get one for you."

Paula was surprised at Rowena's sudden change of tack. "I've got one but there's no service in this area. I had been planning to get a new provider."

"There are still patches where we don't get service. For instance where Dan is now. The agents who visit him out that way say they can't call from there. Now, how long will your parents be staying?"

Again, Paula was taken by surprise at the speed of Rowena's change of topic. It was as swift as her driving. She was glad when they arrived in town and she could get out of the car. Rowena parked in the main street in front of an old two-storey stone building that looked like it may once have been a bank. It gleamed with a new coat of paint on its window frames and pots of flowering shrubs sat cheerily on either side of the polished wood and glass front door.

"Here we are." Rowena led the way. "Dara is doing a wonderful job with this place."

Paula followed her in through the front door where a tinkling bell announced their entrance. They stood in a huge room with high pressed-tin ceilings that ran back deep into the block from the street. All around them, antique furniture sat among pieces that Paula recognised as imports from her experience with her sister's business. There was not a lot of furniture but what was there was well displayed.

Brightly coloured woven mats and tapestries decorated the walls in between pictures and paintings representing various periods and countries. From the outside, it was impossible to know what an Aladdin's cave could be found within, and topping it all off was the wonderful aroma of freshly baked cake mingled with coffee. Rowena had packed them up in such a hurry Paula hadn't had the chance to have a piece of her cake and the smell was tempting her now.

"Hello, Rowena." A thin woman, taller than Paula, emerged from the back of the shop. She had fine dark hair swept back from her face and flowing down over her shoulders. Many couldn't get away with such a severe style but this woman had wonderful bone structure and piercing green eyes perfectly outlined with dark brown eyeliner, and ruby red lips.

"Dara, this is Dan's wife, Paula."

"Hello, Paula." Dara moved forward and the necklaces and bracelets she wore jingled softly as she shook Paula's hand. Up close, Paula could see fine lines etched into her face. She was probably older than she first appeared. "It's lovely to meet you. Welcome to the sticks."

"Thanks, Dara. You've got a wonderful collection here." Paula glanced around again at the contents of the room.

"It's a bit of a sideline. Keeps me out of mischief or I'd go nuts while Chris is at the farm."

"Dara, I'll leave Paula with you. I have some jobs to do and Dan needs me to collect parts from the agent." She looked at her watch. "I'll be back in an hour to pick you up, Paula."

They watched as Rowena swept out of the door.

Dara leaned in closer to Paula. "So, have you synchronised your watches?" She grinned. "How are you getting along with the mother-in-law from hell?"

Paula paused. She wondered if Dara's blunt response had exposed a kindred spirit.

"Put it this way, I don't think I measure up to her idea of what Dan's wife should be."

"Well, you're not from around here so that's one black mark. You're a city girl – that's another – and from interstate as well, oh dear." Dara shook her head.

"You seem to know a bit about me."

"That's all. Which is surprising really. The grapevine must be slipping. I guess I've been too busy redecorating this place."

Paula thought the grapevine was alive and well from what she had discovered already but she didn't want to dwell on that. "It's a credit to you, Dara. You've got some interesting pieces." Paula started to move among the furniture to have a closer look. She stopped in front of a redwood cabinet. "This is delightful. It's Chinese, isn't it?"

"You know your stuff."

"Not really. My sister has an importing business and I've seen similar things in her showroom. I can pick some styles and regions but I'm not as good at judging authenticity as she is."

"I was a flight attendant in another life. That was before Chris swept me away to the never-never." She waved her arms in a wide arc, making the bangles jangle loudly. "I've always been a history buff and collected unusual pieces but they didn't fit into the little house we lived in when we first married. When this old bank came up for sale, Chris suggested we buy it. You should have seen it when we moved in."

"Do you live here?" Paula thought Dara had said her husband was a farmer.

"Yes. I told Chris right from the start I wouldn't survive the isolation of a farmhouse."

"Oh." Dara certainly was frank. Paula wondered if Chris might be a bit henpecked.

Dara's eyes twinkled mischievously as if she could read Paula's mind. "I'm not that much of a witch, Paula. Chris is fifteen years older than me. He's travelled and tried a few different jobs in his time. He likes the farm but it's not his life's work as it is for many around here. His younger brother married a local girl and they've produced a brood of sons to keep the farm going. A lot of my money has gone into this place but it's really only a hobby. Chris is the one bringing in the income. The property's not far from town so he commutes." Dara's look became distant as if she was thinking of something else, then she gave a chuckle. "We've got a huge open kitchen-dining-living area at the back with a lean-to laundry. Then there're bedrooms and a more formal living room upstairs. Plenty of room and no kids to fill it with."

Paula wondered about that but decided to stick to decorating topics. "Have you done all the work yourself?"

"Most of it. I've kept the colours plain in here to accommodate the displays but Chris and I had a wonderful time with colours in the house and Carl is always a good source of inspiration."

Carl again, thought Paula. He appeared to have some influence on the local paint scene.

"Come on. I'll give you a quick tour."

Paula followed Dara into the kitchen behind the shop where there was a clutter of jars and pots, recipe books, and fresh food cooling under net covers. The disorder spilled over into the open living area with magazines, an overflowing bookcase and a desk covered in papers. Upstairs was totally different. Dara and Chris had transformed each bedroom into delightful replicas of past eras.

"This is wonderful, Dara. Do you do bed and breakfast?" Paula tested the comfort of a large rocking chair with a view through the window to the street below.

"Oh, no. We did the place up for ourselves really. I had so many special pieces of furniture to find homes for and we have city friends who enjoy it when they visit. Now, come on, have you got time for a cuppa before Rowena comes to rush you away?"

Paula returned to the shop to select her purchases while Dara went back to the kitchen to make coffee. The bell over the door tinkled. Paula turned and stiffened. Katherine Melton entered the shop, a takeaway coffee cup in her hand.

"Hello, Paula. Taking time off from the busy farm to visit us mere townies?"

Her tone was light but Paula could see a glint in her eyes.

"Just choosing some bits and pieces for the spare room." Paula indicated a cushion and throw rug she held in her hands.

"Dara does have some quaint little things. If I don't have time to shop in the city I've bought the odd little gift here. Mind you, she does have some delightful antique furniture from time to time." Katherine flicked a casual glance over the furnishings.

Paula was annoyed at the obvious dismissal of Dara's talent.

"Hello, Katherine." Dara appeared from the kitchen, all smiles.

"Oh Dara, I'm desperate for lunch. I've been too busy with clients to stop. Have you any of your delightful little pastries? I need some instant energy. I'm feeling lightheaded."

Katherine didn't look like she was about to keel over. She was dressed in flowing cream pants with a matching long-line jacket over a lacy top, all of which highlighted the well-defined curves of her trim body. Her perfectly made-up face glowed and her eyes glittered brightly.

"Sure, I've got a batch of beef and onion pies not long out of the oven. Will that do?"

"Wonderful," Katherine gushed.

Dara disappeared into her kitchen again and Paula seethed quietly. Katherine appeared so condescending and Dara was so nice.

"You're still keeping busy out on the farm then, even though it's seeding time?" Katherine looked her up and down.

"Yes, thanks, Katherine. I am enjoying trying my hand at redecorating."

"I hope you're not overlooking your skin. If you're painting it can do such damage."

Paula was glad her hands were hidden under the rug she was holding. She still had a few patches of paint that hadn't washed off and her nails were a mess.

"I guess you would need something to keep yourself busy." Katherine was touching things lightly without really looking at them and stepping closer to Paula with each word. "When you're not born and bred in the country, it can be difficult to adjust. I was amazed when I heard Dan had married a Sydney girl." Katherine smiled slyly at Paula. "Perhaps it was the temptation of someone new that attracted him. He is such a hard worker. I always thought he was married to the land. I hope he's not neglecting you. He's been too involved in that farm to make a commitment before now. We wouldn't want you scurrying back to Sydney, would we?"

She had moved so close that Paula was drowning in the crisp scent of her spicy perfume.

"I'm not going anywhere." Paula held Katherine's steely look and hoped her voice carried conviction.

"Here you are, Katherine." Dara returned with a small container and Paula took a step back, relieved to be released from Katherine's intense gaze.

"You are a darling, Dara. How much do I owe you?"

"Nothing. You can be the guinea pig. It's a different recipe I'm trying from an old country cookbook that belonged to Chris's mother. They might not be that good."

"If you made them, they'll be perfect. I must dash." Katherine took the bag Dara offered and gave Paula an angelic look. "Now, you take care, Paula. And let me know if you have trouble with your skin. I have the best cream. Dara can vouch for it."

"It is good stuff," Dara said as the tinkling bell signalled Katherine's departure. "I must admit my skin was a mess while we were doing up this place and Katherine gave me a pot of her special cream. It's too expensive for me to buy for myself, though I think she must buy it by the bucket full. Now, show me what you've decided on? The coffee's ready and I don't want you to miss out."

Once again Paula followed Dara out to her kitchen but her appetite for cake had waned. Katherine had unsettled her. Did she treat all newcomers to her malicious sense of humour or were her comments just for Paula? Either way Paula was quite sure she didn't like the woman at all.

★　★　★

After another frenetic journey with Rowena at the wheel, Paula emptied the bags and spread her purchases on the kitchen table. Dara's bright conversation had buoyed Paula's flagging humour and now that she was home she was keen to organise everything. She didn't want to waste time wondering about Katherine.

There was a plain rich-mocha mohair rug to go with the chintzy quilt cover she would put on the double bed her parents were bringing. Luckily the flowers on the quilt were a subtle pink and the tone in the rug should tie it all in with the wall colour. A taupe-and-coffee-patterned floor mat would add some warmth to the wooden floor. She'd picked out a couple of throw cushions, a small tablecloth for the old bedside chest she'd dragged out of the sleep-out, and a bedside lamp.

She hadn't intended spending so much money on the spare room but decided that once it was done there'd always be a place for visitors. Maybe Alison and the children could come for a holiday.

She also had a large checked throw rug to put over the worn leather couch in the lounge. There should be some cushions coming in one of her boxes to go with it and give the old couch a facelift. She had a momentary twinge of excitement at the thought of the trailer-load of things her parents were bringing. There wasn't a lot from her flat that she'd wanted to keep but she did have some favourite pieces and she was looking forward to installing them in her new house along with the beautiful wedding presents.

She thought sadly of some of the lovely things she and Marco had accumulated. He had made sure she left with only a few of them when she'd moved into a partly furnished unit after their breakup. She shuddered as she pictured Marco's smiling face. How could she have been such a fool, to have fallen for his manipulative charm?

"Forget him." Paula spoke out loud and the sound echoed in the empty kitchen. She shook herself, turned the music way up on the radio and packed away her purchases. She had brought home a delicious-smelling pie from Dara's and was going to prepare some special vegetables to go with it. The new man in her life deserved her attention. She just hoped he would be home early enough tonight to enjoy it.

CHAPTER
7

"Dan, where did this mail come from?" Paula waved at the small pile of brochures and envelopes on the kitchen table.

Dan was preparing himself some breakfast and turned to smile at her as he took a bite of toast. Paula's skin tingled under the wind-cheater and trackpants she had pulled on. That wonderful smile turned her to jelly.

"Rowena forgot to give it to you yesterday. She left it with me when she dropped off the shares."

Paula shuffled through the pile, sorting the junk mail from the envelopes. She picked up a letter addressed to her. The neat handwriting was her mother's perfect script. "Why does Rowena have our mail?"

Dan hugged her to him and she could smell the fresh toast he was eating. "That's another thing we have to sort out."

Paula stepped back. "What do you mean?"

"We have a mail bag that's dropped off a couple of times a week. I haven't been in to the post office to apply for one for us yet."

"Why didn't you tell me? I could have called in at the post office yesterday."

"I didn't think of it." He smiled at her again. "Anyway, it's no big deal, is it? Rowena passes on our mail."

"Eventually." Paula could feel her harboured resentment for Rowena's interference surfacing. "It's another thing she has to do for us, Dan. I'd prefer we had our own delivery."

"Okay, the next time one of us is in town, we'll organise it."

"Woodie, this is Tom, are you on channel?" Tom's voice crackled into the kitchen and Dan picked up the handset on the fridge to answer.

"Yes, Tom. Woodie here."

"I'm having trouble with the ute. Can you pick me up?"

Dan looked at his watch and frowned. "I'll be there in about twenty minutes."

"Okay." The two-way crackled and went silent.

"I don't know if it was such a good idea to give my old ute to Tom. He spends every spare minute tinkering with it and then he has trouble getting it going again." Dan gave Paula a kiss on the cheek. "I have to go. We'll sort out the mail soon, okay?" He picked up his food box from the table. "Can you call Rowena and tell her not to worry about lunch today. We'll be on the move and I'm not sure where we'll end up at lunchtime. I've packed some of Dara's pie."

"Why don't you call her on the two-way?" Paula muttered to the back of the door. She jumped as his head popped back round the door and he flapped some crumpled papers at her.

"If you see Rowena today, can you give her these? I keep forgetting."

Paula took the grubby dockets he thrust at her and the door swung shut again.

Her earlier light mood gone, she flopped down at the table. Last night had been wonderful. Dan had been home early enough to eat the meal she had prepared before it shrivelled up. Then they'd gone to bed and enjoyed the pleasure and the luxury of time together. Paula had wanted that closeness to continue this morning and instead she'd turned into the disgruntled wife and Dan had left before she could repair the mood.

There seemed to be a conspiracy to undermine her. Rowena managed the day-to-day running of their farm life and there was little Paula could do. The women of the district knew more about her life than she did.

"Woodie, are you on channel?" Tom's voice filled the kitchen again. There was silence followed by another attempt to get Dan. "Woodie, it's Tom. Are you on channel?"

"Yes, Tom. It's Woodie." Paula listened as the remote words flowed around her. Dan must have reached the car.

"I've got the ute going now. I'll meet you at the corner paddock."

"Okay, Tom. See you there."

The corner paddock. Which corner? Paula wondered how on earth they could come up with such a ridiculous name. How would she ever work out where they were? It was a different language. The two-way crackled and went silent.

Paula pushed back her chair. She was fed up with the radio interrupting her days with its snatches of words and other people's lives. There was always someone asking 'Are you on channel?' How could she be on channel when she felt like she was on a different planet?

She glared at the dials, reached up and flicked it off in frustration. It was all part of the network of things she didn't understand.

She took a deep breath, let it out slowly and unclenched her hands.

"Come on girl, you are an intelligent woman," she said in a whisper, then looked around imagining Dan observing her with his quizzical smile. *If he could see me now, he'd think I'd lost the plot*, she thought. The image brought a smile to her own face. Dan was a wonderful guy. In time she would make sense of his world. She didn't want to sink back into the despair she'd known before she met him.

A mouse shot across the floor and under the fridge. She was amazed at her lack of reaction. They didn't bother her so much any more and she was only catching one or two every so often. She checked the traps regularly, not wanting a repeat of the rotten mouse incident.

The trap that she had set beside the fridge was picked clean. Cunning little creatures had taken the bait without getting caught. She flicked it with her foot to set it off, then wedged another tiny piece of bacon rind onto the prongs. It seemed ridiculous to keep bacon for the mice, when no one else got to eat it. She often ate breakfast alone and when Dan was home there was rarely time for a cooked breakfast. She sighed at the thought of their very short honeymoon. They'd had time for each other and lingering breakfasts then.

Paula pulled back her shoulders. Dan had said tractor season didn't last forever. She'd have her man back to herself before long. In the meantime she had work to do. With the trap back in place she turned and surveyed the kitchen. She'd done very little with it apart from the initial clean up with Rowena. Today she planned to give it a thorough going over. Maybe she would try the oven. Dara's pie had been delicious. Paula decided to try her hand at cooking some different things.

The mail lay on the table where she'd left it. She put the kettle on and picked up the letters. First she'd read the news from Sydney. She had to admit she was missing her family a little. With no internet access she felt cut off from them. It was good of her mother to write. Paula couldn't remember the last time she'd received an actual letter.

Several minutes later Paula dropped the papers back on the table and sat back in a daze. Her mother's letter had been dotted with questions about her new life. Paula had become more and more tense as she'd read. Her mother even wanted to know where she got her fresh milk and bread from, for goodness sake. *She probably thinks I have to milk the cow and bake my own bread.*

"We do have supermarkets and refrigeration in the country," Paula muttered.

It was the last paragraph that had really sent Paula into a spin. The doctor was concerned that Susan's baby may arrive before the due date so her mother had hinted they might come over a few days earlier. Diane promised to phone before they left. Today was Tuesday. Paula was not expecting them until Friday; how much earlier did her mother mean? Had they left yet? Perhaps they were nearly there.

She went to the phone and dialled her parents' number. It rang for a long time then finally went to the answering service. She didn't leave a message. Perhaps her mother was out. Next Paula rang Alison and once more the only response was her voicemail. She could try her brother-in-law at the shop or perhaps even Susan. It was Tuesday though, the day Susan and her husband, Jerry, had to themselves and they usually slept in. Susan was only eighteen months older than Paula and was an accomplished chef who'd won several awards. She and Jerry owned three restaurants and Susan was only slowing down now when her first pregnancy was well advanced. Paula didn't like to disturb her with the baby so close. Perhaps she could try her father's mobile.

She reached for the phone again and it rang under her hand, startling her.

"Hello."

"Hello darling." Paula's relief at hearing her mother's voice was short-lived. "We're in Adelaide. Did Susan call you? We nearly didn't come. Alison has been having a bad time of it with poor little Oscar. He's been very sick."

"I just tried to ring. I couldn't get anybody."

"Alison and Susan both had doctor's appointments this morning. I didn't like to leave them but we're keeping in touch by phone. They insisted we come. The four-wheel drive is very comfortable to ride in. We had a much quicker trip than Dad had expected and got to Adelaide late last night."

Adelaide! Finally her parents' proximity registered.

"I tried to ring you Sunday before we left."

"We would have been at church."

"Oh, that's nice darling. Do you have one nearby? We'll be able to go together. I did ask Susan to let you know we'd left early. She's so preoccupied with the baby she must have forgotten. Now, do you need any supplies from Adelaide? Your father wants to call in on a business friend and I am going to the shops. Do you need any groceries? I can shop for you if you like."

"No thanks, Mum. I've done the shopping." Paula couldn't think what she had in the fridge but she wasn't letting on.

"We'll be there tomorrow, darling. I'm so excited. Here's your father, he wants directions."

Paula's brain scrambled as she tried to take it all in. Trust Susan to not let her know their parents were on their way. They would be here tomorrow and she wasn't ready for them. Her father wanted directions and she couldn't give them. Her hand went to her chest and she clutched at the collar of her shirt.

"Hello, Paula."

"Hello, Dad. You've made good time. How's the four-wheel drive experience?" Paula stalled for time. She didn't want to admit she couldn't direct her parents to her new home.

"It's a good vehicle to drive and comfortable to ride in. I think I've nearly convinced your mother we need one. I've looked at the map. It should only take us a couple of hours to reach you. How do we get to the farm from town?"

"It's a bit complicated, Dad." An idea formed in Paula's head. "Why don't you ring me before you leave Adelaide and I'll wait for you in town by the post office. You'll be able to find that easily in the main street and then you can follow me home."

"Good. We'll probably get away about eight o'clock but we'll ring first. See you in time for smoko, your mother says."

"Yes, bye Dad." Paula hung up the phone. Smoko! Where did her mother get these ideas? She looked around the kitchen and the old familiar anxiety rose and swirled inside her. She needed more preparation time. She'd planned a few more days of getting organised before her parents arrived. Not only that but she couldn't even find her way into town to meet them. She hoped Dan would be able to come with her.

She'd worry about that later. For now she wanted to give the main rooms the once-over. She went into the spare room and collected the painting things she'd left. The window was bare, framing a dull grey sky, and the room was very cold. Rowena hadn't dropped off the curtains she'd promised. Oh, and Dan had wanted her to tell Rowena not to bring lunch. Paula decided to call before she tackled the lounge and then she'd do the kitchen.

She also wanted to do some cooking. There had been a box of recipe books in the pantry. Maybe there were some recipes in there like the things Dara had made. There was a lot to do in a short time. She picked up the phone again to call Rowena.

Two hours later Paula glanced again at the battered little CWA cookbook lying open on the benchtop and hummed along with the radio. With the housework done she'd decided to tackle the cooking. She had selected this book from the collection assuming anything produced by the Country Women's Association would be foolproof.

There was an abundance of tempting cake recipes and with plenty of eggs at her disposal she had settled on a sponge. She had carefully added the eggs, one at a time, then beat the mixture madly with a fork. It was looking good. She cracked the last egg and gasped. A blueish-green blob fell into her mixture and a putrid smell assaulted her nostrils. She gagged.

With a wail she grabbed the bowl and spatula and made a dash for the door to the side verandah. It was a stiff door and she wrenched it with one hand, tipping the bowl and splashing some of the revolting mixture down the front of her shirt. Angry now, she pushed open the screen door and stomped to the side of the verandah where she scraped the remains onto the overgrown tangle of garden. How did she end up with a rotten one among all the other lovely deep yellow yoked eggs?

She washed the bowl, wrapped up the egg shells, changed her shirt and, with fresh determination, turned up the music on the radio and started again. This time it was an apple cake and she took care to crack the eggs into a cup before she added them to the mixture.

The oven was old and the door groaned as she opened it and peered inside. The light didn't work but the interior looked okay so she turned it on to pre-heat and went back to her mixture. The recipe called for two sandwich tins and she had only been able to find an old round cake tin in a cupboard. There was no baking paper. She hoped a good smearing of margarine would prevent the cake from sticking.

Her confidence restored, she hummed along with the radio again and decided she'd try an egg-and-bacon pie next. At least they'd finally get to eat some of the bacon instead of feeding it all to the mice. One of her magazines had a section on old-fashioned recipes which they'd jazzed up with a few new ingredients Paula didn't have. She'd found a similar recipe in a booklet put together by the

Uniting Church Ladies Auxiliary for their centenary. She decided she would serve the pie for lunch tomorrow.

Paula turned from her cake and sniffed the air. Was that burning? She opened the oven door and a waft of smoke puffed out. Flapping madly with one hand she reached up and turned the oven off. She couldn't see anything in the smoky gloom, then she remembered the torch.

By the time she returned the smoke had dispersed leaving an acrid, smouldering smell. She shone the torch into the oven and discovered a small black blob right at the back. Using a pair of tongs she gingerly picked up the cause of the problem. Horrified, she looked at the blackened remains of a mouse. It was stiff and dry. She hoped it had been already dead and she hadn't just burned it alive.

She dumped the residue into the bin, wondering how on earth it could have got into the oven in the first place.

"Now I'll have to clean the oven," she muttered.

She shone the torch into the dark recesses in case there were any other little surprises then went off in search of something to clean it with. It was an old oven and there was plenty of built-up grime that wouldn't budge. She decided to add a little of the pine disinfectant to the hot water in the final rinse then turned away quickly as she gagged. The warm pine smell reminded her of the maggot-ridden mouse. She quickly finished the job, holding her breath.

While she waited for it to heat up again she prepared the egg-and-bacon pie. The recipe simply said plain pastry, so then she had to hunt though the books until she found a recipe for pastry. She'd only ever used frozen sheets before and she didn't have any.

The pastry was very tacky so she added more flour and flattened it out on the benchtop with her hands. She had nothing to roll it out with. Improvise, Paula, she told herself. There was a bottle of chocolate flavouring in the pantry so she used that as her makeshift rolling pin.

The pastry didn't roll well and she had to stretch it and fill the gaps with off-cuts to make it fit the pie dish. She looked at her patchwork pastry and decided it would be covered with the egg and bacon anyway.

The oven was ready for the cake so she put that in. The last directions for the pie made her wail again. 'Cover with rest of pastry and bake in the usual way'. Rest of the pastry! She'd used it all, and what on earth was the usual way? "What kind of person writes a recipe like that?" she fumed.

The name of the person who had supplied each recipe was written in large print underneath. In the space below the egg-and-bacon pie was written MRS P PORKER. Paula's floury hand flew to her mouth. It had to be a joke. She glanced at the names printed under the other recipes. They were WILLIAMS, COLLINS and JONES. She couldn't imagine the ladies who had prepared this recipe book would have entered the name PORKER as a joke.

All the same Paula giggled to herself as she prepared the second lot of pastry. Well, Mrs P Porker, with a name like that you should know about bacon recipes.

She used less flour this time and the final result was a spongy mixture, which sagged into the spaces as she spread it over the top layer of bacon. Somehow Paula didn't think Mrs Porker would approve.

The pie fitted in the oven under the cake and Paula hoped the smell of fresh baking would replace the lingering charcoal odour mingled with a whiff of pine disinfectant. Then, remembering there was still the evening meal to prepare, she rummaged in the freezer and took out a pack of T-bone steak. She put it on to defrost in the microwave and double-checked the settings, not wanting a repeat of the chicken fiasco.

It was getting dark and she needed wood for the fire so she made a trip to the woodheap out past the back gate. She threw the chunks of wood quickly into her basket. There was no sign of any mice but she was sure she could hear them scrabbling under the pile.

Safely back inside, she lit the fire in the lounge and came back to the kitchen in time to remove the cake. There was a faint burning smell but everything looked fine. The top of the cake had risen and browned nicely but the pie was still a bit pale on top so she left it to cook a little longer.

There was no wire rack so she decided to turn the cake out onto the chopping board. But, as she tipped it, the top came away and the bottom stuck in the tin with half the apple. Paula looked at her crumbling creation in dismay and sniffed. She forgot the cake for the moment. There was definitely a burning smell.

She went back to the oven and opened the door. The smell was much stronger but the pie looked fine. She took it out and lifted it up. Through the clear glass dish she could see a blackened bottom.

"Oh no!" she yelped as the heat penetrated the tea towel. The pie dish ended up next to the broken cake and Paula stood miserably surveying the disaster that was her kitchen. What on earth had made her think she could cook? There were dishes piled in the sink, flour and egg shells scattered along the bench, assorted packets and the pitiful results of her labour spread across the table. There was not one decent thing to eat to show for all the mess.

'It's My Party' blared at her from the radio and she did indeed want to cry. Tears of frustration welled in her eyes, but the beeping of the microwave attracted her attention. She lifted out the bag of meat which was now warm and soft and looking nothing like T-bone. There were several bones and she belatedly spotted the label in Rowena's neat print, indicating it was a bag of large chops.

"Argh!" shouted Paula at the mess around her. "I can't even get that right."

"Paula?" Rowena's voice came from the back.

Paula hadn't heard the car. She flung the chops back in the microwave and rubbed at her eyes, cursing under her breath.

"Paula? I brought over the..." Rowena pushed open the door then stopped. She cast her eyes over the kitchen. "What on earth has happened here?"

It was the last straw for Paula. She could no longer hold back the tears. They flowed freely, making little trails down her flour-coated cheeks. She panicked as she felt the old despair wash over her.

Rowena put the bundle she was carrying on the one patch of table that wasn't covered in debris and sat Paula down.

"I'll make you a cup of tea. Don't tell me you've been trying to cook in that pig of an oven, you crazy girl." Paula leaned back in her chair. Rowena's words were like a slap. "It's well past its use-by date. It cooks everything well on the bottom and leaves it raw on top."

Paula watched Rowena as she stacked dishes and wiped benches.

"What were you cooking? Is that apple?" Rowena peered into the cake tin. "Apple cakes can be tricky. You need the apple to be very dry. Looks like the bottom was done but the middle wasn't." She poked at the pie dish with her finger. "We'll have to give that a good scrub. Was this going to be your tea?"

Paula shook her head. "Grilled lamb chops." She pointed at the microwave.

"I don't think the griller works at all." Rowena opened the microwave and pulled out the bag of meat. "Just as well. These are mutton chops, too tough to grill. Much better if you simmer them slowly with some onion and make a gravy. I thought you must have bought meat. We haven't killed a lamb in ages."

She put a cup of tea in front of Paula and started working on the chops. Paula watched her and tried to fathom what on earth killing a lamb had to do with anything and what kind of animal produced a mutton chop anyway? She wasn't going to ask Rowena, so she gave up and sipped at the hot, sweet liquid gratefully. She didn't usually take sugar but she was enjoying this. She realised she was thirsty. Perhaps she'd had a drink with her lunch but she couldn't remember having anything since.

"Feeling better?" Paula looked up and caught a glimpse of a reassuring smile on Rowena's face.

"Yes, thanks. I don't know why I let it get to me like that."

"It's a long day here on your own, with no one to talk to."

Paula didn't want to think about that. She stood up, embarrassed that Dan's aunt had found her, yet again, acting like a weak fool. "Here, let me do that. It's hardly fair you have to clean up my mess."

"That's all right. I called over to drop in those curtains." Rowena nodded at the bundle she had left on the end of the table. "They were my mother's pride and joy. She had a matching set in the second and third bedrooms. Dan's father slept in the second bedroom and I slept in the one you've painted for your parents so they should be a perfect fit. Now, I've still got a lot to do." She looked around the kitchen checking her handiwork. "I need those papers Dan left as well. I can't put off doing the quarterly tax statement any longer. Tomorrow morning I'm out at a meeting but after that I have to tackle it."

"Is that something I can help with? I am an accountant."

"Are you? I thought Dan said you did secretarial work."

"My last job was personal assistant to the company director. I oversaw everything, including the finances. My original university degree was accountancy." Paula left out the 'so there' but she thought it. "I could help with the paperwork."

"No." Rowena cut in quickly. "I've always done the bookwork. Our own accountant seems to think I keep everything in order. You've got enough to do here. There's absolutely no need for you to worry about the paperwork. Are these the receipts?" She hung up the tea towel and gathered up the dockets Dan had left. "I seem to recognise the state of the paper."

"I really would like to help." Paula offered again.

"I'll manage." Rowena's response was firm. "You've got enough on your plate at the moment. I'll have a word to Dan about that stove. He should have replaced that before he brought you here. Typical male, doesn't think about food till it's plonked down in front of him."

Paula didn't think Dan was like that at all. She bridled at Rowena's slur. "We'll sort it out, Rowena. I am capable of selecting a new oven."

"It's more than that. There are finances to consider. Dan's already spent a fortune in the last few months. Some things are more necessary than others."

Did Rowena's tone sound accusing? Paula remained silent. He'd only spent money because of her, or at least that's what Rowena was inferring.

"Anyway, if you'll be all right now I'll be off home."

"I'll be fine. Thank you," Paula replied stiffly.

"Keep an eye on those chops," Rowena commanded. "Let them simmer gently for another hour or so then thicken the liquid with some flour."

"Yes, thanks," Paula said to the empty room after Rowena had bustled out. *She doesn't even think you can manage to thicken a gravy.* Paula returned to the sink and scrubbed at the soaking cake tin. *She obviously thinks you're a useless animal, not worth the good farm money spent on you.*

Surely Dan could afford a new oven. If not, she'd buy it herself. Finance was another thing they hadn't discussed, beyond the wedding costs, which her family had split with Dan. Paula rubbed at the tin even harder. She was highly proficient at managing money. Even with the Marco fiasco she'd escaped without losing everything, although after she left him she'd only had short-term jobs until she met Dan, and now she wasn't earning an income from working. Paula's heart skipped a beat at that. It felt weird not to have paid employment. She hadn't thought much past marrying Dan. Surely there'd be something she could do from home. She glanced wryly at her phone and tablet lying idle on the dresser. If she could get a decent internet connection. At least she had some savings and several good investments still in place.

No time to think about that now. She was exhausted from a day's work that had been mostly unproductive. Tomorrow her parents were arriving. Paula picked up the bundle of curtains with a sigh. They were coming ready or not.

CHAPTER
8

Next morning Paula was out of bed before Dan. She did another check for mice, finding just one in the trap by the fridge, and made sure all of the traps were out of sight. The kitchen was spotless again and she sat down to write a shopping list. Once she got to town she would pick up a few things before she met her parents.

Dan had come home later than she'd hoped last night. She had told him of her parents' early arrival as he ate the stew she'd prepared. Then he'd gone to bed. He was asleep before she could join him. At least he'd agreed to go with her into town to meet her parents. Evidently he needed to pick up some extra chemicals to re-sow a patch that had been damaged by mice.

Paula had tossed and turned all night. By five o'clock she'd given up wrestling with her thoughts. When she was under pressure at work the only thing she could do was to get up and start tackling the job. Eventually exhaustion would catch up with her, but by then the current crisis would be over.

Dan stumbled in rubbing his sleepy face. He yawned and bent down to give her a hug. "You're up early."

"Just making sure everything is ready for Mum and Dad." His eyes were red and bleary and his hair stuck out in all directions. "You will be back to drive me in to meet them, won't you?"

"I'll be back." He yawned again. "I have to help Tom move the equipment on to the next paddock and make sure he gets under way okay."

Once he was gone, Paula showered, dressed and took one last look through the house to make sure all was in order. The room she had prepared for her parents was ready. The curtains Rowena had found were a good fit. The deep maroon and cream stripes were not what she would have chosen but at least there were curtains and they didn't clash too badly with her paintwork. Or should she say Carl's? She just hoped she would be able to find the box of spare bed linen and quilt easily among the containers her parents were transporting from Sydney. So much had happened since she had sorted what to bring and what to leave behind for the move halfway across the country.

The phone rang and Paula looked at her watch as she lifted the receiver. Eight o'clock.

"Hello, Paula."

"Hi Dad, how are you?"

"We're ready to leave. See you at the PO."

"Yes." Paula hoped her reply sounded cheerier than she felt.

"Your mother says to ask if you're sure you don't need anything from the city."

"No, Dad. See you soon." Paula hung up and looked at her watch again. It was nearly a half-hour drive from the farm into town. She hoped Dan would get home soon, so that she could shop before her parents arrived. She'd rung Dara last night and arranged to buy some of her home-cooked pies and cakes. Dara had wanted to give them to Paula but she had insisted on paying.

"You could do a good trade from people like me who can't cook or people like Katherine who haven't time," Paula had joked.

She glanced around the kitchen once more. Her shopping bags and esky complete with freezer blocks were by the door. Outside it was another grey morning. "All threat and no promise," Dan had said, looking at the sky. Paula wasn't sure she understood his preoccupation with water from the sky.

"Woodie Two, are you on channel?" The two-way barked into her quiet kitchen. "Paula, this is Dan, are you there?"

Paula turned and looked at the hated radio on her fridge. She had forgotten they'd added the 'Two' to distinguish between her and Dan. He was 'Woodie' and she was 'Woodie Two'.

"Yes, Dan. Paula here."

"We've had a breakdown. I'm waiting for the mechanic so I can't come home. I'm sending Tom back with the vehicle for you." Paula stared in horror at the handpiece. "Paula? Are you there?"

She pushed in the button. "Yes, Dan."

"You'll have to drop Tom back here."

Paula's head was spinning. She couldn't find her way to town from the house, how would she ever find her way from wherever 'here' was?

"Paula?" Can you hear me?" Dan's voice carried a trace of irritation.

"Yes, Dan." She wanted to remind him that she didn't know her way about and she'd never driven the new dual cab but she couldn't bear the thought of the local ears hearing of her naivety.

"Keep the two-way on in the ute, in case I need to reach you." There was a click and then silence. He sounded just like Rowena.

Paula could have been annoyed but she didn't have time. She was too busy panicking. What was she supposed to do now?

Her parents were on their way. In her head, she'd been playing over the scene of their arrival. She and Dan greeting them in town, then her parents following them home where they would all unload the trailer and Paula would produce one of Dara's delicious pies before Dan returned to work. Now there was no Dan to help her.

No doubt she should be grateful Tom wasn't bringing back the truck or tractor for her to drive to town. Tom. She looked at the pad and pen beside the phone. He would have to draw her a map.

When Paula told him she was a little unsure of her way to town Tom grinned and started to describe the journey. He was standing beside the dual cab drawing pictures in the air with his hands.

"Tom, would you please draw me a map." Paula waved the pad and pen.

Tom went quiet as the two-way crackled to life in the vehicle.

"Woodie Two, are you on channel, Paula?" Paula thrust the notepad and pen at Tom and got into the vehicle.

"Yes, Dan."

"You might as well drop Tom at his place on the way to town. The mechanic will be a while. Tom's got things to do at home and you can pick him up on your way back."

"Yes, Dan," Paula replied meekly, conscious of the unseen ears listening.

"Could you organise some lunch for him to bring back as well? Doesn't look like I'll be home for some time." The radio crackled for a moment. "Thanks, Paula."

Was that an apologetic tone? Paula hooked the handpiece back on to the radio and turned to look at Tom. He was hunched over the paper and pen. Paula looked from the lines he'd drawn to his face. His eyes were downcast and he chewed the corner of his lip.

"I'm not good with a pen," he mumbled.

Paula sensed he was uncomfortable and tried to put him at ease. "Well, I can go one better than you, Tom. I really have no idea of how to get to town and I've never driven a dual cab." She smiled at him and he grinned back.

"The jobs at home can wait," he said. "I could drive you in."

"How about a compromise? You teach me to drive this monster and give me directions."

"Sure." Tom's grin was even wider.

"And Tom." Paula lowered her voice. "If you ever need any help with that paper and pen, let me know."

He met her look briefly then climbed into the ute.

After a couple of lurching, gear-crunching starts they were on their way, both of them grinning like a pair of conspirators.

Paula was amazed at how much she did remember of the journey but there were a couple of corners where she would have made a wrong turn, if it hadn't been for Tom quietly giving directions. Driving the dual cab was a breeze by the time they reached town but it was much trickier to park than her little car.

She shopped for groceries, picked up her food from Dara and still had time before she expected her parents. Tom had followed her about, quietly helping her with her purchases. Dara had insisted he try one of her chocolate chip and macadamia muffins and Paula had been drawn to some beautiful multi-coloured raw silk scarves from Nepal. She bought one for her mother.

Now they sat waiting outside the post office. Paula remembered the mail delivery. She went inside to organise it. The building was very old and, inside, the small public space was filled up with every kind of post and general office need.

She explained about the change in delivery to the short, beady-eyed woman behind the counter.

"It's lovely to meet Dan's bride at last," she said. "He's kept you a real secret." She pulled out a form and began to write on it. "I will need to see some identification, of course."

Two more women came into the shop behind Paula. She reached for her purse, then stopped.

"I have my driver's licence, but it's still got my maiden name and Sydney address."

The woman stopped writing and peered at Paula over her glasses. "Oh dear, that won't do, I'm afraid. You could be anybody claiming to be Dan's wife, you see."

Paula stood looking at the woman. The door opened again and someone else joined the queue.

"Do you have your marriage certificate?" the woman behind the counter asked in a loud voice.

"Not with me." Paula started to back away. "I'll have to come back another day."

"Yes dear. Make sure you bring the correct documentation." She glared at Paula, then tore up the form she had been writing on. "Right then, who's next?" The woman behind Paula stepped up to the counter. Paula turned and made a dash for the door.

"Hello, Paula." She had almost stepped straight into Katherine Melton. "Marg is a bit of a stickler for the legalities."

"Yes…I hadn't thought." Paula stumbled over her words.

"Getting married adds a whole lot of legal documentation. Do come and see me if I can be any help." Katherine smiled her predatory smile.

"Thanks, Katherine. I'm in a bit of rush. Bye." Paula's words ran together and she charged out the door just as Tom was coming the other way.

"Sorry, Paula," Tom said as they narrowly missed each other. "I was coming to find you. Dan just called to ask you to pick up the chemicals at the agents. Looks like we'll be back to work sooner than he thought. The mechanic had the parts to fix the air seeder."

"Why don't you take the dual cab and pick up what Dan needs?" Paula glanced at her watch. "I'll wait here for my parents. Come back for me when you've got it."

Tom got back in the dual cab and pulled away from the curb and Paula walked a few steps along the footpath taking deep slow breaths. She couldn't believe how stupid she'd been in the post office. Something as simple as organising her mail had turned into a major drama. Had she really got her life back together? Where was the woman who could run a busy office single-handed?

"You look like you've got a lot on your mind."

Paula looked up. Jim McInerney was standing on the footpath carrying an armload of envelopes and parcels. He was dressed up again in a shirt, large bright tie and the checked jacket, though Paula thought he looked a bit weary today.

"Hello, Jim. I'm waiting for my parents. They're coming to stay for a few days. Are you doing the errands as well as selling the cars?"

"My office manager is sick and so is my best mechanic. We're all pitching in to hold the fort." He said it so cheerfully that Paula imagined he could be going down with the Titanic and still manage a smile. "The dreaded lurgy is taking its toll."

Paula looked at him.

"The wog," he explained. "There seems to be a particularly nasty flu-type thing doing the rounds."

"Oh, yes. I've heard a few people mention it."

There was a toot and Paula turned to see a four-wheel drive towing a trailer pulling up beside her. She took another deep breath. Her parents had arrived.

"Your visitors are here. They're staying for a few days, did you say?"

"About a week."

"Right then…well…" Jim paused a moment as if he was considering something. "I'll leave you to it then."

"Darling, it's so good to see you." Paula's mother was rushing towards her. She hugged Paula and stepped back. "You still feel so thin. I thought this fresh country air would be good for you."

"It is, Mum. I'm fine." Paula smiled at her father as he walked towards her.

"Hello, Paula." He threw his arms around her. She felt like a little girl again. She had to remind herself she was closer to thirty than twenty. How did her parents manage to make her feel like a child? She straightened her shoulders and stepped back. She looked around for Jim so she could introduce him but he was gone.

"How was your trip?"

"No problems." Her father glanced back at the gleaming white hire car. "The vehicle handled very well."

"The roads are quite good, aren't they," her mother said. "And everything is so well signposted."

"We're not exactly the outback here." Paula defended her new home but at the same time she was thinking about the next part of the journey, with rough dirt roads and hardly a signpost in sight.

"Hello again, Paula. These must be your parents."

Paula turned to meet Katherine's charming smile. In turn she painted a smile on her own face.

"Katherine Melton, I'd like you to meet my mother and father, Diane and Rex Crawford. Katherine is a solicitor." There, she did still have it in her, the perfect hostess on the outside hiding the turmoil within.

"Well, I didn't realise the town would be big enough for a solicitor."

"We have an extensive practice, Mr Crawford. We have offices in two neighbouring centres and one in the city. Since my father died I oversee the whole business, but I have a particular connection here, so this office is the one I like to give special attention to." She glanced meaningfully at Paula.

Paula ignored her. She had enough to deal with at the moment without letting her imagination stray to the Dan and Katherine connection.

"I'm glad to see there are opportunities for professional women in the country. Paula is a talented businesswoman. I am sure she will be looking for another challenge, once she has the homemaking under control."

Paula listened in amazement to her father. How could he think he knew what she would do or how she would feel and how dare he discuss it with Katherine of all people? The visit was going to be a disaster, she could tell already.

"It looks a pretty little town, Paula. I can't wait to see your new home, darling." Her mother squeezed her arm.

"Yes, you're in Dan's grandparents' old place, aren't you Paula?" Katherine said. "Dan must have done a lot of work on it. No one's lived there for years. And of course you've been dabbling with paint yourself, haven't you?"

Paula seethed inwardly but smiled at her parents. "We have made some changes, but I did warn you there's still lots to be done," she explained.

"We don't mind roughing it, darling." Once more her mother squeezed her arm.

"I'm sure it will be quaint. I'd love to see what you've accomplished." Katherine beamed at Paula.

"You should come while we're here, shouldn't she, Paula? We want to get to know Daniel and Paula's friends."

Paula looked at her mother. There she was, trying to organise things again. The last person Paula wanted to invite over was Katherine.

"Those clouds look a bit threatening." Rex was looking skyward. "Is it far to your place? We probably should try to get this trailer unpacked or at least under cover."

Paula was grateful for her father's interruption. The grey day had certainly turned even greyer while they had been standing talking. A premonition perhaps, Paula thought grimly to herself.

"We just need Tom back with the vehicle and we can get going," she said.

"Tom's lucky to have that job. I believe he's virtually illiterate." Katherine's smile was smug. "So nice of Dan to offer the poor boy work."

Paula glared at her. Trust her to give her parents an opinion on Tom before they'd had the chance to meet him for themselves. The dual cab pulled in behind the Crawford's vehicle.

"He's here now. Nice chatting to you, Katherine, but we should be off. You follow us, Dad." Before anyone had a chance for more conversation Paula strode to the dual cab and climbed into the driver's seat that Tom had just vacated.

"I'll introduce you to my parents once we get home, Tom. I don't like the look of this weather." Paula started the dual cab but her eyes were on her father shaking hands warmly with Katherine rather than the clouds building up overhead. She pulled out from the curb, narrowly missing another vehicle, and drove slowly down the road while her parents scrambled to follow.

The drive home was torturous. How would she manage a week with her parents? What would she do with them for all that time? Dan was so busy he wouldn't be around much for entertaining. She slowed as she realised she was leaving her father too far behind.

Katherine's smug smile danced before her. The woman was like a snake. She and Dan had obviously been a couple, Paula knew that much. A striking couple, if the woman at church was to be believed – but that was in the past. Dan had agreed to sort something out after seeding. What could it be? What was the secret that bound them together?

Once they left the bitumen, she had to concentrate to remember her way home. Several times the dual cab bounced through sloshy potholes and snaked around corners. Paula gripped the steering wheel and concentrated on finding her way. She pulled up with a lurch beside the house and realised she hadn't spoken a word to Tom.

"We made it." She gave him a grateful smile.

"Yep."

"Thanks for helping me, Tom. I couldn't have got there and back without you."

"Yep."

"This dual cab isn't so hard to manage."

"Yep...you might just want to watch it on the dirt roads though, especially when it's wet. They can be tricky, but...you'll be right."

Paula looked at his serious face. He was quite pale. "Sorry Tom. I did bounce us around a bit, didn't I?"

"You sure you haven't been having lessons with Miss Woodcroft?" He broke into a grin showing off his crooked teeth.

"Oh, no. Was I that bad?" She laughed, recalling her tense rides with Rowena.

"You'll be right." He turned away and they got out of the vehicle to meet her parents.

"Do you think it's going to rain?" Rex asked after the introductions. It wasn't even lunchtime but the day had become quite dark. The slight breeze had dropped right away.

"Looks like it could. I can help you get your stuff off the trailer, if you like," Tom offered.

"Thanks, Tom. There are a few bigger items. Are you sure Dan won't need you?" Paula was nearly going to add that she didn't want to get Tom into trouble but she stopped herself. He wasn't a slave to be ordered about. He'd offered to help unload. Surely Dan wouldn't be cross about that.

"He hasn't called back since we were in town. It would take a while to fix the air seeder. Its wheels fell off."

Paula looked at him to see if he was joking but his face was back to his usual reserved expression. "Is that the machine he tows behind the tractor?"

"Yep. We were shifting it on to the next paddock and both wheels just fell off. Bearings went."

Paula stifled a smile. Tom was very solemn but the vision his description conjured in her head was amusing. Poor Dan. Now she understood why he would be annoyed and impatient. "If you help my father move the big stuff, I'll put together some lunch for you to take back to eat with Dan. Is that okay?"

"Yep."

Paula gave her mother a quick tour of the house. In each room Diane found something to be delighted in while Paula kept a wary eye for stray mice or protruding traps. Tom helped her dad unload the kitchen dresser, double bed and sofa bed. The rest of her gear was smaller and they could manage it themselves with the trolley Tom had brought from the shed. Paula sent him on his way with a gourmet lunch, courtesy of Dara.

The weather remained threatening but still no rain fell. They stacked the rest of the contents of the trailer in the enclosed verandah and sat down to eat their share of Dara's pie and cake.

"Darling, this is delicious. Does Dara have a shop in town? I must take some back with me when I go."

"She really only does the cooking as a sideline. She has a treasure trove of furniture and knick-knacks, some imports and some locally scrounged pieces. You'd love it, Mum." Paula handed her mother the gift she'd bought that morning. "I got this for you, from Dara's."

"Oh, it's beautiful, darling, thank you." Diane threw the scarf around her neck. The vivid pinks and blues looked beautiful against the hot pink long-line cardigan she wore over a black polo top. Paula could see the tears brimming in her mother's eyes as she stood up and hugged Paula.

"We've got all sorts of things for you in the car, haven't we, Rex."

"Yes, but I think I'll leave you two to go through that. I want to stretch my legs before this weather takes a turn for the worse. How far does your land go in each direction from here, Paula?"

Paula looked out the window at the gloomy day. She had no idea how many of those paddocks belonged to Dan. "I wouldn't go far, Dad. It could rain at any moment. I'm sure Dan will take you for a tour when he's got time."

"It sounds like Daniel works very hard, darling. I hope he's not neglecting you." Diane gathered up their plates.

"Don't be silly, Diane. A man has to work hard to get on. Paula will have to learn that lesson now that she's married him. I'll be back in a while."

Paula watched his departing figure in surprise. Her father was known to be curt at times with her mother, but not usually with her. His comment stung. She recalled he had thought her crazy to break up with Marco but his comment about work was a bit tough.

She knew all about hard work. Her father had taught her that lesson well.

"He's tired from all that driving and you know how testy he gets when he's away from work for too long, darling," Diane soothed.

Paula looked at her mother and wondered why she never stood up to her father. Alison was the same, always giving way and smoothing the path. Susan was the only one who snapped back and gave him some of his own medicine. Paula had rarely borne the brunt of his sharp tongue. Her sisters always called her the spoiled one. The few times in her life she could recall her father losing his temper with her, it had sent her into a hurt, brooding silence. Now she wondered why she just didn't give him his own back like Susan did.

"Come on, let's get the rest of the things out of the car." Her mother was cheerfully oblivious to Paula's tension. "We have more gifts and there are all your wedding photos to look at. They're just delightful, Paula. It was a lovely wedding, wasn't it? You made a beautiful bride and Daniel looked so handsome in his suit."

"Dan," Paula muttered underneath her breath as she followed her mother out to the car.

"Oh and you'll be pleased to to see your coffee machine. I called in and bought you a big supply of pods."

"Thanks, Mum." Paula's spirits lifted at the thought of saying goodbye to instant coffee. She often drank tea but when she drank coffee she preferred it from her machine.

Despite her original misgivings, the afternoon was a lot of fun. Her sisters had sent some extra gifts. One was a beautiful gilt-edged mirror to hang over the mantel in the lounge. Alison had sent her a gorgeous soft blue chenille bathrobe with a note that read 'Something to keep you warm when Dan's not home!' Paula laughed when she opened Susan's gift. Inside the beautiful wrapping paper were two cookbooks by popular television chefs. She got her useless tablet out and stuck in the photographer's USB. While they flipped through the wedding photos Paula told her mother all about her cooking fiasco of the previous day.

"Darling, why don't we go and buy you a new oven?"

"It's okay for now, Mum. Dan and I will buy a new one later." Paula wished Dan could be here now. She flipped back through the photos. Her sisters looked gorgeous in their shell-pink satin. Even though the design of the dresses was slim-fitting, you could hardly see the bulge that was Susan's baby.

"The girls and I had this done for you." Mrs Crawford handed over a flat parcel, delicately wrapped in layers of soft white tissue and tied with a pink ribbon.

Paula opened up the layers to reveal a photo of Dan and Paula on their wedding day. It was a black-and-white photo, framed in gilt similar to the mirror. Paula smiled. "It's lovely, Mum. Thank you." She looked back at the photograph. She and Dan were holding hands as they walked across the lawn at her parents' home. She was laughing up into Dan's smiling face. Her mother was right, it had been a wonderful day.

CHAPTER
9

"You've got such a lovely garden here, Paula."

Paula and her parents were sitting on the old wicker chairs she had placed on the side verandah. Her father had his nose buried in a business magazine. Yesterday's threatening weather had cleared away and they were enjoying a coffee in the weak mid-morning sunshine.

Paula looked out over the tangled bushes and weeds. "Do you think so?" She'd never been one for gardening. Unless you counted the potted palms she'd watered on the terrace of the apartment she'd shared with Marco – she hadn't needed to do anything more. They were on hire and replaced regularly.

"It needs work but there's lots of potential. Would you like me to make a start while we're here, darling? I'd like to do something useful for you."

"Mum, you're on holiday, relax."

"I find gardening very relaxing."

"Yes, when you're getting other people to do it for you." Rex looked over the top of his reading glasses then went back to his magazine. The Crawfords had a beautiful garden. These days they paid a gardener to do all the heavy work but Paula knew her mother had established the garden and still made all the decisions and did a lot of the in-between things.

"What do you think, darling?" Diane went on as if her husband hadn't spoken. "Would you like me to give it a go?"

Paula decided to follow her mother's lead and ignore her father. "Why not? It will give you something to do."

Rex snorted from behind his magazine.

"I mean, there's not a lot else to do here," Paula added quickly, not wanting to sound ungracious.

"Good." Her mother stood up. "I don't suppose you have any gloves?"

There was another snort from behind the magazine.

"I've got rubber gloves in the kitchen."

"They'll do."

Paula gathered the cups and went inside. She wanted to distance herself from her father before she lost her temper with him. Why was he being so negative?

By the time she returned with the gloves her mother was prodding at things in the side garden.

"There was probably a lawn here once." She indicated the ground around her. "And there are some lovely old bush roses here. They just need some attention."

Paula handed her the gloves.

Diane glanced around. "We'll need some secateurs or something similar and a wheelbarrow."

"There might be something in the shed."

Paula made her way from the side garden to the car shed. It was an old stone building set apart from the house. Inside, along the front wall was a solid old workbench and hanging on the wall above it was an assortment of dust-covered tools. Among them, she found a pair of long-handled hedge clippers but nothing else that looked useful for gardening.

She went across the bare yard to the big shed where Dan kept other machinery. This is where Tom had come for bits and pieces to fix the back door. She peered around warily. She had tamed the mouse population in the house but Dan said they were still causing some concern in the paddocks. In the corner, she found an ancient wheelbarrow with a metal front wheel. She dropped the shears into its rusty base and pushed it, the old wheel protesting loudly, back to the side garden.

Her parents were both deep in the bushes, a pile of weeds on the ground behind them.

"We took a couple of knives from the kitchen." Diane waved a large chopping knife at Paula. "I hope that's okay."

Rex took the old shears and began chopping under his wife's supervision, his earlier grumpiness forgotten. Paula began to pick up the foliage they'd dumped on the ground and relaxed a little. Perhaps her mother was right. Gardening could be therapeutic for them all.

★ ★ ★

A few days later they were all outside when Rowena arrived.

"You must come over for dinner while you are here." Rowena was inspecting the garden with Diane while Paula watched, with her father, from the verandah.

"That would be lovely. Thank you, Rowena." Diane replied for all of them.

"I'm on my way to Adelaide but I'll be back on Sunday. How long are you staying for?"

"We can't stay too long. I have to be back for a meeting later next week."

"We will stay until Tuesday though, won't we, Rex? You did say we could have a week."

Rex folded his arms over his rounded stomach. "Don't forget the driving time."

"Shall we make it Sunday night?" Rowena suggested. "I'll be back by then."

Paula smiled. There was still the weekend to fill and no sign of Dan being home for long. He had put in brief appearances for meals and had promised to take them on a tour of the property but so far it hadn't eventuated. They had gardened for two days and Paula was amazed by the transformation of her garden under her mother's careful supervision. The nights were quiet though. At least a meal at Rowena's gave them something else to look forward to.

"Do you drive to Adelaide often, Rowena? It's quite a distance." Diane's prying was a match for Rowena.

"Oh, it's not far. I only go when I'm not needed to manage things here." She looked at Paula, who bristled. What was Rowena implying?

"It must be a relief to know Daniel has Paula to look after him now."

"Daniel?" Rowena frowned. "Oh, you mean Dan. Yes, although I brought him up to look after himself."

Yes, Paula thought murderously. That's why you still run around after him. Out loud she asked, "What time would you like us on Sunday, Rowena? We don't want to be a bother. Are you sure you wouldn't rather come here?"

"No, Paula. I'm not sure what we'll have yet. I'll probably pick up dessert at one of those cheesecake places. Come over about six pm. Tell Dan I'll make a take-home pack for him, if he's still on the tractor. Now I must get going. The Crows play tonight and even though we've got members' tickets, you have to get there early to get a decent seat."

"It must be impressive to watch at the Adelaide Oval." Rex fell into step beside Rowena.

"It's certainly wonderful for the game but parking's a nightmare."

Paula trailed behind as her father and Rowena talked the pros and cons of the facilities.

They all waved Rowena off. In the distance they could see a tractor moving around a paddock, turning the light brown soil a deeper shade of brown in its wake.

"Is that Daniel?" Diane asked.

"He's called Dan, Mum..." Paula hesitated. She had no idea where Dan was working at the moment. Since her parents' arrival she had hardly had a chance to talk with Dan alone. Last night she'd fallen into bed before he came in. "I'm not sure. Probably not."

"He said he was moving to a paddock closer to the house today." Rex took a few steps in the direction of the tractor.

Diane went back inside the yard to continue with the garden. Paula stayed with her father.

"When did Dan say that?"

"Last night. I was still reading by the fire when he came in. We had a good talk while he ate his meal. It's a big business this farm, Paula. So much depends on things beyond Dan's control, like the weather, grain prices, stock prices, governments..."

"I know, Dad."

"Do you? It's a large monetary commitment. You wouldn't want to lose any more should things go wrong."

"I'm sure Dan knows what he's doing." Paula wasn't going to talk about personal finances with her father when she hadn't discussed it with Dan first. She started walking towards the front gate where her mother had tamed the lavender bushes on either side, creating a living frame for the path stretching up to the front steps.

"Yes, but do you?"

Paula kept walking and ignored her father's last words. The strong scent of lavender filled the air as she brushed past the bushes. She hoped her father hadn't been discussing their finances with Dan. She had lost money in the breakup with Marco. Even though she had some personal investments he had wrapped their shared assets up so well that she had walked away losing her share of the apartment altogether. She didn't care in the end. She had simply wanted to be rid of him.

But she and Dan were different. If things went wrong with the farm she was prepared to do what she could. Paula stopped and looked back over the lavender and the wire gate, to the tractor making its way around the distant paddock. Her father was looking that way as well. She had assumed he meant if things went wrong with the farm but maybe he had meant with her marriage. He hadn't wanted her to marry Dan so quickly. Well, he was wrong if he thought she and Dan wouldn't last. They loved each other. They would work out the rest as it came.

The sound of an approaching vehicle brought Diane to the steps and they all watched as an old green car sailed past the front of the house and round the side, towards the back gate.

"You don't very often see a working EJ Holden these days." Rex's voice carried a hint of admiration and he walked off to follow the car.

"Who's that?" Diane asked.

"Uncle Gerald," Paula called over her shoulder as she went inside. "I suppose I'd better put the bloody kettle on again," she muttered to herself. Rowena had arrived just as they were getting up from the breakfast table, so they had offered her a cup. Now Uncle Gerald would want a cup of tea. They would never make it into town this morning.

An hour later they were standing in the middle of Dara's shop. After Rex had admired Uncle Gerald's car, the old man had had a quick conversation about the prospect of a storm and then been happy to drive off again without stopping for a drink. Rex had driven them into town, then left them to their own devices.

"Dara, this place is just delightful."

"Thank you, Mrs Crawford."

"Do call me Diane. You have such a wonderful eye for display." Diane picked up a small hand-knitted vest. "This is gorgeous. I could see Oscar in that."

"Do you have some of your delicious food we could buy?" Paula gave Dara a hopeful look.

"I'm sorry, Paula, I haven't started the baking today."

Paula detected a weary note in her voice. "No, I'm sorry, I should have phoned first."

"You don't have to. Normally I bake every day but Sunday. I'm late starting today. I have some things in the freezer if you don't mind taking home frozen food."

"Please don't worry on our account, Dara." Diane put the vest and an embroidered bib on the counter. "Rex and I did enjoy the pie that Paula bought from you on our first day but we can cook our own."

Paula would have laughed and said "Not in my oven", but something was wrong. Dara's dark hair flopped around her pale face and the fine wrinkles in her skin looked more pronounced. She wasn't wearing her usual carefully applied make-up.

"Would you like a cuppa?" Dara's offer lacked her typical bubbliness.

"No…"

"Yes…"

Paula and her mother answered at the same time.

"We don't want to hold you up," Paula said.

"If you don't mind sitting in the kitchen while I work, I'd like you to stay. I wouldn't mind some company."

"You show me where everything is, I'll make the tea." Diane bustled forward. "Paula can go without but I need my cups of tea to get me through the day."

Paula held her breath waiting for her mother to add the line about getting to know Paula's friends but they followed Dara into the kitchen in silence.

The normal clutter of jars and fresh food on the big old kitchen table had been replaced by neat stacks of papers, cheque books and ledgers. The benchtops were clear and gleaming and the assorted glass containers for flour and sugar were placed neatly along the open shelves above the sink. Paula looked around in amazement. The whole place sparkled and a delicious smell filled the room. A large pot simmered on the stove top.

Dara looked up from the papers she was moving into bigger piles trying to make space on the table. "Chris has been home."

Paula looked at her, not understanding.

"He's the tidy one. When he's not busy on the farm he loves to cook, he's responsible for the vegetable soup." Dara nodded towards the stove. "But he's even better at cleaning up."

"What a wonderful husband. I hope you appreciate him." Diane's smile turned to dismay and Paula looked on in concern as her friend slumped down on a chair and put her head in her hands.

"I do. He's a wonderful man and we are so lucky in many ways. But I don't know what to do. He's so unhappy on the farm." A tear ran down each of Dara's cheeks.

"What do you mean, unhappy?" Paula sat down beside her.

"Chris is the oldest of two boys. He's travelled and worked at other things but he's always come back to the farm. He's the oldest son and it's expected of him. Since we married he's stuck at it but his brother's children are getting old enough to help and they're all keen to farm. We don't have children. We both decided it was too late for us, when we married. Without someone of his own to follow on, Chris no longer has the heart for farming."

Diane brought steaming cups of tea to the table. "Can't Chris sell his share and do something else?"

"It's all so complicated. They've had a few tough years and the property struggles to make enough for one family, yet it pays for three. His brother, us and his retired parents."

"What about your shop?" Paula asked.

"It's a sideline really. I've put money into stocking it but I just make enough to be able to buy more."

"Could you move somewhere else to find work?"

"It might come to that. But we've put so much work into this place."

"It's a pity you're so far from the city," Diane said. "Do you get any tourists out this way?"

They were interrupted by the bell over the shop door.

"Oh no!" Dara rubbed at her face. "I must look a sight."

"Let me go out," Paula said. "You stay and finish your tea."

Paula walked through to the shop where a man and a woman dressed in smart, casual clothes were browsing among the furnishings. They had the relaxed look of tourists.

"Can I help you?" she asked.

"Well, we hope so. We're looking for something typical of this area." The drawl of the man's American accent tweaked Paula's curiosity immediately.

When she walked back into the kitchen, Dara and Diane were just returning from a tour of the upstairs rooms.

"It's a wonderful place, Dara. Such a pity you don't get tourists. You could have this place filled up all the time, if you were close to Sydney." Diane enthused. "Oh, there you are, Paula. You didn't see your father out there, did you?"

"No." Paula hadn't given her dad another thought. She looked from her mother to her friend's face. Dara's usual sparkle had returned. Paula wondered how she would take the news.

"Why don't you keep Dara company a bit longer and I'll go for a stroll and see if I can find him." Diane took a fifty dollar note from her purse. "This is for the vest and the bib. Don't worry about the change."

"Your mum's lovely," Dara said after Diane left. "She shouldn't have much trouble finding your dad. There can't be many places for him to be. Most shops shut before lunch on a Saturday and it must be nearly that now."

"Oh, are you closing soon?"

"I usually shut my doors too. The whole town will be dead by midday. Everyone will be at the football. It's an away game."

"An away game?"

"In another town. I don't follow it but Chris goes sometimes. They can play anywhere up to an hour or two's drive away."

"Dara, I hope you don't mind, but I've got you some customers for lunch and I need to know more about the lady who knitted the home-spun jumper." Paula watched her friend's face anxiously. She had a vague shape of an idea forming but it might not be at all to Dara's liking.

"I think I'm going to need another cup of tea to make sense of what you're on about." Dara put the kettle on while Paula explained.

"Your customers are American tourists. They were in looking for a souvenir from this part of Australia. They're touring in one of those camper vans. I had no idea what to show them until I came across those beautiful home-spun hand knits you've got."

"You didn't sell one?" Dara stopped making the tea and stared at Paula.

"Did I do the wrong thing? They didn't say not for sale."

"You sold one of those two hundred dollar jumpers?"

"They're beautiful, probably worth a lot more. The wool is so fine and the colours are gorgeous."

"They're Monica Brown's. I told her they were worth more but I never thought we'd sell one, here. I suggested she look for interstate markets."

Relieved, Paula went on. "Well, it was just what the American couple were looking for. If your friend Monica had been spinning the wool straight from the sheep's back, you probably could have sold them more. They were most interested in the whole process. Anyway, they asked me where they could get a good Aussie lunch and I invited them to come back here." Once again, Paula paused and watched Dara's expression anxiously. A little colour had returned to her friend's face and she'd obviously brushed her hair and put on lipstick while Paula had been in the shop.

"You want me to give them lunch, here?"

"Not give them lunch, charge them."

"I haven't got anything to sell them."

"You've got that delicious-smelling soup, and you said you had stuff in the freezer. They're after home-style food and local conversation and they're happy to pay for it. I said it would be thirty dollars each and they didn't murmur. They'll be back at twelve-thirty."

"Thirty dollars each!"

"Sounds like an interesting opportunity to me," a male voice said.

Paula and Dara both turned to look at the tall, solid man framed in the back doorway.

"Chris! You're home early."

Dara's husband nodded and crossed the room to give her a hug. "It's going to rain and we're low on fertiliser. Decided to call it quits for today."

"Chris, this is Paula."

He took off his hat, revealing a balding pate, and offered his hand. "Pleased to meet you, Paula."

He was a big man but his grip was gentle. Paula thought his eyes reminded her of a faithful dog's, deep, brown and trusting. "Hello, I seem to have overstepped my welcome, I'm afraid." She chuckled.

"Well, I'm curious. Tell me more."

They all sat down at the table and Paula told them about her conversation with the American tourists and how Dara's set-up was just what they were after; a good home-cooked lunch, in a kitchen, with real conversation. By the time her parents came back to collect Paula, Dara was well on her way to creating a gourmet feast and Chris had showered and was preparing the table for their guests.

At least Dara was much happier than when Paula had first arrived, which was more than she could say for her parents. She climbed into the back seat, clutching the container of soup Dara had insisted she take. Her father jerked the vehicle away from the curb, making the soup slop wildly from side to side. Luckily, the lid was well sealed.

The sky had become quite cloudy and grey and light rain was beginning to fall. The atmosphere inside the car was just as gloomy. Diane was looking out the side window at the disappearing town as they left it behind and Rex was looking directly ahead. Paula could see the outline of his jaw jutting firmly forward.

"What have you been up to this morning, Dad?"

"Your father has organised a surprise for you, darling." Diane jumped in quickly.

Alarm bells rang for Paula. Her father's surprises were second only to her mother's in conjuring up less-than-delightful bombshells for the recipient.

"He's bought you a new oven and organised for it to be installed. You can get rid of that dreadful old thing you have. Won't that be so much better?"

Paula looked towards her father but he continued to watch the road directly ahead. "Dad, there was no need. Dan and I..."

"Nonsense, darling," Diane cut in. "We wanted to give you a present that would be useful. I'm so glad your father was able to find something suitable in town. They've got quite a good electrical shop, haven't they?"

Paula didn't know. She hadn't been in the electrical shop herself, yet. But she did have ideas for doing up her own kitchen. Ideas she wanted to share with Dan so they could make the decisions together. She wondered what arrangements her father had made and if it was too late to change them.

"The shop assistant said you were so lucky," Diane continued. "They've got a couple of deliveries going your way on Monday morning and they can fit the stove in. The electrician can't come that quickly but he did say sometime next week he'd call you. They all knew the farmhouse. People are so friendly here, Paula. You're so lucky to live in such a pleasant place."

Diane stopped to draw breath and Rex glanced around.

"You needed a decent cooker," he said firmly.

Diane turned back to watching the view and Paula sat back in her seat, nursing the soup. She was going to hate the new stove, she knew it. Why did they have to go ahead without consulting her? It was something she and Dan should do together. And how would he take the news that her parents had gone out and bought them a stove? She knew her parents' visit had been going all too smoothly, something had to happen.

"What was that?" Diane squealed. "It looked like a mouse. Did you see that, Rex? Look there's another one. It is a mouse. They're running across the road."

"Relax, Diane, they're not in the car. Dan said there was a bit of a problem with mice eating the seed in the paddocks."

"Oh dear," Diane wailed. "I hope we don't get any in the house."

Paula pushed back further into her seat. Yes, she thought, all too smoothly.

CHAPTER
10

Dan knew Paula wasn't home as soon as he entered the house. He was already accustomed to the difference her presence made. Even if it was late and she'd gone to bed, there was always a sense of her being there. He couldn't feel it now. She must have gone somewhere with her parents. From what he'd seen in the brief times he'd been at home, Paula was getting on okay with them. He was glad her fears of their visit not working out had been unfounded. It was easier leaving her each day, knowing she had some company.

He took off his boots, left them in the back porch and walked into the empty kitchen. It was dark and cold. He turned on the light and looked in the fridge for something to eat. There wasn't an extra plate left from last night's roast chicken as he had hoped. Paula wouldn't have thought of it. Planning meals wasn't one of her talents. He grinned. Not that he minded. She had plenty of others.

He suspected her mother had cooked the roast. It had been delicious. He wouldn't call himself a fussy eater and he didn't mind

Paula's cooking but he did enjoy solid, hot food at this time of the year. It helped him to keep going. He was tired, a deep weariness that invaded every part of his body down to his toes. Something warm for lunch would have been nice.

He frowned. Sometime this week he would have to organise some sheep to be killed. Rowena had reminded him a few days ago that their meat supply was low. If this rain kept up he could fit it in but the forecast hadn't been very promising. He'd really only stopped because he was so tired, Paula's parents were here and Tom was busting to go and watch the footy match. He didn't think the rain showers would amount to much.

There were still a few embers in the lounge fire, so Dan stirred them to life, put on some more wood and went off to have a shower. The warmth of the water thawed the chill from his body and eased his tired mind.

They'd had a few setbacks with breakdowns and the mice had done a bit of damage but so far the seeding was progressing okay. If they could just get a decent return this year, he could borrow enough to pay Katherine off and get her out of his life. Then he would be free to make a fresh start with Paula. Rowena was right: he really should have sorted out the mess from his past before he'd contemplated the future.

The talk on the radio this morning had been worrying. The outlook for grain prices wasn't good with a predicted worldwide downturn. It was hard enough, with all the other variables, to get a decent return, and now his profit margin would be even narrower. It would mean less money to maintain and improve the farm let alone all the other costs that accrued, good or bad year.

Dan went back to the kitchen and made himself a sandwich. He took it into the lounge where the fire was burning strongly now. He looked up at the large gilt-framed mirror Rex had hung over the mantelpiece. Dan thought the mirror a little fancy for the room but no doubt Paula's decorating talents would soon remedy that. The throw rugs and bright cushions on the old couch had already improved the look of the furniture.

He glanced across at the jumper Paula's sisters had sent him, still lying in its paper where he had left it when he'd unwrapped it a couple of nights ago. It was a navy pure wool hand knit. The Crawford family certainly were generous.

He turned on the television. The football was about to begin. Dan looked up at the wedding photo on the mantel as he took a bite of his sandwich. Paula was looking like a princess and laughing up at him. He settled back into the lounge, reminding himself how lucky he was. The siren sounded from the television signalling the start of the football game. Within five minutes of the first bounce he was asleep.

★   ★   ★

Paula looked down on Dan's sleeping form. She glanced at the television then at the partly eaten sandwich on the plate beside him. He must be so tired. He hadn't heard her call out as she came in the back door. She bent down and kissed him.

He opened his eyes, his face curved into a smile and he stretched his arms towards her. "Hello, Sweet Pea."

"Here you are." Diane came into the lounge from the passage. "We wondered where you'd got to, Daniel."

Paula went to speak but Dan winked and blew her a kiss. "Yes, here I am home at last. I'm sorry I haven't been around much…"

"No, don't apologise. Paula told us you would be very busy. I'm just glad we've been able to do a few things to help you two get started."

Paula held her breath thinking her mother was going to blurt out the story of the new oven before she could tell Dan herself.

Diane warmed her hands by the fire. "Will this rain keep you home for a while?"

"I don't think there's much in it, Diane. I'll probably be back on the tractor tomorrow. Just thought I'd spend an afternoon with my family." He put his arm around Paula's legs.

"Oh, Daniel, is this your lunch?" Diane picked up the plate and inspected the sandwich Dan had taken one bite from. "You need more than that. Did you put Dara's soup on to heat, Paula? You got one of those food grill things among your gifts didn't you? Where have you put it? We can toast this sandwich for Daniel and get him some soup."

Paula rolled her eyes at Dan and followed her mother to the kitchen.

"Don't fuss, Mum. And his name is Dan, not Daniel."

"Yes, I keep forgetting. I've never been one to abbreviate names. Paula, you really should take better care of Dan. He's working long hours and he needs to be well fed."

"He's not an invalid." Paula defended herself but she did feel a little guilty as she retrieved the grill from the pantry. She didn't have anything to do but look after Dan and the house. She really would have to get some kind of routine into her life and organise meals better but not one day had been the same since she'd arrived. She recalled Dara's revelation that her business was only a sideline. Paula hadn't intended she'd be Dan's fulltime housekeeper. She'd have to find herself something else to do but what that might be she had no idea.

"Can you get out your toaster as well, Paula?" Diane cut into her thoughts.

Paula took the toaster from the cupboard under the sink and plugged it in beside the grill.

Diane squashed Dan's sandwich in the grill. "Dad will probably be happy with toast and soup and so will I. What will you have?"

"Just some soup." Paula set the toaster going with the first lot of bread. "Where is Dad?"

"Putting away his things. He'll be here in a minute."

Diane put in more bread and buttered the first lot of toast. She dropped the knife, fumbled the lid on the butter container and kept glancing towards the passage door.

"Mum, is everything okay? You and Dad…"

"We're fine. I'm so glad we've had this chance to spend some time with you." Diane patted Paula's arms. "I know you and Dan haven't had long on your own but this was the only time your father would take time off and if I'd let him delay it, goodness knows how long it would have been till we could come over. Susan could have the baby any day, then I'll be needed there. She really is still doing too much you know."

Paula could see the tears brimming in her mother's eyes.

"Susan's tough, Mum, and I'm sure her baby will be too, it wouldn't dare not be! Anyway, it's worked out well having you here. I certainly wouldn't have been able to transform the garden from a shambles to something from *House & Garden*." She laughed, trying to lighten the mood.

"I don't know that you're quite ready for open inspection but you're very lucky. Someone once put a lot of time into that garden. There was a definite layout under the jungle and some hardy plants." Another lot of toast popped up and Paula rescued Dan's sandwich from the grill.

"I'll take Dan his lunch." She carried a steaming bowl of soup and the now-toasted sandwiches into where Dan still sat by the fire watching the television. "Here you are, your majesty."

"Thanks, I could have come out."

Paula bent and kissed him. It was a wonderful feeling to have him home during the afternoon. "We can all eat in here. It's much warmer."

As she turned to go back to the kitchen, she heard her mother give a pitiful scream and then the sounds of a chair being dragged and something thudding to the floor.

Paula and Dan burst through the door into the kitchen at the same time as Rex came in from the passage. Diane was standing on a chair, there was a plate of toast on the floor and wobbling around beside it was a mouse.

"A mouse." Diane's voice was a mere whisper.

Dan moved towards the mouse and Rex went to his wife's side.

"It's all right, Diane. It can't reach you." Rex's tone was gentle as if he was talking to a little child.

Diane brushed at her hair with her hands. "It was in the toaster."

"It couldn't have been, Mum. We've cooked a couple of lots of toast today."

"It was in the toaster," Diane repeated. "It just popped out with the toast."

Paula's hand flew to her mouth. She didn't know whether to be disgusted or amused. The mouse had stopped wobbling. Dan held it in place with his foot, picked it up by the tail and took it outside.

"It's gone now, Diane. You can get down." Rex had an arm around his wife and held her hand to help her down.

"There might be more." Diane kept brushing at her hair.

"No, it's gone now. Come down before you fall," Rex said soothingly and she allowed him to help her down. "Come and sit by the fire." He led her to the lounge and Paula bent to pick up the plate.

Dan came back inside. "I've got rid of it. It must have been in the bottom of the toaster eating the crumbs. It was quite groggy from the heat and its fur was singed on top." He stopped beside her, brushing his hands together. "I told you to keep the pets locked up while we've got visitors," he whispered.

Paula smirked.

"Your mother would like a cup of tea." Rex had come back into the kitchen.

"Is Diane all right?" Dan asked.

"She'll be fine. It was the suddenness of it, that's all. She can cope with mice as long as they don't surprise her like that one obviously did."

Dan inspected the cupboard where they kept the toaster. "These old cupboards share the wall as their back. There are a couple of gaps."

"But I don't have food in there."

"Doesn't matter. I've seen mice eat the chipboard shelves out of a cupboard when there's nothing else."

"What if there's more? I can't have Mum going into hysterics again."

"It couldn't be helped, Paula. She'll be all right. It's a fear she's had all her life." Rex's tone was almost gentle. "When she was a little girl she stayed with her grandparents during a mouse plague. She woke up one night with mice in her bed and her hair. There was no electricity and it took a long time for her grandpa to light the old kero lamp and come to help her."

Paula shuddered. That explained why her mother had always had a fear of small creatures, even those big brown moths with the eyes painted on their backs that had been in a holiday house when Paula and her sisters were kids. She recalled the fuss her mother had made about getting them removed.

"I'm sorry, Dad. I did my best to make the house mouse-proof, and I did try to warn you we weren't ready for visitors."

"Your mother will be fine. She knows we can't rid the world of all small creatures, although it surely wouldn't hurt if there were no mice."

"I'm with you there," Dan said.

"Oh, and she's worried about your lunch going cold in there."

"I'll go and wash my hands."

"Dad, you go and sit with Mum. I'll finish getting the lunch and make her a cup of tea."

"I don't think she'll want any toast." Her father gave her a wink and went back to the lounge.

No, thought Paula, I don't think any of us will be having toast until I've given the toaster the once-over. She threw all the offending pieces in the bin, put the kettle on and used the electric grill to toast some cheese sandwiches. She was glad to see the smile on her father's face again. Pity it took a mouse to put it there.

Later that afternoon they set off with Dan for a tour of the property.

"This vehicle is very nice, Daniel. The interior still smells new. Have you had it long?" Diane asked from her seat in the back of the dual cab beside Paula. Rex sat in the front with Dan.

"Only a week."

"What made you decide on the dual cab?" Rex asked. "Wouldn't something like I've hired be more appropriate for a family vehicle?"

"This has to double as the family car and the work vehicle. I did a lot of research on them. Jim McInerney, our local car dealer, reckons this one is the best value for performance and money at the moment."

"Yes, well, he wants to make a sale."

Paula tensed. Her father was being very presumptuous.

"I know car dealers don't always have a good reputation but I've found Jim to be as honest as the day is long. He's been in the business for over forty years. You wouldn't last that long out here if you made bad deals."

"It's a big vehicle for Paula to drive. She should have —"

"I've managed it fine, Dad," Paula cut in. "And Jim McInerney struck me as an honest man."

"You thought that about Marco and look where that got you."

Paula sat up rigid in the back seat. Heat flooded her cheeks. Had her father gone mad? How could he mention Marco's name again, and in front of Dan? It was unthinkable.

"Oh, Paula. Did you tell Daniel about the oven?" Diane tried valiantly to change the subject.

"No, I…"

"It's our gift to you both, Daniel." Diane filled the silence. "We wanted to get you something while we were here and that old stove has had it so Rex has organised for a new oven to be installed."

"I hadn't had a chance to tell Dan about it yet." Paula's eyes met Dan's in the rear-view mirror. His serious mask had returned and she couldn't tell how he was reacting.

"It's very good of you, Rex," he said.

"Oh! Look at the lambs, aren't they gorgeous." Diane lowered the window.

Dan slowed and they watched as tiny lambs wobbled on unsteady legs behind mothers while older and stronger ones frolicked in little groups.

"They're my first lot of autumn lambs," Dan said. "I've always had spring lambs but this year I've got one mob lambing early to see how it goes."

"Tell me a bit more about the sheep market," Rex said. "You were saying the other night that current prices are good. Are these animals for meat or wool?"

"Both. They're bred for their good body size and their increased fleece weight."

Paula sat, miserably listening to Dan's careful explanation of his breeding program. Her father could match Rowena in the speed he delivered bombs and then changed the subject. She wasn't sure how much more of this roller-coaster visit her nerves could stand.

Later that night, tucked up in their bed, Paula tried to explain. "I'm sorry my parents are making their presence felt. The oven was a surprise to me as well. I hadn't had a chance to tell you about it."

"They are very generous," Dan said. "I feel bad about that old oven. I should have put a new one in before you came. You know I would have got around to it once seeding was finished."

Paula put her fingers over his lips. "Don't worry. I could have managed. Anyway, only a couple more days and they'll be gone." She kissed him gently. "Then we can be alone again."

"We're alone now." He rolled to meet her and she melted into the wonderful sensation of his embrace.

CHAPTER
11

"Dan's not with us, Rowena. He's back on the tractor." Paula and her parents had driven over to Rowena's together for the Sunday evening meal.

"I know, he called me on the two-way. He can work himself far too hard, my dear nephew. He'll be here in time for main course, I insisted. Now, come through to the lounge. I've got the fire going in there."

Paula gritted her teeth. *If Rowena says jump, we all have to ask how high.* They followed her past the kitchen and the delicious smell of roast meat to the living room.

Rowena's house was more compact than the old farmhouse. It had a small galley kitchen with a casual eating area at one end just big enough for four. The lounge was a large room and through double sliding doors was a formal dining room. The furniture was a mixture of neat and comfortable except for one battered vinyl recliner rocker with a throw rug over it drawn in close to the fire. It was the only thing that looked out of place.

"Do sit down, everyone. Rex, have the recliner." Rowena straightened the rug. "It's quite comfortable. Dan always sits in it in his work clothes but the rug is clean. Now, what will you have to drink?"

They decided on a bubbly red. The bottle was open and Paula wondered if Rowena had drunk a glass or two already. She seemed more relaxed, almost vibrantly happy. Her barely pink shirt was crisscrossed with white lines and had tiny frills edging the pocket and collar. It gave Rowena a much softer, more feminine appearance.

"Your Crows played a good game last night." Mr Crawford raised his glass in a mock toast.

"Yes, it was an exciting evening." Rowena's cheeks glowed and there was a sparkle in her eyes.

"You are a real fan then," Diane said. "I'm afraid I don't understand the game. Rex enjoys it though, don't you, darling. Daniel seems to like it too. It was nice to see him relaxing with Rex last night. You're right, Rowena, he is a very hardworking young man."

"Dan was a handy footballer himself for our local team but he injured his knee and decided he'd give up playing." Rowena's look was wistful. "Sad for him really, he was a damn good ruckman."

Dan and Rex had watched the game on television the night before, and Paula and her mother had worked on setting up the beautiful antique dresser they'd placed in the kitchen. It was just right to display some of the special wedding gifts and Paula had one or two things of her own that fitted in quite well.

She had already decided the kitchen would be her next project, once her parents left. There wasn't much she could do about the built-in furniture but the table would be better at the end of the room in front of the window and a coat of paint on the walls and cupboards would give the room a new lease of life. She would have to keep a strict eye on Carl's colour mixing though.

The football talk continued and Paula got up to inspect the photos Rowena had dotted around the room. They were mainly of Dan at various ages; a portrait shot of him as a baby, a black-and-white snap at about primary school age where he was in footy gear, shaking the hand of a man presenting him with a trophy, and a high school photo where he looked thin and gangly and uncomfortable in an ill-fitting blazer. On the old upright piano there was a picture of him as a teenager with a serious-faced older man. It had to be his father, they were so alike.

"I think we'll have our soup now. The roast is nearly ready and Dan will be here soon."

Paula marvelled that Rowena could be so sure. She trailed behind the others into the dining room where they sat at the beautifully set table.

Rowena produced another bottle of the red bubbly. "Will you top up the glasses please, Rex?"

Over soup, the conversation was all about Sydney. Rowena had been there several times. It seemed they had a few favourite restaurants in common and Paula was mildly surprised at Rowena's obvious enjoyment of the Bondi lifestyle. She hadn't really pictured her there. There were some layers to Rowena that she only got glimpses of.

Another bottle of wine was opened and Diane rattled on about some of her favourite shops. Paula found herself picturing some of the shopping trips she'd had with Alison and was engulfed in a sudden pang of homesickness. She was pleased to see Dan come in.

"Ah, Dan, just in time to carve the roast." He had barely a chance to say hello and plant a kiss on top of Paula's head before Rowena whisked him away to the kitchen.

It was a magnificent meal accompanied by a fresh bottle of red, a Clare Valley shiraz this time. Paula marvelled at her father and

Rowena, who were tossing back the wine. Dan had a couple of glasses but the earlier bubbly had been enough for Paula and she stuck to water.

"That was delicious, Rowena." Rex raised his glass in a toast.

"Thank you, Rex. I do prefer mutton to lamb. It has more flavour. But that was my last roast." Rowena turned to Dan. "I hope you will find time to organise a kill this week, Dan. There's not much left in my freezer."

"I'll see how the weather goes. They're predicting heavy rain by the end of the week. If I can keep at it I should almost have the seeding finished by then."

Paula's heart skipped a beat. There was a light at the end of the tunnel. Dan's long hours would soon be over.

"Do you mean you have to kill your own sheep?" Diane's voice was slightly raised. She'd had several glasses of the red as well.

"That's how you survive on a farm, Diane." Rex gave a snort. "You can't run to the shops every five minutes from here."

"But a lamb?" Diane glanced around the table, her eyes wide. No doubt, like Paula, she was imagining those dear little creatures they'd seen frolicking in the paddock.

"By lamb we mean a young sheep, not a baby." Rowena stood up and began clearing away the dishes. "At any rate things are a bit more civilised these days. Our local butcher does the killing at his abattoirs and the cutting up and mincing for us, all we have to do is pack it. But I used to help my mother do all the preparation when I was a girl. Dad would kill the sheep and cut it up and we would mince and season and pack."

"That must have been a big job." Diane helped carry the plates. "I don't know if I would have the stomach for it."

Paula watched as the two women disappeared into the kitchen and wondered what would be expected of her. She didn't like the sound of mounds of raw meat but at least it explained the hand-labelled bags of meat that were already in her freezer.

"Well, with everyone being so busy it is just as well I organised a few things for you while I was here." Her father's tone was serious and Paula felt a sudden apprehension.

"It was generous of you to buy the stove —"

Rex cut Dan off. "Oh, that was nothing really, just an extra wedding present. No, I have at least had time to organise Paula's financial affairs since you two have obviously not got around to it."

His words rocked Paula as surely as if there had been a real explosion.

"What do you mean, Dad?"

"There's a lot at stake here and it's obvious that you two haven't given too much thought to financial matters. I spent some time with the local solicitor getting some papers drawn up for you both to ensure your financial security."

"Dad, you're still not making sense. What have you done?"

"You are totally reliant on Dan for income, for everything. You should be included as a partner."

"Dad!"

"You're stuck out here by yourself. You've left behind any prospects of a decent job. You don't even have a car."

"I still have my car in Sydney. I'll sell it eventually. I'm hardly spending any money anyway. Just a few groceries and bits and pieces for the house."

"If you keep spending your savings on daily needs you won't have anything left."

"We haven't had a chance to talk these things through. You had no right to interfere. It's Dan's and my business." Paula's voice was rising. She glanced briefly at Dan. His face was expressionless as he sat silently looking at her father. "We will organise our own affairs."

Rex snorted and Paula noticed his cheeks had a ruddy glow. "Like you did with Marco? You ended up losing out there, my girl."

"You have no right!" Paula jumped to her feet, almost knocking over her chair.

"Which solicitor did you see?" Dan's quiet voice silenced them both. They turned to look at him.

Rex took another sip of wine. "I went into the local practice in town, here."

"Yes, but who did you see?" Dan asked again. Paula had never before witnessed the smouldering anger that she could see in Dan's eyes now. It frightened her.

"I asked to see that nice young woman. What was her name, Paula? You introduced us to her on the first day here."

"Katherine Melton." The words slid from Paula's lips.

In the silence that followed Dan rose to his feet, looked down at Rex and slowly shook his head. "I'm sure you meant well, Rex, but you shouldn't have interfered. You really shouldn't have."

"I think it's time for sweets." Rowena strode into the room carrying the cheesecake on a platter like a trophy, a flustered Diane following in her wake carrying some plates. They had obviously heard the last part of the conversation.

"I'm sorry, Rowena, I'm tired and I've got a very early start in the morning again. I won't stay for sweets." Dan turned to Paula. "No need for you to come, stay and finish the evening."

"Dan, I'm sorry, I..."

"We'll talk later." He kissed her on the cheek and left.

"Touched a raw nerve there, did I?" Rex asked in mock surprise. "He didn't let me finish. Katherine wasn't available so I saw the other chap who works there."

"We don't do business with that firm any longer, Rex." Rowena's voice was clipped. "If we need a solicitor there's a practice in Adelaide that we use." She passed out slices of cheesecake but Paula had lost all interest in food. "You will have to excuse Dan." Rowena looked directly at Rex. "He does take his responsibilities very seriously and this is a particularly trying time of year." She spoke quietly but there was no sign of the earlier, gentler persona. Her head was high and her eyes glittered. "I manage the financial matters of our business but Dan and I are partners. We never do anything without consulting each other. Paula says she is an accountant so I am sure she will recognise good business practice. One does not sign over a share in a business without some consultation. In their haste to get married, Dan and Paula may have overlooked some of the details but I am sure they will work it out in time." She sat and waved her arm at Paula. "Do sit down. Eat your sweets. I'll send a doggy bag home with you, for Dan. He often takes life too seriously."

Paula slumped into her chair.

"Paula will make sure Daniel has it for his lunch won't you, darling?"

Paula looked at her mother through weary eyes. "Dan, Mum. His name is Dan. He hates being called Daniel. When will you remember that?" she snapped.

"Oh, I'm sorry, I keep forgetting, I…"

"Lots of people call him Daniel. It's only natural," Rowena said. "When he was born his father, my brother Daniel, wanted him to be named after him. His mother would only allow it if there was a variation, so Dan it was. He's never been anything else to me. I've been looking after him since he was three years old."

Rowena held Paula's gaze for a minute before Rex spoke.

"You should understand, Rowena, I have the best interests of my daughter at heart. I will not see her lose out like she did with a previous relationship."

"I understand exactly where you are coming from, Rex." Rowena looked him directly in the eye. "I won't allow Dan to become any more encumbered than he already is." She smiled sweetly. "Now, please open this bottle for me. It's a particularly nice dessert wine."

"And this is a particularly nice cheesecake," Diane said. "I usually make my own but you would never know this wasn't homemade. Perhaps I can buy some on our way back through Adelaide, Rex. Do you think we'll have time? Which shop did you say you bought it from, Rowena?"

The conversation flowed around Paula like waves over a rock. Her head reeled, yet she felt numb. She looked at the three of them carrying on a polite exchange about food, as if none of the previous dialogue had taken place. The cheesecake was beyond her but she tipped down the glass of wine that her father poured and helped herself to another.

★   ★   ★

Paula opened her eyes. Her head felt fuzzy. She couldn't remember how many glasses of wine she'd drunk last night. What a nightmare! She was hoping she'd wake up to find none of it had happened. But the reality flooded back with her consciousness.

On the way home last night, her father had tried again to explain the legal document he'd had drawn up and her mother had sat in silence for once. It was some kind of arrangement to keep Paula's investments separate from Dan. It was almost like a one sided pre-nup agreement, only they were already married. Paula had yelled at them both, ranting and raving about their interference. When they had arrived home she had marched into the house then crept miserably into bed where Dan was already asleep. She vaguely recalled him getting up early this morning and here she was, alone in the bed again.

There were sounds coming from the kitchen and it was only seven. Paula sighed deeply, dragged herself out of bed, pulled on her new dressing-gown and wrapped it tight to fight off the cold.

She could hear her mother's voice murmuring softly as she approached the kitchen, then her father's voice, much louder.

"I want the finances to be tidied up so she can come home with some collateral, once this country fling is over, that's all."

"I know what you mean Rex, I just think —"

Paula pushed open the door. The heater was on in the kitchen and there was a smell of toast mingled with a hint of pine. Her parents both stood at the sink. She glared at them.

"Good morning, darling." Her mother gave her a weak smile.

"Are you feeling better this morning?" Rex asked.

Better? What did he mean? He obviously didn't care how she felt if he could describe her marriage to Dan as a 'country fling'. All kinds of words flew around her fuzzy brain. She wasn't going to put up with his meddling any more. She tried to think of something to say to hit back but all she could think of was how well she'd cleaned the toaster yesterday. She wondered if her mother had eaten any toast or perhaps her father had been the one to use it.

"We're heading home this morning, Paula," Rex said. "Your mother is worried about Susan."

Now she focussed.

"What's wrong? Have you heard something?"

Paula looked at her mother but she wouldn't make eye contact. They'd rung her sisters on Sunday morning and everything had been fine then.

"Nothing new, but I think you can manage here without us and we don't know when this baby might turn up. Your mother wants to be there, and you don't seem to need us here."

"I see." Paula spoke quietly and her mother looked up expectantly. You're darn right I don't need you, Paula thought. She opened the fridge. "Have you packed something to eat in the car? It's a long trip."

"We'll stop along the way. Now, come on, Diane, once we drop this trailer off at the depot in Adelaide we will make much better time. We could be almost home by tonight. Are the cases ready to close up?"

Diane followed her husband out the door, without speaking. Paula looked around the kitchen. Everything was neat and in its place. Her mother had done the dishes and put everything away except the offending toaster, which sat alone on the bench.

Paula sat down. Her head ached. She had been right to worry about her parents' visit. It had turned into a disaster. It was probably best that they left early, before they could do any more damage.

Diane came into the kitchen and patted Paula's shoulder. "I'm sorry it's a bit of a rush, darling. I want to be home in case Susan needs me. You understand."

Paula stood up and forced a smile onto her face. "Of course, Mum. I'm fine here. You're better off there, where you can be of some help."

Diane flinched. She stepped back.

That was probably a bit rough, Paula thought to herself. Anyway, Susan would surely have paid Paula to keep their mother away a bit longer. She certainly wouldn't be expecting to see their parents a few days early.

"Darling..." Diane's eyes were watering. "I'm sorry about the solicitor thing. I did try to warn your father but..."

Paula turned away. She couldn't face a tearful scene. Her sleeve caught a plate and it crashed to the floor and broke. "Bugger!"

"Paula," Diane chided. "Your language has deteriorated since you moved to the country."

Paula looked up from the pieces she was picking up and glared at her mother. "No, it hasn't. I'm not a little girl any more, Mum, and I can swear if I want to."

Tears brimmed in her mother's eyes again.

"Here you are." Rex stuck his head round the kitchen door. "The car is packed. We must get going, Diane." He gave Paula a kiss on the cheek as she stood up. "You don't have to do anything with those documents if you don't want to but I think it would be wise to at least read them. I've left them in the bedroom. Take care."

Paula turned to her mother. They looked sadly at each other for a brief moment then Diane stepped forward and hugged her tightly.

"Yes, take care, darling. Make sure you eat properly. You're still so thin."

"Come on, Diane, she's a grown woman, she can manage her own food. Now we don't want any teary goodbyes." Rex propelled his wife through the door. "Don't come out, Paula, it's damp and cold outside."

Paula smiled weakly and sat down as if she was a ten-year-old again.

In the quiet she heard the four-wheel drive start up and move off down the track. As the sound of the motor faded she looked across the table in front of her to the old dresser. She recalled the evening she had spent with her mother unpacking the china, glassware and wedding gifts, while the men watched the football on television. She had enjoyed the relaxed camaraderie she had shared with her mother then.

On display was a large white platter painted with abstract flowers in various shades of blue and touches of green, the bright colours reflected in the other gifts of coffee mugs and assorted bowls and plates they had placed along the shelves around it. She was glad she'd asked for the bright colours instead of plain white as her mother had originally suggested. This drab old kitchen needed a lift and the dresser and its contents had begun the process.

A momentary flush of excitement sent her thoughts tumbling over colours she could use to complement those in the dresser and give the whole room a fresh look. Then the crackle of the two-way reminded her she was alone, with no vehicle and no idea of when Dan would be home. The prospect of the long week ahead made her feel listless. What would she do?

"Woodie, it's Croft. Dan, are you on channel?" Rowena's voice burst into the kitchen.

"Yes, Rowena."

"I forgot to give Paula the leftovers for your lunch. Would you like me to bring them out later?"

"Yep, that would be good."

"See you about twelve."

"Okay."

Paula stood up and snapped off the two-way. Dan didn't need her when he had Rowena to run after him, feed him, do the paper-work. What was the name Jane had given her and Paula, 'new blood'? Well, if producing children was all he'd married her for, Dan could think again. Thank goodness for modern medicine and the pill. Paula looked around her empty kitchen and misery washed over her once more. But what was she going to do with her time?

She brushed at the tablecloth. There were a few dirty marks on it. Washing. That's what she'd do. She'd strip her bed and her parents' bed and give everything the once-over. Happy to have a plan at last, she went to her parents' room. On the bedside table she noticed a large envelope. It bore her name, written in her father's bold handwriting. She picked it up, turned it over and wondered how she was going to sort this out with Dan. They had been so happy. Why did her father have to interfere?

The phone rang. Paula went back to the kitchen, dropped the envelope on the dresser and picked up the receiver.

"Hello, Paula? It's Jim McInerney speaking."

"Hello, Jim."

"Look, I'll get straight to the point. I know you've got visitors but I am desperate. My secretary, Heather, is still sick, in fact she's in hospital and I'm nearly going under here. Dan mentioned a while back that you knew a bit about office work and I wondered whether you could spare me a few hours."

Paula was stunned. It was the last thing she'd imagined hearing. She smiled to herself, thinking of Marco's empire that she had managed. "I have spent a bit of time in an office but…"

"I don't care if you can type or not, just some filing, phone answering, banking and mail. Only a few hours a day, I don't want to keep you from your visitors, and I'd pay you, of course. I know it's a bit cheeky to ask, Paula, but I've tried a couple of other people. Seems everyone's sick or covering for someone who is sick and I thought of you. It wouldn't be all day… "

"Hang on, Jim." Paula jumped in. This could be just what she needed. "My parents left this morning. I could possibly do it…"

"Wonderful, how soon can you be here?"

"Well, I'm not even dressed so I'd need a few minutes and then… oh!"

"What's the matter?"

"I don't have any way of getting there. Dan has the dual cab."

"Don't worry. I've got a rookie who needs to take a vehicle for a test run. He can take it your way and pick you up. I'm sure I've got a car here you could borrow to get you home."

"Oh no, Jim. That wouldn't be right…"

"Look, Paula, you are doing me a favour. It's the least I can do.
Will half an hour be enough time? I can have young Brad out there
by then. We'll sort out the rest when you get here."

Paula looked at the phone for a minute before hanging it up.
What had she done? What would Dan think? She hadn't even had
the chance to ask him. Still, he was busy and Rowena had his lunch
under control. Paula would go in to town, sort out Jim's office and
be home before anyone knew she was gone. Maybe there would
be time to repair some of the meddling her father had done and
Dara might even have something delicious she could bring home
for their evening meal. She hummed as she left Dan a note on the
slight chance that he arrived home before her. Yes, this was definitely what she needed.

CHAPTER
12

It didn't take Paula long to familiarise herself with the way Jim's office ran. She felt relaxed sitting in the comfortable leather chair behind the counter. It made her remember her first observation about Jim. He ran his business with style.

She was thankful that she'd chosen to dress in her black knee-length skirt and the pink-and-black floral knit which she tucked in at the waist. The smart outfit had boosted her confidence and made her feel good after months of not working. Heather's systems had been easy to follow and by mid-afternoon all that was left to do was the post. Paula slipped her double-breasted coat back on. There had been no need for that in the warm office but outside the day was bitterly cold.

She felt she had everything sorted and organised as she stepped confidently up to Marg's counter.

"Oh, hello dear. Paula isn't it?" Marg's beady eyes inspected her shrewdly and then scrutinised the bundle of mail Paula had placed on the counter. "I didn't recognise you. Running a few errands for Jim, are you?"

"I'm managing his office while his secretary is away." It didn't take long for word to get around.

"That's nice for you, dear. Katherine Melton was in earlier and she was saying it was kind of Jim to give you a bit of work, to keep you occupied. It can get very lonely on the farm during tractor season."

Paula looked down at the packets and envelopes she had put on the counter. How did Katherine know about the job and what did she mean? Paula wasn't a child to be kept amused with toys while she waited for her man to come home. She stood up straight and looked directly at Marg.

"I've noticed a couple of things in the mail log that would be better for Jim's business if they went Express Post."

"Oh yes, Heather didn't care for it much. I did try to…"

"And I couldn't find any record of a monthly account. Surely a business the size of Jim's would have one of those."

"Heather didn't…"

"I think it would be much more efficient if you set one up."

"Perhaps when Heather gets back…"

"She's in hospital, poor thing. I'd like to have things organised before she gets back to save her some work. I'm sure you understand how much more efficient it would be."

"Well, of course but I don't like to…"

"I'll be in tomorrow to finalise the details." Paula turned to leave then looked back at Marg's puce face. "Oh, and can you have the paperwork ready for me to change over the mail delivery at the farm by tomorrow. I'll bring in my change of name details but I won't have much time. I'd appreciate it if you had it ready for me to sign. See you then." Paula turned and strode out of the post office leaving an open-mouthed Marg in her wake.

She stopped outside the door and took two deep breaths before continuing on her way back to Jim's. Perhaps she'd been a bit hard on Marg. Paula had gone in with the intention of discussing why Heather didn't make use of the obvious time and money-saving services available. But at the mention of Katherine's name Paula had lost all sense of reason. That bloody woman! What was it about her that she kept such a close eye on their affairs? She was obviously an old girlfriend but if Dan didn't still care for her what bothered him so much?

Paula stopped. Katherine had been away for a while. Maybe she had broken off their affair, not Dan. Perhaps he still harboured feelings for her but had married Paula on the rebound. She'd had friends who had been in similar relationships, but at least they hadn't married and were able to walk away from the misery. That would explain Dan's reaction at the very mention of Katherine's name.

A yell from a passing child interrupted Paula's wild thoughts. Was she going crazy? Dan loved her, she knew it. Just because she'd had a bad experience with Marco didn't mean it would happen again. She strode off along the footpath trying to concentrate on what was left to do before she went home.

"Paula, thank you so much for today." Jim beamed at her as she tidied up the front desk. "Are you able to come back tomorrow?"

"I should think so. That's if I don't get a better offer."

"Oh, I said I would pay you a good wage."

Paula laughed. "I was joking, Jim. Where else would I be, except home alone? I've really enjoyed being here today."

"Good." His momentarily displaced smile returned. "Now, we need to find you a car to borrow."

He took Paula through to the huge workshop area out the back. There weren't as many vehicles lined up as there had been when she'd come with Dan to get the dual cab.

"I've got two mechanics off with this flu bug as well. We've had to cut back on work. Thankfully, I'm expecting them both back tomorrow. Now let me see what we've got on the block that we can lend you."

Jim went off and talked to a mechanic and Paula wandered around the shed until he caught her up.

"I've got a ute that has just been traded. It's in good condition so you should be fine in it, or..."

Paula listened carefully to the 'or'. She didn't fancy a ute after experiencing Dan's.

"There's old Mrs Johnson's Audi."

"That will do nicely."

Jim got keys and they headed off into a far corner. "I don't know why she bought it. It wasn't practical for her and I wouldn't recommend them for our roads. She loved it though, racked up thousands of kays going from here to the city and interstate then traded it for a RAV4." Jim laughed. "She'll be eighty next birthday and is quite eccentric. Anyway I haven't been able to sell it here so I'm going to try Adelaide."

Paula expected an old chunky-looking car but instead they stopped beside a sleek jet-black, three-door sedan. Jim opened the door and Paula could detect the smell of leather as she slipped into the driver's seat and gripped the steering wheel. Now, this was a car. And she noted there was no two-way radio.

Paula felt she had a new lease of energy as she pulled up in front of Dara's shop.

"Paula, I've been going to ring you all day." She was met by Dara's enthusiastic welcome as soon as she stepped through the door. "Thank you so much for sending that American couple to us. They were great and we got on so well. We ended up cooking them an evening meal and they stayed the night. We had such a good time and the bonus is they insisted on paying, and very well I might add. It lifted Chris's spirits. I can't thank you enough for that."

Over coffee Dara gave Paula all the details. The local hospitality idea had been a success and Paula was pleased it had worked out. With their fine food and cheerful welcome, Dara and Chris could have a good business although they'd have to do something about their coffee. Dara had used the machine on her shop counter to make it this time and it had been rather bland. Paula explained her presence in town and Dara insisted she come for lunch the next day.

"Jim can't be such a slave driver he doesn't give you a lunch break."

"He's a nice man," Paula replied. "He's even let me borrow a car to get back and forth."

"So he should. You're helping him out."

Paula had a quick wander around the shop while Dara served some customers; they all wanted food. There were several ideas gelling in Paula's brain about Dara's place.

She was still mulling them over as she zipped along the bitumen, the radio beating out catchy drive-time music and a container of Dara's mutton curry nestled on the seat behind her. Paula felt her cheeks heat up at the recollection of her question regarding which animal mutton came from. Dara had been kind enough not to laugh but Paula had felt like a fool when she'd said it was sheep but an animal older than lamb, and tastier in her opinion. Paula shook her head. Some things were so simple and right in front of her face and yet a trap for the girl from the city.

It was getting late and by the time she reached the dirt turn-off, the sun was setting. Ideas for Dara's business were still dancing in her head and she had gone some distance before reality hit. She had never driven herself out here in the dark. She peered ahead, looking for something to give her a clue about the right roads to take.

It all looked so different in the gathering darkness and as the last bit of light left the sky, she stopped. The headlights pierced the dark of the road ahead but all around her was blackness.

She turned off the radio. The car was warm and purred as gently as a cat. Overhead a thousand stars twinkled in the night sky. She was all alone out here. For all she knew she was the only person left in the world. She slid down in the driver's seat. What should she do?

In the distance she could see the glow of headlights. She sat up, her confidence returning. Perhaps she could stop whoever it was and ask directions. She watched. The lights moved but didn't ever seem to get any closer. Off to her right she could see another set moving slowly. She thumped the steering wheel. Tractors! They were bloody tractors going round and round in paddocks. Miserably she watched their progress then noticed a third one out in the distance in front of her. She was surrounded by machines but they were no help.

The lights of the tractor in front disappeared and reappeared. Each time it looked to be closer. She stared hard. The lights flashed at her. It wasn't a tractor, it was a car and it was coming along the road towards her. She searched the dash and found the hazard lights, hoping the driver would stop and be able to give her directions. A familiar battered old ute pulled up across the road from her and a gangly young man got out.

Paula jumped out of her car. "Tom!"

"Is that you, Paula?"

"Thank goodness. It got dark so quickly and I couldn't find my way."

"Lucky it was me that came along. You might want to dip those lights. People get a bit aggro around here when drivers use high beam."

"Oh." Paula ducked down and searched the dash again. "Sorry, Tom, I'm not used to this car yet."

"Is this old Mrs Johnson's car? I thought it would have been sold by now." Tom ran his hand over the roof. "It sure is a nice car."

"Yes, but it's got a silly driver who can't find her way home."

"You've come a long way past the first turn-off but there are several ways to your place. Follow me and I'll take you back this way." He jerked his thumb over his shoulder. "Do you want me to call Dan on the two-way…"

"No." Paula jumped in. "He might not be home yet."

"Oh, I think he will be." Tom lowered his eyes and poked the dirt with his boot. "He was going in for tea, he said, then having an early night."

Paula's shoulders slumped. Dan had probably calmed down and wanted to talk and she wasn't home. She pulled open the car door. "Well in that case we'd better get going. I've got his dinner in the back."

She waited while Tom turned the ute around and cursed her own stupidity for leaving town so late. Now not only Tom knew about her losing her way but Dan would as well and then probably Rowena. She should have told Tom to radio ahead. The whole district would know soon enough.

After some distance and a few sharp turns, Tom pulled over into a driveway. Paula didn't recognise her own gatepost until she pulled up beside him. He wound down his window and she waved her thanks. She hadn't worked out the window buttons yet.

She drove on alone down the corrugated driveway and pulled the car into the empty shed. There were lights on in the house but none outside so she had to feel her way in the dark. The thought of the mice that could still be scurrying around made her hurry and she caught her toe in a crack near the back door. She juggled the curry, lost her balance and hit the door with a thump. Straightening up, and with the food safe, she opened the back door into the verandah at the same time as Dan burst through from the house.

"Paula!" The relief on his face quickly changed to a frown. "Where have you been? I've been ringing all over the place. I was worried you were in a ditch somewhere. Jim should never have let you have that car, it's not practical."

Paula stiffened. Her beloved Dan was sounding just like her father. "I left you a note. I was…"

"I know. I've only just found that. But I had tried to call you on the two-way several times during the day and eventually Fred Martin replied and said you were in town working at Jim's."

"Who is Fred Martin? And how does he know me?" Paula tried to think of the male customers she'd served at Jim's. Most of them had introduced themselves but she didn't remember any Fred Martin.

"He doesn't know you but his wife Jackie was in town shopping and she ran into a friend, who had heard that you were at Jim's."

"Well, if you knew where I was, why were you so worried?" Paula was suddenly weary. This wasn't the evening she had planned.

"When I got in it was dark and you weren't here. I found your note then saw your parents' things were gone and I wondered how you were getting home. I rang Jim and he said he'd loaned you that fool of a car that used to belong to…"

"Old Mrs Johnson." Paula said it for him and wondered if there had ever been a time in Mrs Johnson's life when she hadn't been old.

"Anyway, Jim said you'd left hours ago."

"I went to Dara's for coffee and a chat and I picked up some curry." She waved the container in his face and stepped past him into the passage. She was tired and cold. It was embarrassing to get lost but now she was just plain angry.

Dan followed her to the kitchen. "I rang Dara, she said you'd left just before dark. That's nearly two hours ago. The roads are pretty rough with the rain and that car isn't…"

Paula banged the cupboard shut and turned to glower at Dan with a saucepan in her hand. "All right! I forgot the time. It was getting late and I got lost. Luckily Tom came along and showed me the way home."

They glared at each other across the kitchen. Paula lifted the saucepan. Silence surrounded them, then Dan's serious face broke into a grin.

"Well now, little lady," he said in that dreadful American accent. "You weren't gunna throw that pan at me, were ya?"

Paula looked down at the saucepan in her hands then back at his beaming face. Who could resist his smile and soppy charm? She grinned. "Any more questions and I might. You were sounding like my father."

He crossed the room in two strides and wrapped her in his arms. "I'm sorry about last night. I behaved badly. Your parents must think I'm a real country hick with no manners who can't look after their daughter."

Paula struggled from his embrace. "Now let's get some things straight. My parents are always interfering and this time they just went too far…oh!"

"What's the matter?"

"The oven was supposed to be delivered today. I forgot all about it."

"Don't worry, if they'd have brought it there would be a box at our back door. Pearson's Electrical are notorious for not turning up when they say."

Paula looked earnestly at Dan. "I didn't ask my parents to get a stove."

"I know, but they're right. Rowena said the same thing. I should have been more organised and had the kitchen usable at least."

"It is. I just need more practice. Thank goodness for Dara."

"That's another thing, I haven't thought about how you are paying for groceries. And as for a partnership, there are a few financial restraints on the farm at the moment. I wasn't trying to keep you out. I just don't think it's fair to burden you with my obligations."

Paula wondered what he meant by obligations but she didn't want to spoil the moment with more questions. She put her hand to his lips. "It doesn't matter right now. We'll sort it out. Don't try to take over from my father. I'm your wife, not your child."

He held her at arms-length and looked into her eyes for a minute. Then he slowly drew her towards him.

"In that case, wife, I've got the fire going in the lounge," he whispered in her ear. "It wouldn't take long to fill the bath and there's a bottle of wine in the fridge."

"Don't open it for me." Paula found it hard to concentrate as he nibbled on her ear. "But I'd love a soak in the bath." She snuggled in close and sighed as he shuffled her backwards to the door. The one good thing about arguing was the pleasure of making up.

CHAPTER
13

Paula was up early the next morning having breakfast with Dan and scribbling notes on a pad.

"You are taking this job seriously. Do you think Jim will want you this early in the morning?" Dan asked between bites of toast.

"I don't have to be in till ten. I'm working on an idea for Dara's place."

"What kind of idea?" Dan raised an eyebrow.

"A way for her to earn more of a living from her business. Would you say you get many tourists in this area?"

"Not really. They tend to go to the coast. It's a half-hour drive the other side of town and the main highway goes straight there. There's no need to come this way."

"What things could entice them this way? I mean, besides good accommodation and food."

"We're all farmers trying to make a living. There's nothing special here."

"Dara had some beautiful hand-knitted jumpers. She said a Monica someone did them."

"Monica Brown? She and her husband have a farm nearer town. She has a merino stud. I've heard she does all kinds of things with the wool. Spins and dyes it herself. Then I guess there's that alternative couple out the other side. Hobby farmers. They're supposed to be growing all kinds of flowers. I haven't been there but lavender is the main thing I think. There are other farms about that specialise."

"City people are interested in farm life. They don't usually get to see it close up."

"What, the mud and the shit and the mice? I'm sure they'll be flocking to see it." Dan laughed and kissed her head. "Speaking of which, I'd better get back to it. Promise me you'll drive carefully and get Jim to swap that car for something useful."

Paula stood up and started to clear away the table. "I'll be fine, Dan."

He kissed her again, on the lips this time, and she felt her toes curling.

"You'd better go or neither of us will get to work."

"I'm away." Dan gave her a wink and left. Paula hummed to herself and picked up the bag of bread they'd opened for breakfast. The door swung in behind her and Dan stepped just inside.

"Perhaps you'd better crumble that and leave a trail so you can find your way home again tonight."

She pulled a face and threw the bag at his departing back.

★ ★ ★

Paula was pleased with herself. It had been a good week and she had achieved so much. Jim's office ran well. Thanks to the absent Heather's good practises, Paula had only a few suggestions to help improve the running of the place. Her main job had been to catch it up. It was Friday and Heather was recovering and due back at work on Monday so Paula was making sure all was in order for her return.

Pearson's Electrical was between Jim's and the post office so there had been time to pop in and look at the stove her father had ordered. Surprisingly, Paula quite liked it. She would have preferred the metallic finish instead of white but it would match the fridge and freezer and the brand was reputable. For once she agreed with his choice. If they didn't deliver by next week she'd get the dual cab and pick it up herself.

At least it had been a conversation point when her mother had rung to say they'd arrived home safely and Susan was still in one piece. Paula had jokingly reported that the stove's progress was no closer than Susan's baby. She was able to avoid discussing anything more serious and nothing was said about the financial papers her father had left. Diane sounded the same as always and asked a barrage of questions about the progress of seeding, the mice and Dara's shop before Paula had finally been able to end the call.

At the post office she'd managed to smooth the waters with Marg, who assured Paula that the roadside delivery was organised and would begin next week. Yes, Paula thought to herself, a most productive week.

"All ready to leave me, I see." She looked up into Jim's kind face, smiling at her over the counter.

"Well, not quite. I'll come back after lunch for a while but I did want to talk with you, if you've got a minute."

"Of course." Jim, with his trademark checked coat flapping over his ample tummy, came round the counter and pulled up a chair beside her.

"I am an accountant, or at least I was in another life and…"

"You're kidding. You mean I've had an accountant here answering the phone and running to the post office. Wait till I tell the wife. I expect you'll want more pay."

"No, nothing like that. I don't want to meddle with your financial advisor, but I did notice a couple of things among your records that you could be doing smarter, and they'd save you money."

Jim was most interested in her suggestions and planned to follow them up with his accountant. Paula was pleased. There were just a couple more things she wanted to achieve before she went home today. Next stop was Dara's for lunch.

In between answering Jim's phone and doing the paperwork, she had kept her ear to the ground about local industry and points of interest. She had put together an idea for Dara's business and today she was going to show her friend the plan.

The winter sun was shining, but there was a dull feel to the day and the distant skyline was a murky grey. The weather didn't dampen her spirits as Paula set off for Dara's, hugging her coat close and humming as she walked, head down into the wind.

"Hello, Paula. It looks like rain, can I give you a lift?" Katherine Melton was certainly capable of changing her mood. She was dressed immaculately, as usual. Today, she wore black trousers and a blood-red turtleneck jumper, under a long leather coat. She carried a briefcase and stood in the middle of the footpath, in front of Paula.

"No, thanks Katherine, I'm only going as far as Dara's. I'll be fine."

"Have you been enjoying your little job at Jim's? Nice of him to get you off that farm. I suppose Dan is up to his usual workaholic frenzy." She smiled slowly like a cat who had just found a mouse.

Paula squinted up at Katherine. There was grit in the air and it was affecting her eyes. "We're both busy. I must keep going." She went to step around Katherine, who moved to block her way.

"Just a minute. I see your father has had some kind of agreement drawn up regarding the farm."

"That's none of your business."

Katherine lowered her face closer to Paula's. "You may think you've snared a fortune in property but you can't cut me out that easily. There are some ties stronger than money."

She glowered at Paula for a minute, then turned briskly away and walked towards her car, leaving Paula standing alone on the footpath. Paula's anger at Katherine shifted to Rex. What on earth had been in that paperwork that had raised Katherine's hackles?

She rolled her shoulders, physically trying to rid herself of Katherine's oppressive presence, and watched as the sleek silver Pajero pulled away from the footpath. Suddenly the anger left her and she had the urge to giggle. *One thing a week at Jim's has taught you, girl, you know your vehicles now.* A month ago, she wouldn't have known one four-wheel drive from another.

Paula continued on her way as another blast of grit stung her face and Katherine's Pajero roared away down the road. Then she imagined Katherine going through the files reading their personal information. How dare she pry into paperwork that was none of her business. Perhaps Paula had been hasty in casting the papers aside. She should at least read what her father had drawn up. She didn't have to act on it. What had Katherine meant about some ties being stronger than money?

Paula shuddered, but not from the chilly wind. Katherine's tone had been menacing. She didn't want to mention the meeting to Dan but who else could she ask about Katherine? She didn't know Jane well enough and she certainly couldn't ask Rowena. Maybe there was a way she could broach the subject with Dara.

Paula hurried across the street and into Dara's welcoming shop. Wonderful spicy savoury smells reached her as soon as she clattered through the door.

"Well, look what the cat dragged in." Dara chuckled from the middle of her shop where she was arranging stacks of brightly coloured woven baskets.

"You might say the cat spat me out," Paula replied with a grin.

Dara's dark eyebrows arched. "Don't tell me Jim's turned into a tyrant on your last day."

"Oh, no, nothing like that." Paula ran her fingers through her hair and glanced towards the window. "It's very stormy looking outside. Do you think we'll get any rain?"

"Now, there speaks a farmer's wife, hopeful of getting her man off the tractor." Dara's bracelets tinkled with her laugh as she beckoned Paula. "Come into the kitchen. My man is home already and has promised to mind the shop for the afternoon. We can look at this proposal of yours uninterrupted."

They ate lentil burgers garnished with fennel, chilli sauce and sour cream and Paula laid out her plan around them on the kitchen table. Chris kept one ear on her explanation in between serving and when Paula finished he was the first to speak.

"You have put a lot of homework into this, Paula. I had no idea it would be possible for us to make an income from bed and breakfast."

"That would be the icing on the cake, Chris. It's your food. That's the drawcard. You and Dara have a wonderful talent for producing fresh, wholesome country food with the odd multicultural touch." Paula hesitated and glanced from one to the other. "I hope you're not offended by my suggestion of an improved coffee machine."

"That little machine was second hand from the bakery when they upgraded." Dara raised her eyebrows. "I hadn't imagined I'd use it much."

"If you make fantastic coffee it would be a drawcard I'm sure." Paula waved her hand over the remains of their lunch. "Bakeries are well and good but sometimes people want alternatives to pastries and buns."

Chris picked up the plan Paula had drawn up. "And you think if we turned half our floor space over to a dining area, customers would pay to come in and sit down to eat."

"You've got a huge space out there. Dara has some lovely items but you said yourself you only make enough to keep turning them over." She looked at Dara, who had so far remained silent. "You could still maintain your stock on one side with some things interspersed among the tables. You could have a couch and coffee table and magazines for those who want a quiet coffee and different sized tables and chairs for people to eat at, so it didn't end up looking like a dining room and…"

"Whoa! Steady up. We need to go a bit slower." Chris laughed.

"It would be a big step." Dara spoke for the first time, looking at Chris.

"Do you like the idea?" he asked.

"We would need to think it over a lot more. It would mean a lot of changes for both of us."

Paula sensed a sadness in Dara that she hadn't anticipated. She had thought her friend would be as enthusiastic as she was about the business idea.

"Look, I've still got some things to finish for Jim and some jobs to do before I head home, so I'll leave it with you." She looked hesitantly at Dara. "It is just an idea."

"Of course, Paula, we know." Chris put his arm around his wife. "And thanks for working on it. There's a lot for us to digest but we will definitely look it over."

"Yes, thanks, Paula. We do appreciate what you've done." Dara smiled a farewell.

Outside, the sun had disappeared under a dirty grey haze and the wind had strengthened, whipping Paula's hair across her face and dirt into her eyes. She hurried back to Jim's to put away the last of the filing.

"Paula, I've been checking out the suggestions you made." Jim smiled at her over the counter. "They're very useful and I am indebted to you for stepping into Heather's shoes. I hope you'll forgive me for thinking you were just an office girl."

"Now, Jim. There's no such thing as 'just an office girl'." Paula wagged a finger at him. "I'm sure Heather is more to you than that. Titles don't matter, it's whether you can do the job that counts."

"Well, you have certainly done the job and I am most grateful. If there is ever anything I can do in return..."

"As a matter of fact, there is. I want to buy a car."

Jim's eyes twinkled. He was always the salesman. "What did you have in mind?"

It was only four o'clock when Paula left for home but the day was dark with dust. She peered anxiously through the windscreen at the sky, as another gust of wind rocked the car. She had thought the haze was rain coming and it had been hard to believe when Jim corrected her and said it was topsoil from paddocks, near and far. Peering into the gloom, she couldn't imagine how there could be any dirt left.

She smiled as she recalled the deal she'd done with Jim to buy the Audi. He'd tried to talk her out of it but she'd fallen in love with the car. It suited her much better than the dual cab.

She knew how much the Audi was worth; she'd seen the paperwork. Her father had reluctantly agreed to sell her Mazda when she'd called to ask. That, along with the sale of a small parcel of shares, would cover it. Jim had given her a very good price after complaining he'd probably never be trusted to sell another vehicle to Dan again if she went home with this one.

Tucked away in the boot were tins of paint. She'd paid Carl a visit, explained what she wanted for the kitchen, watched him carefully as he prepared it and opened every tin before she left the store.

He had feigned hurt at her suggestion that he had mixed the wrong bedroom colours, insisting he had been in the business for years and he would have mixed exactly what she'd asked for. She giggled as she recalled his long low bow in the middle of the shop with his assurance, "The customer is always right, Mrs Woodcroft." He certainly was a character.

As she neared home, the wind that had been pushing her all the way suddenly stopped, and, by the time she got out of the car the haze had cleared, leaving the sky lighter than it had been for hours.

She carried in the steak she had bought. She'd had a sudden memory of her mother's braised steak as she'd searched the meat section of the supermarket and decided that's what she'd cook for their evening meal. She had just struggled in with the last of the paint when she heard a car and rushed back outside, hoping it was Dan home early.

Rowena's vehicle pulled up beside the gate.

"I've picked up the meat from the butchers," Rowena called as she got out of the car.

Yes and hello to you too, thought Paula.

"I picked up some extra plastic bags in case you need them," continued Rowena. She opened the boot of her car.

Paula walked over to see what she was talking about and stared in amazement at the crates of meat filling the boot.

"What is this?" she asked, feeling stupid as soon as she'd said it.

"Your meat, my dear. The butcher does most of the work but it doesn't come neatly packaged like it is in the supermarket. Here, you carry this one in." Rowena pointed to a crate and waited for Paula to lift it out before reaching in and picking up another. They made two trips, stacking the crates along the kitchen benches.

"You'll need the table for sorting and packing." Rowena paused and looked at Paula's clothes. "I'd forgotten you've been at Jim's. If you're going to work in town perhaps I could do some housework for you."

Was that a criticism, Paula wondered. She glanced around her kitchen, which was neat and tidy except for the meat they'd carried in and the bags of shopping she'd left on the floor. "I'm fine thanks, Rowena, besides that job's finished now. Jim is expecting Heather back next week."

"Oh, didn't I see old Mrs Johnson's Audi in your shed? I thought you would have to return that once you'd finished."

"It's no longer old Mrs Johnson's Audi. It's now young Mrs Woodcroft's Audi." Paula grinned.

Rowena stared at her as if she'd gone mad.

"I've bought it," Paula said with a flourish.

Rowena sniffed and pursed her lips. "Well, I don't know what Dan will have to say about that, finances are —"

"Dan doesn't have a say, Rowena. I bought it with my own money."

"I see. Does your father know?"

Paula seethed. "He is selling my car in Sydney. Not that he has any say in it either."

Rowena held her gaze a minute before she spoke. "I wouldn't mention it to Dan tonight. After today, he won't be in any mood for surprises. I'd better be off and package my meat then. You seem to have everything under control here."

"Yes, see you later." Paula listened as the back door banged shut and then marched over to the kettle.

"Old bag," she muttered as she flicked the switch. What I need is a nice cup of coffee, she thought to herself. What had happened to Dan today? She hoped it was nothing to delay the seeding.

She looked at the plastic shopping bags she'd left on the floor by her feet. She should put the steak on. It would take a while to cook and the temperature was dropping quickly so she had to get the fire going in the lounge. She avoided looking at the crates of meat. Goodness knows what she was going to do with all that.

While she sipped her coffee, she braised the steak and left it to simmer. The wood basket in the lounge was empty. Outside, the wind had picked up again and dark clouds were rolling in. She filled the basket quickly and noticed the supply of wood was getting low. Vaguely she wondered where it came from but she had to make a dash for the house as a sudden strong wind hurled rain and bits of leaves and debris all around her.

She leaned against the inside of the back door, clutching the wood basket and catching her breath, as outside the wind howled and the rain crashed down on the tin roof of the verandah. The sudden ferocity of the weather frightened her. She listened as the old verandah creaked and wondered whether it could withstand the force. The house was more substantial. She would feel safer in there.

Once she had the fire roaring she checked the steak. Happy to see it simmering gently, she went to change out of her good clothes, which were now damp and flecked with wood chips. The lights flickered and she was reminded of the last storm they'd had. After that night Dan had brought her a rechargeable lantern from the shed. Knowing it was in the pantry, alongside the torch, was reassuring.

Back in the kitchen, she began peering into the boxes Rowena had delivered. There were huge plastic bags of mince, sausages, chops and legs. The size of it all overwhelmed her but she couldn't leave it sitting on the bench for too long.

The back door banged. Saved by my man, she thought as she went to meet Dan. They could have a lovely evening together by the fire. The sight of him brought her up with a start.

"Are you all right?"

The man who stood before her didn't resemble Dan at all. His hair stood on end as if it had been gelled in place and he looked at her through red-rimmed eyes from a face covered in dirt. His clothes were filthy and his arms and hands were smeared with mud. "What have you been doing?"

"Trying to contain bloody lunatic sheep while I watched our farm blow away." Paula saw him grimace as he bent to pull off his boots.

"Are you hurt?" She took a step closer. He looked terrible.

"Just landed funny when I jumped off the back of the ute. I must have twisted my knee."

"What were you doing?"

He didn't reply but kept tugging at his boots. Paula wanted to hug him but she hesitated. There was an indiscernible barrier between them and she didn't know how to deal with it. She refrained from asking any more questions.

"I've got tea cooking. Why don't you soak in the bath and I'll bring you a drink."

"Thanks. That's a good idea." He gave her a faint smile, dropped the last boot and went through the end door to the laundry.

Paula returned to the kitchen where the crates of meat still waited. She poured Dan a drink and served up their meal. It was the only useful thing she could think to do.

They ate by the fire and between mouthfuls of food Dan quietly explained his day to Paula.

"I knew it wasn't going to be a good day for seeding and I was checking the stock when the north winds hit. At first, it just dried the soil out and nothing much moved, but by lunchtime, the wind was so strong, it was taking the topsoil with it. Tom and I were trying to fix a damaged fence when we realised we had sheep out on the road. Conditions were so bad we could hardly see more than a couple of metres in front of us. We got the sheep back in and fixed the fence but…" Dan sighed deeply and stopped.

Paula watched him. Her heart ached to see his wretchedness.

He looked up at her. "I'm afraid I wouldn't be signing any financial agreements that bound you to this place. It's not worth a cracker at the moment. I don't know how much I'll have to re-sow, that's if I do it at all."

Paula didn't know what to say. Her previous work had involved looking at markets, predicting sales and investments, but this was so much more intangible. She looked on helplessly as Dan continued.

"When the wind dropped, Tom and I did another quick inspection of the stock and we found a dead ram. They get agitated and all push together. Anyway, this one must have spooked in the wind and run into the fence at an odd angle, broke its neck. Then we found a blocked water trough just as the wind changed and the storm hit from the south. The rain pelted down. But only for a few minutes." He shook his head slowly and looked back at Paula, the tiny hint of a smile gleaming in his bloodshot eyes. "A man has to be mad to be a farmer and a woman has to be even madder to marry one."

She hugged him then, so tightly. "Dan, we'll get through this." But she didn't really understand and there was no conviction in her voice.

"I'm sorry, I'm not good company. I'm bushed. I'll take myself off to bed."

"Dan, I need…" He turned and looked at her, his normally straight torso drooping at the shoulders. "I need to clean up first. I'll be there in a minute."

She wanted to ask him about the meat but it was insignificant in comparison to his day. Well, Mrs Woodcroft, life on the farm, lesson number ninety-nine, how to package meat, she said to herself as she looked balefully at the crates lined up on her kitchen bench.

It took her till midnight but she got it done. Every bit of meat was in a bag and in the freezer. The crates were washed and stacked up on the sink and she'd done the dishes as well. On her way out of the kitchen she passed the envelope her father had left, still lying on the dresser. She picked it up, turned it over once then dropped it into the drawer and pushed it firmly shut. She really didn't want to know what the envelope contained.

Exhausted, she fell into bed beside Dan who tossed and turned restlessly, keeping her awake, in spite of her tiredness.

CHAPTER
14

Paula woke late the next morning. The sun was shining and the day looked positively cheerful after the devastation of yesterday. She could hear male voices coming from the kitchen. Curious, she pulled on jeans and a jumper before going to investigate.

Dan, Tom and Bruce were sitting at the kitchen table drinking coffee produced from her machine by the look of the nearly empty water tank. Dan had decided her coffee machine made better coffee than instant.

"Hello, sleepyhead." He greeted her with a wink and she was pleased to see the smile back on his face. "We're having a commiserating drink."

"Hello, Paula." Bruce raised his cup. "Nothing stronger than coffee at this hour of the morning, I promise."

Tom smiled shyly at her. Paula smiled back, happy to have some company in her kitchen. She refilled the tank, made herself a coffee and joined them at the table.

"We're going to inspect the damage. Bruce assures me he doesn't think it's as bad as I thought," Dan said.

"Plenty worse off than us," Bruce said. "I reckon we might be some of the lucky ones."

"Yeah, but you pig farmers are used to being dealt shit." Dan smirked at his friend across the table.

"Unlike you sheep farmers who just have shit for brains." Bruce leaned across the table to give Dan a mock cuff across the head.

"Ahem." Tom cleared his throat gently and nodded in Paula's direction.

"Oh, sorry, Paula. Come on Dan. What were you thinking? There's a lady present." Bruce grinned. His dark features were full of boyish charm.

Paula laughed. She was enjoying their friendly banter. "Don't mind me. I've heard things around the boardroom table in Sydney that would make one of your legendary shearers blush."

"Dan said you're still getting the mice inside." Tom quietly changed the subject.

"Yes, one or two. But, thanks to you, there aren't as many getting in."

"They were only Dan's pets to get rid of the mother-in-law." Bruce laughed.

"Hey, steady up," Dan said.

"Sorry, Paula, I was only kidding. The toaster story was a beauty. No offence meant."

"None taken," she replied. "I would have laughed myself but my mother is really terrified of mice."

"One good thing about this storm, it might have killed the little buggers off." Bruce's face was serious again.

"It would have knocked their numbers, but I think we're stuck with them for a while yet." Dan stood up. "Do you want to come for the ride, Paula?"

"Yes." She collected his cup with her own but Bruce and Tom had already carried theirs to the sink.

"What did you do with the meat?" Dan pointed to the empty crates. "I'd forgotten Rowena was collecting that yesterday."

"I packed it all away in the freezer."

"It must have taken ages. You could have left it till this morning. It's cold enough in this kitchen overnight." Dan opened the freezer door and looked in. "Did you label any of it?"

"No, should I have?"

"It helps when you're trying to work out which lump of frozen meat is which. Although it looks like we'll be eating the same thing for a week."

"Why?" Bruce peered over his shoulder. "Oh, I see. Now that's what I call meat."

Dan pulled a large bag of mince from the freezer. "How did you think we were going to use this much mince at one time?" He hefted the bag up and down.

"Or sausages or chops." Bruce was still peering into the freezer.

"I divided it into smaller parcels." Paula felt defensive of her effort.

"Yeah, but this much meat should last us for months, Sweet Pea. We don't want to cook it all in one go." Dan's lips twitched.

"Well, I thought we'd break off what we needed."

All three men looked at Paula for a moment.

"Feed the man meat." Bruce broke the silence and gave Dan a pat on the back.

"In future, you can do it yourself if you don't like the way I do it." Paula glared at Dan.

"Don't get upset. We can still break it into smaller packages. Some of it's not frozen solid yet. What's a bit of meat between friends?"

"I've already spent half the night doing it," Paula snapped. "Why don't you do it?"

"That's my cue to leave." Bruce grabbed his hat. "I'll 'meat' you outside."

Paula picked up the frypan she'd left draining on the sink the night before. "One more word about meat!" She waved the pan in the air.

"Don't do it, Bruce." Dan put up his hands. "She's armed and dangerous. We'll catch you up in a few minutes. This won't take long."

Paula kept one hand on the pan and watched as Bruce and Tom beat a tactical retreat.

"I'll shift the not—so—frozen packs into the fridge. We can deal with it after our drive," Dan said, his nose already back in the freezer.

Paula stayed at the sink rinsing the cups then followed Dan outside when he'd finished transferring the meat. She wasn't really cross. She was thankful to see him smiling and enjoying the company of his friends, even if it was at her expense.

She did feel a bit silly about the meat, though. If only she'd thought about it last night she would have realised she was packaging far too much for the two of them to eat in one meal. It had been an exhausting week and Dan's distress had upset her. She hadn't been thinking straight.

Bruce and Tom were wandering back from the paddock close to the house.

"There're some sandy ridges in that one that have drifted." Bruce jabbed his thumb over his shoulder. "You might have lost some seed in patches there."

"That's a wheat paddock. I only finished it Thursday." Dan turned away.

They all got in the dual cab to check out the rest of the property.

"I see you've still got old Mrs Johnson's Audi." Tom spoke from the back seat where he sat beside Bruce, as Dan drove onto the track that crossed their farm.

"I noticed that in the car shed," Bruce chipped in. "What are you doing with that, Dan? Going all up-market on us?"

"Jim let Paula drive it while she's been working for him."

"He certainly couldn't sell it to anyone," Bruce said.

"It's a pretty nice car." Tom's voice was full of admiration.

"There speaks the young and naive." Bruce chuckled. "Jim would have trouble giving that lemon away."

Paula looked at Dan, whose eyes were on the track ahead. "I've bought it."

"Cool!" Tom exclaimed.

"Good choice." Bruce's response wasn't anywhere near as exuberant.

Dan kept his eyes ahead and didn't say a word.

After that the conversation remained firmly on the condition of the land and the state of the weather.

A few hours later Paula and Dan stood together waving off Bruce and Tom. "So, you've bought the Audi," Dan said.

"I'll use the money from the sale of my car and a small investment to pay for it. Jim has kindly let me keep it until we can sort out the finances."

They walked to the car shed and Dan made his way slowly around the Audi. He kicked the tyres and rocked the body, then looked in through the window. "It's a nice-looking vehicle. Not one I'd pick, living where we do, but I'm sure Jim wouldn't sell it to you if it wasn't mechanically sound."

"No." Paula couldn't help but recall Jim's reluctance to sell her the car. "I find it much easier than the dual cab."

"It's your money."

Paula couldn't tell from the odd look on his face whether he was annoyed or amused. "I do love it and it means I can get around when you're not here."

"Speaking of which, there's no point in getting back on the tractor today." He turned his back on the car. "Bruce asked me to go to golf. It's Sponsors' Day at the local club. I said I didn't want to leave you on your own again."

"That's silly, Dan. You should go." Paula tried to sound enthusiastic. She didn't want to be a clinging wife who wouldn't let her husband do anything without her, but they'd hardly had any time alone together, just for themselves.

"I suppose I could go just for the game," Dan said. "Jane will be home with the kids. Why don't you go and visit her?"

"Oh, no. I couldn't just call in. Anyway, I've got things to do here."

"If you're sure. I'll come straight home after the game. Maybe we could have another of those deep baths to ease my golfer's aches." He reached his arms around her and nuzzled at her ear.

Paula turned to escape his embrace and kissed him firmly on the mouth. "You'd better get going, Mr Golfer, I've got work to do. If you stay here I'll give you a brush. I plan to start painting the kitchen today." She smiled bravely but she didn't feel it. Underneath, she was wishing he would stay home.

"I said I'd pick up Bruce so I'd better get going."

"What about your lunch?"

"They always have a good spread at Sponsors' Day. I'll eat when we get there."

Paula fiddled in the backyard while he got ready. She tugged out a few weeds and snapped off some dead branches. The garden here remained untamed by her mother's green-fingered touch. Once again, it must have been a lawn edged by roses, like the side garden. Dan's grandmother obviously liked roses.

"I'm off. I won't be late." Dan kissed her and jumped into the dual cab.

She was glad he had shaken off the doom and gloom of yesterday and waved him goodbye, but the silence once the vehicle departed was absolute. She wandered into the kitchen, thinking she would have some lunch. The crates piled on the sink reminded her of the meat in the fridge. Dan had said they would repack together.

"Bugger," she muttered. With a sigh she dragged the meat to the sink where she pushed and probed and hacked with a knife to make smaller parcels of meat, then repackaged it and pushed it into the freezer. It wasn't till she'd shoved in the last bag that she remembered the labels.

"Bugger," she muttered again. "Too bad." She glanced around the kitchen and thought of the paint tins stored in the middle bedroom, ready for her to begin – but her heart wasn't in it any more.

She wandered into the spare room her parents had occupied and realised she still hadn't stripped the bed. While she was pulling off the sheets she looked at the curtains. She had noticed a musty smell to them when she'd hung them. Going closer she could still detect it. It was a sunny, breezy day and she might as well wash them too.

Once the machine was loaded up, she went into the lounge. The only thing out of place was the lovely blue hand-knitted jumper that was Dan's gift from her sisters. A momentary pang of homesickness gripped her as she picked it up and glanced across at the box of wedding photo proofs, sitting on the side table. She wondered what her family were all doing today.

Then she recalled Jane's request to see her wedding photos. Perhaps she could drive over and see her as Dan had suggested. She'd have to ring first to get directions.

Having a purpose to her day lifted her spirits and she made herself some lunch while she waited for the washing machine to finish with the sheets and curtains. As soon as the machine stopped, she dragged out the bundle of wet things and carried them outside.

She pegged the sheets firmly then hoisted the curtains over the line. The stiff breeze pushed the wet material into her face and she had to fight to get the pegs in place. With the last peg attached she ran her hands down the material and then stopped in alarm. Among the pattern, in lines down the curtains, she noticed patches. She looked more carefully. Intermittently she could see frayed spots along the length of the curtains. They must have been sun damaged, Paula thought, and Rowena's words replayed in her mind. *They were my mother's pride and joy.*

"Oh no! Why did I wash them?" Paula wailed out loud. I wish she'd never given them to me, she thought. Here was another black mark for the new bride. I've wrecked the precious family heirlooms.

Nothing she could do would fix them so Paula reluctantly left them to blow in the breeze and went inside to ring Jane.

Jane was pleased to hear from her and welcomed the idea of an afternoon together. "If it's good enough for the men, it's good enough for us," she joked.

Paula gathered the directions she'd scribbled and the wedding photos and walked out to the car with only a passing glance at the tattered curtains on the line. She'd worry about them later.

In the Audi, she turned the key in the ignition but got only a fleeting click from under the bonnet. She tried again, thinking she hadn't turned the key properly, but got the same result. Again and again she tried, then she stopped and thumped the steering wheel. What could be wrong? It had driven beautifully yesterday.

Back inside the house, she rang Jane.

"I'm sorry Jane, I've got car trouble. Would you like to come here instead?"

"I would, Paula, but James has just gone down for a sleep. We've had some terrible nights with him lately and I don't want to pick him up. How about I call you when he wakes?"

"Okay." Paula hung up and tears brimmed in her eyes. "Get a grip, girl," she said and bit her lip.

The sound of a vehicle sent her scurrying to the back door. If it was Rowena she'd have to hide the curtains. She wasn't up to explaining the demise of the family treasures.

Paula glanced out the window at the vehicle. It was Tom's ute. She went out the back in time to see a plump middle-aged woman wearing a billowing floral skirt and rubber boots getting out of the passenger side. She carried a bundle in her arms. Paula blinked. She must be Tom's mum.

Tom waved over the roof of the ute.

"Hello, Tom. Aren't you playing football today?" Paula asked.

"We've got a bye." He came to the gate and held it open. "This is my mum, Rita."

"Pleased to meet you, Mrs Woodcroft."

Paula held out her hand. "Call me Paula, please." Rita took one hand off the bundle and rubbed it down her skirt before she gave Paula's hand a quick clasp.

"I shoulda called by sooner, but I have my work cut out lookin' after this lot." She jerked her head in Tom's direction.

Tom stood silently behind his mother, holding a bag of dog food and shifting awkwardly from foot to foot.

"Stop fidget'n', Tom," Rita barked over her shoulder then she turned back to Paula. "Young Tom here says you've been hav'n' trouble with mice."

"Yes, we have a bit. But thanks to Tom's help they're not as bad."

"I brought you a present." Rita thrust forward the bundle she was carrying. Paula looked down in surprise as the lump of rags landed in her arms and began squirming.

"Our Bluebell's the best mouser there is and any pup of hers always follows in her footsteps. This little fella should look after you fine." Rita pulled back a corner of the raggedy cover to reveal a bright little face with deep brown eyes and a pointy snout.

"This is very kind of you, Rita." Paula looked from the pup to Rita. "But I don't know…"

"Dan might not want it, Mum. I didn't get a chance to ask him."

"Rubbish, Dan doesn't get a say. If Paula wants it she can have it. Don't need to go askin' her husband's permission. Anyway it's a weddin' present and you can't give back a present."

Paula looked back at the sweet little face gazing quizzically up at her. Beneath the rags she could feel its back quivering. It didn't look frightened, so she presumed it shook from excitement.

Dan had an old farm dog that went with him when he was working with sheep. Paula rarely saw it. Rocket, it was called, although Dan laughed that it no longer had turbo power. It still lived at Rowena's where there was a big enclosed wire dog kennel. It would be nice to have something to talk to other than herself when Dan wasn't around and Rita was right, she didn't have to ask his permission.

"Thank you, Rita. It's a lovely present. Would you like to come in for a cuppa?"

"I'm not really dressed for visit'n'. Only young Tom thought you might be on your own this arvo, so I thought it was time I popped over and said hello."

"Please come in. Actually, Tom, I've got a bit of a problem with my car. If you've got time, perhaps you'd look at it for me."

"Course he will. Young Tom's a whiz with mechanicals."

Tom grinned and Paula led the way into the house.

Paula and Rita enjoyed a cup of tea and a chat while Tom tinkered with the Audi. Well, at least Rita did the chatting and Paula listened and they nursed the pup between them. Rita had an opinion on every topic and Paula found out a lot about neighbours she'd never met.

Rita leaned in close. "How you gett'n' on with Miss Woodcroft?"

"She's been a big help." Paula didn't think it right to speak disloyally of Dan's aunt to Rita.

"Don't you stand any of her bossiness. She's a strong woman, that one. Done a darn good job of raisin' Dan on her own. Pity she never had her own kids. She'll be glad Dan's got you. Means she can let go and live her own life, now that he's got a fitt'n' wife."

Paula was held by Rita's direct gaze, uncertain how to respond.

"Your battery's had it," Tom declared solemnly from the doorway. "Dan's got a spare over in the shed at Miss Woodcroft's. I could go and get it for you."

"Oh, no. Thanks, Tom, I'll wait for Dan."

"Do you need a ride somewhere?" Rita asked. "Tom could drop you off."

"No, thank you both. I don't need to go anywhere." Paula smiled valiantly but she felt deflated. The Audi had given her a new autonomy. Apart from Jane's she had nowhere to go really, it was just the freedom of being able to go if she wanted to. Now she'd had her 'wheels' removed, she felt isolated again.

"We'd betta get goin' then." Rita stood up. "Come on, Tom." She walked in her socks to the back door where she'd left her boots.

"See you, Paula." Tom smiled his shy smile.

"Thanks for that nice cup of tea, Paula." Rita patted Paula's arm and leaned in close. "No matter what anyone says, you're the right one for Dan, I can tell. You're a nice person. Just what Dan needs."

Paula smiled back at her, unsure of what to say. The puppy squirmed again in her arms and she looked down.

"Oh, and don't throw out those rags yet." Rita laid a plump hand on the bundle. "They've got Bluebell's smell on them. It will help to settle him in, till he knows you."

Paula pulled back the rags again as the ute drove away and the sweet little face looked expectantly up at her. "Okay, little guy. It's just you and me. What am I going to call you and where will you live?" She nestled the little bundle on the floor in a corner and opened the door into the old sleep-out. Among the bits and pieces she thought she'd seen an old basket.

There was a snuffling near her feet and Paula jumped, expecting to see a mouse. Instead the pup had wormed out of the rags and was eagerly sniffing the sleep-out floor at her feet.

"You're living up to Rita's expectations already. There are probably plenty of mice in here." Paula laughed as she watched the little animal scurry along on its short legs, sniffing and sticking its snout into every nook and cranny. She found the basket and called the pup.

"Pup! Here boy."

He came quickly at her call and nuzzled her leg. She bent down to pick him up and carried him with the basket outside where he boldly explored the weeds around her. Once the basket was ready, she sat the pup in it and tucked the rags back around him. The little dog whimpered once then looked expectantly up at her again.

"All that's left is to name you. I can't keep calling you Pup."

Paula lifted the basket up to her face and dog licked her cheek. The things she'd hung on the line flapped in a gust of wind and caught her attention.

"Oh, no," she wailed. The curtains were blowing in the breeze and she could see the garden through them. Great lengths had ripped in lines down the material. They must have given way as they'd dried. "Well, Pup, we could be excommunicated if Rowena finds out about this. It will be our little secret, okay?"

The pup looked up at her expectantly, blinked and gave a little yip. Paula laughed at her co-conspirator. She didn't like the idea of a dog living in the house but she didn't have anywhere outside to keep it, so she decided to clean out the sleep-out.

She sorted through the furniture that was left in the room. Rowena had been right, it was mostly junk. Paula dragged a lot out and made a pile in the backyard. Back inside she surveyed the all-but-empty room.

"This will do until Dan can make you a kennel outside," she spoke to the pup, who watched her from his basket.

Paula took up the broom and swept the cement floor, raising a cloud of dust which made the pup sneeze sharply several times in a row. "Sorry, little guy, nearly finished."

In the corner, she stacked some old chests of drawers and a cast-iron bed frame; apart from that the only thing worth salvaging had been an old wooden trunk. It was empty but in good condition and she had plans for it in the lounge.

She put an old blanket on the floor and wedged the basket in a corner between the wall and the drawers. "I hope this will be snug enough, little guy."

His eyelids were drooping and his snout was resting on his small paws. She covered him gently with the rags then shut the door and hoisted the old trunk into the lounge. It would make a good table for magazines.

The wood basket was empty again and once more she made the trek outside and filled it with the last of the wood. The tattered curtains were a depressing reminder of the damage she'd caused. Defiantly, she pulled them off the line and wound them into a bundle. With any luck Rowena would never ask after them and Dan wasn't likely to.

The pup was awake and scratching at the sleep-out door as she stumbled inside with the wood basket and the bundle of curtains. At the sound of her footsteps, he whined pitifully.

"Just a minute," she called and it stopped but as she went on into the house she heard the whining begin again. In the lounge, she dropped the wood basket as the pup's pleas turned into a pathetic howl. Hastily, she lifted the lid of the chest, shoved the curtains inside and went out to rescue the miserable animal.

"Now, what's your problem?" she asked as she opened the door a little. The pup pushed through and danced at her feet excitedly. "Do you need to go outside?" Paula had no idea how often pups needed a toilet stop.

Outside, the dog explored the jungle of garden around the clothesline on its short stocky legs while she brought in the rest of her washing. She carried the sheets into the laundry and before she could turn around the pup was there, sniffing at her feet.

The phone rang. Paula looked down at the little face tipped sideways looking back at her. Unable to resist, she picked the dog up and answered the phone.

"Paula, it's Alison."

"Has Susan had the baby?"

"No. I'm just ringing to say hello. How are things on the farm?"

"Good." The pup settled on Paula's lap then shut its eyes. "I've got a pup."

"Oh, how sweet. Is it a sheep dog?"

"No. It looks a bit like a Jack Russell. It's a wedding present."

"What did you think of the things we sent?"

"They were lovely, Alison. Didn't Mum tell you? I should have emailed." Paula scrunched up her nose and looked at her tablet lying on the dresser. "Well, at least I would if I had a decent connection. I've been busy working."

"Mum was a bit vague about the visit. She didn't mention you were working. It's great you've found yourself a job already. Mum and Dad were home a bit sooner than expected. Did everything go all right?" Alison's tone was curious.

"I didn't get the job till after they'd left." Paula didn't want to go into the reasons for the hasty departure. "Mum was worried about Susan having the baby early."

"Oh, I can't see that happening. Jerry has put his foot down and banned Susan from work and she's complaining that she's sitting at home, bored and growing fat. At least the poor baby has a chance to fatten up now that she's slowed down. Mum goes over with a sympathetic ear and fusses over her. I can't stand it. I hope you'll make a better mother-in-waiting."

"No babies here thanks," Paula jumped in quickly. "We're not ready for that."

"Where is that gorgeous man of yours? Still on the tractor? Mum did say he worked hard."

"We had terrible weather here yesterday. He's gone to golf."

"Golf! And left you home alone?"

"I've got plenty to do here." Paula put on a brave front.

"So what was the work that you found? I didn't imagine you'd find it easy to get something but it's great you have. You'd soon be bored in the kitchen."

"It wasn't permanent." Paula hadn't had the chance to be bored but today she felt the isolation of her existence keenly.

"Paula, don't be too tough on Dad."

Alison's sudden mention of their father took Paula by surprise. "What do you mean? He's the one who's tough. He interferes too much."

"He was very generous in helping Julian and me when we needed it."

"Yes, but you didn't have a big failure like Marco to make up for."

"He only has your best interests at heart."

"Ali, I have to go." Paula cut her sister off before she could say any more. "I'm expecting visitors, so I'd better get organised. Thanks for ringing."

"Call me any time if you want a chat won't you, little sis. We miss you."

Paula hung up quickly as the tears brimmed in her eyes for the second time that afternoon. The movement woke the pup on her lap. He lifted his head and opened two sleepy eyes to look adoringly up at her.

"Just as well I've got you." She patted his head and put him on the floor. "Come on, we've got work to do."

By six o'clock Paula sat dejectedly on the couch watching the news alone. The pup was asleep again, in his basket in the laundry. There had been no word from Jane.

Paula had kept herself busy with housework. The beds were freshly made and she'd closed the old blind in the spare bedroom and swathed a sheet across the top of the window so it didn't look so bare.

The fireplace in the lounge had been overflowing with ash and it had taken her several loads to get rid of it all. Both she and the pup had been sooty by the time she'd finished. The fire flickered brightly now but she'd used the last of the wood in the basket and there were only scraps left outside. She had no idea where to go to find more.

A roast sizzled in the frying pan in the kitchen and the vegetables were prepared, ready to cook when Dan came home. She wished he would come home now. What was the point of her being here, if not to be with him?

She turned the television off and played a CD instead, moving restlessly from the lounge to kitchen. The sounds of Pachelbel's Canon floated after her. Prodding at the roast, she decided she would put the vegetables on. Surely, Dan would have to be home soon.

The kitchen curtain was still open and she went to close it. The blackness beyond was total. In the glass she could see her own reflection. Despair washed over her and she pulled the curtain across sharply. How did other wives tolerate it? Maybe if they'd been brought up in the country it was different. It sounded like Jane had a role to play on their property beyond the house but Paula was no help to Dan. She didn't understand the first thing about what he did all day. Behind her the phone rang.

The pup came skittering to her feet as she answered it.

"Paula?" She was pleased to hear Jane's voice. "I'm sorry I didn't get there today. I tried to ring a couple of times but you were engaged or not answering."

"It's been a busy day." Paula tried to sound light-hearted.

"Bruce and Dan are here. We wondered if you'd like to come over for tea…" Loud laughter echoed in the background. "They've had a few drinks but I could come and pick you up and you could drive Dan home later."

Paula didn't feel the slightest bit cheery. She looked across at the frypan where the roast still sizzled and then at the table she had set with their new dinner setting and flowers from their garden. "I don't think so Jane, thank you. I'm cooking a roast and…" The pup sat right in front of her looking up adoringly with those big brown eyes and Paula suddenly felt overwhelmed. Tears began to roll down her cheeks. "I'm sorry," she sobbed.

"Are you all right?" Jane's concern only made Paula feel worse.

"Yes, I guess I'm just very tired."

"You've been on your own long enough." Jane's voice was reassuring. "I'll get Bruce to drive Dan home. They won't be long."

Paula picked up the pup and stroked his back. "Now she'll think I'm a weak fool who can't even spend half a day on my own without turning into a gibbering mess."

The pup relaxed and was soon asleep again. She tucked him into his basket and shut the door, then went back into the kitchen where the small blow heater was struggling to warm the room. Perhaps they could eat in the lounge by the fire. A quick check in there revealed the last log crumbling into coals. Perhaps Dan would be able to bring some from wherever he had the wood stashed.

Back in the kitchen she began serving up the roast. That's if Dan's in any state to eat it, she thought. By the time she had dished up and cleared away the mess, she heard a vehicle approaching. She put the two plates of food into the oven to keep warm just as a bang at the back door announced Dan's return.

The chill in the back porch made her shiver as she was met by a smiling Bruce.

"Hello, Paula. Sorry we're late. Dan let his hair down a bit."

"Where is he?"

"Pit stop." Bruce pointed towards the toilet. "Are you okay? Jane wanted me to check you were all right."

"I'm fine. Thanks for bringing him home, Bruce."

Bruce turned to go then looked back at Paula. He lowered his voice and spoke earnestly. "He needed to unwind. Let go of his troubles a bit." The toilet flushed. "Anyway, I'd better get home myself."

So lighten up girl, she told herself. You've been home alone all afternoon, done housework and cooked a nice meal and now your grateful husband comes home late and inebriated by the sound of it. She went back to the kitchen to look for the bottle of wine.

There was a crash and a yelp from the laundry. She stuck her head through the passage door in time to see Dan struggling out with the pup attached to the leg of his jeans.

"What is this?" he asked and stumbled another step forward. "Have you been breeding killer mice?"

She went to rescue the pup, or was it Dan's jeans? She wasn't sure which. "It's our wedding present from Rita."

"Bloody hell. Don't tell me Bluebell's still spitting out pups." He laughed and fell against the wall, waggling his leg. "Let go of me, Fang."

Paula removed the pup and patted him gently. "It's only Dan," she soothed. "Did you think he was a burglar?"

"Lucky it didn't bite my leg off, silly mutt. Old Rocket will probably think it's a mouse." He staggered up straight and swayed towards the kitchen. "Now, Jane mentioned roast and I'm starving. Damn it's cold in here. Have you got the fire going?"

Paula ignored him and went back to the laundry with the pup, settled him back in his basket and returned to the kitchen. Dan wasn't there. The sounds of her CD had been replaced by the voices of football commentators from the television. Looks like we'll be eating in the lounge, she thought, glancing ruefully over to her beautifully set table.

She removed Dan's plate from the oven, put it on a tray with the cutlery and carried it through. The wood basket was lying on its side and the fire was little more than a faint glow of crumbled ash. Dan was stretched out on the lounge, snoring gently.

"Dan." She bent closer and spoke gently in his ear. The smell of beer and stale smoke wafted around him. "Dan." She spoke louder and shook his shoulder.

"Hmmm?" He opened his eyes. She saw a look of recognition register and a goofy smile spread over his face before he closed his eyes again, mumbling, "Hello, Sweet Pea."

"Dan!" She shook him harder. "Are you going to eat this?"

He opened his eyes and half sat up. "Yes. I'll just get the footy scores." This time his eyes didn't focus and he slowly sank down and began snoring again.

Paula looked down. The pup had snuck in and was watching at her feet. "Looks like it's still just you and me." She went back to the kitchen. At the door she turned. The pup was stretched out on the floor between the remnants of the fire and the couch, his head resting on his paws. "Then again," Paula said sadly. "I guess it's just me." She went into the kitchen and ate her meal alone with the blow heater at her feet.

CHAPTER
15

"Good morning," Dan's warm lips nuzzled at Paula's ear and she opened her eyes. He was leaning over the bed smiling at her. The inviting aroma of toast and coffee wafted in the air.

"Good morning to you." She smiled and kissed him before he straightened up. A breakfast tray sat on the table beside the bed.

"I'm sorry about last night." His face was full of concern. "I hope I wasn't too obnoxious."

She smiled at him. He was wearing his work clothes and that serious air surrounded him again. "Well, you make a pretty useless drunk." She pulled back the covers and patted the bed. "But you could make it up to me."

He leaned down and kissed her. The prickles from his usually clean-shaven chin brushed against her cheek. She wrapped her arms around his neck and breathed in the fresh smell of his recently showered skin but he gently pulled away.

"I'm sorry, Sweet Pea, I have to go out."

"But it's Sunday."

"I know. Tom's picking me up. I've arranged to help Fred Martin move some stock and there are a few jobs I promised Rowena I'd do."

Paula watched him cross the room. He always had something to do. She didn't think she could face another day alone. She sat up, the chilly air seeping in around the edges of the covers. "We need more wood. The pile is empty." She pulled the doona tighter around her.

"Really?" He looked back. "Already?"

Paula frowned. "It's been so cold. How else do you expect me to keep warm?"

"I didn't realise the pile was getting low."

"Just tell me where you keep more. I can get it."

"We have a ready source but it's scattered all over the property."

Paula stared at him. "You mean I have to go looking for it?"

He smiled. "I tell you what. You eat some breakfast. I should only be an hour or so. Then, once I've got the dual cab back I'll come and get you. I wouldn't mind an offsider and we can collect some wood while we're at it." He winked and left. She listened to the sound of his bootless feet creaking down the passage. Then he called to her, "And don't be too long. I've been entertaining Fang here, but I think he's looking for you."

Paula heard a little bark and then the passage door shut. Her spirits lifted. She had forgotten the pup for the moment. They really would have to think of a name for him. She stepped out of bed onto the mat, pulled on her dressing-gown and took a sip of the coffee Dan had left. *Come on girl, lesson number one hundred and sixty-four, there's always work to be done on a farm.*

Dan had come back for Paula as promised and they had set off across the property checking stock and loading up wood as they went. He had a chainsaw and used it to cut up old branches along the edge of a scrubby section where he'd made piles of dead wood. Each time he started up the chainsaw, the pup had cowered in Paula's arms.

"You're a real brave little mutt, aren't you, Fang?" Dan laughed.

To Paula's untrained eye the paddocks didn't look much different. "Will the crops be okay?"

"We won't be too badly off if we can get some rain," Dan told her. "I think we've only lost seed in that sandy paddock close to the house. Some of the other paddocks have bare patches but as long as the seed is still there and we get some rain soon they should come back."

The back of the dual cab was loaded high with wood by the time they drove along the track to Rowena's, the pup sitting on the back seat. Dan pulled in behind Rowena's empty garage. She had gone to Adelaide again. They unloaded a pile of the wood for her.

"Rowena said there was a bit of mail for me in her bag," Dan said when they'd finished. "She left it on the kitchen table. Can you go in and get it while I pick up the spare battery?"

Paula looked at him in surprise. She'd forgotten all about her flat battery.

"Tom told me about it when he picked me up this morning." A small smile played at the corners of Dan's mouth.

"He said it was just one of those things," Paula said defensively. "Batteries wear out without warning sometimes."

Dan held up his hands, palms towards Paula and put on his fake drawl again. "I'm just offerin' a spare battery, ma'am."

"Thank you." She turned on her heel and went to Rowena's shed to collect the spare key.

Inside the house was dark and cold. Paula turned on the light in the kitchen. The benches were clear and gleaming, not a thing out of place. The small table at the end was, by contrast, a clutter of papers, books and pens.

Paula walked over to look for the mail. Rowena must have been doing bookwork. There were piles of accounts clipped together, bank statements, cheque books, notes in Rowena's neat handwriting and computer-generated pages of crisp figures, all in ordered groups on the table. Paula couldn't help but glance at them. She was sure she could help Rowena with the task of keeping the farm books.

Suddenly a name leapt off the page at her. Katherine Melton. Paula ran her finger across the entry. A payment had been made to her just last month. Quickly she scanned back up the list. Each month, for the last three, a payment had been made to Katherine. The paperwork only went back that far.

Paula sat down and looked more closely through the lists. She looked through a snapshot of their farming finances; payments to the bank, to agricultural suppliers, to fuel companies, to local businesses. And there were airfares, wedding accounts; everything that had happened to Dan and Rowena in the last three months was listed here via their accounts, including the payments to Katherine.

It was a large amount of money. What could it be for? What was it that Katherine had said the other day in town? Paula tried to think back. Something about not cutting her out and some ties being stronger than money.

Paula looked back at the papers in front of her. Katherine was receiving regular payments from Dan, which didn't give the impression she was being cut out. Why would he be giving her all that money?

Rowena's garden gate squeaked and Dan's footsteps came closer along the path. Paula looked around quickly for the mail. There were several envelopes addressed to Dan in a pile to one side. She grabbed them and stood up just as Dan reached the door.

"There you are. I thought you were lost. Anything interesting?"

Paula snapped off the kitchen light. "Like what?" she asked guilt-ily. Perhaps he'd seen her snooping.

"In the mail."

"Oh! No...or at least I think it's all farm stuff." She handed over the pile, thankful he couldn't see the confusion on her face in the semi-light.

The pup waited in the dual cab and wagged his whole body as Paula got in. She patted him and he settled on her lap. She wished she had the courage to ask Dan straight out what had happened between him and Katherine but she'd seen his reaction to the men-tion of Katherine's name. Paula didn't want to be responsible for changing the mood.

"That's a terrible name."

Paula looked at Dan in horror. Had she said Katherine's name out loud?

"Well, it's not that bad," he said, backtracking at her reaction. "But you can't keep calling it Pup. It's going to get a bit bigger." He grinned and Paula realised she had been talking to the pup out loud, as she thought about Katherine.

"I don't know what to call him. I've never named anything before."

"What about 'Fang'?"

Paula looked down at the pup's sweet little face. One eye was open and one ear was half-cocked, as if he was listening for their decision. "That sounds mean and tough. How about Rupert?"

"Rupert?" scoffed Dan.

They laughingly swapped names all the way home but couldn't agree on anything.

In their own yard, they worked together to unload the wood and stack it. The pup darted around between them sniffing at every scrap of wood and barking, before he disappeared into a dense patch of bush and weeds on the other side of the woodpile.

Paula looked up at the sound of several quick barks.

"He's probably found a mouse," Dan said.

There was a loud rustling in the bushes and another little bark.

"Perhaps he's lost in the jungle." Paula peered into the tangle of ivy and weeds.

Suddenly the pup's tail emerged near her feet, then his back and eventually the rest of him was revealed, pulling backwards on something he held in his mouth.

"If that's the jungle," Dan chuckled, "I think we've just found Tarzan."

The pup had backed right out of the bushes now and was dragging a large ivy vine. His back legs propped as he pulled and worried at the vine, trying to drag it out further.

They both laughed as the pup continued to tug and pull at the vine, sometimes swinging off its feet.

"Tarzan it is," Paula said, happy that they had a name at last.

"Now, let's get this wood inside," Dan said. "I think we're going to need a nice cosy fire tonight." His eyes sparkled and he reached for Paula and wrapped her in his arms.

Whatever secrets those eyes held, Paula didn't want to know. He was with her now and that was all that mattered.

CHAPTER
16

"You don't think it's too much?" Paula stood anxiously watching Dan's reaction as they looked around their newly painted kitchen in the late afternoon. She had to admit to having second thoughts about the colours she had chosen for the old kitchen cupboards; the drawers were Bistro Green and the doors Blast Blue. Now that it was finished she thought it a bright contrast to the old honey-yellow tiles but she liked the effect all the same.

There were a lot of cupboards running the length of one wall. Each cupboard had a drawer above it. The colours reflected the blue and green design of the new plates. The old benchtop laminate was off-white and patterned with blue, green and yellow squiggles.

"You've kept everything else cream. It gives the whole room a lift. I don't think we'll need to replace the tiles and once we get this old floor polished and some curtains in the window, it will look first rate. Another decorating masterpiece by Mrs Woodcroft." Dan laughed.

"I couldn't have done that ceiling without your help." They looked up at the patterned pressed tin ceiling high above them. Dan had painted it white over a couple of evenings. Paula knew he was very tired but he'd offered to help out. At least he had been working shorter hours over the last week. Seeding was almost finished. Now they needed rain.

"I didn't do much. There's a lot of wall space you've painted and I wouldn't have the patience to tackle those cupboards. I would have bought new ones."

Paula leaned against him. He was warm in an old jumper and trackpants and smelled good from his recent shower. She on the other hand was very tired and still covered in splotches of paint. It had been a busy week of painting and then working on the floor. She'd discovered wonderful wooden boards under the old linoleum and had spent a day uncovering it and cleaning it up. They'd need a sander in but it didn't look too bad.

The new stove was installed. Luckily, the electrician had been able to come only a day after it was delivered, which was a minor miracle according to Rowena, who had popped in a couple of times to check the progress of the kitchen.

Now Paula had no excuse not to cook. Except that she wasn't keen on the idea. She'd stocked up on Dara's food this week with a couple of trips into town for decorating supplies.

As if on cue, Dan patted his stomach. "What's for tea? I'm starving."

Paula looked around at her gleaming kitchen. Once again, she hadn't thought ahead. There was a freezer full of meat but it was all rock solid. She hadn't taken anything out to defrost.

Dan pulled her in close. "I know it looks nice, but it is a kitchen. We are going to use it, aren't we?"

She sagged in his arms. "I'm so tired," she wailed. "How about toasted sandwiches? Or some of Dara's veggie soup?"

Dan patted his stomach again. "What happened to feed the man meat?"

"Now, don't you start that again." Paula turned on him and wagged her finger under his nose.

"Okay, my shout. Why don't we go into town for a meal at the pub?"

Paula smiled then turned her head. "Was that a car?"

Dan listened. "I can't hear anything. I'll go and throw on some clean clothes."

"I need a shower," Paula said to his disappearing back. She looked down at her chipped fingernails and paint-splotched hands. Just as well Katherine can't see those, she mused, then frowned. She hadn't given Katherine a thought since she'd looked over Rowena's paperwork last Sunday; why did she have to think of her now and spoil her happy mood?

Paula looked up as Tarzan gave a long low growl. He got out of his basket and trotted to the passage just outside the kitchen door where he stopped, ears pricked and eyes staring in the direction of the back door. Paula hesitated as he growled another long low rumble. It had to be more than a mouse. Thank goodness Dan was here. She backed towards the door that led to the lounge, planning to sneak through that way to the bedroom.

There was a loud crash from outside followed by a yell. Paula screamed, Tarzan barked furiously and Dan came running, tucking his fresh blue shirt into his jeans.

"It's only us, Paula. Is Dan home yet?"

Paula raised her eyebrows and Dan shrugged as they recognised Bruce's voice. There was a bit more scuffling noise and a whispered command. Paula picked up Tarzan and watched as Dan walked out to the verandah to open the back door.

"Surprise!" A chorus of voices called out.

Tarzan whimpered and Paula held him close as Bruce pushed past Dan with an esky in one hand and baby James tucked up in the other. Dan stood back as Jane followed with a plate of food and Andrew.

"Happy house-warming." She went on into the house as more people followed behind her.

Dara and Chris came through, loaded with containers. "Happy house-warming," they echoed.

"I can't wait to see all the redecorating." Dara grinned as she followed after Chris. "Is the kitchen finished?"

Jim McInerney struggled through the door with a battery in his hands.

"What's this, Jim?" Dan asked. "It's a bit late for house calls."

Jim put the battery down against the wall and looked at Paula.

"I heard about the battery in the Audi. I'm sorry," he said.

"It wasn't your fault," Paula hastened to reassure him.

"This is your house-warming gift." He gave Paula a quick hug before she could reply, then turned to the short plump woman in a flowery dress and navy jacket who stood behind him. "This is my wife, Mary."

"Hello, Mary," Paula said. There wasn't time for any more conversation as others pushed in through the door. They all greeted Dan and he introduced Paula and they continued on into the house.

Tom came in grinning shyly, and also loaded down with containers of food.

"Careful with those cream cakes, Tom." Rowena was right behind him. She kissed Dan on the cheek.

"Did you organise this, Rowena?" he asked.

"Nothing like a good party to brighten things up. Happy house-warming." She smiled broadly at him, moved on to Paula and went to present her with a parcel. Rowena frowned at Tarzan. "I'll pop this inside. Now, you might not like it but Dara assures me you can take it back if you don't. Welcome to Wood Dell." Rowena leaned in and surprised Paula with a kiss on the cheek then she swept on after Tom.

"Wood Dell?" Paula looked quizzically at Dan.

"Gran's name for this place, I think. It was before my time."

Loud voices echoed from the kitchen.

"Looks like we're not going anywhere." Dan patted his stomach. "I hope there was some decent food in some of those containers."

"At least you're showered and changed." Paula held out her arms. "Look at me, I'm still covered in paint."

"You look beautiful to me." Dan pulled her close for a hug and sandwiched Tarzan between them as he kissed her.

"Come on, you two," Bruce called around the kitchen door. "Time for snogging later. Let's party." He waved a can of beer at them.

Paula tucked Tarzan in his basket and shut the laundry door. She planned to whip up to the bedroom and change before she followed Dan into the kitchen. Someone had found the CD player and disco dance music blared from the lounge.

"There you are, Paula." Dara offered a glass of champagne. "Come on, they want to toast the newlyweds."

"I want to change first."

Dara looked her up and down. "Okay. We can't have the new bride looking too dishevelled. You go and change and I'll hold them off."

Paula escaped to the bedroom. The bed was in a jumble. Quickly, she straightened the sheets and threw over the quilt. Then she pulled on a soft pink jumper and camel twill jeans. She brushed her hair, dabbed on some perfume and applied some mascara and a splash of pink lipstick. Too bad about the hands, she hoped no one would notice them.

Back in the kitchen, more people had arrived. The table and benches were loaded with food and eskies lined the passage outside the kitchen door. Through the lounge door were more people and she could see all kinds of parcels piled on the old wooden chest.

"Here she is," Chris called above the noise.

Someone gave a long wolf whistle and Dara pushed a glass of bubbles into her hand. There was a sea of faces in her kitchen, all looking at her. Gratefully she glanced up at Dan as he appeared at her side and put his arm around her.

"Okay everyone, a bit of quiet," Bruce called from the other end of the kitchen. People around him stopped talking but the noise and music still echoed out from the lounge.

"Cut the music," someone called. It stopped and more people pushed through the lounge door.

"As the best man," Bruce began.

"The missing best man," Dan scoffed. "Never there when I really need you."

"I'm still the best man, mate." Bruce grinned. "Just as well I'm already married or Paula wouldn't have looked twice at you."

There were cheers and yells and whistles.

"Get on with it, Bruce, we're getting thirsty," a male voice called from the lounge.

"Okay, okay. As the best man, it is my job to propose a toast to the bride and groom." He waved his can at Paula. "Welcome, Paula. You're a brave woman taking on this big lug. But I reckon you've made a good choice. As mates go, Dan is the best. He's a true friend who always helps out and I'm sure he'll make a good life partner. You must have what it takes to be a farm wife. Seeding is almost over and you're still here!"

A few female voices echoed support.

"Dan can be difficult to put up with," Bruce continued, "but you've managed so far, so I reckon you two will be okay."

"Come on, Bruce!" the voice called from the lounge. "It'll be harvest before we get a drink."

"Yeah, get on with it," yelled another.

Bruce ignored the interjectors and lifted his can high. "We wish you both a long and happy marriage and may your home soon fill with the patter of little feet —"

"Many." Jane raised her glass.

"A footy team," a man shouted from behind Bruce.

"Give them a chance," called another voice.

"Ladies and gentlemen," Bruce bellowed above the noise. "I ask you to raise your glasses, cans and bottles, and drink to the bride and groom."

"To the bride and groom!" Voices echoed loudly all around them.

Dan hugged Paula close and she smiled up at him. She reminded herself again how lucky she was but the children part worried her. Did he really want her to produce offspring so soon?

"Don't frown, Sweet Pea, this is a party," he murmured in her ear, then kissed her.

"Go, Dan," Bruce yelled, accompanied by a wolf whistle and the popping of a cork.

Lids were lifted from containers, the new oven was warmed up and soon plates of delicious-smelling food were being passed around. Dan introduced Paula to several people. She recognised a couple called Olive and Frank Williams from church. Olive had given her the plate of homemade biscuits. Tonight she'd brought two plates of dainty pink lamingtons filled with cream.

"There's a little plateful for you to put in the fridge for tomorrow, dear." Olive indicated the smaller plate. "You probably won't get a chance to try them tonight."

"Did you get much rain this week, Dan?" Frank asked.

"Only two mils," Dan replied. "Hardly worth mentioning."

"That blow do much damage?"

Another woman began talking to Olive and Paula glanced around her kitchen. Dara and Chris were at the other end. She hadn't had a chance to speak with them properly since she'd left them with her business proposal. Each time she'd called in at the shop, Dara had been busy with customers. She began making her way towards them.

"What were you thinking with these colours, woman?" A belligerent voice growled at her elbow.

Paula turned to look at a rough-shaven man, with bleary eyes and a sly grin. She remembered Dan had introduced him earlier as Ted Watson. Standing beside him was a neatly dressed woman. She was very thin and there were dark shadows under her eyes.

"This is why I'd never let my wife loose with a colour chart." He jerked his head towards the woman next to him and then flicked his hand in the direction of the kitchen cupboards. "Looks like a Smartie box."

Paula bristled. She hadn't liked the way he'd hung on to her hand when Dan had introduced them. Now here he was being rude about her decorating.

"Now, Ted." The woman smiled apologetically at Paula. "I'm Heather. I want to say thanks for taking my place at Jim's."

Ted gave a little grunt.

"I'm pleased to meet you." Paula shook Heather's small hand warmly. "I hope everything was okay when you got back."

"It was great, thank you. I was worrying about all the things I'd have to catch up and you had left it all organised. And your talents go beyond the office. I like what you've done in here." Heather nodded at the room and Ted gave another little grunt.

"I guess it's not to everyone's taste," Paula said.

"Taste!" Ted snorted. "Never let a woman make choices. I hear you bought old Mrs Johnson's Audi. A city car for a city woman. I hope you last a bit longer than that car will."

"Ted, can I interest you in one of my sausage rolls?" Rowena pushed a plate of food under Ted's nose and Paula stepped back. For once, she was grateful for Rowena's interference; she didn't think she would have been able to remain polite to Ted for much longer. Heather seemed so nice. Paula didn't understand what she was doing with such an obnoxious man.

"Paula, we want to thank you."

She turned, and was pleased to see the friendly faces of Chris and Dara behind her.

"What for?"

"Your business suggestion." Chris draped an arm around his wife and pulled her close. "We've talked it over a lot, in fact we've talked of nothing else since you visited us, and we really like the idea."

"We've gone over our finances again and again," Dara said.

"I'm going to put it to my family, once seeding is finished. Dara and I want to run the place in town as a proper business. I can still help out on the farm when they need me."

"We're not getting too excited yet, but it would be wonderful if we could make a living here and not have to move." Dara gazed wistfully at Chris but his look was elsewhere.

"Well, well. What's she doing here?" he murmured.

Paula turned and felt her smile fade as she watched Katherine Melton pushing her way into the room with a tall, well-dressed man in tow. Paula recognised his type. He had city written all over him.

"She probably came with Monica and Rod Brown," Dara said. "Katherine and Monica are as thick as thieves at the moment."

Paula watched as Katherine threw her arms around Dan and kissed him on the lips. Dan undid her arms and listened as Katherine indicated the man with her.

"She's a bit up front, our Katherine," Dara said. "She and Dan used to be an item. She still carries a bit of a torch for him. Not that he's the slightest bit interested any more and certainly not now he's got you."

Paula forced herself to turn away and look back at Dara who was smiling sympathetically.

"For a smart woman, she doesn't always do things in good taste." Chris gave a slow shake of his head.

"She's all right. Oh, there's Monica," Dara said. "Now you must meet her, Paula. She's the one who has the fine wool stud just out of town and she spins and knits those beautiful jumpers. Chris, you'll get us a refill, won't you?" Dara waggled her empty glass at him.

Chris smiled benevolently at his wife, then looked at Paula. "Where's your glass?"

"Oh, I must have put it down." She glanced around.

"I'll get you another one."

Chris set off to work his way to the drinks.

Dara leaned in close to Paula. "I was worried about Chris. He's putting on a brave front but it will be hard for him to tell his family. They've never understood his travelling and trying other jobs. I didn't want him to take on the business just because of me. We've done a lot of soul-searching and it's what we both want. Sink or swim, we're going to give it our best shot." She gave Paula a warm hug. "Thank you."

"We'll have another party once you're up and running," Paula said.

"You bet." Dara chuckled and looked around. "Now let's find Monica. You'll like her."

Paula followed Dara. She couldn't help glancing in Katherine's direction. She was still talking animatedly to Dan who had his back to Paula, while the fellow Katherine had brought with her stood slightly to one side, looking coolly over the crowd.

Dara introduced Paula to Monica. She was a slightly built woman, beautifully made up and wearing an open vest over a black turtleneck jumper. The vest held Paula's attention. It had been woven in various rust colours with traces of black and gold and had delicate beads sewn into it. The vest was exquisite and, to Paula's amazement, Dara explained Monica had spun the wool, dyed it and knitted the vest. Paula was also interested to know she managed the stud on the property she ran with her husband.

"I studied animal genetics at university," Monica said. "Producing fine wool has always been a passion. Rod is more interested in cropping so we make a good team. Dara has been telling me about your ideas for her shop. Sounds like you've got a good head for business."

Paula felt her enthusiasm grow as the three of them discussed ideas for Dara's shop. People filled the house with noise. Food and drinks were passed around in a continuous flow while the music pounded a beat from the lounge room. Paula was staggered by all the food. There were lots of homemade sausage rolls, pizza, toasties with delicious toppings, pin-wheel savouries and little quiches. At least Dan would be getting something to eat.

She looked around for him. He was no longer in the kitchen but coming towards her was Katherine. She was dragging the tall man behind her and waving a small parcel in her other hand.

"There you are, Paula," she called. "This is Simon, from our Adelaide office. He's up for a little stint in the country, so I thought I'd show him how we party out here."

"Hello, Simon."

Simon replied, but his voice was lost in some sudden loud laughter from the group of women sitting at the kitchen table. He glanced haughtily at them, then stood silently beside Katherine.

A real bundle of laughs, Paula thought.

"Now, this is for you." Katherine pressed the small parcel she had been carrying into Paula's left hand and at the same time grabbed her right. Her beautifully manicured nails were painted a deep red. "Just as I thought," she said holding up Paula's hand. "You haven't been looking after your hands. My mother always said you could tell a lady by her hands. This cream is a miracle cure for hardworking hands. I always have extra pots."

"Thank you." Paula took the parcel and tucked her hands behind her back.

"Katherine, I wouldn't have thought you'd bother to make the trip out." Rowena pushed through with a plate of food. "Can I interest you in a spring roll?"

Paula took the opportunity to edge away. That was twice Rowena had saved her from a tricky conversation. Was it just coincidence or was Rowena purposely extricating her?

Jane was sitting at the table holding James. There was a group of women around the table and all were fussing over a girl who nursed a tiny baby. Paula slid into a spare seat.

"Hello, Paula," Jane welcomed her. "Do you know everyone here? Nothing like taking over your house and filling it with strangers."

Paula nodded around the group, remembering the faces of everyone but the young woman with the baby. She must have arrived while Paula was getting changed.

"This is Cassie, Tom's younger sister."

"Hello." Paula tried not to stare but Cassie only looked sixteen or seventeen. Perhaps the baby wasn't hers.

"Cassie's only been home a week with her dear little baby," Jane said.

Paula couldn't believe this girl, who looked barely more than a child herself, was responsible for the tiny bundle in her arms.

The other women resumed their conversation. It was all about babies. Paula listened, uncomfortably aware she had nothing to contribute.

The phone rang and someone waved the handpiece in the air, calling out for Paula. Saved by the bell. She excused herself from the group and made her way to where the hand held out the phone.

"Hello?"

"Hello, darling. What's going on there? I'm ringing to let you know Susan has had her baby."

Paula could hardly hear her mother's excited voice. Someone shouted out behind her and the music seemed to get louder.

"Hang on, Mum. I'll go into the bedroom."

In the bedroom, Paula shut the door and left the main light off. She made her way to the bed in the pale moonlight, sat on the edge and turned on Dan's lamp.

"Can you hear me now?"

"That's better," her mother said. "It sounds like you're having quite a do there. Now, let me tell you all about your new nephew, he's just gorgeous. Susan only went into labour this morning and she'd had him by early evening. Not bad for a first but then she always does things in a hurry."

"Is everything okay?" Paula tried to get a word in.

"Wonderful, darling, they're both wonderful. Everyone says he looks like Jerry but I think he's like Susan as a baby. He's got dark hair and long fingers and toes. Susan is up and about and giving poor Jerry orders already. Alison is with them at the moment and she's got Oscar and Isabelle with her. Susan has a lovely room. It's not a bit like a hospital. She says she's going home tomorrow."

"Does my new nephew have a name?" Paula cut in when her mother drew a breath. She had a sudden desire to be back in Sydney.

"They're still discussing it but I think it's going to be Rupert. Rupert is Susan's choice and Jerry's bound to give in. He's besotted."

Paula remembered the discussion she and Dan had about naming Tarzan. She was glad she hadn't stuck with Rupert if that was to be Susan's baby's name.

"The babe is a good size. About seven pound, which isn't bad considering they were worried Susan would be early and the baby wasn't growing much."

"Has Dad been in?"

"Of course, darling. We've all had a nurse already. I wish you were here. You will come back for a visit now, won't you? You'll have to meet the new baby."

"It's a long way, Mum. I can't come right now." Paula tried to sound detached but she would have loved to jump on a plane there and then, and fly home for a visit. "I'll get there sometime soon."

"I hope so, darling. Anyway, I must keep phoning. I haven't let your aunts or Grandma know yet. I'll let you get back to your party. Best love, darling."

"Say hello to Susan for me." Paula didn't know if her mother had heard before the line went dead.

She hung up and remained still, listening to the distant sound of the party raging in the other rooms. It would be an effort to go back. Maybe they wouldn't miss her if she curled up and pulled the quilt over her head.

Stop this. She stood up. She had Dan and a house full of his friends who, with a few exceptions, were fast becoming hers. She should get a grip and enjoy the party.

She hadn't been to a party since their wedding. Glancing around the bedroom, she reminded herself again of the effort Dan had put in, to make this room nice for her.

There were brass hooks behind the door and two small paintings on the wall beside her. The wood floor had been stripped and polished. There were small mats on each side of the bed and one larger, fringed mat in the space at the end of the bed in front of the window. The furniture was all old and wooden. The pieces didn't match but suited the room. In the corner stood a beautiful carved dressing table, complete with lace doilies and a framed picture of Dan and Paula on one of their early dates. A delicate chair had been placed alongside.

He had gone to a lot of trouble for her and here she was lurking in the bedroom. "Come on, girl," she muttered. "You've got a party to go to." She turned off the lamp and made her way slowly to the door as her eyes adjusted to the semi-darkness.

Just as she reached for the handle there was a sudden eruption of loud voices and music from the passage as the door from the lounge opposite opened. The noise dulled again as the door clunked shut. There was a scuffle, the sound of muffled voices and then she recognised Katherine's voice.

"We need to discuss the future."

Paula clasped a hand to her mouth as she heard Dan reply. "We don't have a future any more, Katherine. You know that." His response was brusque.

"We have to." Katherine, by contrast, spoke in charming tones. "There are some things we can't ignore."

There was a soft thud on the other side of the bedroom door. Paula stepped back in alarm. There was silence for a minute. What were they doing?

"Stop it, Katherine. Someone might see us. You've already kissed me publicly tonight. I don't want Paula to know about us."

Paula jumped as he said her name so close. What if they came into the bedroom looking for a place out of sight and found her eavesdropping?

"There's plenty your precious bride doesn't know about you." Katherine dispensed with the charm. "How long do you think you can keep her in the dark?"

Paula's hand flew to her mouth again.

"She doesn't need to know about us. It's over." Dan's reply was gruff.

"Oh, Dan." Katherine's clipped tones changed back to silken honey. "This was the baby that was supposed to save our relationship."

"Well it didn't and now I want to be rid of it."

Paula's head spun. They had a child? A child Dan didn't want to acknowledge? What if he hadn't met Paula? He might have been prepared to. She gripped her head in her hands tightly as the realisation hit her. She was responsible for a child being denied its father.

The sounds of the party erupted into the passage again.

"Here you are, Katherine. I think it's time to go." Simon had obviously had enough of the country party scene.

"You're right, Simon," Katherine snapped. "This party is over."

The front door opened and closed. Paula held her breath then slowly let it out as she heard Dan walk away down the passage followed by the gentle thud of the internal door.

She stayed where she was. She couldn't face the crowd now. Did everyone know Dan and Katherine had a child? Paula gathered that Katherine had been away from the district for a while and that she came and went from Adelaide often. Perhaps she kept the child there. That would explain the regular payments Dan made to her.

Why couldn't Dan have been honest about his past, instead of hiding it? What else was there she didn't know about?

She twisted her wedding ring around and around her finger. Doubts bubbled up inside her. Had she made another mistake? Perhaps Dan wasn't the man she thought he was.

"Paula?" She jumped as his voice called down the passage. "Paula?" he called again.

"Coming." There was nowhere to hide. She couldn't stay shut up in the bedroom, people would wonder where she was. She drew herself up, opened the door and stepped straight into Dan.

"There you are." His face lit with that beautiful smile but her stomach didn't do its usual butterfly flip. He looked at her closely and frowned. "Is everything okay? Jane said you had a phone call."

Paula dismissed his concern. "Susan had a baby boy today. Everything's fine and Jerry is besotted."

"That's good news…"

"Just like all fathers should be," she rushed on.

Dan looked at her. "That's why I've come."

"What…why?" Paula was bewildered. She wanted him to explain it all to her and make it right. She didn't want to believe he was heartless but she wasn't sure she could cope with any more tonight.

"Babies. That's why I've come," he said again.

Paula stepped back.

"Not ours, of course," he grinned. "Not yet anyway. The women want to know where Cassie can go to feed and change her baby and Jane was hoping to put James to sleep somewhere. Should they use our room?"

Paula pushed past him into the passage to hide her confusion. She had thought he was about to explain all about Katherine and their baby. "I think the spare room would be better."

Jane stuck her head around the end passage door. "Can we use a bedroom, Paula?"

"Yes, of course, come in." Paula hurried along the passage, turned on the light in the spare bedroom then stepped back to let Jane through with James. Dara came behind carrying Jane's basket then Cassie followed and another woman – Paula recalled her name was Sarah – followed after her with Tom bringing up the rear, pushing a stroller.

Cassie had a bag thrown over her shoulder and she was struggling with the baby capsule.

"Here, let me help." Dan stepped forward to take the capsule from Cassie. He carried it with ease, in one hand.

"You look like you've done that before." Sarah laughed. "It suits you. When are you and Paula going to have your own?"

"Well, I…" Dan handed the baby capsule over to Cassie.

"Dan and I have things to sort out before we can even think about children." Paula said from the doorway. "They aren't commodities that can be ignored or got rid of. You shouldn't just produce them on a whim. Once you have them, it's a lifetime commitment. You can't change your mind or shirk your responsibilities when the going gets tough."

She stopped and the room was very quiet as the four women, Tom and Dan all stared at her.

"I see you chose not to use my curtains." Rowena squeezed past Paula into the bedroom.

Paula's heart skipped a beat. She'd forgotten all about the bloody curtains.

"I like what you've done with this room," Dara cut in quickly. "The colours are very inviting."

"Decorating is Paula's department. I just do as I'm told," Dan said.

Rowena turned to him. "Bruce is looking for you."

Dan gave Paula a lame smile and ducked off. She stayed planted in the doorway. Did as he was told? When had she ever told him to do anything? She had been on her soapbox about children. Perhaps it had touched a nerve. She hoped so. She didn't want to believe she could have fallen in love with someone who was so cold and calculating as to cut his own child from his life.

The two mothers and their babies were fussed over by the other three women. Tom stood back awkwardly. Paula watched them all from the doorway feeling every bit the outsider she was. Rowena, the maiden aunt who'd probably never had sex, let alone a baby, helped Jane organise James. There was Dara, who had made the decision not to have children, clucking like a hen, and then there was the other woman, Sarah. Paula vaguely remembered her joining in the pregnancy tales so she must have children.

Paula watched as Cassie laid her baby on the bed. She looked so young and self-conscious and there were dark rings around her eyes. Suddenly the speech Paula had made a few minutes earlier flew back at her. What had she said about having babies? She had intended her words for Dan. Paula didn't know anything about Cassie. She looked like she'd been through enough without having a mad women preaching about responsibilities and commitment.

Quietly moving back, hoping no one would notice, Paula slipped through the house into the laundry. Tarzan lifted his head then flopped it back down again and covered his face with a paw. The door closed behind her and Paula spun around to face Rowena.

"Don't be too quick to judge others, before you know the full story." Rowena's voice was soft but carried no trace of gentleness. "Cassie has had a tough time. The young lad who fathered her babe made off just before the birth, so I don't think she needs to be reminded about responsibility. Sarah in there runs the family property with her father. Her husband's a truck driver. It's the busiest time of year and on top of all that she's just had her third try at IVF. She only came home yesterday. I don't know how she will cope if it's not successful this time, so commitment is not something she needs a lecture on."

Paula was devastated. Her aim had been to shake Dan's conscience, not upset the others. "It wasn't my intention to criticise Cassie or Sarah."

"Nor mine to criticise you. I just thought you should know a bit of background so —"

"So I don't put my foot in it again."

"If you like." Rowena held her gaze for a minute then rubbed her hands together. "Now come on, it's cold in here. Don't hide in the laundry. This party is for you and Dan. There are parcels to open. You should be out there with your husband enjoying yourselves." She opened the door and strode back to the kitchen.

Paula pushed the door closed again and sank down onto the floor. She patted Tarzan, who opened one sleepy eye and half-heartedly wagged his tail. Rowena must surely know all about Dan's past. Who else knew? How could she face people now? A million thoughts crowded her head.

"What did you call him?" She looked up into Tom's gentle eyes. She hadn't heard him come in.

"Tarzan." She gazed down at the sweet little dog asleep without a care in the world.

"Has he caught any mice yet?"

"He's sniffed out a few in the house but outside he goes berserk. There have been several little bodies dumped at the back door."

"I thought he'd do okay. Cassie has his sister. They make good watch dogs and they're very loyal."

Paula stood up feeling very embarrassed. "Tom, I hope Cassie didn't think I was referring to her when I went on about babies, I..."

"I think she's too tired to register what anyone's saying at the moment."

"She does look exhausted."

"I didn't think she should come but Mum thought it would be good for her to get out for a while." He paused. "Things are a bit tense at our place. Dad went off his tree when Damo ran out on her."

"That's hardly her fault."

"I know. I didn't think he had much guts and this just proves it. She'll be better off without him, in the long run."

"I guess so." Paula wondered about Dan's child. She didn't even know if it was a boy or a girl. Perhaps it would be better off without Dan in its life. But how could she live with that?

"Did you try one of Mum's powder puffs?"

Paula looked at the lopsided smile slowly spreading over Tom's face. "No."

"She sent some specially for you. She wins prizes at the show for her powder puffs."

Paula's recollection of Rita didn't gel with the image of a delicate powder puff. "I'd better try one then." She shut the door on the sleeping Tarzan and followed Tom back to the kitchen.

The rest of the party was a blur. She opened the presents people had brought. Rowena's was a set of filmy sheer white curtains, sprinkled with blue flowers. They would be perfect for the main bedroom. Dara had brought some scatter cushions for the lounge and Jane and Bruce had given them a rustic photo frame. There were many other things. People she'd never met before had been very kind.

Every time she saw Dan he seemed to be tipping a can of beer down his neck. She drifted from one group to the next, hovering on the outside, not really joining in the conversation. By the time the last of the revellers had left, it was three in the morning. Dan followed them outside to see them off and Paula went into the kitchen where she was amazed to find everything washed, dried and tidied away. Apart from a pile of empties, an assortment of leftovers in her fridge and a stack of clean dishes and cups, it would have been hard to know there had been a party.

She switched out the light and checked on Tarzan and the dying fire in the lounge. There was a bit more debris in there where the diehards had continued to drink and tell stories close to the fire.

In the bedroom Dan was lying on top of the quilt. She hadn't heard him come back inside. He was still fully clothed except for his shoes. His hands were clasped across his chest and he was snoring gently.

Paula couldn't help but grin, in spite of the uncertainty she felt. He could never be accused of being a noisy drunk. Unless you counted snoring, she thought, as he gave an extra-loud snort. She took the throw rug from the end of the bed and spread it over him, then undressed and climbed in between the sheets.

Perhaps it was just as well he was asleep. She didn't know how she could face him tonight.

CHAPTER
17

"What are you going to get up to this week, Paula?" Jane's cheerful voice asked from the phone.

"I don't know," Paula said. "I think I've had enough redecorating for a while although I would like to find some curtains for the kitchen. Is there anywhere local I could find something?"

Jane laughed. "Not locally. Dara has the odd thing of course, but for furnishings we have to go further afield or online. I think it would be worth a trip to Adelaide. I've got a ready babysitter there. Mum loves the chance to spend some time with the boys and you and I could have a day's shopping."

"That sounds great. I want to find something to send to my sister for her new baby." Paula hesitated. "I'm a bit reluctant to go too far at the moment. Now that seeding's finished, I was hoping to see a bit more of Dan. We've got a few things we need to organise."

Paula didn't want to elaborate. She had spent a miserable week-end trying to find the courage to ask Dan for the truth but she hadn't been able to do it. She loved him but she felt their marriage was now hanging by a tenuous thread. She didn't want to destroy that thread. It was all she had.

Jane chuckled. "I'm sorry, Paula. Dan is probably not working the five am to eleven pm shift any more but you'll find he's still gone most of the day. He might appear more regularly for meals but he'll always have something to do. You put your foot down, though. Dan is such a hard worker sometimes Bruce and I worry he does too much. We were so glad when he married you. He needs something else in his life besides work."

"Oh, well. I guess I'll get used to being a farmer's wife eventually." Paula tried to mimic Jane's lightness.

"Of course you will. It's not easy giving up the working life you're used to but give yourself a chance to settle in. You're so resourceful, Paula, you'll find something to occupy your time besides running around after Dan." Jane's warm chuckle echoed from the phone. "And one thing you must do is give yourself a break. So when would you like to go to the city?"

"Any time. You say. You've got more to organise than me."

"Bruce needs me to help with the pigs for the next few days. We could go after that..." Jane paused. "But you've got shearers soon, haven't you?"

"Shearers?"

"I'm sure I heard Dan say something at the party. Maybe it was next week. Anyway, we can work around it once you know. I'd better get off the phone. Bruce will be in, looking for his lunch and I haven't got far with my jobs yet."

"Bye, Jane." Paula hung up. She glanced around her tidy kitchen and knew the rest of the house was in a similar state. She had a bit of washing in the machine to hang out, but apart from that, she had nothing else to do. Dan's lunch was even prepared.

He had gone off after breakfast to do something with sheep and had promised to be back for lunch. Then he said he had shed work to do. She wondered what jobs Jane had to keep her busy. And then there was her mention of shearers. What had she meant by that?

Paula fidgeted restlessly then picked up her tablet. She went to the middle bedroom where she had stored boxes of her things that she hadn't unpacked and anything else she hadn't found a home for. She took the wireless router she'd bought from its box and went back to the kitchen. She had to unplug the phone to use it. Maybe she could do some internet research on tourism for Dara, and perhaps investigate online accountancy. She got it all connected but it was responding very slowly.

"Paula?" Dan's call from the back door surprised her. She hadn't heard a vehicle.

She went out to meet him "You're early for lunch."

"I'm not coming in yet. I've sent Tom off in the dual cab. His ute's got a flat tyre and I need to go and check another mob of sheep. I'll have to take your car."

"Can I come too?"

"Of course, but I have to go now. Rowena called me. She was on her way out and she noticed some sheep in bother. It's the mob with the lambs."

Paula grabbed her keys and jacket and followed Dan out to the car shed. Tarzan trotted faithfully at her heels.

Dan drove and Paula noticed the look of concern on his face. "What do you think is the matter?"

"I don't know. Rowena said she saw a few ewes pushed up in the corner and the rest of the mob running around. Could be a break-away group. There were still a few who hadn't lambed. Or, they could be sick or there could be a fox or a dog about."

He concentrated on the track and Paula tried to pay attention to the landmarks along the way. They were close to Rowena's house. There were a couple of gates to pass through and Paula opened and closed them each time. One more loomed as they reached the paddock with the sheep.

"I'll get this one," Dan said.

"No, I can do it." Paula jumped out of the car before Dan could say any more.

This gate was different. It was more like a continuation of the fence and it was hooked to a thick post at one end with a wire and wood contraption at the top that had Paula puzzled. She wiggled and pushed at it and then, just as she heard Dan open his door behind her, the wood popped free, flung out of her hands and the gate collapsed at her feet. She bent down and dragged it back but it scrunched on top of itself making it difficult to move. There was enough space for Dan to drive the car through then he came back to help her.

"These can be a bit tricky for the beginners." The skin crinkled around his eyes and his lips turned up in a small grin.

"Well, if you show me how I can do it next time." Paula stepped to the side. She wasn't going to be beaten by a gate. She watched as he picked up the iron dropper, pulled the wire tight and dragged it back to the post where he hooked the bottom of the dropper into a wire loop and then wound the stick through the top.

They got back into the car and she was wondering how hard it could be when she glanced over to see the tiny grin still lurking at the corners of Dan's mouth. At least he was smiling, even if it was at her expense.

He drove across the paddock to the main mob of sheep. They were gathered together in a big huddle. He drove slowly around them looking carefully.

"Something has spooked them," he said. The mob reluctantly split and he drove among them. "Can't see any that look sick or injured though and I don't want to stir them up any more."

He wheeled the car away from the scattering mob and headed off across the paddock to the distant fence line, which was dotted with trees following a road.

"There's one."

Paula looked in the direction he pointed but all she could see was a clump of rock and a bush. As the vehicle got close, the rock moved and a lamb stood up beside it. Then Paula realised it wasn't a rock but a sheep struggling to get up.

"Damn it." Dan jumped from the car as soon as it stopped and Tarzan raced after him.

"Get out of it, dog. Paula, get this mutt back in the car," he yelled then turned and raced after the lamb, which was hobbling away quite quickly.

Paula called Tarzan back and shut him in the car as Dan came towards her carrying the lamb.

"This little fella looks okay. Can you hold it while I check out the mother?"

Paula took the struggling bundle in her arms. It was surprisingly strong for something so small and gangly. It gave some desperate little bleats and the mother raised her head and gave a weak reply.

"Bloody hell!"

"What is it?"

Paula went to stand beside Dan who was bending over the back of the sheep. She had blood and exposed flesh down both of her back legs. "Oh. How can that happen?" Paula stared in horror at the mangled mess. "The poor thing."

"Dogs," Dan said. "Fred Martin lost a couple of sheep last week. He lives just over that way." Dan pointed across the road to another property.

"I thought farmers had dogs that worked sheep, not attacked them."

"This is the work of a rogue dog or a pack that's had a taste of killing. They might be farm dogs but most farmers lock their dogs up. This must be a pet dog that's allowed to roam."

The sheep gave another feeble bleat and struggled to get up again.

"Easy, old girl." Dan checked her out carefully. "I don't think she'll live." He got back to his feet.

"You can't leave her here to die."

He frowned at her. "Of course not. I'll take you home and come back."

Paula gripped his arm. "What are you going to do?"

"I'll have to shoot her. Put her out of her misery."

"The poor thing. How awful." Paula hugged the lamb in tightly. It lay quietly in her arms. "Are you sure we can't save her?"

"I can take her home, try cleaning her up and keep her in the shed, I suppose. She might be able to feed the lamb a bit longer. If we keep that alive, it cuts the loss."

Paula recoiled inside. Dan was so cold about it. This poor animal was in misery and he was worried about the cost.

"We have to try," she said.

"I don't know what's in your boot but that's the only place I can put her. You'll have to nurse the lamb."

"Okay." Paula didn't care about the car. She couldn't bear to see the sheep in such a terrible state.

Dan backed the car in close to the injured ewe. Paula shut the lamb in the back of the car with a stern warning to Tarzan not to terrorise it and went back to help. They hefted the feebly struggling animal into the boot and shut her in.

"Will she be okay in there?"

"She's not going to be any worse off. I'd be more worried about the nice upholstery if I was you," Dan said.

Paula climbed through to the back seat and picked up the lamb, which had piddled on the floor. Tarzan watched closely from the centre panel but he didn't attempt to get in the back with Paula until she called him.

All the way home she talked softly to the lamb and Tarzan. Dan had to open and close the gates. The pup cuddled in close to Paula and rested a protective paw on the lamb's leg.

Back at the house yard, Dan drove on to a distant shed. The shed was built on a slope. On the low side there were stilts holding it up and on the other side small wooden yards joined what looked like mini paddocks.

"I'll put her in the shearing shed with the lamb. At least she'll have shelter and feed and we can see what happens from there."

The interior of the shed was divided into several small yards opening out into a long open area, with a wooden floor and machinery hanging from the low ceiling, backed by a row of little doors. Paula recalled pictures she had seen of men shearing and Jane's earlier mention of shearing floated briefly through her mind before the injured ewe and the pitiful bleating of the lamb regained her attention.

"Should I bathe her wounds?" she asked as she and Dan leaned over the rails looking at the forlorn pair. "Or should we ring the vet?"

"I don't think you can save her, Sweet Pea. The nearest vet is a long way away and I'm pretty sure the vet would agree with me. There's too much damage."

Dan's concerned face melted Paula's heart.

"We've got to try," she pleaded.

"Okay. But don't get your heart set on a recovery. It would take a miracle."

Paula went back to the house to gather her supplies. She bathed, disinfected and bandaged the mangled legs of the ewe and then she could see there were more wounds all around its back. It was impossible to deal with them all. She did the best she could then put feed in a container on top of the grated floor close by. Finally Paula trickled water into the ewe's mouth and gently urged her to fight.

Dan worked quietly in the shed behind her. Eventually, when she sat back on the dirty floor surveying her handiwork, he came and urged her away.

"You've done all you can. You've given her a chance, there's nothing more you can do."

Arm in arm they went back to the house for a late lunch. Tarzan skittered between their feet chasing leaves and insects as they walked. Paula leaned into Dan and he hugged her close.

They'd barely eaten when Tom returned and Dan went off with him to change the tyre and check more sheep. It wasn't till they'd driven off that Paula realised she hadn't asked about the shearing. She decided cleaning out her car was more pressing and armed with disinfectant and hot water she set off to scrub it clean.

She'd just finished when an approaching vehicle made her look up. Tarzan went barking down the track as Rowena's car turned into view.

"Tarzan! Here, boy." Paula called him back.

The pup came running to sit at her feet, uttering a low growl.

"I know how you feel," Paula muttered. "But we have to be nice to Dan's aunt." The car pulled up beside them. She turned and pulled her face into a smile. "Hello, Rowena."

"Did Dan find out what was happening with those sheep?"

"Yes, he thinks they were attacked by dogs."

"Damn them." Rowena slapped the steering wheel. "Much damage done?"

"We could only find one that was hurt, a ewe and her lamb. The ewe's been badly bitten all over her back and legs. We put her in the shed and I've patched her up a bit."

"Don't get too attached. In my experience, they rarely survive the shock. I suppose Dan is hoping to save the lamb. How old is it?"

"Dan thought about a week," Paula replied, thinking the poor ewe didn't stand a chance with all the negative vibes from Dan and Rowena. Paula had high hopes for her nursing skills. Besides, the ewe had a lamb to live for.

Rowena got out of the car. "I've upgraded our mobile phones and bought one for you."

Paula stared in amazement at Rowena's back as she rummaged in her car.

"Since I was buying three I got a very good deal." Rowena lifted out a large plastic bag.

"I have a phone," Paula mumbled as Rowena shoved the bag at her.

"But you said it didn't work here. These phones have pretty good coverage. All the information's in the bag and your new number. They said in the shop Dan could simply put in his sim from his old phone." Rowena waved a dismissive hand. "You'll know what to do with it all."

"We should pay you for them —"

"The business pays for them," Rowena cut in.

Paula peered into the bag. Her other phone was out of contract and was a few years old. She would have liked to have selected her own new phone.

"While I'm here, we may as well discuss the shearing arrangements." Rowena was on to the next topic.

"Shearing?" Paula questioned. She was still thinking about phones.

"Dan has employed shearers with a reputation for being fussy about their food. Hasn't he told you?"

Paula didn't want to admit he hadn't mentioned it. "I do remember something," she said vaguely. "When are they coming again?"

"They're planning to start on Thursday. It will depend on the weather and how they get on at the previous place. Our usual contractors weren't available so I hope this lot are okay. I can bring over lunches. They'll want a hot meal, so it will be handy to use your kitchen for some of it. I've got cakes and slices in the freezer already."

Paula had no idea what she was talking about. Shearing was to do with sheep, not meals. "I'm not sure what you mean."

"You are green, aren't you?" Rowena chortled. "While the shearers are here we have to provide morning and afternoon teas and lunches. Lunches don't have to be as big as they were when I was a girl but this group is old-fashioned. They like a hot lunch each day."

"How many of them are there?" Paula felt a tinge of nerves building in her stomach.

"Three shearers and a roustabout. Dan and Tom will do all the other jobs. But that means six to feed every day."

"For how long?" Paula was in panic mode again now. Cooking was not her forte and she definitely wouldn't rate highly with fussy eaters.

"If everything goes well, they should only be here three or four days."

Paula quailed. Four days of cooking for six other people. Why hadn't Dan warned her?

"Now, don't worry." Rowena rubbed her forehead. "I can do most of it."

"That doesn't seem fair."

"Nonsense. The shed is by your house so you'll have the brunt of the to-ing and fro-ing and washing up. Cooking for shearers is a part of farm life." Rowena frowned and leaned back against her car.

"Are you all right?"

"I can't seem to shake this headache. I've had it for days. It's most unlike me. I felt a bit dizzy for a moment but I'm fine now. I'll head off home and get a good night's sleep. We can discuss the food again tomorrow."

The car door slammed shut and Rowena reversed away with her usual burst of speed. Paula watched until her car was out of sight, then rushed inside. In her kitchen she dragged out all the recipe books she had, including the old ones she'd found in the pantry. She searched frantically for ideas about what to cook. In one old cookbook she found a recipe called 'Shearer's Cake'. From the ingredients she gathered it was some kind of heavy fruit cake but the cooking instructions sent her into hysterics. 'It should be baked in two petrol tins cut sideways.'

Tarzan put his paws on her knees as she laughed. She patted her lap and he jumped up. "I don't know, Tarzan. These country women certainly do things differently. I won't be making that one. I don't have any petrol tins handy." Stroking his soft ears she continued to search for suitable recipes.

By the time Dan came home she had the debris of her work spread everywhere in the kitchen, trays of biscuits in the oven and a cake waiting to go in but nothing organised for their evening meal.

Dan stood in the doorway surveying the chaos.

"Don't you start, Dan Woodcroft." Paula wagged a floury finger at him, a smile wavering on her lips. "Why didn't you tell me I had to cook for shearers?"

"I didn't think of it." He put up his hands. "Rowena usually does it."

"I'm here now."

"Yes, but Rowena is a partner..."

Paula cut him off. "And I'm not."

"Of course you are." Dan rushed to her side. "I haven't been thinking straight, I should have told you. I couldn't get my usual contractors and it's been a hard slog getting these guys here. I didn't really want them yet but it's the closest time I could get. Look, how about I make us scrambled eggs."

"That would be good." Paula grimaced. "If we had any eggs left. Will soup and toasties do?"

"Whatever," Dan said. "I'll get the fire going."

"You have your shower. I'll deal with this and do the fire."

Time had gotten away from her. It was almost dark and the rest of the house, away from the frenzy she had created in the kitchen, would be cold. He gave a nod and left her to it.

By the time she had finished cooking and cleaning up and they'd eaten a picnic tea in the lounge by the fire, it was after nine o'clock.

"Did you check on the sheep?" she asked as she leaned back against Dan in a relaxed state of mild exhaustion.

"No change. I looked in on them before I came inside."

"Can we look again? I'd like to see them before I go to bed."

"It's freezing out there."

"Please, Dan." She pulled on his hands to stand him up.

He gave in and they rugged up and took the torch to make the trek across the yard to the shearing shed. Dan turned on the lights and Paula rushed to the rail to look into the pen.

"Dan," she whispered excitedly. "She's standing up and the lamb is drinking from her."

Dan came to stand beside Paula. "She's a good mother."

"It's a positive sign, isn't it?"

"We'll see."

Paula watched fascinated as the lamb tugged at the ewe's teats. Its little tail wagged so hard it looked like it would spin right off.

Paula said a quiet prayer for the ewe and her baby as Dan dragged her away and back to the warmth of the house.

CHAPTER
18

Rowena sipped her honey and lemon tea then rested her head back onto the soft cushions of her rocking chair and shut her eyes. She felt lousy. Blast, she thought to herself. I haven't got time to be sick now. There's too much to do.

Her earlier conversation with Paula didn't make her feel any easier. Dan should have explained about shearing and the meals but even so Paula didn't seem to be much of a cook. These contractors had a reputation for walking out if the food wasn't to their liking. Getting shearers was hard enough without worrying about them staying the distance.

Rowena's head throbbed and she reached for the headache tablets she'd left on the table. She hated taking drugs of any sort but she was feeling desperate.

Paula was still such an enigma. Sometimes she seemed so sensible and acted as if nothing could faze her and the next she panicked and flew off the handle at the slightest sign of difficulty.

And her speech the night of the party! Rowena could not understand what that had been about. Whatever had set the girl to prattle on about babies and responsibilities was a mystery. Paula didn't strike Rowena as totally tactless but on Friday night she had put her foot right in her mouth and nearly swallowed it.

Rowena had organised the surprise party to help Paula get to know a few of the locals. Apart from Rowena, no one from the local community had been at the wedding. Some of Dan's city and interstate friends had been there and one had been a last-minute stand-in for Bruce as best man. She'd thought it important that the newlyweds had a good country party to start their married life.

It had been a good night although it was a surprise to see Katherine there. That woman had more front than David Jones. And Rowena had noticed Dan's drinking. He'd certainly consumed quite a lot by the time she left. It was most unlike him to drink excessively. He'd done it a bit in his younger days but thankfully hadn't kept it up like some did, drinking themselves into oblivion every week.

He was a steady, reliable man and she was so proud of him and what he had achieved with the farm. Rowena hoped his determination to pay off Katherine, without involving Paula, wouldn't be his undoing. Too many secrets were not a good thing.

"Blast," she muttered. The pounding in her head had not abated at all. She stood up and the room spun briefly. A small wave of concern washed over her. She lived alone now. What if she passed out? Carefully, she took herself off to bed. A good night's sleep was the best cure for everything.

*   *   *

Paula looked up from the breakfast table as Dan came in the door but he couldn't match her smile. He knew she would be upset by his news.

"What is it?"

"The ewe didn't make it."

"No!" Paula pushed her chair back. "She was improving last night. Are you sure she's not just resting?"

Dan grabbed Paula's arm as she rushed towards the door. "She's dead, Sweet Pea. I should have finished her off yesterday. It was worth a try but the damage was too great." He pulled Paula close. He should have shot the poor sheep when they'd found it. He didn't like to see animals suffer but euthanasia wasn't a job he enjoyed either and he'd let Paula's enthusiasm dissuade him.

"What about the lamb?" she asked.

Dan smiled. He took in her trembling lip as he brushed a tear from her cheek. He wanted to protect her from the often cruel reality of life on the farm. Working with animals could be distressing at times. "It's okay for now. I've handfed lambs before, but sometimes they don't make it. Rowena's probably got all the gear we need at her place. We had a lamb we bottle-fed last spring."

"Did it live?"

"No." Dan watched the hope fade from Paula's face. "But its mother had deserted it at birth and only fed the twin. It was very weak and hadn't had any colostrum. This one's age and a few days of the ewe's milk might be enough to keep it alive."

"The poor little thing. Where is it now?"

"Still in the pen. I'll have to corner off a bit of the backyard so it's close for feeding. It's a four-hourly job to start with."

"But it's so cold at night. Why don't we use the sleep-out? It's only a cement floor and it's grotty anyway. I can clean it out afterwards."

Dan looked down at the eager face of his wife and he couldn't resist kissing her. "Promise me you won't get too attached, Sweet Pea. It might not make it."

"You're such a pessimist. Think positively."

He put an arm around her shoulders. She was right in a way. He didn't think of himself as a pessimist, just practical. The odds were against the lamb's survival, and there wasn't room to get too emotional. It only made his work harder.

"Okay." He grinned. "But I want to remind you that only a few weeks ago you said you drew the line at sharing our bed with animals. It seems to me that we will soon be sharing our house with a dog who has taken over the laundry and a lamb in the sleep-out. I worry about what you're planning next."

"Nothing at this stage and certainly nothing extra in our bed." She poked his chest with her finger.

"Not even our own children?" Dan sensed immediately that he had said something wrong. Paula pulled away from him and the sparkle left her eyes.

"Especially not that."

There was silence between them. Paula looked at him expectantly but he didn't know what to say. The phone rang and she hurried to answer it.

He recalled the night of the party and her words about babies and responsibilities. He had thought at the time they were directed at him but he didn't understand why and she hadn't mentioned it since. They'd never discussed having children. Perhaps she genuinely didn't want them. Children were something he'd assumed he'd have with the right person. Paula was definitely the right person but if she didn't want children, he could live with that too.

"Dan!" He turned at her appeal. She had obviously called him before and he hadn't heard her. She was holding the phone out towards him, worry all over her face. "It's your aunt. She doesn't sound well."

He was by the phone in two strides. "Rowena? What's up?" He couldn't recall the last time Rowena had been sick. She was the toughest person he knew.

"I've got a terrible headache I can't get rid of and I feel like I've been hit by a truck." Rowena's voice shook. "I've made a doctor's appointment but I feel a bit dizzy. I know you're flat out getting ready for shearing but I don't think I can drive —"

"Of course you won't. What time is your appointment?"

"Eleven o'clock…" Rowena broke off into a rasping cough.

Dan looked at his watch. "Will you be all right till then? I can come over earlier."

"I'll be fine. See you then."

Dan listened as the line went quiet.

"What's the matter with her?" Paula asked.

"I don't know. It could be that nasty flu virus that's been doing the rounds. She must be feeling bad, she rarely sees a doctor."

He looked at his watch again. He had sheep to shift and things to get ready for the shearers. It would take him and Tom all the time between now and when the shearers arrived to be organised. He'd lose half the day taking Rowena in and out to the doctor.

"Does she need driving? I can take her."

Dan smiled gratefully at Paula. He was so used to managing things himself. He was beginning to give Tom a bit more responsibility. Now there was another person in his life he could rely on.

"Thanks. You'll probably need to leave here by quarter past ten, her appointment's at eleven."

"Thank you, Dan. I think I can manage the timeline."

"Perhaps you could take the dual cab. I've got some fencing wire and some chemicals to collect at the stock agents. It will save Tom or me a trip. I can go with Tom in the ute to move the sheep."

He pecked her on the cheek, relieved that was all sorted and strode out the door already planning his next movements and directions for Tom.

★   ★   ★

Paula shook her head and sat back at the breakfast table to finish her tea. For a moment she had thought the opportunity had come to talk to him about Katherine and their child. Rowena's phone call had put an end to any discussion they might have had. She really needed to get it out in the open. It was building an invisible wall between them.

Tarzan scratched impatiently at the door.

"You must be eating too much." She let him outside. "I wonder if Carl stocks dog doors. That's what we need, Tarzan." Then she remembered the lamb. She went outside and collected up some of the old furniture she'd dumped when she'd cleaned out the sleep-out for Tarzan. She carted it inside to block off a corner of the old room for the lamb. She lined the inside of the makeshift pen with newspaper. The pup was a close shadow watching everything she did.

Next she went up to the shearing shed. The lamb was alone, a bundle of legs in the corner of the pen. Dan must have disposed of the mother. The sound of the pen gate opening brought the little creature to its feet and it bleated pathetically. Paula gathered it up and carried it back to the house, talking to it all the way, with Tarzan following patiently at her heels.

She put the lamb down gently on the paper and it stumbled around, once again bleating pathetically. The pen looked so barren and uninviting. Paula had thrown out the rags that Tarzan had arrived in. He still slept on the one old blanket she had. What could she use to keep the poor little creature cosy and warm? Then she remembered the tattered curtains she'd stuffed in the chest.

Tarzan tipped his head on one side and looked quizzically at Paula as she giggled at the sight before her. There was the lamb, bleating feebly from the box, all tucked up in the nest she had made with the family heirloom curtains.

"I'm sorry, little lamb. I promise I'll bring you home something to eat. I'll be back as soon as I can."

She hurried away to clean up so she could drive Rowena into town.

★ ★ ★

Paula glanced anxiously at Rowena as they reached the outskirts of town. She had been shocked to see how ill the older woman looked when she'd arrived to collect her. Rowena had sat in a chair and directed Paula to the laundry to find the box of lamb feeding gear. Normally Rowena would have bustled about not letting Paula delve into the cupboards at all.

Now, she sat in the car with her head back and her eyes shut. Every now and then she coughed a dry rasping cough. Pain lines etched in her face each time. Paula reluctantly asked for directions. She didn't know where the doctor's surgery was.

When they pulled up, Rowena accepted her help to walk in. Paula left her with the young receptionist while she went off to find the stock agents to buy formula for the lamb and collect Dan's list of items.

She finished there quickly so she decided to call in at Dara's and see what she could buy from her for lunches. By the look of Rowena she wouldn't be doing much, and Paula didn't want to let Dan down. She was determined to feed the shearers well.

An hour had passed by the time she got back to the doctor's surgery. Several other people sat in the surgery flipping through magazines. Paula was conscious of their gaze following her as she stepped up to the reception desk. There was no sign of Rowena.

"Hello, Mrs Woodcroft." The young receptionist spoke to Paula with a wary glance towards a door to the side. "Miss Woodcroft is waiting in the room next door." Once more her gaze slid in that direction. "The doctor said he'd like to see you, Mrs Woodcroft."

"No need. I've just got a dose of the flu." Rowena's voice growled from the other room followed by a bout of coughing. One of the women sitting closest to Paula smirked, lifted her magazine higher and nudged the man next to her.

"If you wouldn't mind waiting, I'll let Dr Hunter know you're here." The receptionist picked up the phone.

"Thanks."

Paula entered the side room. It contained a small desk with an eye chart hanging on the wall above it. There was little else but two chairs. Rowena was sitting on one of them tapping her foot

"What did the doctor say?" Paula asked

"I'll live."

A door opened somewhere beyond reception, a murmur of voices came closer, and a small man of Chinese appearance stuck his head in the door.

"Hello, you must be Dan's wife," he said.

"Yes, I'm Paula."

"Lachlan Hunter." He shook her hand. Paula thought he was perhaps not much older than her.

Rowena had another spasm of coughing.

Both Paula and the doctor looked at her.

"I thought you said I needed to go to bed. I can't if you two are chinwagging," Rowena snapped as soon as she caught her breath.

"Won't be long, Miss Woodcroft." The doctor smiled and ushered Paula into his office, indicating the chair beside his desk. This room was busy with furniture including an examination table, spare chairs and a bookcase full of medical books. There was one small window and all the walls were covered in charts of various parts of the human body.

The doctor got straight to the point. "I know this is a big ask of you, Paula, but Rowena lives alone and I am concerned for her health. I would like her to be in care. She refuses to go to hospital and frankly at this stage there is nothing they can do for her there that can't be done by someone at home. She needs bed rest, fluids and some TLC. She has a particularly nasty bug and there is little I can do for her unless it causes secondary problems that will respond to antibiotics. But I don't think she should be alone at the moment."

"Of course not, Dan and I wouldn't dream of it. She can come and stay with us until she's well." Paula was shocked by the doctor's serious tone.

"It's a matter of keeping her temperature down and the pain at bay and seeing if anything develops. She's a strong woman and she should shake it off. Trouble is you never know who will succumb to the flu. If the symptoms change or she gets any worse, let me know."

"We will."

He stood up. "Have you and Dan had your flu jabs?"

"I haven't. I don't know about Dan."

"Rowena overlooked it this year. I recommend you have them." Paula thanked him and helped the grumbling Rowena out to the car.

"The bed is made up in the spare room. The doctor wants you to stay with us for a few days."

"He can say what he likes. You can take me home to my house. I want to sleep in my own bed."

"He's worried about you," Paula said. The day had come in cold again and she put the car heaters on as they left the town behind and followed the bitumen towards home.

"Piffle! I've got a touch of the flu. I'll be fine by tomorrow. I shouldn't have gone in to see the young worry wart. Take me straight home."

"You need someone to look after you."

"Rubbish. I've been looking after myself for more years than you've had hot dinners. No need to change now." Rowena fanned her face with her hand. "Do we have to have these heaters on?" She burst into another round of the racking dry cough.

Paula glanced at her in concern. The older woman looked quite flushed as she shut her eyes and leaned her head back in the seat. Paula turned off the heater and drove on, wondering what to do. Rowena was so determined. Paula didn't like to disobey her but she was worried about her staying alone.

Then Paula had an idea. She turned on the dreaded two-way radio and picked up the handset. The dual cab swerved slightly as she juggled the unfamiliar contraption.

Rowena opened her eyes. "What are you doing?"

"Calling Dan." Paula's reply sounded calmer than she felt. "I can't imagine what he'll say if he knows I've taken you home when the doctor wants you to stay with us."

Rowena snapped off the two-way. "Do you want the whole district to know my business? I'll have every old busybody within cooee visiting and bringing me chicken broth." She coughed again. Paula hung on to the handpiece and waited for her to stop.

Rowena flopped her head back and Paula saw her lips move.

"Pardon?" Paula leaned closer.

"I said all right. Take me home to Wood Dell."

Paula glanced at Rowena again, wondering what she meant. Then she remembered Wood Dell was the old family name for Dan and Paula's place. Her lips twitched. Well, you can have that round, Paula, she thought to herself. But her smugness was short-lived. The notion of Rowena under her roof didn't exactly fill her with joy.

CHAPTER
19

Paula took Rowena in through the back door. They had to step around a plastic bag. Paula noticed there was a note attached. She didn't have time to investigate. They were greeted by the miserable bleats of the lamb from the sleep-out and a prancing Tarzan who shot between their legs and out the door.

"That's all I need," Rowena grumbled. "A room in a zoo."

Paula ignored her complaints and settled her on the couch in the lounge. Another coughing fit from Rowena sent Paula scurrying for a jug of water and a glass to put beside the invalid, who refused offers of anything else.

"Don't fuss over me. You do what you have to do. I want to sleep." Rowena promptly shut her eyes.

Paula's fingers itched in irritation. Right at the moment she could easily have given Rowena a piece of her mind. Looking after Rowena was the last thing Paula wanted to do but they were stuck with each other. She was distracted by the cries of the lamb.

Back in the kitchen, Paula followed the instructions on the packet to make up the lamb's formula. She frowned over the directions, worried she would make up the wrong proportions. The guy at the stock agents had urged her to be exact.

Tarzan was scratching to be let back in.

"Sorry," she said as she opened the door. "I forgot to find out about the dog flap."

He turned his head to one side, peering up at her with a forgiving look. Once more the pathetic bleating drew her attention.

Tarzan followed her into the sleep-out and watched as she climbed over the barricade and started feeding the lamb.

"You poor little thing." The lamb sucked frantically until only the dregs remained in the bottle. "You must have been hungry."

The newspaper was wet and mucky in parts. Paula replaced it and met Dan and Tom coming in the back door as she'd finished.

"How's Rowena?" Dan picked up the plastic bag that still sat just inside the door.

"The doctor says she has the flu. He thinks we should have flu shots."

"I haven't had one before."

"Neither have I."

"We're young and fit." Dan winked at her.

"The doctor wants Rowena to stay here until she's feeling better. She's in the lounge."

"I'll go and see her. Tom and I haven't had lunch yet. Any chance you could rustle us up something?"

Paula glanced at her watch. It was nearly two. She realised she was hungry as well. "I'll wash up then I'll get something."

"Can I see the lamb?" Tom asked.

"Sure, then go into the kitchen and I'll organise some food."

Dan and Tom both came in as she put a plate of sandwiches and bowls of Dara's soup on the table.

"Rowena says she doesn't want food but she's asked me to collect some clothes from her place. I don't like to go through her things. Would you mind going, Sweet Pea?"

"I don't like the thought of going through her things either." Paula's voice rose in protest.

"Yes, but at least you're a woman. It's female stuff."

Paula held his pleading look for a moment. "Okay."

"That lamb looks like it's doing okay," Tom said. "No sign of scouring yet."

"It would have only had one feed of formula." Dan piled sandwiches on his plate.

"What's scouring?" Paula asked between mouthfuls of Dara's old-fashioned beef broth.

"Their stomachs don't always tolerate the change from ewe's milk to formula," Dan said.

Paula looked up from her soup expectantly. She still wasn't sure what scouring meant.

"It goes straight through them," Tom mumbled, his mouth full of sandwich. "Comes out the other end as liquid poo and runs everywhere. Poor little things poop themselves to death."

Paula's stomach lurched and she sat back from her bowl of soup.

"Sorry, Paula, excuse me. But so far there's no sign with this one," he added reassuringly and went back to chomping his way through another sandwich.

"It's early days yet." Dan's voice was gentle, though the look in his blue eyes was sad. "Don't get too attached."

Paula carried the remains of her soup to the sink. Suddenly she didn't fancy beef broth any more.

★　★　★

It was strange going into Rowena's house, knowing Rowena wasn't there. The last time Paula had come she'd taken a quick look at the farm books. Now she immediately felt like a snoop.

Rowena had given her a list of items to collect from the bedroom. Sleepwear, clothes and underwear, a hot-water bottle and some slippers and dressing-gown. Paula stepped into the large front bedroom and stopped. Like the rest of Rowena's house it was well furnished but this room definitely had a more feminine stamp.

The walls were a soft buttercup yellow and the double brass bed was covered in a quilt of deeper yellow, patterned with pink flowers. The curtain fabric matched the quilt but there was nothing else flowery in the room. Above the bed was a series of pictures, all the same size and framed identically in honey-coloured wood. Paula looked more closely to see they were paintings by Tom Roberts, all scenes of Australian pioneering days.

The quilt was thrown back and an old-fashioned wicker bed tray sat to one side with the remains of Rowena's breakfast still on it. Paula picked up the thick maroon dressing-gown from the end of the bed and put it in a bag with the slippers from the floor.

Then she took the tray to the kitchen and washed up the breakfast dishes, before returning to the bedroom and making the bed. That was the easy part. There was still the rest of the list of items Rowena had requested.

Paula crossed to the old tallboy and tried to remember which drawers Rowena had told her to look in for the other items of clothing. She felt like a thief digging through the drawers.

The underwear was easy, all neatly folded into the top drawer. A tracksuit was in exactly the spot described in the third drawer, but it was the pyjama drawer that surprised Paula. It was a neatly organised collection of bed wear, from full-length flannelette pyjamas to beautiful lacy cotton nightdresses. There were also two or three embroidered satin negligees with matching robes. Paula ran her fingers over a midnight-blue silky number.

"Well, well, Rowena, very sexy," she murmured. "You never should judge a book by its cover."

She left the satin gear and shoved some flannelette pyjamas in the bag with the other things and then remembered the book and tablets Rowena said were on the bedside table. They lay between the only other things on the table, a lamp and a photo frame. Paula glanced at the photo. A rather handsome man had his arm around a smiling Rowena. He was slightly taller than her with a thick head of dark hair greying at the temples. It was a fairly recent photo judging by Rowena's appearance. Paula wondered who the man was.

It wasn't a brother. Dan's father was her only sibling. Perhaps a cousin but Dan had never mentioned other relatives. Maybe he was a family friend. Paula looked back at the photo after she'd added the book and the tablets to the bag. Rowena's eyes sparkled from the picture.

Paula thought about Rowena's frequent trips to town. She loved the football and had a member's ticket for the Adelaide Oval where she often sat with a friend. Paula had assumed that the friend was a woman but maybe it was a man. Surely Dan would know. She felt a little guilty prying in Rowena's private life but her curiosity was roused. She closed the curtains, picked up the bag and left the room keen to ask Dan what he knew.

★ ★ ★

The microwave whirred as it heated the formula. Paula rested her head on the wall as she watched it go round. It was five in the morning and she didn't feel as if she had slept at all. The kitchen was very cold. The little blow heater struggled to warm the big space and no curtains in the window left a large expanse of cold glass.

She could hear the faint bleating of the lamb in the distance. She'd fed it at nine o'clock and then one o'clock and now here it was, wanting to be fed again.

"What are you doing?"

She jumped. She hadn't heard Dan enter the kitchen behind her.

"Feeding the lamb – again."

"It should only be four hourly."

"That's what I'm doing. I swear it's got a clock inside it that goes off at the exact minute four hours is up."

"But you've been out of bed more than that."

"Your aunt has been coughing and coughing. I've been in to her several times. The room is so cold but I don't want to heat it because the tablets don't seem to be lowering her temperature much. One minute she's shivering and the next she's throwing off the quilt. I'm worried about her."

"You poor thing." Dan pulled her in close. "Why didn't you wake me? I could have done something."

"I don't know what…" Another bout of distant coughing joined the bleating of the lamb. "There she goes again. All she's had are sips of water and cordial. She says her throat is raw and her chest hurts."

The microwave beeped to announce the formula was ready.

"Why don't I feed the lamb and you see to Rowena. Then you should go back to bed for a while. I don't want you getting sick as well."

"Thanks." She smiled gratefully at him then pulled her dressing-gown tighter around her and left the warm kitchen for Rowena's bedroom. Just as well Alison sent the dressing-gown, she mused. It wasn't something Paula had thought she'd have much use for.

She tapped on the door and entered the spare room. The bedside lamp was on and Rowena was standing shivering by the bed.

"What are you doing? Are you okay?" she asked.

"Oh!" Rowena spun around and swayed on her feet.

Paula rushed towards her.

"I'll be fine." Rowena held up her hand up. "Don't fuss."

"I heard you coughing again." Paula was very tired and she'd just about had enough of Rowena's churlish behaviour. "I wondered if you needed anything."

Rowena swayed again and sat down heavily on the side of the bed.

"I'm sorry, Paula. Between that blasted lamb and me you've probably had no sleep either. Don't worry about me. I think my temperature is lowering at last but now I'm saturated and the sheets are too." Rowena shivered. The room was very cold.

"Why don't you go into the lounge and change?" Paula suggested. "I've kept the fire going in there, and I can change the sheets for you."

"I can change the sheets."

"Rowena, really, it's okay. It won't take me long. You go into the lounge and get warm."

To Paula's amazement, the older woman gathered her things and left without another word. *Well, wonders will never cease, Mrs Woodcroft. You may be able to soothe the savage beast yet!*

★ ★ ★

Bright morning light shone around the blinds. Paula struggled to open her eyes. She blinked briefly, trying to recollect what day it was. Her head was hazy from lack of sleep. She glanced at the bedside clock and sat up with a jolt. It was ten o'clock.

Her dressing-gown lay across the end of the bed where she'd left it only a few hours earlier. *You and me are becoming old friends,* she thought, as she dragged it on and made her way down the passage. Rowena's door was shut and there was no sound coming from inside but as she opened the passage door she could hear the bleats of the lamb. It had been at least five hours since Dan had fed it for her.

In the kitchen were the remains of breakfast. Dan would have gone off to work ages ago. She quickly mixed another lot of formula. The strong smell made her empty stomach squirm.

"Here I come, little fella," she said as she pushed open the door. The lamb rushed towards her. "It hasn't taken you long to work out where your next feed's coming from...oh!" Paula gagged at the sight of the brown muck caked down the lamb's legs and the smell of the liquid manure that it had spread everywhere with its little hooves. "Don't tell me you're not well."

Paula leaned over the barricade to feed the lamb and used her other hand to cover her mouth and nose. The lamb devoured the bottle as quickly and happily as usual. Its little tail, which whizzed back and forth, was also caked in the putrid brown liquid.

"What am I going to do with you? You're filthy."

She decided bathing it was the only option. In the laundry she put some warm water in the old cement trough, then she added some liquid wool wash. Gingerly holding the struggling lamb at arms-length, she carried it to the laundry and, standing it in the trough, used a rag to wash the muck from its backside, legs and tail.

"This will clean you up. And I'm only using the best quality wool wash." Her giggles turned to concern as the lamb struggled. She didn't want it to get wet all over. The only towel was an old beach towel Dan used to wipe his hands. She used that to dry the lamb off.

Its box and bedding were still clean and dry so she tucked it back in and carried it into the kitchen to put it by the heater. Then came the revolting job of cleaning up all the putrid newspaper and laying out fresh sheets.

Back in the laundry, she'd just put Rowena's sheets in the machine when a scratching sound at the back door reminded her she hadn't seen Tarzan this morning. Dan must have let him out.

She opened the door to reveal a small dog the same size as Tarzan but it was dark brown all over, with hardly a white patch on it.

"Tarzan! What have you been doing?"

The little dog sank down on all four legs and lowered its head to its front paws.

"Now I'll have to wash you as well." With a fresh lot of water in the laundry trough she put Tarzan in and washed him. "You'll have to have the royal wool wash treatment as well. I don't have any dog shampoo."

Tarzan didn't seem to mind her ministrations. She rubbed him down with the towel and he gave himself a vigorous shake, took a couple of bites of dog food then pattered off to the kitchen. By the time Paula followed him he was curled up by the lamb's box in front of the heater, fast asleep.

She cleared up the breakfast dishes and hummed to herself. Her two little charges were fed and washed and sleeping peacefully. Once she straightened up the kitchen she'd be ready to start the day. The plastic bag Dan had carried inside yesterday still waited on the dresser.

Paula looked at the note. 'Sorry we missed you. I used these before I got my new lounge curtains. They might do for the kitchen till you find what you want. Jane.'

Paula tugged open the bag and pulled out some calico curtains on rings. She'd have to give Jane a call to say thanks. It was kind of her and the curtains certainly would help for now.

"Dan made me some breakfast."

"Rowena, you startled me." Paula looked up from her parcel. "Are you feeling better?"

"My cough's chesty, my nose is streaming and I feel giddy when I stand up."

I'm glad I asked, thought Paula, then she saw Rowena sway and moved quickly towards her.

"What have you been doing?" Rowena stared disdainfully at the front of Paula.

Paula looked down. The front of her pretty blue dressing-gown was covered in brown smudges and smears. Whether it was poo or mud she couldn't be sure.

"Damn!" She looked reproachfully at the two sleeping animals.

"I'm going to need more things from my place today." Rowena lowered herself carefully into a chair. "I've got one of those little oil-filled heaters at home. It's so cold in this house and I want my hankies. I can't tolerate tissues. There should be mail today and you'll need to get the food from the freezer for the shearers. Have you planned what you're giving them yet?"

"I've got a couple of Dara's meat pies." Paula glanced at the fridge. She'd forgotten about preparing for the shearers this morning.

"You'll need more than that," Rowena said. "They'll be starting at seven thirty tomorrow morning. You'd better make a list and ..." She broke off into a bout of coughing that left her struggling for breath. Tarzan jumped to his feet and the lamb began to bleat.

"I think you'd better go back to bed. I'll organise the food today."

Rowena dragged herself up without a word and went slowly to the door. Paula heard her mutter something about a 'blasted menagerie'.

The orders are flying again, so she must be feeling a bit better, thought Paula as she waggled her head at Rowena's back.

The older woman stopped at the door and turned back. "And I'd remove those animals from the kitchen. Shearers won't like them at their lunch table." She turned and continued back to her bed.

"Bloody shearers," Paula muttered. "I don't like them already."

CHAPTER
20

Paula pulled up outside the shearing shed at nine twenty-five the next morning. She tipped her head back, shut her eyes and took a deep breath. She felt as if she'd done a day's work already.

By the time the lamb had cried for its early-morning feed, she had decided it was time to get up for the day. Dan had gone off to make sure everything was ready for the shearers and she had begun in the kitchen. At least she hadn't heard Rowena cough so much in the night.

Now here she was about to run her first test. Dan had said morning tea was at nine-thirty exactly. She couldn't carry everything across the long stretch of yard to the shearing shed so she had loaded up her car boot.

Rocket was sleeping by the door and he hobbled to his feet expectantly as she approached, his deep brown eyes looking soulfully up at her.

"Sorry, old boy. No titbits yet, maybe after morning tea."

Paula climbed three steps to enter the large iron-clad shed, her arms wrapped around the basket she'd filled with containers. She paused inside, immediately distracted by the hum of activity going on around her. Three men were bent double over sheep jammed between their legs. The machinery over their heads whirred and she watched, fascinated, as the wool slipped away from the sheep in long strokes.

The yards close to the shearers, where Paula had administered first aid to the lamb's poor injured mother, were now packed with sheep and the air was filled with a mixture of animal smells, the shuffling of the feet, the occasional low bleat and the click and whir of the shears.

Tom was bundling chunks of dirty wool into a big bag and another lad of about his age was carrying an armload of wool to a large table where Dan was picking at a fleece. She put her basket down and watched as he folded the fleece and deposited it in a bag hooked up inside a machine.

Behind her, the whirring noise reduced. One of the shearers had switched off his shears and was now bending and stretching. Dan came and took the basket. He carried it to a clear spot off to the side where there was a rough table and a plank over a couple of drums served as a seat.

He looked over the food containers in the basket. "Did you bring the kettle?"

"Yes, the rest is still in the car —"

"I'll get that while you set this out." He hurried off, preoccupied.

Paula took the lids off the containers to expose the sandwiches that Rowena had insisted she make. After that she set out the cake and the slice. The thick chocolate cake was Rowena's but Paula was pleased her fruit slice had turned out rather well.

The last shearer switched off his shears and in the sudden silence the bleats, murmurs and shuffles of the sheep packed into the shed were louder and Paula could hear the more distant sounds of those outside, already shorn or still waiting their turn.

Dan carried in the box with the kettle and coffee and tea-making things and another container of biscuits. Paula set it all out. By the time she'd finished the men were gathered quietly around her.

"This is my wife, Paula. This is Max and his offsiders, Johnno and Brad." Dan indicated the older of the shearers and the two men standing next to him. Then he pointed towards the lad alongside Tom. "And this is young Stuart."

Paula smiled and said hello to them all then stood back as they moved in on the food. She glanced at her watch. It was twenty-five minutes to ten. Dan had explained the shearers stuck closely to their two-hourly schedule. Lunch would be at twelve and afternoon tea at three. Paula's job was to keep the food coming.

The men kept up a friendly banter. Max was only a bit taller than Paula but he was solidly built and had a face that crinkled all over when he smiled. He was the boss and the one Dan said they had to keep happy. By the way he was devouring the sandwiches, Paula thought at least they were to his liking.

She wandered away from the men to look at the layout of the shed and the talk behind her became a bit more animated. She stopped by the big table made up of wooden rollers where Stuart had spread the last fleece. The thick wool looked grubby on the outside but when she parted it, her fingers revealed soft, oily, finely crimped strands.

"I'm hoping that's our future." Dan had come to stand beside her.

She looked up at his serious expression and followed his proud gaze as he looked across the fleece spread over the table.

"This is some of the best wool we've had. I've been working on a breeding program since Dad died. It's quite a business selecting the right rams, looking for ewes that produce twins, breeding and culling. There's a lot involved to produce this fine wool."

Paula looked back at Dan again. There was a toughness in his eyes, a grim determination about him that made her uneasy. It was a part of his character she didn't understand.

"Glad I'm not a sheep then," she said lightly. "I'm not interested in producing offspring. You might cull me."

Dan looked at Paula with a surprised expression and behind them the pen doors clanged and the machinery started up again as the shearers resumed their work.

"I'd better clear away the morning tea." Paula was embarrassed that her attempt at a joke had fallen flat.

"I've got to shift some sheep." Dan turned away to talk to Tom.

Paula lugged the containers out to the car where Rocket still waited.

"Hardly anything left to give you." She tipped a few crumbs and sandwich scraps in front of him. He licked at the ground half-heartedly then pricked up his ears.

There was a loud whistle from the other side of the shed. "Rocket," Dan called.

Rocket sped off, leaving Paula amazed that he could still live up to his name.

"No rest for the wicked," she mumbled and got into her car.

"How did you go?" Rowena was coming out of the bathroom as Paula carried the morning-tea things back into the house.

"They ate nearly everything. All the sandwiches, cake and slice are gone. There are still biscuits left but there was a whole packet of them."

"They always go for the homemade things first. Are you organised for lunch? I can help."

Paula looked at Rowena closely. She had some natural colour back in her cheeks and her eyes had more of their normal sparkle. "You shouldn't overdo it. You've been very sick."

"Nonsense! I've only just got out of bed. I'm feeling much better today —" Her words were chopped off by a bought of chesty coughing.

Paula got her a glass of water.

"Thanks," Rowena said a little more meekly, once the cough had passed. "If I could just shake this cough, I'd be fine. I've finished my book and I can't bear lying in that bed any longer."

"Well, I would appreciate some help."

"Good. Come on then, what needs doing?"

Rowena washed up while Paula fed the lamb again. She was pleased that since she had cleaned it up there had not been much more sign of the scouring, but the enclosure was badly in need of another clean out. It would have to wait until later.

Back in the kitchen, Rowena had her nose in the fridge.

"Did you say you were giving them Dara's pies for lunch?" she asked.

"Yes, that's what I'd planned." Paula wondered what was wrong with that.

Rowena stood up. "That should be enough if we do plenty of mashed spud and veggies. What about dessert?"

Paula hesitated. "I was going to give them more cake."

"I'll make a baked pudding if you like. Have you got ice-cream?"

"Yes."

"Good. Better to keep your cake for the tea breaks. Now if you get me a bowl I'll get started."

Rowena came to a stop at the fridge, flicked on the two-way radio with a click of her tongue then bustled on into the pantry.

Paula gritted her teeth and opened a cupboard to dig out a bowl. Behind her a male voice crackled from the two-way. Paula had been in the habit of turning it off when Dan wasn't home. The crackling drove her mad when she was working in the kitchen.

Rowena cracked an egg into a cup then tipped it into the bowl with some sugar. Paula recalled her fiasco with the sponge.

"How do you end up with some eggs being rotten?" she asked.

Rowena began to beat her mixture. "Our eggs come from my chooks. I have a couple of roosters. If an egg is fertilised and left for too long it can start to develop then it goes off. I've spoiled a few cakes by not cracking into a cup first."

If only I'd known that, Paula thought. She would have been saved a lot of bother had she cracked open each egg separately.

"Hello."

Paula and Rowena both looked around at Uncle Gerald, who was standing in the doorway.

"Hello, Uncle Gerald," Rowena shouted. "We're all a bit busy today. Dan's got shearers, you know."

"I wondered what all the cars were doing up by the sheds," he replied. "They'd better have plenty under cover. Looks like a chance of stormy weather coming." He looked at Paula. "Is the kettle on?"

"Paula's too busy today. Why don't you pop up to the shed and say hello to the men."

"It's all right, Rowena. Uncle Gerald can have a cup of tea before he goes." Paula noticed the little smile on the old man's face as she turned to put the kettle on. It was a brilliant contrast to the frown on Rowena's.

The kitchen was a frenzy of activity but they had the food ready with time to spare. Uncle Gerald had drunk his cup of tea and eaten a piece of cake before heading off to the shearing shed.

Now it was almost lunchtime and Paula was about to set the table but she stopped and looked down the kitchen towards the bay windows. She had managed to get Jane's curtains up on the old rod and she had tied them back with a couple of her bright scarves. They made a perfect frame to the sunny day outside. Paula could see no sign of Uncle Gerald's predicted storm.

"You've done a good job with this room, Paula. I like your colours."

Paula wasn't used to praise from Rowena. "I was thinking I'd like to have the table down in front of the window."

"It would give you more room up this end for working. Shall we do it now?" Rowena began moving chairs out from the table and Paula joined in.

"Is this yours?" Rowena lifted the tablet Paula had been trying to access the internet with. She tried to recollect what day that had been. Monday! It seemed so long ago now.

"I was hoping to find some work I could do online...to keep my hand in."

"You won't have much joy with internet connection until you get a satellite connection like I have." Rowena fixed her with a sharp look. "If you're interested in account keeping I am sure there would be work among the local farms."

Paula felt a surge of hope. She really wanted to be included in the paperwork for this farm.

"Not ours, of course. I can manage fine," Rowena added, "but I know a few older farmers who would probably happily pay for someone to visit them and help with their books. Even after all this time, they've never got used to all the paperwork involved with the BAS."

"I'd better put it away for now." Paula took the tablet from Rowena and noticed the bag with the phones was also still leaning against the wall where she'd left it. She'd forgotten all about the mobiles. Hoping Rowena hadn't noticed, she took everything into the other spare room. Tarzan was at her heels as usual and she decided to heed Rowena's warning and shut him in the laundry on her way back to the kitchen.

By the time the men came in for their meal the kitchen was tidy and the table was placed in front of the window, spread with a cloth and set ready for them to begin. Rowena had worn herself out and had retired to the lounge to eat her meal in peace.

"This looks good," Dan murmured in Paula's ear as he passed.

She smiled happily as she served up their meals. Just as well Rowena had suggested lots of vegetables. Each serving of pie hadn't looked that big on their plates and they all consumed their share of the pudding and ice-cream. Dan and Tom left straight away to shift more sheep and the contractors thanked Paula very politely for the meal before they left.

Rowena returned from the lounge carrying her empty plate as Paula sank down at the table.

"Time to get this cleaned up then it will be afternoon tea."

Paula groaned.

"Have you eaten?"

"I don't feel hungry."

"You've got to eat, woman. There's not enough meat on your bones as it is."

Paula looked across at the remains of Rowena's lemon pudding. It had smelled delicious as she'd served it. "I think I'll have some pudding and ice-cream."

Rowena raised her eyebrows but said nothing as she started on the dishes.

By the time they were finished, Rowena had nearly worn her pointy little nose away with blowing and her cough sounded worse. She decided to take herself back to bed for a while.

I can obviously be trusted to organise biscuits and cake for afternoon tea by myself, Paula thought wryly.

★ ★ ★

"Thanks, Sweet Pea."

"What for?" Paula asked sleepily. She was snuggled up to Dan on the couch. It was late and they should have gone to bed but neither of them had been inclined to move after Rowena had said goodnight and left them to the fire.

"You have earned us a big tick with Max. He wasn't too happy when a few of the early sheep had seeds in their wool but your food and, to quote Max, 'happy disposition', smoothed the way. You're a hit with the shearers. I should have got me a pretty wife years ago."

She poked him in the ribs. "I can't take the praise for the cooking. Hardly any of it was mine. Dara and Rowena were the ones who saved the day."

"Never mind." Dan moved his other arm and pulled her closer. "I didn't marry you for your cooking."

Paula stiffened. They'd been so busy with shearing and Rowena and animals that the business with Katherine had been buried for a while, but Dan's comment reminded her. She really did need to talk to him about it.

She took a breath. "Dan?"

He nibbled at her ear. "Mmmm?"

"We need to talk."

"Mmmm." His warm lips were travelling down her neck.

"It's important."

She tried to pull away but his hands were already under her jumper, his lips on hers. She returned his kiss. There was always tomorrow.

★ ★ ★

Paula hummed as she watched the lamb drain another bottle. She was doing very well. Paula had named her Lucky because everyone who had seen her said she was lucky to be alive.

Dan had found an old wooden packing case that he was putting in a small pen by the shed so she could move Lucky out of the house now that the lamb didn't need to be fed quite so often.

Paula wondered what was taking Dan so long. He had gone to organise the new lamb accommodation once they'd come back from church. That was about an hour ago.

She went to the kitchen to wash out the bottle. Rowena had gone home yesterday but had said she wouldn't go to church with them while she was still coughing so much. Paula was glad to have the house to themselves again. It was hard to relax with Rowena around, even if she was sick.

"Paula?"

She went outside to see what Dan was up to.

"I've rigged up some more undercover yard space at the old implement shed. I need you to help me shift in some sheep. I don't like the look of this weather."

Paula hadn't noticed but now she took in the big dark clouds moving in from the west. Perhaps Uncle Gerald had been right.

"I thought we needed rain."

"We do, but not during shearing. You can't shear wet sheep. I've got a mob ready to go into the shed but I think I'll bring up a second lot now that I've got a bit of protection for them. Another pair of legs would be helpful."

"I'll bring mine then." Paula smiled, hoping to get a similar response from Dan but he was already heading back towards the gate.

"I'll meet you at the shed," he called over his shoulder.

"Aye, aye, captain." She gave a mock salute and went to collect her coat.

Dan had been restlessly watching the weather all weekend. Paula had thought the weekend break before the shearers finished off on

Monday would be relaxing but Dan had been in and out of the house doing jobs.

The first two days of shearing had gone well. Dan was flat out classing and sorting wool, keeping the sheep up to the shearers and shifting the shorn animals back to the paddocks, but he was pleased with the way things were going and with the quality of the wool.

She glanced up at the darkening sky as she crossed the yard to the shearing shed. It did look like it might rain. If rain meant a delay with the shearing, she could understand why Dan was getting twitchy.

The sheep he wanted to bring in were a few paddocks away from the shearing shed. They drove for a distance along the track that connected their place to Rowena's before Dan stopped in front of a gate.

"I guess that's why I'm here." Paula got out to open it.

"Pull it back onto the track and leave it open," Dan called as he drove through. He pulled up on the other side, motor running, and let Rocket out of the dual cab. "I'm going to bring the sheep back through this gate. You stay back a bit, in the middle of the track and make sure none of them go the wrong way. Grab a stick," he yelled and drove away.

Paula shivered, partly from the cold and partly from nerves. She watched as Dan in the vehicle and Rocket on his old legs rounded up the sheep and moved them back across the paddock towards her. What if they wanted to go her way and she couldn't stop them? She'd heard of people being trampled by cattle. Could she be overrun by sheep? Was the stick to protect her? Surely Dan wouldn't have asked her if it was dangerous.

She could hear him whistling and calling to Rocket, who seemed to understand the instructions. Gradually the bleats from the sheep grew louder and the smell of wool and manure reached her on the strengthening breeze.

With a thumping heart she stepped away from the gate and into the track as the first of the sheep edged towards her. Dan urged them forward with the dual cab. She lost sight of Rocket but could tell where he was as a bunch of sheep leapt forward. The leaders jumped over an imaginary obstacle and ran up the track away from Paula.

She sighed then stood rigid again as some of the following sheep slowed and looked in her direction. Dan called an order and suddenly Rocket slipped through the fence and stood beside her. His tongue lolled from the side of his gaping mouth as he panted quickly, not taking his eyes from the sheep. The reluctant group moved on.

"Thanks, Rocket," she said.

Dan called again and Rocket ran off as a small group, still in the paddock, tried to break away from the mob. Another lot coming through the gate veered in her direction. She yelled and waved her arms, the stick whooshed through the air and they turned and ran up the track. Paula grinned. So that's what the stick is for. With her new-found confidence, she urged any hesitating sheep on up the track and soon Dan and Rocket were also through the gate beside her.

Paula got into the vehicle beside Dan but Rocket hesitated when Dan opened the back door and called him in.

"Come on, Rocket, you stupid dog."

Paula flinched. Rocket climbed into the back and sat up panting quickly, not offended by Dan's abuse, his eyes watching the sheep ahead.

"Silly old boy. He still thinks he's young. I'm trying to save his legs," Dan said as they slowly followed the sheep up the track.

Once they reached the shed yards, Dan let Rocket out again and asked Paula to shut the gate across the track behind them. The gate was a wire contraption, like the thing she had struggled with the day they'd found Lucky. It lay stretched out along the fence. She walked to the end of it, lifted it up, kept the wire pulled tight like she remembered Dan had done and walked backwards to the joining post, dragging the gate with her.

She struggled to get the narrow gate post, made of wood rather than iron this time, into the loop of wire that held it in place at the bottom. Once it was in she had to strain hard to get the top end close to the joining post and then manoeuvre the wooden handle through the top of the fence to hold it in place. Carefully she let go of the gate. It sagged a little but stayed up.

Paula let out a slow breath. "Thank goodness." She looked up and could see Dan was out of the vehicle working with Rocket to get the sheep into the yard he had made around the old shed.

"Damn!" Paula kicked the dirt at her feet. She was standing on the wrong side of the gate.

She strode to the other end where it joined the wooden rails surrounding the shearing shed and climbed over into the holding pens. She was on top of the next lot of rails when there was a twanging sound behind her. She looked back in time to see the gate spring undone and fall down to the ground.

"Damn!"

"Paula!" She looked up at Dan's shout. There was a small group of sheep running flat out in her direction. She jumped down from the rail, landing heavily on one ankle. A sharp pain shot through her lower leg as she hobbled to the middle of the track, waving her arms and yelling. The breakaway mob split in two and ran either side of her, leaping the fallen gate and racing away down the track.

Dan was yelling at Rocket and swearing like she'd never heard him before. There were more sheep heading in her direction. Quickly, she ran to the gate and winced as another sharp pain grabbed her. She picked up the gate, pulled it straight, hooked the bottom in the wire and held on tight. The frightened sheep milled in the other corner and Rocket arrived to turn them back towards the shed.

Dan came and took the gate post from her. "Why the hell didn't you tell me you couldn't shut it?" he snapped.

"I thought I had shut the bloody thing," she shouted back then turned and hobbled away from him.

"What's the matter?"

At least he sounded concerned. "I'm fine," she said. "I twisted my ankle."

"Can you get back to the house? Rocket and I can manage now. I'll get the other sheep later."

Paula watched him stride back towards the mob.

"Yes, thanks for your concern," she muttered to his back. Then she turned and limped away, her pride damaged more than her ankle.

Much later, when Dan returned to the house, he was more relaxed and concerned for her welfare. He insisted she put her foot up and wrapped a packet of frozen peas in a tea towel to act as an icepack. The ankle wasn't that bad but she enjoyed his attention and his attempts at silly jokes made her laugh.

They had another of their picnic teas in the lounge in front of the fire.

"Rowena is improving. I called in when I took Rocket back," Dan said.

"I rang her this afternoon. She's coming over to help me with lunch again tomorrow. She's cooking a roast." Paula was still amazed by the quantity of food they were supplying and even more so that Rowena was allowing her to serve supermarket frozen fruit pies to follow the roast. Paula had expected to be told it had to be homemade but Rowena had simply replied that it was a good idea.

"There will probably be an extra for lunch. Ted Watson is coming over to lend a hand."

"The name rings a bell. Was he at the house-warming party?"

"Yes, he and Heather came. He's a gingery-haired fellow, stocky build, ruddy complexion."

Paula recalled the obnoxious man with the clinging handshake. "I remember. He didn't like what I'd done with the kitchen."

"Ted can be a bit of a big mouth but he's a good bloke and he's experienced with sheep." Dan put his arms around Paula. "Anyway, that's tomorrow. We're alone again and I reckon one of those baths would be just what your ankle needs."

"Do you?" Paula held him off. His reference to being alone reminded her of Rowena and the photo Paula had seen in her bedroom. "Dan, do you think Rowena has a man in her life?"

"No." He gave a snort. "My aunt hasn't been out with a man for years."

"How do you know?"

"If she so much as sneezed at a man it would be round the district in a flash."

"What if the man was in Adelaide?"

"South Australia is a small state, Sweet Pea. I'd still hear about it."

"What about the friend she goes to football with?"

"There are a couple of different ones but they're all women."

"Are they?"

"Well, I've never met them. I just assumed…" Dan hesitated and looked closely at Paula. "Do you think she's got a boyfriend in Adelaide?"

"There's a recent photo of her with a man. She has it beside her bed. I think there's a part of your aunt's life that you don't know about."

"Really? Well good on her. I hope she has got someone. She's devoted her life to Dad and then me, it's about time she took some time for herself."

Another thought entered Paula's head. "So, it is possible to have a secret the rest of the district doesn't know about."

"Possible." Dan laughed. "But highly unlikely." He took her hand and looked at her with his serious expression. "Now, I've got a few secrets I want to share with you."

Paula stiffened. This was it. At last he was going to tell her the truth about his past with Katherine.

"They're not bad secrets." His eyes were like deep pools drawing her to him, his lips turned up in the smallest of smiles. "But they do involve removing clothes." He trailed his lips down her neck to the top of her breasts. She melted at his touch. He lifted his head and she returned his kiss as his lips found hers, then he pulled away. "Hold that thought. I'll go turn on the bath."

Paula reluctantly let him go. He winked and let himself out the door. She gazed into the fire. They were so happy again she had almost convinced herself there was nothing between Dan and Katherine. What was the point of bringing it up? Any fears she had about Dan's past had to stay buried.

*　*　*

Sunday's grey clouds only produced some light showers of rain. Dan had enough sheep undercover to get the shearers started. The sky was clear and sunny again so the remaining sheep would soon be dry.

Rowena arrived just before lunch with the roast meat, gravy and potatoes. Paula had cooked the rest of the vegetables and they served up together.

"We've got Ted for lunch, I believe." Rowena nodded.

"Yes." Paula grimaced. "He has already expressed amazement at my cooking ability. Something about how he thought city girls could only open cans."

"His mouth runs away with him, that man."

"He held onto the plate I offered at morning tea a bit too long."
Paula shuddered. "He gives me the creeps."

"He's all talk. They've had some tough times on their property.
Poor Heather, she really works hard to keep that family together."

"I can't understand why Dan likes him. I find him offensive."

"Men don't always notice these things about other men. Anyway, Ted is good with sheep and Dan respects his opinion when it
comes to selecting breeding stock."

"So we have to put up with him."

"I guess we do, yes."

The sound of voices interrupted their conversation and the two
women set to work to serve up the lunch.

Paula did her best to avoid Ted, as she had done at morning
tea. In her previous career she had developed a manner at meetings that had enabled her to blend in with the surroundings when
necessary. People often forgot she was there, allowing them more
freedom in their opinions, which often worked in her favour. She
had found this approach had worked well with the shearers. They
relaxed more in their breaks and resumed a more natural discussion when they thought she was busy with other things and not
listening.

Ted wasn't quite so prepared to let her fade into the background.
Once the roast was served, Rowena disappeared into the lounge to
catch something on the television and Paula quietly tidied up the
kitchen and set out the dessert bowls.

"Don't know how you blokes can eat in here without your sun-
glasses." Ted's remark rose above the voices of the others. "The
technicolour of this room could blind you."

Paula kept her back to the table and held her breath. There was
a slight pause in the conversation, then it resumed as if Ted hadn't
spoken.

"Guess you don't come in here if you've got a hangover, Dan." Ted persisted. He gave a derisive chuckle.

"You know I don't drink," Dan joked. "What did you think about that last lot of ewes? I thought the quality of their fleece was looking pretty good."

Dan drew Ted's attention and Paula gave a small sigh of relief. Ted's comments had a knack of making her hackles rise. The rest of the meal progressed with only a few minor remarks in her direction. Paula managed to keep her cool and was relieved when the shearers left and Ted followed Dan and Tom out the door. She began to clear away the lunch dishes and stack them ready to wash up.

"Dan and Tom will be a few minutes. I thought I'd wait in here."

Paula turned, startled by Ted's voice behind her. "Have a seat." She nodded towards the freshly tidied table and chairs. Her heart was thumping. She didn't feel comfortable alone with Ted.

He came and stood close behind her. "Perhaps I could wipe some dishes."

"That's really not necessary." Paula kept busy with her dishes. He didn't strike her as the type to lift a finger with household jobs. She wished he would go away.

"Am I not good enough for the fancy city girl?" Ted's voice carried a hint of malice.

Paula turned to face him.

"I didn't mean it that way, Ted. Can I get you another cup of tea?" She tried to deflect him, wondering frantically what had happened to Rowena. She normally came back in to help Paula with the dishes.

"No thanks." Ted folded his arms across his chest and leaned against the table watching her. "Dan shouldn't be long. Just trying to be helpful while I wait. You've got a bit to learn about country life."

Paula looked at him, wondering what he meant.

"You and your fancy city ways," he continued. "Jim's been on to Heather about making changes."

"The changes were intended to make improvements in Jim's business and Heather's job easier."

"Marg at the post office said you were in there changing things behind Heather's back. My wife's got enough to do with me and the kids, without having to do extra for Jim."

Paula felt a twinge of guilt. She hadn't intended to make things difficult for Heather. The changes should have helped. Paula thought back to the night of the party when Heather seemed to be genuinely grateful for Paula's assistance.

"I hope Dan's got enough sense to stick to his plans and Rowena's still got her hands firmly on the books." He glared at her. "We wouldn't want you interfering with farm stuff that you know nothing about." His tone had underlined the 'nothing'.

"We're ready to go, Ted." Tom had poked his head around the kitchen door.

"Righto, mate." Ted followed Tom through the door.

Paula leaned back against the cupboard. She'd outmanoeuvred a few boardroom thugs in her time but Ted had unnerved her. Everything he said had sounded so spiteful. She couldn't understand how Dan could be friends with the man. And poor Heather, who probably worked all day at Jim's and all night for her family with little support from Ted.

Rowena burst through the door from the lounge. "Can you believe it? I nodded off in front of the television. Sorry to have left you to the cleaning up."

"They've only just gone." Paula turned back to the sink. She smiled to herself, thinking of the change of fate that made her welcome Rowena's bossy presence.

CHAPTER
21

Dan looked up from the piles of paperwork he had spread all over the kitchen table. "Would you like to go to Adelaide this Friday?"

He had been at it all morning, sorting papers, calculating figures and making phone calls. Paula had kept herself busy with housework, curious about what he was doing but not wanting to interrupt.

She looked at him now over the washing she was folding. "Jane and I were planning to go once shearing was finished but I guess we can do that another time."

"I could go alone." He hung his head in mock dejection.

She leaned over his shoulders and hugged him. "I'd much rather go with you."

"Good. I've got a big load of wool to deliver and several jobs to do."

Paula didn't think it sounded very exciting but at least it was a day with Dan. She'd helped him and Tom load the huge bales onto the truck. It was one of several jobs she'd helped with about the place and, apart from her sheep-moving experience, she'd managed quite well. Gradually, she was gaining little snippets of understanding of Dan's work.

Another passing shower of rain darkened the day and Paula turned on the kitchen light.

"Send it down." Dan leaned forward, peering out the window.

Paula looked out at the grey day. Helping Dan outside was one thing but Paula still had a long way to go when it came to understanding the weather. One day he wanted rain, the next he didn't. There was an old rain gauge on their side fence. Dan checked it and wrote the details in his little pocket diary every time it rained. His preoccupation with something he had no control over seemed futile to a city girl, whose only previous thoughts about rain would be to know if she needed her umbrella or not.

"You've changed your tune," she said.

"I didn't want wet sheep while we were shearing but we've finished and the crops badly need it. There are still some patches that have been slow to recover from that bad wind we had."

"What about the next poor farmer who's shearing now?" Paula put her arms around his neck and kissed his cheek.

"Well, I hope it's not raining at his place, but the rest of us need it."

Paula shook her head. Every conversation she heard Dan have with other farmers inevitably had a question about how much rain they had received. Then there would follow a lengthy discussion about how much more or less it was than what Dan had recorded. The night of the party she'd heard the same conversation over and over again.

She left Dan to ring Jane.

"We'll go another time." Jane's response was practical when Paula explained Dan's offer.

"I was hoping you could tell me a few places to look for curtains and baby things in the city."

"Is there something you haven't told us?"

"They're not for me," Paula added quickly. "Well, the curtains are for the kitchen, but I still haven't sent my sister and baby Rupert a gift yet."

"I can tell you the places to look but I'm not sure that you'll get a chance."

"What do you mean?"

"You'll be taking a load of wool so you'll be in the truck and Dan will have a list of other things he will need to do. It'd be a safe bet that you won't be passing any major shopping centres or getting into the city."

"Oh, well." Paula tried not to sound disappointed.

"Will you be in town tomorrow?"

"Yes. I have to restock the pantry after those shearers. I'm astounded at how much they ate."

"You certainly had a baptism of fire there. Most shearers these days charge a bit extra and supply their own lunch."

"Really! Why was I the mug?"

"It's hard to get shearers. People aren't exactly lining up for the job. I guess Dan had to take whoever was available. Shall we meet at Dara's for coffee tomorrow afternoon? I can fill you in on the best shops, just in case you get the chance."

* * *

It was still dark when they left home Friday morning. Paula sat quietly in the truck willing her queasy stomach to settle. She had made a couple of quick trips to the toilet first thing and now she felt empty and a bit flat. Dan was so cheerful in spite of the early hour and she didn't want to let on that she wasn't feeling well. The truck was warm and surprisingly comfortable.

Paula put her head back, shut her eyes and was dozing before they'd reached the bitumen. She dreamed she had a baby in a pram. She was pushing the pram quickly trying to get somewhere and people kept stopping her to look at the baby. Every time someone looked in to inspect it there was a lamb looking back from the pram.

"Come on sleepy head, what do you want to do today?" Dan was patting her shoulder.

Paula opened her eyes to the morning light and saw that they were approaching the outskirts of Adelaide. She felt refreshed and her stomach had settled. A shiver of anticipation ran through her. It was hard to believe she could feel excited at the prospect of a trip in a truck to deliver a load of wool. She would really have to make the effort to get out more.

"I'm not sure." She tried to focus on her surroundings.

"I thought you wanted to go shopping."

"I do, but…" Paula looked out at the industrial area they were passing through. "I don't know where I am."

"I'm not going to drop you here, but I can closer in. You could catch a bus into the city, or a taxi. You'll have a boring day with me. I've got an appointment in the city later this afternoon. I've organised a place to leave the truck. How about we have a meal together after my meeting?"

It was all a blur to Paula. She had no idea where the city was from here. She made a sudden lunge for her bag.

"Damn."

"What's wrong?"

"I've left my phone home. It was flat and I've left it on the charger."

"We should have done something about getting you a new one."

Paula grimaced. "Rowena did. Last week. Then she got sick and we had shearers and I'd forgotten all about it. I don't want to lose all my contacts so I was going to see about swapping the sim or at least merging mine. She bought you one as well."

"It's something I've been meaning to do. Trust Rowena to do it without including you. Anyway, it doesn't matter for today. I know there's a coffee shop on the corner of King William and Hindley Streets. I'll meet you there at four o'clock."

Dan found a place to pull over. Paula wasn't worried about finding her way but they had no way of contacting each other if something went wrong.

"This is where my appointment is." Dan pulled a dog-eared business card from his wallet. "If something happens and I'm not with you by four thirty find a public phone and ring their office. I'll make sure I get a message to you there."

"It's all so complicated. Maybe it would be easier if I stayed with you. I can go to the city this afternoon when you do."

"You'll be bored silly with me." Dan's response was abrupt. "Go and enjoy yourself in the shops. The bus that follows this route should take you direct to the city. I promise I'll be there at four. The phone number is a precaution, that's all. You won't need it." He was all but pushing her out the door. "I can't stay here for much longer with this load or I'll have a policeman on my tail."

Paula picked up her bag and coat and climbed out of the truck. The chilly Adelaide morning made her shiver after the warmth of the cabin. She had barely stepped away when Dan waved and drove off. She felt a little disappointed. A day on her own wasn't what she'd expected, even if it did involve shopping.

She walked further up the road to the bus stop. Huddled in the corner of the deserted shelter out of the wind she hoped the bus wouldn't be long and that it would, as Dan had said, take her directly to the city.

★   ★   ★

Sitting at a window table in the coffee shop, Paula watched as people hurried in all directions over the busy city intersection outside. Like her they were rugged up against the wind, which had strengthened as the day went on. The weather hadn't bothered Paula though. Her earlier fears had disappeared as the bus had indeed deposited her right in the city and she had easily made her way to Rundle Mall to visit the shops that Jane and Dara had suggested.

The mall had been busy but not as frantic and crowded as Sydney's. She had found her way around easily enough and made her purchases. She'd had a very productive morning. In the bags at her feet were assorted baby clothes in various sizes for Rupert. She'd found most of them in a small shop that Jane had recommended, tucked away in an arcade. Then she hadn't been able to resist some books and a small squeaky giraffe. She'd ended up with quite a bundle for her new nephew.

Finding the curtains had been a little more difficult but she had eventually settled on some striped fabric in the same green and blue as she'd painted the kitchen cupboards. At least she hoped they matched and would look right in the kitchen.

She'd bought herself a dark navy denim skirt and a blue and maroon striped top along with a few other bargains she hadn't been able to resist. Who knew when she'd get back to the city? Then she'd lingered over the bunches of brightly coloured flowers in a well-stocked street stall but she'd run out of hands to carry anything more and who knew how long it would be until they arrived home?

Now she was waiting in the coffee shop for Dan as arranged. She hadn't ordered yet. The unsettled feeling in her stomach had returned to plague her. The magazine she'd bought to read hadn't held her attention for long and she stuck it back in her bag and looked at her watch again.

"Hello, Sweet Pea? I'm only a few minutes late. I hope you haven't been waiting long." Dan sat down beside her and reached for her hand. His hands were cold but his eyes were bright. He looked so happy. "Have you ordered? I wouldn't mind a coffee." He leaned closer across the table. "Are you okay? You look a bit pale."

"I'm just tired. I've done a lot of shopping." She indicated the pile of bags at her feet.

"You sure have. What did you get?"

"Things for Rupert and the house and a couple for me."

"Let me buy you a drink."

Paula decided on tea. Dan placed the order at the counter then inspected her parcels.

"My day has been quite boring by comparison." He smiled and his whole face shone.

"Tell me about it."

"Nothing much to tell, just farmer stuff and a dull meeting."

Their drinks arrived, coffee for him, tea for Paula and a couple of sweet biscuits. Dan changed the subject to where she'd like to go for their evening meal. He made several suggestions but she shook her head.

"Come on, Paula. We won't often get to the city." He picked up a biscuit, bit it in half then washed it down with the last of his coffee.

"I'm feeling really tired, Dan. Can't we just grab takeaway on the way home?"

"You can't be tired, that will spoil my surprise."

Paula frowned. She really had gone off the idea of surprises.

He took both of her hands in his and gave them a squeeze. "I think you'll like it and I'm sure it will get rid of your tiredness."

"Can't you just tell me?"

"No. Come on, collect your bags. We've got a little walk and then all will be revealed." He wriggled his eyebrows up and down.

Paula grinned as he gathered up some of her bags. She had to admit she was curious. They both stood and he put his free arm around her, directing her out of the shop and into the icy wind blowing along King William Street. Paula shivered with the cold.

"I promise you'll like it," he whispered mysteriously and walked her on down the street and around the corner onto North Terrace.

Eventually they turned in at a large hotel. Paula didn't even see the name as Dan hurried her to the lifts and they rode up several floors. She could see his secretive smile reflected in the mirrored walls. When the lift stopped, he led her out and along the corridor until he stopped in front of a door. Producing a key card from his wallet, he held the door ajar with his shoulder then turned and scooped her up.

Paula cried out in surprise as her carried her through the door. "What are you doing?"

"We are continuing the honeymoon we didn't finish."

"Oh, Dan." Paula didn't know whether to laugh or cry. This was not what she'd expected at all.

He set her down on the edge of the bed then sat down himself and put his arm around her. "I'm sorry you've had such a tough start on the farm but I did warn you it would be different to Sydney life. There's been so much to do and I know I'm not the easiest person to live with. Rowena often tells me I'm too serious." He tipped Paula's face towards his with his fingertips. "I want you to know I love you."

She kissed him. They fell back onto the king-sized bed and rolled towards each other. "This is a lovely surprise," she whispered in his ear and then began to nibble it gently.

Dan rolled onto his back taking Paula with him. "We've only got one night here," he murmured. "Let's make the most of it."

* * *

They slept in the next morning and had a late breakfast.

"I've got one more appointment this morning," Dan said as he tucked in to bacon and eggs.

Paula was sticking to toast and tea. The queasy tummy was coming and going. Last night she had enjoyed the meal they'd eaten out but now she felt a bit flat again.

"Shall I come?" she asked.

"There's no need. We've got a late checkout. Why don't you stay here and relax. I shouldn't be too long. Perhaps we could have another of those spa baths before we leave."

His eyes shone at her across the table and she grinned, remembering the fun they'd had last night.

After their breakfast, they strolled down to the river and over the footbridge. It was a cold day but they were rugged up and it was lovely to meander along without a purpose. Once Dan had left for his meeting, Paula lay back on the bed to read a magazine but it didn't hold her interest for long. Hotel rooms were really quite boring on your own, she thought, even if they were fancy.

She packed up their things. At least when Dan came back they could have that spa and relax again until it was time to go. The thought of it made her restless. She looked at her watch. He'd been gone an hour. She could walk down and meet him but she didn't know where he was.

Then she remembered he'd said he was at the same place he'd had the meeting yesterday. Paula dug in her purse for the card he had given her. It was for a solicitor and the address was a building on King William Street.

She picked up her bag. Instead of waiting for Dan she would go to meet him. It would be a surprise and would give her something to do. Besides, if she missed him she could always come back to the room.

There was a little chocolate shop along the way and she stopped and bought a selection of their beautifully displayed treats. It would be something delicious for the journey home. Then she continued on along King William Street looking for the number of the building on the card. It was on the other side of the road but further along. She stayed on the sheltered side watching the numbers until she saw the building she wanted opposite. It was a typical office block, with nothing much to distinguish it from the buildings either side.

Paula continued on to the lights and waited with a small group of pedestrians, their heads down against the wind. When she got to the other side, she noticed a little coffee shop on the corner. She was tempted to take refuge in there as the wind whipped the hair back from her face. The building she was looking for wasn't far, only a couple of buildings down from the corner. She recognised it just as a tall blonde woman walked out of the front doors and down the steps to the footpath.

Paula stopped. The woman was well wrapped in a long black leather coat with a vivid red scarf swathed around her neck. Her straight blonde hair was pulled back with a smaller scarf of matching red. Katherine Melton. What would she be doing coming out of the same building Dan had his appointment in? Surely it was a coincidence? There must be many different offices in the building. It was several storeys high.

Paula stepped back close to the front of the little coffee shop and watched. Katherine faced back towards the doors as if she was waiting for someone. Her face was partly turned towards Paula, who saw Katherine smile as a man came down the steps. A man Paula knew. It was Dan.

She put her hand to her mouth as he reached the bottom of the steps and Katherine hugged him. Paula leaned back against the glass behind her and closed her eyes. What was going on?

Then she panicked. What if they came this way and saw her watching them? She opened her eyes but they were gone. She searched frantically then saw the red of Katherine's scarf further down the street. They were walking away from her. Paula relaxed against the glass again.

She had almost forgotten all the doubts and insecurities that had formed in her mind about Dan and Katherine. Now they billowed up inside her again in a giant cloud of confusion. Nausea swept over her. What would she do?

She looked up and down the street, then turned full circle to face the coffee shop. Three pairs of amused eyes stared back at her. The coffee shop had a bench running along its front window so people could sit and look out. She had been standing a foot away from three men in suits, who had obviously been watching her every move through the glass.

She turned and made a dash across the street as the pedestrian lights began to blink red. A car about to turn the corner tooted at her, adding to her embarrassment. Once she'd reached the footpath on the other side she tried to blend in with the people walking in her direction.

She followed the crowd into the mall and walked until she noticed the familiar facade of the David Jones building. She turned in and made her way down to a coffee shop where she ordered a sandwich, but she didn't touch it. Her head was too full of whirling thoughts and her stomach churned in sympathy. Everything she had heard about Katherine and Dan resurfaced and replayed in her mind. She didn't understand why Dan would have a secret meeting with his old girlfriend. If he couldn't tell Paula about it, he must have something to hide.

Was he making a fool of her? Perhaps he and Katherine were still managing to have some kind of relationship because of the child. Katherine was capable of it but Paula didn't want to believe it of Dan. Not the man she knew.

She looked at her watch. It was nearly checkout time. He would probably be back at their room, wondering where she was.

Paula didn't want to go back but what else could she do? She had to meet Dan. She had no other way of getting home.

CHAPTER
22

Jane pouted with mock jealousy when Paula told her about Dan's surprise. "How romantic. Bruce would never think of that. I'll have to get Dan to whisper in his ear."

Paula cringed underneath the veneer of a smile she had put on for Jane's benefit. The two women were sharing a midweek cuppa in Paula's kitchen. Andrew played with his trucks again and James was lying on a blanket trying to roll over. Tarzan had been shut outside because he kept licking James's face.

Dan was obviously acting out a charade. Paula would too until she could sort out what she should do.

"It was only one night, Rowena wasn't keen to feed Lucky for longer than that, and I've hardly seen Dan since. He turns up at mealtimes and comes in late. Last night he had a meeting and didn't get home till midnight and he's still chasing after sheep and mumbling about crops in his sleep." Paula didn't mention their long silences and their strained hugs and half kisses.

"Oh, dear. So he's not perfect then. There's another illusion shattered."

"I haven't been feeling well, actually." Paula changed the subject.

"What's the matter?"

"I've had an upset tummy for a few days now."

"Oh, oh, throwing up first thing in the morning?" Jane raised her eyebrows.

"No, I can't be pregnant if that's what you're implying," Paula's response was emphatic. "I'm not chucking anyway, it's the other end and it comes and goes."

"So to speak." Jane laughed. "How's your sister that had the baby getting on?"

"Okay, I think. I've spoken to her briefly on the phone. Mum rings with regular updates. She wants me to go to Sydney for a visit."

"You must miss them. Will you go soon?"

"I don't know. I don't want to go and leave Dan right now." Paula played the part of the perfect wife but she'd get on the plane today if she didn't have to face her father's 'I told you so'. He had been right and she had been wrong but she wouldn't admit it.

"Dan would survive. He's managed before and there's always Rowena to keep an eye on him."

They both sipped their tea and Andrew, dressed in red trackpants and a black and yellow Batman cape, brought a clump of trucks for Jane to untangle.

Paula watched the little boy return to his game, then summoned the courage to ask Jane the things she couldn't ask Dan. "Jane, did you see much of Dan and Katherine together?" Paula saw the look of surprise cross Jane's face before she answered.

"Where did that come from?"

"I just wondered. Katherine seems to turn up a lot..."

"Like the proverbial bad penny." Jane's eyes opened wide. "But surely not on your romantic weekend."

"It was one night," Paula corrected. She didn't want to go as far as telling Jane she'd seen Dan and Katherine together in the city. It would seem as if she had been spying. "Dan gets so tense at the mention of Katherine's name. I wondered what had caused that."

Jane gave a wry grin. "Katherine doesn't want to let him go. She's a spoiled brat, really. Her father was a nice man but he indulged her every whim. She and Dan were a hot item for a while. I think it was more about sex than..." Jane stopped and put her hand to her forehead. "That wasn't very tactful. You should talk to Dan about it. Bruce would wring my neck if he knew I was talking to you about them."

"I never imagined Dan was celibate until he met me, Jane. I'm just not sure how to deal with Katherine."

Jane reached down and wiggled a toy in front of James, who was beginning to grizzle. "Dan broke off the relationship but Katherine has had trouble accepting the decision. She can't cope with being denied something she has her heart set on. If she found someone else she'd forget about Dan in a flash. It's as simple as that. I don't think she ever really loved Dan anyway but now that he's been taken away from her she's acting like a spoiled child. There have been rumours but there always are. You don't want to take any notice." Jane picked up James then she turned back to Paula. Her expression was solemn as she jiggled the baby. "You don't need to worry about Dan. He's as honest as the day is long and anyone can see how much he loves you. Katherine will find something else to distract her eventually."

Paula sipped some more tea. If only she could believe Jane. There had been no sign that she knew of anything more between Dan and Katherine than what she had said. If there was a child, Paula didn't think Jane knew about it. But that seemed strange given the way everyone always knew everyone else's business in the district.

Garbled voices crackled from the two-way. Paula had been trying to ignore them all afternoon. Usually she turned the radio off when Dan wasn't there but she'd been distracted when Jane had turned up with the boys.

"Dara and Chris really look set to have a go at this cafe and bed and breakfast thing," Jane said.

"They are such a talented couple. I've been thinking about the type of advertising they could do. We need something to divert the tourists on their way to the coast. Once they get the people in I'm sure their reputation will spread."

"Paula, are you there?" Dan's voice emitted from the two-way.

Paula picked up the handpiece. "Yes, Dan."

"Can you come and get Tarzan? He's up at the shearing shed."

"Okay." Paula helped Jane and the boys to the car. "Tarzan is getting braver. He wouldn't leave the yard before. Now he takes any chance to explore a bit further."

"Plenty of good smells around a shearing shed," Jane said.

Paula waved her off and then went to retrieve the errant Tarzan. Surely Dan could have dropped him back instead of calling on the radio, she thought.

Dan's serious mood had settled on him like a cloak again. He had been surprised when she had returned late to the hotel room. She'd made up an excuse about doing some last-minute shopping and, once they'd retrieved the truck, she had pretended to sleep on the way home. They had been politely avoiding each other ever since.

★ ★ ★

Dan shut Tarzan in the dual cab and went back to the sheep pens. He had just got the rams yarded and the damn dog had come sniffing under the rails and sending them into a stink. Dan wasn't used to having a dog as a pet. His father had bought Rocket and Dan was very fond of the old dog but he worked for his living. Dan had accepted Tarzan because he was company for Paula and good at killing mice but away from the house he was a nuisance.

The rams stood defiantly in a corner of the yard away from Dan. He watched them closely. Ted should be here any minute. Dan wanted his opinion on which ones he should keep and there were a few more jobs he needed to do before dark. He looked at his watch. Tom was out spraying and if Ted didn't hurry up it would be time for Dan to take over. Tom had football practice and he had some things to do in town, so Dan had said he could leave early today.

What Dan had really hoped for was to be in at a reasonable hour tonight. Poor Paula. He could tell by the way she reacted that she must be wondering what had got into him after their great weekend. He had wanted to celebrate getting a settlement sorted out with Katherine – at last – but he didn't want to tell Paula until he knew all the legalities were tidied up and the papers signed.

It was just as well he hadn't told her. Katherine had rung not long after they'd arrived home and said she'd changed her mind and wasn't ready to sign yet.

Dan had thrown himself into work, angry that she had the power to hold him to her like this. He wanted to tell Paula everything but his pride wouldn't let him. There had to be a way to sever his ties with Katherine so that he and Paula could be free of her, but it was all so complicated. Her demands were making life very difficult.

He looked at his watch again. "Come on, Ted." He slapped his hand on the wooden rail. One large horned head turned his way, stepped forward from the rest and stamped its hoofed foot.

"And the same to you, mate." Dan glared at the ram then turned at the sound of an approaching vehicle.

CHAPTER
23

"Get up quickly. I need you to come with me."

Paula opened her eyes. Dan was a blurry figure standing at the side of the bed. She felt as if she had been drugged.

"What time is it? I must have gone back to sleep." She started to sit up and was hit by a thud of pain as the headache that had developed last night slammed her waking brain.

"Quickly, Paula, I need your help." Dan grabbed her clothes from the chair and passed them to her. "I've been calling you on the two-way radio but you've turned it off again."

The thudding in her head slowed her thoughts but she was sure his voice had taken on an accusing tone. That damn two-way. She was sick to death of it intruding in their lives. If he needed to talk to her, he could come and see her like he was doing now. He didn't have to whistle her up like he did Rocket.

"We've got to get over to Bruce and Jane's quickly." He was hovering as she struggled with her clothes. What had happened to her tender and adoring bridegroom of last weekend? She looked at Dan through groggy eyes. He still had on his hat and boots. He rarely wore his hat inside and never his boots. The boots were always side-by-side inside the back door and the hat hung on the hat rack.

"Why? What's the matter?" She glanced at the bedside clock that showed eight am. She fought to remember which day it was. Sunday. Sunday! What had got into him?

"There's been an accident. Jane needs our help. I'll fill you in on the way." Paula's heart missed a beat. She looked up quickly from the sock she had been tugging over her foot and grabbed the end of the bed for support as the room spun. Her throbbing head couldn't cope with the sudden movement. Dan didn't notice. He strode off, leaving her to finish dressing. The stomach upset that had plagued her all week since their trip to Adelaide had eased but now she had a headache.

They rattled along the rough piece of road that connected their farm to Bruce and Jane's. Dan managed to avoid the worst of the potholes but each rattle of the dual cab compounded the ache in Paula's head.

His explanation, that Bruce had got caught up in the auger and was on his way to hospital, filled Paula with horror. She had watched Dan use their auger. She imagined the long steel worm that moved the grain. The strong, seemingly unstoppable mechanism would make a mess of soft human flesh. She shuddered.

Dan glanced at her as they turned into the Freemans' drive. "Are you okay?"

The hint of concern in his voice was enough for Paula to forgive his earlier brusqueness.

"Yes. Just a bit of a headache." She gave him a weak smile.

He looked away to manoeuvre over the grid. Paula closed her eyes and clenched her teeth as the shudder it caused vibrated though her.

There was already a vehicle parked outside the house gate. Rowena had arrived before them. Dan was out of the dual cab and through the gate before Paula had undone her seatbelt. He waited at the back door for her to catch up and then went straight into the house without knocking.

They walked through the enclosed verandah, stepping around piles of clothes and over assorted toys. This room served as Jane's laundry and was also a playroom for Andrew. In the kitchen Rowena was bending over Jane, who was sitting at the table with a mug of something hot clasped in her hands.

"Good, you're here." Rowena was always one to state the obvious. "I'll drive Jane to the hospital. Paula, you stay here with the children. Dan, you should get out to that auger and see if there's anything that needs doing. The pigs still need to be fed." Rowena gave her orders like someone is accustomed to organising.

"Right." With a half-smile at Jane and a brush of his lips past Paula's cheek, Dan left.

Jane rose from her chair. "Thanks for coming, Paula. I shouldn't be too long. Will you be okay with the kids?"

"Of course she will." Rowena rattled her keys.

Paula willed the headache away. "Don't worry about anything here, Jane. You go and be with Bruce, we'll be fine."

With a sharp nod Rowena ushered Jane out of the house. Silence followed the departing car. Paula took Jane's seat. She rested her elbows on the table, let out a sigh and held her head gently with her hands.

"Woodie Two, are you on channel?" The two-way snapped at her from the nearby benchtop and from another room she heard the baby begin to cry. Paula stayed where she was, unmoving.

"Woodie Two?" There was louder crackling, a distorted voice and then it cleared. "Paula, are you there?"

When she realised it was Jane's voice speaking from the two-way, Paula moved quickly. She snatched up the handpiece. "Yes, Jane, I'm here."

"I forgot to tell you, I gave James a breastfeed a couple of hours ago. When he wakes up he can make do with cereal and crusts. I've left it on the sink. There's expressed milk in the fridge if you're desperate." Jane's voice reached Paula in snatches and she could imagine Jane's hand clutching the speaker in Rowena's vehicle as they sped into town. Rowena only had two speeds, flat out and stop.

"I'll find it, Jane. Don't worry about the children." Paula hoped her voice sounded convincing. Not only for Jane's sake but for the ears of the rest of the district. Nothing was private on the two-way.

"Call me at the hospital if you need me to —" Jane's voice was cut short by Rowena's background orders.

"She'll manage, Jane..." There was a crackle then silence.

Paula knew Rowena had the same misgivings about her ability to cope. Maybe this was Paula's chance to prove she could manage. She might be a city girl but she was made of tough stuff and she had been a darn good organiser in her job in Sydney. It was a distant past life that had happened before she married Dan and it didn't seem to count for much with these people she'd come to live among.

James cried again, quickly weakening her resolve. Babies were another thing altogether. Paula had looked after Alison's children sometimes but she had rarely changed a nappy.

She had nursed James before and he had always been content to lie in her arms and gaze up at her. Now he had worked himself up. His cries were a series of sharp wails. She went to the cot. He was kicking his legs fiercely. His fists were clenched and his eyes were scrunched shut.

Paula spoke soothingly and reached to pick him up. His eyes flew open and he stopped crying. She looked into the deep brown eyes looking back at her with such trust. She cuddled him. He was wet from the waist down.

"Is that your trouble, young man," she murmured. She looked around for clean nappies. There was a changing table with drawers underneath. "Don't tell anyone but nappy changing is not my forte." She laid him on the table. Immediately he began to kick and cry again.

"Where's Mummy?"

Paula turned to see Andrew standing in the doorway. This time the Batman cape was over his pyjamas.

"Hello, Andrew. Mummy and Daddy had to go out for a while." Paula tried to sound reassuring. "I've come to stay until they get back. You'll be okay with me." She turned back to the wailing, squirming James.

"James likes this." Andrew appeared beside the table with a brightly coloured squishy clown that made funny noises when he squeezed it. James stopped crying and clutched at the clown. With Andrew's help Paula managed to remove the wet nappy, replace it and find a change of clothes before James began to grizzle again.

"I'm hungry," Andrew said.

"I think we all are," Paula replied. "Let's see what we can find." Her headache was fading. If she could settle James, she might be able to get some housework done for Jane.

Andrew ate cereal, happily talking to himself and pushing a toy tractor back and forth on the table next to his bowl. Paula drank tea and tried to interest James in the food Jane had left for him. He would try it then push it away. He began to grizzle.

"Yoo hoo! Are you there, Paula?" A tall, angular woman with long brown hair pulled back in a ponytail sailed into the kitchen with a tiny baby strapped to her chest in some kind of sling. "I'm Jackie Martin. We haven't met before. Fred and I are northern neighbours of Bruce and Jane's. I hope you don't think I'm interfering but my Fred was coming over to give your Dan a hand, so I thought I'd come too. I might be some help with young James." She brushed a large hand down James's tear-streaked cheek and gave a wave to Andrew. "Hello, Andrew. I've left my boys with their gran." She looked at Paula, who hadn't moved since she entered the room. "I knew there'd be enough going on here without adding my tribe. Now, I thought I heard Jane say something on the two-way about expressed milk in the fridge. That might settle her James." She turned to investigate the fridge.

Paula put her hand to her mouth to make sure it wasn't hanging open. She wondered how many other flapping ears had been listening and waiting to see how the city girl managed.

"Thanks, Jackie. I'll go and tidy the bedrooms." Paula moved slowly to the door, watching Jackie in amazement as she scooped James up from his high chair and balanced him on one hip while she prepared the bottle with her other hand. The tiny baby strapped to her chest didn't move. Paula was startled as a small hand slid into hers. She looked down into Andrew's worried face.

"I'll come with you," he said in a quiet little voice.

"You're my best helper." Paula smiled and together they tackled the bedrooms.

They took the wet baby clothes to the washing machine and began sorting the rest of the washing.

"How are things going?" Dan wrapped his arms around her and she turned and hugged him back. It was their first cuddle since they'd come home. "Are you managing?"

Paula stepped back and put her hands to her hips. "I'm managing fine. Did you think I wouldn't?"

"No. It was simply an enquiry after your personal wellbeing, ma'am." Dan did his American drawl.

Paula looked up into his twinkling eyes. She wanted so desperately to go back to their happier days. Why did there have to be secrets?

"I'm feeling a bit as if everyone's waiting to see how I cope." She turned back to the washing. "I guess I'm being a little paranoid. Jackie is in feeding James."

"She'll sort him out." Dan lowered his voice. "She's the local earth mother."

"More like Amazon woman." Paula chuckled and he hugged her close again. There was a pushing between them and two little arms wrapped tightly about her legs. They looked down.

"Dan, this is my best helper."

"Hello, buddy." Dan lifted Andrew into the air and sat him on his shoulders. "He's my best helper outside some days."

Dan carried the little boy into the kitchen and put him down. There was no sign of Jackie.

"I have to make some phone calls. I want to get a few blokes over to sort things out. We don't know how long Jane will have to manage on her own."

"Does Bruce have family?"

"His parents live on the property but they left for an overseas holiday just before our wedding. They're not due back for a few more weeks. Bruce only has one younger sister and she lives in Adelaide." Dan poured drinks for himself and Andrew.

Paula's thoughts went back to Bruce and his injuries but the phone ringing interrupted her. Jane didn't have a phone in the kitchen, it was in the passage.

"Hello, Paula, how are you managing with James?" Jane's voice wavered down the line.

"He's fine, Jane. How's Bruce?"

"The doctors haven't finished with him yet. But they don't think too much serious damage has been done. It's a mess but at least he still has a foot." Jane sounded very tired. "I don't want to leave him yet. He may have to go to Adelaide."

"We're all fine. Jackie is here. You stay with Bruce." Paula reassured Jane, who gave her more detail about Bruce's accident. Paula was silent as Jane quietly explained how she hadn't been able to get Bruce out of the auger, how Dan had heard her call for help on the two-way from his vehicle and how he had come to their aid.

Between them Dan and Jane had managed to get Bruce's foot out of the auger and strap it up. Dan had gone back to the house to call an ambulance and arranged to meet them halfway, checking on the sleeping children while he was there.

"Thank Dan again for me, Paula. If he hadn't heard my call on the two-way and responded so quickly..." Jane's voice faltered. "Things might have been much worse."

"I will," Paula said softly. "Give Bruce our best wishes."

Paula stared at the phone she'd replaced in its cradle. She was mortified. Dan had done all that and not a word about it. She had always hated the intrusion of the two-way in their lives. How often did she turn it off once Dan was out of the house? Sometimes she remembered to turn it back on before he came home, other times Dan did it. She didn't want to think about what might have happened if he hadn't heard Jane's call for help.

Back in the kitchen Paula hugged Dan tight.

"What was that for?" He raised his eyebrows and gave her a cheeky grin.

"Jane just told me what happened. It must have been awful for the two of you trying to get Bruce out."

"Worse for Bruce. How is he?"

Paula relayed Jane's message.

"Thank goodness. I wasn't sure how bad it was. There will be a few families out there waiting to hear." Dan left her to make his calls and Andrew trailed out after him.

Paula sat at the table and rested her head on her arms. The headache had faded but not left completely. Dan was so organised, he knew just what to do.

In her office in Sydney she would deal with all kinds of daily events and crises. She realised now that she had arrived with a naive view of what life would be about on the farm.

She liked to be organised and follow routines but so far hardly one day had been the same as another. Just when she thought she was getting the hang of something, the weather changed or machinery broke down, people turned up unexpectedly or not at all, animals caused disruption and accidents happened. There was so much variety, yet somehow she felt it all followed an underlying network of codes and rules that she wasn't privy to.

Paula shook herself. Jane needed her help. There was no point in worrying about things that couldn't be controlled. I can surely organise things to make Jane's life easier at home, she thought. I might not know the locals but Jackie does.

Paula stood up and giggled softly to herself for the first time in a week. First she had to find Amazon woman.

Jackie was settled on the couch with the sleeping form of James cuddled in alongside her. Her own baby was sucking at her breast. "James will probably want his mother the next time he wakes." She waved a spare hand at the empty bottle beside her. "He wolfed that lot down."

"Do you think he'll be okay with Jane at the hospital? She doesn't want to leave Bruce yet."

"Best place for them all. I wouldn't take Andrew though. He would soon be bored and be another worry for Jane."

"I could drive James in to the hospital."

"He'll need a car seat. If you want to take my car I can stay here with Andrew."

Dan and Andrew were back in the kitchen when Paula went through to organise a bag for James. Dan had a sheet of paper in his hand.

"This is a list of phone numbers and names. All the blokes I spoke to said their wives were happy to help. Just give them a call. I've got to get back to the sheds." He nodded at Paula, gave Andrew a pat on the head and left.

Andrew saw Jackie coming through the other door and hid behind Paula, clinging to her leg. "When's Mummy coming back?"

His tiny sad voice melted Paula's heart. He was usually such a happy little boy. "She'll be home later, Andrew." Goodness knows what he was making of all this. She thought for a minute. He was obviously feeling insecure. She didn't want to leave him and there were things she could organise for Jane if she stayed. Bending down, she gave him a hug. "You and I have jobs to do before Mummy gets back."

She spoke to Jackie who was waiting in the doorway, the tiny baby back in the sling, fast asleep again. "I think Jane should have her own car. Then she and James can come and go when they want. We need someone who can drive James to town in Jane's car." She gave Dan's list to Jackie. "Who can I ask on that list?"

The rest of the afternoon was a whirl of activity for Paula, the devoted Andrew never far from her side. She rang Olive and Frank Williams, who lived between town and the farm. They came and collected Jane's car and took a grizzly James and drove to the hospital.

Paula made a pile of sandwiches and Jackie whipped up an amazing slice which they fed to the men helping Dan. Paula rang the women on Dan's list and asked them if they could make a meal to be delivered for Jane's freezer. She filled them in on Bruce's condition. Sometimes the phone rang with offers of help from people not on her list. Paula was amazed by the generosity of the people she spoke to, many of whom she'd never met but they all knew Jane and Bruce and wanted to help.

By mid-afternoon things were organised both inside and out. The men had a roster system drawn up to help feed the pigs and keep an eye on the rest of the farm and Paula had the domestic help under control. Jackie went home and Dan came in to find Paula again.

Andrew was getting restless. He was asking for his parents and not easily side-tracked by Paula's diversions.

Dan sat down on the floor and played trucks with him. Paula made them a drink and watched as Dan interacted with the little boy. He was so good with Andrew it reminded Paula that he had his own child somewhere. How could he not want to devote time to it? She sighed in frustration. Perhaps she should just tell Dan she had overheard the conversation with Katherine. Blurt it out. At least he might be able to tell her about it and perhaps unlock the secrets from the past that threatened their happiness.

"Hello?"

"Mummy." Andrew was up from the floor and running for the kitchen door as Jane came through it, carrying a sleeping James. He flung his arms around Jane's legs.

"Let me take James." Paula reached out her arms.

Dan struggled up from the floor. "I'll put the kettle on."

Jane nursed Andrew and explained to him that Bruce would have to stay in hospital for a while yet. He had a very sore foot.

Dan asked more detailed questions about Bruce's surgery and expected recovery. Jane did her best to answer. She looked very tired and Andrew kept demanding her attention.

Satisfied that his mate was doing okay, Dan rose from the table. "I'll go and feed the pigs if you ladies can manage without me."

Paula smirked. "We'll try."

"Don't do anything silly like Bruce," Jane said.

"He probably shouldn't have been using that old seed bin."

"Of course not, but you know what he's like."

"I can't preach. I cut corners sometimes."

Paula looked up in alarm as Dan patted Jane on the shoulder and left. She hadn't thought Dan was in any danger when he went out to work each day.

"Don't look so worried," Jane said. "I'm sure Dan wouldn't take the risks that Bruce does sometimes. My husband thinks he's bulletproof..." Tears welled in her eyes. "He was so lucky, Paula. It could have been much worse. That stupid auger could have chewed his foot off and even his leg."

"Don't cry, Mummy." Andrew's little arms wrapped around his mother's neck and he hugged her. James began to stir in Paula's arms.

"I think it's bath time for you boys." Jane took in a deep breath. "Come on Andrew, you can help wash your brother."

Paula handed over James. "Can I do anything?"

"You and Dan have done so much. I really appreciate it and I know it will help Bruce to rest more easily if he knows things are being looked after here. The boys and I will be fine now. You and Dan should go home. We've taken enough of your time."

Paula showed Jane the list of helpers they'd organised and helped her bath the boys before she left in search of Dan. The sun was setting and the outside air was cooling rapidly.

She walked away from the house towards the rows of long low sheds where Dan was feeding the pigs. Long before she reached the first shed the smell hit her. It pervaded the air, leaving her in no doubt she was heading in the right direction. She couldn't understand how anyone could work with such smelly creatures.

"Hello." Dan appeared carrying a metal bucket in each hand. "Ready to go home?"

"When you are. Is there much more to do?"

"I just have to hose out this yard."

Paula put her hand over her mouth as Dan used a hose to squirt out a mixture of straw and mud and pig manure.

"Don't you like it?" Dan held up a hand coated in brown muck and gave her a wicked grin. He moved towards her. "It's supposed to be good for the complexion."

"What are you doing?" Paula stepped back.

"Giving you a face mask."

"No, don't." Paula squealed as Dan darted at her and ran his finger down her nose. She pushed away from him and lurched backwards but her feet stuck and she sat down with a thud in the soft, wet mud.

"Are you okay, Sweet Pea?"

She groaned. He bent down and offered her a hand.

"It was only a bit of mud," he said as she took hold of his hand.

Paula tugged on his arm and caught him off balance. He tumbled down in the mud beside her.

She laughed at him as he tried to wipe the mud from his shirt. "It's only mud," she mimicked.

He whipped his hand up and smeared her cheek and she squealed again and managed to wipe some mud down his face before he trapped her hand in his.

"Well," he said looking at her sternly. "There's only one consequence for this behaviour."

"What's that?"

"We'll have to have another one of those baths when we get home."

Paula laughed at him and they struggled up together. She looked into the clear blue eyes of the man she loved. Were those eyes capable of deceit? She didn't want to think so as he hugged her in close and they made their way home.

CHAPTER
24

"Paula?" Rowena was calling but Paula didn't want to be found. She was hidden away, furiously looking through the farm paperwork, but the figures kept blurring. It was hot and the light was dim. Paula peered closer at the book in front of her.

"Paula, are you there?" The sharpness of Rowena's call cut through Paula's dream and she sat up quickly on the couch. The room spun and she had to grip the seat until it stopped. She had no idea what the time was. She'd only meant to shut her eyes for a minute, to give the painkillers a chance to ease the throbbing in her head.

Rowena was in the kitchen. "Paula?" she called again.

"I'm in the lounge." Paula rose carefully to her feet. The fire had burned low but she didn't feel cold.

"There you are. I've been trying to ring all morning but you've been engaged. Then I tried the two-way but I only got Dan out in the paddock."

"I was using the internet earlier. I forgot to plug the phone back in."

"I don't know why you'd want to waste your time with that. You know you can use the internet at my place to check your email until you get a satellite dish installed."

Paula drew in a breath. She really wasn't in the mood for Rowena today. "I'm looking for work I can do from here."

"I would have thought you had enough to do looking after Dan and helping around the place."

"I'm only looking." Paula's head thumped and she shut her eyes but only for a minute. The room started to spin. It was better if she had her eyes open.

"Are you all right? You look flushed."

"I've got a bit of a headache."

"I hope you're not getting that wog like I had. You probably caught something visiting Bruce. Hospitals are full of germs."

Paula couldn't believe Rowena's arrogance. If Paula did have a wog, it was more likely she'd caught it from Rowena than from a five-minute visit to Bruce in the hospital. "I'll be fine, Rowena. What did you want?"

"I wanted to contact you so I thought I would try your mobile, then I realised I didn't know what your number was. I put the paperwork in with your phones." She held her own phone up in her right hand.

"I've got it written down out here." Paula led the way into the kitchen. She was glad she'd remembered to get the phones out the day after Bruce's accident.

Rowena keyed the number into her phone. "Did you get any of that rain that went through last night?"

"I can't remember what Dan said. Maybe it was twenty mils."

"Good grief! That would be a downpour. Are you sure he didn't say twenty points?"

"Perhaps he did. I don't know. Why were you trying to contact me?" Surely it wasn't to discuss the rain, Paula thought as she sat down at the table. Her legs felt like jelly.

"I'm going away for a few days. Dan's so caught up looking after Bruce's place, I was hoping you'd feed the chooks and see to Rocket if Dan doesn't have time."

"Of course I can. Dan and I will sort it out." Paula couldn't resist asking more in spite of her headache. "Are you going far?"

"Only to Adelaide. I'm helping a friend prepare for a special birthday celebration."

"Is it someone Dan knows?" Paula probed. "Should I organise a card?"

"No. Dan doesn't really know my Adelaide friends." Rowena slipped her phone back into her handbag. "I wanted to speak to you about Frank and Olive Williams. Do you remember them?"

Paula recalled the short round woman who had given her sweet homemade treats and her husband who was of equally round proportions. They'd been the ones to drive Jane's car to the hospital on the day of Bruce's accident. "Yes."

"I talked to Frank about your bookkeeping skills. He was quite keen to have you look over his books and perhaps help keep them up to date. He has an accountant but prefers to do things his way. He and Olive don't have children to hand their property on to and they don't want to sell up and move to town. They're happy running the place for now but they've never got their heads around the growing paperwork. You could help them out, couldn't you?"

Rowena was a strange woman. She didn't seem keen on Paula finding other work beyond the farm, and their own farm books were strictly out of bounds, yet here she was, trying to get Paula to look over someone else's paperwork.

"I guess I could," she replied vaguely.

"Well, you don't have to. I thought you were wanting a little extra to do."

"It's fine, Rowena. Leave me their number and I'll contact them."

Rowena handed over a note and inspected Paula closely. "I'd better get going but I think you should take it easy. Get Dan a simple lunch and have a lie-down. I'll see you when I get back."

"When will that be?" Paula ignored the obvious instruction that Dan was to be taken care of before she saw to her own needs.

"Sunday evening probably, the party is Saturday night."

Must be going to be some party, thought Paula, it's only Wednesday.

"Are you sure you're okay?" Rowena asked again. "I could make the lunch before I go."

"I'm fine."

Rowena picked up her bag and stopped at the door. "Oh, did Dan tell you I sent a heap of old sheets and towels over for rags?"

"No." Paula wasn't sure what that had to do with anything.

"You always need them for something on a farm. I noticed when I was feeding your lamb you were obviously short of old things."

Rowena's eyebrows arched and Paula felt a glow in her cheeks. She'd forgotten about the curtains.

"Of course, if you don't like things that are given in good faith, you can simply return them, you know. I told Dan I preferred you didn't use the good furnishings for animal bedding."

She sailed on out the door. Paula sank down onto a chair and put her head in her arms.

★ ★ ★

"Paula! This bloody dog has been up at the sheds again." Dan marched through the kitchen door with a muddy Tarzan tucked under his arm. "He'll end up getting squashed by something or run over."

"Look at you, Tarzan." Paula took him from Dan. "You're all muddy again." She'd left the pup in the backyard after they'd come back from feeding Lucky, but there were too many holes in the old fence. "Can't we make the backyard dog-proof? Then he couldn't escape when I let him outside. He could even have a kennel out there."

"I haven't got time to do those types of jobs now." Dan went to wash his hands and Paula followed him into the laundry and ran some water to wash the muddy pup. "I put a bag full of rags in the corner there."

Paula looked at the bulging black garbage bag Dan pointed to on the floor.

"Rowena's given me a lecture about using good household stuff instead of rags." He looked at Paula shaking his head. "I don't know what she was going on about."

"Her curtains."

"What?"

"I used her curtains to line Lucky's box."

"Bloody hell, Paula. Why?"

"I washed them and they fell apart. They must have been rotten." She glared at him. "Curtains don't last forever, you know."

"At least you could have told her what happened."

"I needed something in a hurry for the lamb and they weren't any use for anything else." Paula saw the corner of his mouth twitch but he turned away.

"Well, she wasn't happy." He headed for the kitchen. "What's for lunch?"

Paula ignored Dan and finished cleaning up Tarzan. He looked at her with big eyes as she gave him an extra-long rub-down.

By the time she followed Dan into the kitchen she had calmed down. He was sitting at the table, eating the lunch she'd prepared.

"Aren't you eating?" he asked.

"I'm not feeling hungry. I think I might be getting that wog Rowena had."

"Perhaps you'd better go to bed."

"It's just a headache and I feel a bit off. I had been planning to visit Jane today but now I don't think I should. Have you seen her?"

"She's managing okay. I talked to her this morning after I'd fed the pigs. Her mum is coming tonight to stay for a few days."

"That's good." Paula was a little envious. She felt totally washed out and wished her own mother was close enough to come and stay. You must be sick, girl, she thought wryly.

"I've given Tom a couple of days off. He's taking Cassie to Adelaide. She's going to live with their older sister for a while."

Paula recalled the tired young girl from the party. "That poor kid. An unplanned pregnancy is so avoidable these days. Why do people bring babies into the world if they're not wanted?"

"I don't think it was as simple as that. Cassie and Damo probably planned this baby."

"Is Damo the father? Didn't he leave her?"

"He's a nice enough bloke. He and Cassie have been together since they were about fifteen."

"She doesn't look much older than that now."

"She's eighteen or nineteen, I think. Little more than a year younger than Tom. For some reason Tom and his old man never thought Damo was the right one for Cassie. I think Damo left because they were putting pressure on him to marry her. Wouldn't surprise me if he turns up in Adelaide once Cassie's there. I think, in this case, the baby will be the thing that pulls them back together."

"Isn't that often the way?"

"I don't know." Dan's face had become serious again and he stood up from the table. "You're right about one thing. People shouldn't bring babies into this world if they're not wanted."

He turned away from Paula and she could no longer see his face. What was he hiding? If it was a child with an old girlfriend surely they could deal with it, plenty of other people did.

Paula took a deep breath. She couldn't live like this any longer. "Dan, we've got to talk."

He turned back towards her.

She looked into his serious eyes and her resolve faltered. But she couldn't stop now. There were things that needed to be brought out into the open. "Dan, I love you but sometimes past events need to be sorted out."

"We agreed the past was best left there when we first met."

"But if something from that past affected our future surely we could work it out."

"We could...but not now. I've got to get back to the spraying. I haven't got Tom to help me."

"But, Dan —"

"You should have a lie-down. You don't want to get as sick as Rowena did."

Paula watched miserably as Dan walked to the door. Then he paused and she thought he might come back.

"I've let Tom take the dual cab. I'll use the ute while he's gone." He took another step then turned back again. "Oh, and Ted will be here for a bit while Tom's away."

Paula stiffened. "Why?" She didn't like the man at all and she couldn't understand why Dan did.

"I need the help. He knows sheep and he could do with the money."

"Why?" she asked again.

Dan looked at her quizzically. "Ted's land is more marginal than ours and he's paying off a big loan. Any extra cash he can get is a bonus. He's got four kids to feed and clothe."

"Can we afford it?"

"Things are tight and the current season hasn't been shaping up that well so far but the wool prices are good." He frowned. "What's all this about? You don't need to worry, we'll manage."

"I'm not worried but both you and Rowena have said things that have intimated finances are tight. Of course I'm not allowed to look at our financial records so I wouldn't know." Paula knew she was being perverse but she couldn't help herself. "If Ted is costing us extra money perhaps I could help out while Tom's away."

A little smile softened the corners of Dan's mouth again. He patted her hand. "No offence, Sweet Pea, but sheep work isn't really your thing yet."

Paula snatched her hand back. "I can learn."

"Of course you can but Ted has a good eye for sheep. He's been helping me with my selective breeding program for a few years now."

Along with Katherine, what a trio, thought Paula. And there was poor Heather with four children to look after. "So, he's not good with money but he's okay with breeding."

"That's a bit tough." Dan looked at her in surprise. "Ted's finances are his own business but if he's struggling it's not necessarily because of financial mismanagement. Farming is far more complicated than that. He's had to sell off a lot of stock through the last couple of dry years and now that demand is so great, they're too expensive to restock."

Tarzan began to bark.

"That will probably be Ted now. You go to bed. You don't look well."

His words echoed in her sore head as she sat alone at the table, looking out across the valley. Their whole conversation had been one of mixed messages and half-truths. She longed for their first carefree days together when they were so in love and the rest of the world, past or present, didn't matter.

Paula dragged her gaze back to the kitchen. What was she thinking? They were still in love, weren't they? That hadn't changed, had it? She looked around the empty room and a wave of sadness swept over her as the truth hit her. It had changed. She had to face up to it. Dan's past haunted them and so did hers. There had been a time when she had thought Marco was the man for her. That hadn't worked out either. Her father had been right. She had been too hasty in marrying Dan before they'd had a chance to get to know each other properly.

She put her hands over her face and held her pounding head. "Stop it. Just stop it," she muttered to the empty room.

CHAPTER

25

A couple of days later, Paula struggled to get out of bed. She'd had a restless night feeling hot and flinging off the quilt, then waking up later shivering with cold. In between she'd been plagued by weird dreams and an aching body. By morning, she was exhausted.

Dan had made her a cup of tea and toast when he got up but it sat cold beside the bed where he'd left it a couple of hours ago. He had gone off on a bus trip. Paula tried to recall what he'd said. Something about inspecting crops.

She thought perhaps if she got up and had a shower she might feel better but she sank back onto the bed, weak from the effort. She dozed but the fever continued to rage through her. Once or twice she coughed but the pain that cut through her chest almost made her wish for the headache back.

By the middle of the day, she summoned enough energy to get off the bed and struggle out to the kitchen where she sipped some water down her parched throat. It made her feel queasy so she sat in a chair and waited for her stomach to settle.

Lucky's bottle drained on the sink. Dan must have fed her before he left but she would be hungry again now. Paula prepared another bottle and went out to the back door where she kept an old pair of shoes. Dan had propped the back door open so that Tarzan could get in and out. The door that led directly into the laundry was also open so he could get into his food and bed but not into the rest of the house. There was no sign of the little dog.

It was a sunny day but a chilly breeze blew, making her pull her dressing-gown tighter as she made her way across the yard to Lucky's enclosure. The lamb was certainly pleased to see her and bleated loudly. Tarzan materialised, attracted by the noise.

"What have you been up to?" Paula fed the lamb and at the same time reached down to pat Tarzan's head. The world spun and she clutched at the fence instead. Lucky emptied the bottle very quickly. Paula turned to go back to the house. It looked such a long way and she didn't have the energy. Her legs felt like rubber. She sank to the ground with her back against the fence. The tall grass was wet but she didn't care. She shut her eyes thinking a quick rest would gain her the energy to make it back to the house.

Little paws walked across her legs then pressed on her stomach and a warm rasping tongue licked her nose.

She opened her eyes to see Tarzan's curious brown eyes looking right back at her. "It's okay, boy." She patted him gently. "I'm not feeling too good but I'll be okay in a minute." Tarzan settled on her lap. "I'll rest here a little bit longer," Paula whispered and shut her eyes again.

The sound of an approaching vehicle and Tarzan's barks brought her back from a crazy dream world where she was chasing after sheep that she couldn't stop from running through her house.

She opened her eyes to the afternoon sunshine and wondered where she was. The empty bottle beside her reminded her that she'd come out to feed the lamb.

The dual cab pulled up across the yard beside the house. Thank goodness Dan was home. She had no idea how long she'd been sitting outside but she was damp and cold and she didn't know if she could get up. Tarzan had run barking towards the vehicle, then back to Paula.

She looked up and saw Dan was walking quickly across the yard towards her.

"Paula? What's happened? Are you all right?"

Paula shook her head. The voice was Tom's, not Dan's. Perhaps she was still dreaming. She looked past Tom, who was kneeling beside her, to the dual cab. "Dan?" she whispered.

Tom took her hand. "It's Tom, Paula. What are you doing out here? Did you fall?"

Paula looked down at her dressing-gown. Why wasn't she dressed? Her head spun. "I'm feeling a bit sick. I should go back inside."

Tom put his arm around her and helped her up. She felt stupid being so weak. What on earth must he be thinking?

"Where's Dan?" Tom asked as he supported her slowly back across the yard.

"Isn't he with you?" Paula tried to think.

"I've been in Adelaide."

She pulled up abruptly and looked up at his worried face. "That's right. I forgot you had the dual cab. Dan's gone on a bus trip." Her lips felt dry and cracked. "I really need some water."

They reached the gate and Paula gave a cough. The pain took her breath away and she crumpled against Tom.

"Paula? I think you should see a doctor."

"No, I'll be okay," she mumbled into his jumper. "Just help me inside."

Tom guided her to the couch and got her a glass of water. She was very dry but she could only manage to sip a little before nausea swept over her.

"I'll ring Miss Woodcroft."

"She's away." Paula sank back onto the couch and shut her eyes. "Dan will be home soon."

Strange dreams continued to haunt Paula's sleep. Faces peered at her and asked her stupid questions but her mouth couldn't shape the replies. Dan and Tom came and went during her restless sleep and even Dr Hunter featured. She kept pushing at blankets that made her too hot, then reaching for them again when she was racked with shivers. Soothing voices whispered in her ear and eventually she slept a more peaceful sleep.

When she opened her eyes next, early-morning sun filled her room but she was disoriented. The window wasn't in the right place. She blinked hard and tried to think where she was.

"Hello, Paula."

She turned her head to see a woman in a nurse's uniform standing beside her. She struggled to sit up but her weak body failed her.

"Steady on," the woman said. She was older than Paula and well built. She had what Diane would have called an ample bosom. "You're looking a lot better but you're not ready to get off that bed yet. You're in hospital. Do you remember being brought in?"

Paula stared at the woman then glanced around the room. She shook her head. It certainly looked like a hospital room but was she still dreaming?

"My name's Jenny. I'll be looking after you today. Do you think you could sip a drink for me?"

Paula sat forward and felt a strange sensation around her nose and ears.

"Careful," Jenny said. "You'll need that oxygen for a while."

She readjusted the tube then checked the bag suspended from a pole. Another tube snaked down from the bag to Paula's arm.

"Is that a drip?" Paula croaked.

"You were very dehydrated when they brought you in yesterday —"

"Yesterday?" Paula struggled to sit up again.

"Take it easy. I can prop you up a bit more if you like but you're still very weak."

Paula tried to make sense of what Jenny was saying as she watched her pull up the rails on the side of the bed then adjust the bed and pillows behind her.

"Tom March brought you in and Dan was here half the night. They had a bit of trouble tracking him down. You had everyone worried."

Paula remembered feeding the lamb and sitting down in the grass and then Tom coming but she couldn't recall much after that. "It's just the flu, isn't it?"

"That would be bad enough but you've got pneumonia. At least your temp is close to normal again. Dr Hunter will be in to see you soon. Take a few sips of this."

Jenny helped Paula put a straw to her mouth and she sipped on some lemon cordial. It was wonderfully soothing over her parched throat.

Lachlan Hunter came in as she flopped back on the pillows.

"Good morning. You're looking brighter. How did she go through the night, Jenny?"

They looked at her chart and Jenny helped Paula to sit up so the doctor could listen to her chest.

"Have you ever had pneumonia before?" he asked once she had been lowered back onto the pillows.

"No."

"Well, I'd say you were very lucky Tom came along when he did. Pneumonia is not something to be mucked around with. You'll have to stay here until I'm sure it's cleared up."

Paula didn't have the strength to argue. She didn't care where she was as long as she was in bed.

"You need to keep drinking. Once your fluid level has improved we can remove the drip." He turned to give instructions to Jenny and Paula closed her eyes.

The next time she opened them, Dan was standing beside her, his face full of concern. She was so pleased to see him.

He bent down and kissed her forehead. "Paula, why didn't you tell me you were so sick?"

She frowned. Was it her fault? "I didn't realise myself. I thought it would pass if I rested. It must have mucked up your day."

"I never would have gone at all if I'd known. Rowena's given me a dressing-down over the phone. She was ready to forget the party and come home but I said there was nothing she could do at the moment."

Paula could imagine Rowena going on at him. "Poor you." She smiled sympathetically and her lips cracked. "Can you pass me the drink please?"

Dan sat beside her, telling her all about the bus trip and the various crops and techniques he'd seen. Then he told her how they'd eventually got a message to him via the phone on one of the properties they'd visited. He hadn't realised his phone was on silent. The wife of the farmer showing his property had driven out and told him Paula was in hospital and then taken him back to get the ute which, of course, had been difficult to start.

Paula drifted off to sleep with Dan holding her hand and talking quietly beside her.

The days passed slowly. The aches and pains faded and she was able to drink enough to have the drip removed. She needed the oxygen less but she still didn't eat much. Her appetite was nonexistent but she knew she had to eat or they wouldn't let her go home.

Hospital was a boring place once she started feeling better. Dan came every evening. Tom and Rita called in and Jim came with fresh oranges from his tree. Dara visited a few times, bringing special treats she had made to encourage Paula's appetite. She'd even brought in a dressing-gown for Paula and taken hers home to wash. Jane rang but she had taken Bruce home the day Paula had been admitted and couldn't fit in a visit back to the hospital just yet. Looking after Bruce was like having another baby in the house, she'd joked.

Then of course there was Paula's mother, who rang every evening to check on her progress. Paula's room was dominated by a huge arrangement of flowers her mother had sent.

Sunday evening she was eagerly awaiting Dan's arrival. The staff had hinted she might be able to go home the next morning and she wanted to tell Dan so he could organise to come and get her.

When Dan arrived Rowena was with him. She brought Paula a pretty posy of violets from her garden and a little parcel.

"Are you feeling better?" Rowena sat on the only chair in the room. "I would have come home and looked after you myself. I've already told Dan what I think of his nursing skills." She was wearing a smart tailored jacket and skirt in navy fabric. The jacket was nipped in at the waist and the lapels were trimmed with two white stripes giving it a nautical look. The outfit suited Rowena well and combined with the sparkle in her eyes and the glow in her cheeks Paula thought she looked years younger.

"I am much better, thanks." Paula smiled. Dan hovered at the end of her bed squirming like a chastised schoolboy. "I might be able to come home tomorrow."

"What time?" he asked.

"I don't know. After the doctor has been, I suppose. Why?"

"I've got a full day spraying tomorrow. That's if the weather is as forecast."

"I can come and pick Paula up," Rowena said.

"I could always get Tom to spray while I come in. He's only working on some fencing." Dan moved to the other side of the bed and took Paula's hand.

She smiled hopefully. She would have preferred Dan to collect her.

"Nonsense. I'll do it. I have to do some shopping anyway. I'll make you a meal so your tea will be organised and Dan will be home early, won't you." Rowena fixed him with one of her stares.

"Yes, of course."

"How did the party go, Rowena?" Paula changed the subject.

"Very well. It was a quiet affair really. Only about fifty people and it was catered, so not too much work."

"Whose birthday was it, did you say?" Paula hoped Dan would take an interest.

"One of my city friends." Rowena's reply was evasive. "No one you've met."

"Is there anything you'll need Rowena to bring in?" Dan asked.

Paula sighed. He was still thinking about tomorrow and hadn't taken any notice of the party conversation. "Perhaps something for me to wear home. Otherwise I'll have to go home in this dressing-gown, just like I came in."

"We mustn't tire you." Rowena stood. "Get a good night's sleep and I'll see you tomorrow. I'll ring first and check what time. Come on, Dan. I need an early night myself."

She sailed off out the door. Dan bent down to kiss Paula.

She threw her arms around his neck. "I miss you," she whispered.

He kissed her and smiled. "See you tomorrow, Sweet Pea."

The next morning did not go as Paula had hoped. Lachlan, as the doctor had insisted she call him, wanted her to stay one more day. He wasn't convinced she had regained her appetite well enough and her oxygen levels were still fluctuating.

"We want to make sure we've hit this on the head. No point in you going home and ending up back here again. We'll do blood tests then see how you are tomorrow."

Paula was disappointed. She rang Dan's mobile but got his message bank, so she rang Rowena who agreed with the doctor — of course — and said she'd drop off Paula's clothes when she came in to do the shopping.

"An extra day will give me a chance to do a bit of housework for you."

"There's no need." Paula had tried to deflect her but Rowena had insisted on tidying up before Paula went home.

* * *

Dan was disappointed when he eventually got the message that Paula wasn't coming home that day. Tracking in to the hospital every night was wearing after a long day and conversations always felt disjointed and unnatural. He still felt guilty about not being there when she needed him and he missed her. He wanted Paula to be home.

He'd had a long conversation with Diane the night before. He'd just arrived home from visiting Paula when the phone had rung. Diane had been very concerned that Paula needed better medical attention and wanted her to fly to Sydney. He had managed to reassure his mother-in-law that Paula was in good hands and making a steady recovery.

Diane had gone on about Paula getting sick too easily and not taking care of herself properly. She'd hinted at a previous illness that had taken a while to shake but she didn't elaborate and Dan had the impression that Diane blamed the illness on Paula's lifestyle at the time. Perhaps the woman was insinuating that he wasn't looking after Paula properly. It was hard to tell. Paula's mother asked more questions than Dan had the chance to answer. He had placated her by saying Paula would be home today and now he would have to explain that she had to stay longer in hospital.

By the time he got home, it was late and he was tired. He'd had a few problems with the tractor, which had held him up, and now he'd have to go back and finish the job tomorrow.

Tarzan came jumping at his feet as he had every time Dan had returned home since Paula had been away. Dan had been shutting him out of the house during the day and letting him into the laundry to sleep at night. Once he had finished spraying, he'd try to get time to fix up the house yard so Tarzan couldn't escape. The silly mutt liked to roam and several times it had run at vehicle wheels.

Dan headed inside then remembered the drums he had in the back of the dual cab. They would have to be unloaded in the shed before he drove into the hospital. He looked at his watch then jumped back in the car. If he did it now he could have a shower and enjoy the meal Rowena had left for him before he drove in to town.

He heard the bark turn to a sickening yelp as the dual cab moved forward.

"Bloody hell."

Dan jumped out of the car and ran around to the other side. The little dog lay on the ground beside the back tyre. Tarzan's eyes were wide with pain. He tried to stand but his leg wouldn't hold him.

Dan knelt down beside him. "You bloody stupid mutt," he murmured.

There was no sign of blood. Dan ran his hands gently over Tarzan who whimpered when his back leg was touched.

"Damn. Have you broken that leg?"

Dan shook his head at his carelessness. If only he hadn't been in such a rush he would probably have noticed the poor little bugger. He hoped there would be no other injuries.

The nearest vet was in the next town. He pulled out his mobile and rang the out-of-hours number. The vet arranged a time to meet him. Next Dan rang the hospital and asked them to let Paula know he'd be late.

With the plan in place he took an old towel from the back of the dual cab and carefully wrapped Tarzan in it. He placed him in a box on the front seat then climbed in beside him. Tarzan whimpered again. His head was the only part of his body visible. Dan could see he was quivering.

"Hang in there, little buddy." Dan placed a gentle hand on the dog's head. Tarzan settled, let out a small whine and closed his eyes.

Dan rested his head against the steering wheel. If only he'd shut the dog back in the house. He should have been more careful. What would Paula say? She loved the little mutt. How was he going to tell her he'd injured her dog?

* * *

Paula was sitting in a chair when Dan finally arrived. She looked so much better tonight. Lachlan had probably been right to make her stay in hospital one more day.

She stood up as Dan came through the door but her smile froze when she saw him.

"What's the matter?" she asked.

"I'm sorry, Sweet Pea..." he hesitated.

"What? What is it?"

"It's Tarzan. He's been injured. I'm so sorry."

Paula looked at Dan and he could see the confusion on her face. "Injured? How?"

"He...I..." Dan looked at her, his distress at what he had to say making him stumble over his words. "I ran over him."

"Oh!" Paula slapped her hand to her mouth.

"He's going to be okay. He dislocated his leg but there don't appear to be any other injuries. The vet put the leg back in and she's keeping him overnight."

"I still don't understand how."

Dan wrapped her in his arms. He felt so bad. He needed Paula to understand it had been an accident. "He ran at the wheel. I didn't know he was there."

Paula pulled away. "You ran over him?"

"Yes, I thought he was in the yard —"

"But you know the fence has holes. It doesn't keep him in." Paula glared at him, her eyes wild with anger. "How could you be so careless?"

"I don't know..." Dan faltered at her fury. "It was an accident."

Paula glared at him a moment longer, the look full of recrimination, then she climbed onto her bed and lay down.

Dan pulled up the blankets. "Can I get you a drink? It's a nasty shock."

She looked away.

Dan gripped his hands together, struggling for something to say.

Finally Paula broke the silence. "You must wish you'd done a better job."

Dan could see the tears pooling in her eyes.

"What?"

She looked at him. The tears rolled down her cheeks but her eyes were dark, icy. "Killed him," she said. "It would have saved the vet fees."

He shook his head. "You can't mean that, Paula. It was an accident."

"I'm sure it was. I don't think you did it deliberately, but you never liked Tarzan. He's always been a nuisance to you."

He knew this wasn't his rational Paula speaking. She was hurting. He wanted to hug her and tell her how sorry he was but her look warned him not to.

She turned away from him again. He stayed by her bed not knowing what to say. The pain of her reaction stabbed him like a knife. She was wrong. He did like Tarzan. The little dog had been a nuisance at times but he was a loveable mutt and Dan had become quite fond of him. He wanted Paula to know he shared her distress.

Silence stretched out around them. Dan made a couple more faltering attempts at small talk but Paula didn't respond. Eventually, he stood up.

"I'll go home. I'll ring in the morning to find out what time to pick you up." He bent to kiss her but she didn't respond. "Good night, Sweet Pea." He hovered a moment and once more wished he could hug her and make everything all right again. But he couldn't, so he left.

CHAPTER
26

"Darling, you still sound rather flat. Are you sure you're okay? Why don't you come home to Sydney for a while? I could look after you and you'd meet Rupert. I feel terrible being so far away, when you're sick."

"I'm not sick any more, Mum." Paula caressed Tarzan's silky ears with her fingers as he lay curled on her lap. "I've been out of hospital for over a week."

"Perhaps the doctor let you out too soon. I'm not sure those country doctors are up with the latest treatments."

"I'm much better, Mum. Lachlan and the staff looked after me exceptionally well. It's taking me a while to get my energy back, that's all."

"I still think a holiday here would soon help with that. Dan's probably too busy to look after you properly and —"

"How's Rupert?" Paula asked, knowing that the mention of her latest grandson would deflect the topic away from Paula. She listened while her mother filled her in on Rupert's every move, then she managed to end the phone call without too much reference to her own health again.

Dan came in as she hung up. He had worked till after dark nearly every night since she'd come home. She had got into the habit of going to bed as soon as she'd cleared up after their evening meal and she was usually asleep before he followed her. They were both being very polite to each other.

"Who was that?" he asked.

"Mum."

"Is everything okay over there?"

"Fine. Evidently Rupert is smiling." Paula placed Tarzan in his basket. "Mum nagged me again about going over."

"Why don't you go?"

Dan stepped towards her but she turned away and stirred the curry she was cooking for their dinner. She could tell he wanted to hug her, but she still nursed her hurt about Tarzan and had added it to all Dan's other riddles. They all festered together like an infected wound. If she let him get close, she knew she would fall into his arms and let him distract her from the secrets he was hiding. She wasn't prepared to let him do that any more.

"I don't know if I feel up to it yet," she said. "I need a certain amount of strength to cope with my mother."

They ate their meal, between disjointed conversations. Dan had been to see Bruce, who was frustrated about not being able to resume work yet.

"I don't know how Jane puts up with him. He's like a bear with a sore head...or foot." He gave a half-hearted grin. "Perhaps we could have them over for a meal when you're feeling better."

"I am better," Paula replied. "I don't think I've got the energy for entertaining yet, that's all."

"Maybe later."

They ate the rest of their meal in silence. Dan cleared away the plates and got out some mail and papers to read, while Paula did the dishes alone. He offered to wipe but she said they could be left to drain.

When she was finished, he had his head down looking at accounts. The *Stock Journal* lay on the table beside him, the headline story outlining the effects of low rainfall around the state.

She watched Dan for a moment. Even from the side, she could see his face was set in the serious mask he often wore these days. He shuffled the accounts into a pile, the notebook where he recorded the rainfall lying open and empty of figures.

She wished he could have shared his burdens with her but now there was an invisible wall between them. It frightened her but she didn't know how to begin to break it down, so she said goodnight instead and went to bed.

Paula didn't feel that tired but there was nothing else to do. The days were hard enough. She'd contacted Frank Williams and made a time to visit him and she'd looked at various options she could work on via the internet. Dan had helped her apply for a satellite dish to be installed so they could get better online connectivity than the phone line gave them. She'd even finished the advertising ideas she had for Dara's place and dropped them in to the shop but her heart wasn't in any of it.

She felt empty, like she had when she realised her relationship with Marco was finished. That was the thing that scared her. She had left Marco. He had continued to chase her, pledging his undying love. He was always dramatic and full on. She'd given him two weeks' notice at work and even when that was up it took him a while to realise she wasn't going back to him, no matter what he did. She'd taken a partly furnished flat instead of going home to her parents and juggled temp jobs while she looked for something permanent. It had been a low point in her life. She'd lost weight and felt miserable.

Finally she'd been getting back on track and feeling better when she'd met Dan. Now, here she was drifting away from him. Maybe the problem was her. Perhaps she wasn't capable of maintaining a long-term relationship. She'd been naive enough to believe being married would make a difference. Now she realised it only added more complications.

The phone rang but she didn't answer it. Dan would get it in the kitchen. It rang several times. She sighed. Perhaps he'd gone outside. She picked up.

"Hello?" Dan's voice echoed loudly from the kitchen extension. He must have picked up at the same time she did. She was going to hang up until she heard the voice on the other end.

"Hello, Dan." Katherine's honey tones dripped down the line.

"What do you want, Katherine?"

"Now, that's no way to greet your lover."

Paula clamped her hand over her mouth so she wouldn't make a sound but she couldn't make herself put down the phone.

"Past tense." Dan's voice was a growl. "I'm tired, Katherine. What game are you playing this time?"

"I think I've worked out a way we can tidy up our 'little mistake', as you like to call it."

"I can't give you any more money than I already have. You'll just have to take the monthly payments. That was our original agreement."

"But the other week you were ready to buy me out."

"And you backed out of the deal. I don't have the money any more. I've invested it elsewhere."

"But I've made other plans."

"So have I."

"This way the whole mess will be out of your life for good."

"It already is, Katherine."

The clunk of the phone was loud and startled Paula. Dan had hung up. She quickly replaced her handset.

She lay alone in the dark for a long time, thinking over what she'd heard. Dan had obviously tried to get rid of Katherine and her child with one large payout instead of the monthly amounts. That must have been what their meeting was about in Adelaide, but something had stopped Katherine from going through with it. Now she had changed her mind and Dan didn't have the money any more.

And what was the other investment that Paula wasn't privy to? Her head began to pound as she tried to make sense of it all. Finally, she'd worked herself up so much she felt ill. She needed to get away from the farm and Dan and think it all through. First thing tomorrow, she would make arrangements to go to Sydney. Perhaps she'd be able to sort her life out from there.

As soon as Dan left the next morning, she checked flights to Sydney on the internet. There was a seat on a flight that night. She hesitated. It was a lot of money and it didn't give her much time. She typed in her credit card details then hesitated again as her finger hovered over the 'process' button.

Dan and Tom would be gone for most of the day. She would have to leave Dan a note. It was a cowardly thing to do but he had suggested she go, and if she told him she was going he would try to help and probably want to drive her to the airport. She wanted to avoid that. She clicked the button.

Tarzan pattered into the kitchen, gazed at her a moment and then settled himself into his basket. Thankfully he was making a good recovery but he still needed to be kept quiet for a few weeks, the vet had said. How would he take to a long flight in the bottom of an aircraft?

Then there was the problem of getting to the airport. She didn't want to take her car. That would mean leaving it there. There was a bus that left from the front of the post office in the early afternoon. If she could catch that to the city she could take a taxi from there and still be at the airport in time for her flight.

It was just a matter of getting to the post office. If she drove in to town she could leave her car with Jim but he would think it strange that no one had given her a ride.

In the end it was decided for her. Rowena called in and saw her bags at the door.

"Dan said you were thinking of flying home to see the new baby. I didn't realise it was today. Is he taking you to the airport? I thought he and Tom were fencing on Harvey's place today."

"Dan is busy and it was short notice so I decided to take the bus to Adelaide." Paula felt awful but she wasn't actually lying. She just hadn't told Dan she was going.

"How were you planning to get to the bus?"

"I'll drive in and leave my car at Jim's."

Rowena noticed the dog cage at her feet. "Surely you're not taking Tarzan?"

"He needs rest and care. Dan's not around."

"He can stay with me."

"Oh…no…" Paula stammered.

"The flight could be very upsetting for him. I'll take good care of him. I'll enjoy the company. Now why don't I drive you in to town. I have some banking to do and bills to pay. I'll pick up Tarzan on my way home."

Paula hesitated. She hadn't imagined Rowena the type to have a pet.

"Dan should really have taken a bit of time off to see you to the bus."

"He's been so busy, Rowena." Paula made up her mind. She needed to make a move in case Dan turned up. "Thanks for the offer. I'll check I've got everything. Won't be a moment."

She walked through the lounge on her way to the bedroom. There was no fire. They hadn't lit it since she'd come home from hospital. Neither of them spent any time in there any more. She paused in front of the framed wedding photo on the mantelpiece. For a moment her resolve weakened. She traced Dan's smiling face with her fingertip. Then she sighed, turned her back on the photo of her wedding day and went to the bedroom for a final check.

Rowena helped her carry her bags to the car.

"You're taking a lot for a holiday."

"I didn't know what I'd need and I've got presents for the baby." Paula had never got around to posting the things she'd bought in Adelaide. That reminded her of the special night she and Dan had enjoyed there. Then she remembered the meeting she'd witnessed between Dan and Katherine and she climbed into Rowena's car, determined to leave. She needed some thinking space.

Rowena chattered most of the way into town about trivial things. It wasn't like her. Rowena rarely said things without a purpose. Paula was relieved when they pulled up across from the post office. Rowena ceased her chatter and they'd arrived safely. Cause for a double celebration.

"You are planning on coming back, aren't you?"

Rowena's question caught her off-guard. Had she seen through Paula's masquerade? "That's a strange question," Paula replied evasively.

"I need to know. You see, I've got a close friend, a male friend, in Adelaide, and he's asked me to marry him."

Paula looked at Rowena in astonishment then she forced a smile. "That's wonderful, Rowena. Have you told Dan? He hasn't said anything."

"I haven't told him because I didn't want anyone here knowing before I made up my mind. I've enjoyed having a part of my life that no one from the district knew about."

"And you're telling me, so you've decided to accept?"

"I wanted to make sure Dan was settled."

"Are you saying he's not?"

"On the contrary, I think he is but…he's not always good at opening up about what's on his mind."

"Perhaps not."

"He's very much like his father. Daniel kept things to himself too much, bottled them up. He was a wonderful man, my brother, but he was too soft. I think Dan's tougher than he was but I wouldn't like to see him hurt."

Paula looked at Rowena, unsure where the conversation was leading. Rowena looked steadily ahead. Suddenly she shifted in her seat and turned her whole body towards Paula, resolve on her face as if she'd made up her mind about something.

"Dan's mother was an Adelaide girl, very pretty," Rowena said. "She was tall, glamorous and had the most wonderful smile. Dan looks a lot like her."

Paula couldn't recollect seeing any pictures of her among the collection at Rowena's, and Dan didn't have any photos except those of him with Paula. "Why aren't there any photos?"

"Daniel got rid of them all when she died. It was his way of dealing with his loss. It nearly broke my heart to see young Dan sobbing for his mother and not even a picture to remind him of her pretty face, but Daniel wouldn't allow it."

Paula's heart ached for her husband. He would have been Andrew's age. "It seems so cruel."

"It was Daniel's way of coping with his grief. He tried to go on as if she'd never existed but of course that didn't work. When he died the doctor said his heart was diseased but I really think the old saying 'died of a broken heart' fitted him better."

Paula looked up to see if the bus was coming. "What has this got to do with you getting married, Rowena?"

"I don't want Dan to pine away, a lonely old man."

"He's not likely to do that."

"There's something that Dan doesn't know."

Paula shook her head. "Not more secrets."

Rowena looked at her quizzically. "I think you should know. Dan's mother was a city girl. She loved my brother but she couldn't settle in to farm life. We hoped having Dan would help but as he needed her less, she spent more and more time in the city with her friends. The day she was killed in the accident the car was loaded up with her things and Dan's. She was going back to the city. Thankfully, she didn't take Dan with her, we don't know why, but she dropped him off with my parents as she was leaving. She said she'd be back for him the next day but, of course, she died before she reached the city. She left Daniel a note. It was a cowardly thing to do, not telling him to his face that she was leaving him."

Paula thought guiltily of the note she had left on the kitchen dresser for Dan. But this was different. She wasn't leaving him for good. She needed some space to think things through and maybe he did too.

"I brought this...in case you changed your mind." Rowena reached around and pulled Paula's letter to Dan out of her handbag. She gave it to Paula as the bus arrived across the road.

"I'm only going home for a holiday, Rowena. I'm not running away. This letter explains that."

"Of course, and that's what I'll tell Dan...to his face. And I'll also tell him that you made a spur-of-the-moment decision to go and that you'll ring him and explain, once you've arrived safely at your parents' home." Rowena patted Paula on the hand. "Now, we had better get your bags out or you'll miss the bus."

Paula struggled with her bags and tugged at her coat. She was cross with Rowena for interfering but at the same time she was troubled by the sad story of Dan's parents.

Rowena organised a ticket from Marg in the post office. Then they stood to one side of the bus and waited in an awkward silence as the driver loaded up the luggage and assisted other passengers.

"You have a safe trip and give my regards to your parents." Rowena surprised Paula with a quick hug.

Over Rowena's shoulder Paula could see Marg watching them from the post office window. "Thanks for the ride."

"Appearance is very important you know." Rowena straightened Paula's collar. "You're right, there have been too many secrets. It's about time Dan knew the truth about the damage that lack of communication caused in his parents' lives." Rowena glanced behind her at the post office. "Some people have long memories and believe history repeats itself. I subscribe to the theory that says we can learn from the mistakes of the past."

Everyone else was on the bus and Rowena stepped back as Paula climbed the steps. "See you soon, dear," Rowena called loudly behind her.

Paula looked back at Rowena. The older woman stood at the bottom of the bus steps, her tall frame bent slightly forwards. A wisp of hair fell across her eyes. She flicked it back and leaned closer.

"I never did like those curtains, you know. Mother loved them but I thought they were ugly."

Paula stared as Rowena strode away, her shoulders back and head held high. The bus door closed and Paula had to move quickly to find a seat. She watched the now-familiar buildings of the town slip by and it wasn't till they passed Dara's shop that Paula realised Rowena hadn't given a definite answer about whether she had decided to marry her friend, or not.

★ ★ ★

Rowena stood on the road and waved cheerily at the departing bus, then got into her car and sat back in the seat, letting out a long sigh. Had she done the right thing? Matters had obviously deteriorated between Dan and Paula but Rowena had thought they would have come to their senses eventually. When she realised Paula was leaving, she had to do something. She couldn't physically stop her.

Rowena felt partly responsible for keeping the poor girl in the dark. Dan had been so stubborn, saying he didn't want Paula to be responsible for his debts, and Rowena had agreed to continue to run their finances until he had a deal sorted out with Katherine. It was not that easy, of course. Katherine was determined to keep her hands on Dan in any way possible. He should have just explained everything to Paula from the beginning, but he wouldn't listen to any words of wisdom from Rowena.

Tonight he was going to have to. She was going to cook his evening meal and he could eat it and listen to what she had to say. He might not like all the things she was going to tell him but she should have done it long ago, including letting him know about Austin.

Rowena started her car and drove to the supermarket. Roast chicken was one of Dan's favourites. That would be their meal tonight and she would dish it up with a good serve of home truth.

CHAPTER
27

"It's so lovely to have all my girls together again."

Paula looked up from the picture she was colouring with Isabelle. She was sitting on the floor of her parents' lounge leaning over the coffee table. The thick cream rug was soft beneath her and the winter sun sparkled on the distant harbour and warmed the room, as it had done every day since she'd arrived. No one looked anxiously out at the sky for rain here. Her mother was smiling at her.

"Susan is here with baby Rupert, and Alison with Oscar and Isabelle and now Paula home from the outback, I am so lucky."

"Mum, you do go on. Paula lives on a farm a few hours from Adelaide. You could hardly call that the outback." Susan stood up, arched her back and rearranged her clothes. She had fed Rupert then given him to her mother to burp. "Although it does seem a long way from decent shops and I bet you don't have a good restaurant handy." She groaned and rubbed her lower back. "Honestly, Alison, does your body ever go back to normal after having babies?"

Alison laughed. "Get used to the aches and pains. Trust me, nothing will ever be the same again."

Susan groaned again then gently ran her fingers over Rupert's dark head of hair.

"It doesn't matter, does it, darling?" Diane cooed at Rupert whose little rose pink cheeks were plump from his feed. He lay contentedly in her arms gazing up at her. She looked around at them all. "You're all worth it, even when you've grown up."

"Now, come on Paula, spill the beans about life in the country." Susan sat on the other side of Isabelle and picked up a pencil. "We hardly hear from you, so you must be busy. What can you possibly get up to all day long? All that fresh air and a gorgeous man must be good for your sex life."

"Susan, the children." Diane rebuked.

Alison laughed. "I don't think they'll be corrupted, Mum. Come on, baby sister, tell us what you get up to all day. It must be so different to the life you had here."

Paula looked up from her paper, unsure how to explain her life to her perfect sisters whose days were so well organised. "I don't know, the days fly by. I've done some redecorating, I've picked up some freelance accounting and I've kept up the work on the garden Mum started. Sometimes I help Dan, there are animals to feed, machines to shift, a trip into town can take half a day. Some nights I look back and don't know what I've accomplished."

Alison looked at her closely then smirked at Susan. "Sounds a bit like having children. The time just disappears."

"Tell me about it. The other day I waved Jerry off in my dressing-gown, Rupert started crying, the phone rang, the washing machine was full, the place was in a mess and before I knew it Jerry was home again and I was still in my dressing-gown. I have no idea where the day went."

"The toughest fall the hardest," Alison said.

"What's that supposed to mean?" Susan looked up at her sister.

"Where are the nappies, Susan? This baby needs changing." Diane was undoing Rupert's all-in-one. "Are you sure you've got enough clothes on him?"

Paula watched her mother and sister haggle over how many layers the baby needed but her thoughts were back on the farm. She wondered what Dan was doing now. Did he miss her? He hadn't rung. Perhaps he was angry with her for leaving without telling him.

She'd wanted space to think and she'd certainly had time to do that. The bus trip had taken two hours, then the wait at the airport and the late evening flight to Sydney had allowed her plenty of time to go over the events that had conspired to hasten her departure.

She tried to ring Dan once she arrived at her parents' home, but there had been no answer and she was relieved when his mobile transferred to message bank. She'd been able to let him know she'd arrived safely without having to speak to him. He hadn't rung her back.

She'd done little in the days she'd been in Sydney except sleep and spend time with her mother and sisters. The infection had left her feeling listless and lacking appetite. Her mother had made all kinds of tempting morsels for her but she could only eat small amounts.

Susan and Diane had planned a festive meal for the next evening. It was the first chance all the men had to join them and it was a double celebration, a welcome meal for Paula and a wedding anniversary for her parents.

Paula had hardly seen her father since she'd come home. He had picked her up from the airport but work kept him away for long hours each day. She was glad. Diane chattered and fussed over Paula and worried about her health but didn't ask too many questions about Dan, other than who was going to feed him if Paula wasn't there. Paula knew her father would want more detail. She didn't want him asking questions that she didn't know the answers to.

★ ★ ★

A night later the whole family was relaxing in the Crawford's lounge after enjoying the delights of Susan and Jerry's culinary skills. Diane hadn't been happy for anyone else to be in her kitchen but they'd given her the job of minding Rupert while they cooked.

"Come on, Paula, have you gone teetotal? What happened to the party girl?" Susan waved a bottle of wine in Paula's direction.

"I don't seem to have the stomach for it since I had the flu."

"Leave the poor girl alone, Susan." Jerry wrapped his arms around his wife. "Nursing mothers aren't supposed to drink either, are they?"

"I've only had one glass."

"Small amounts are good for milk production, aren't they, Mum?" Alison said.

"Isn't that an old wives tale?" Jerry asked. "From what I've read —"

"Oh here we go." Susan groaned. "Jerry's an expert on everything. He's read every book on child rearing that was ever written."

"Not quite."

"I had a glass of sherry every night when you girls were little." Diane cut across their teasing.

"That explains it." Jerry laughed. "The three of them have been pickled since birth."

"Charming." Susan's tone was indignant but she had a smile on her face.

Jerry reached around and kissed her tenderly on the cheek. "Do what you like, my darling. You are a wonderful mother."

"Please, Jerry," Alison scoffed. "Susan gets in a flap if Rupert poops out of routine. I think it's a bit early to bestow the royal order of motherhood on her just yet."

"Where's that wine, Susan?" Julian asked. "I'm not breastfeeding and I think it's Alison's turn to drive home."

Alison smiled at her husband. "I did rather overdo it last week-end at the Carsons' party."

"Never mind, honey, you created some wonderful dance moves."

"Ali! Go girl!" Susan enthused.

"Where's the port, Diane? I don't know if I can put up with any more of this prattle." Their father grumbled, but with good humour. "We've been married all these years and produced this disorderly bunch. Please don't tell me you were dancing on tables, Alison."

Diane looked horrified and everyone else laughed, except Paula.

She had been enjoying the evening but suddenly she felt very alone. Watching her sisters and their husbands joking and enjoying each other's company opened up the ache she had been hiding since she'd left the farm. Her mobile rang. Her heart gave an extra thump at the sight of Dan's name on the screen. She stepped out into the passage to answer.

"Hello, Dan."

"How are you?"

"I'm okay, still tired, but okay."

"I've been getting in late and I didn't like to ring then...I've missed you."

Paula's heart ached for him but she couldn't bring herself to say so. "I wanted to catch up with my family. You said I should come."

"I know. It was just a surprise when you went so suddenly."

Paula hesitated and loud laughter echoed from the lounge room.

"Sounds like a party."

"Only the family. It's Mum and Dad's wedding anniversary."

"I'd better let you go then. I just wondered how you were."

There was a pause. Paula could picture Dan with the phone pressed to his ear, perhaps at the kitchen table where he often sat to make calls.

"How long do you think you'll stay?" he asked.

"I don't know. It's been good to see Susan and Ali and the children. Now that I'm here, it seems silly to rush back."

"You're right." Dan paused again. "Still no rain here. Are you getting any over there?"

"No." The sound of loud voices and clinking glasses carried from the lounge and Rupert began to cry from the bedroom. "I'd better go."

"Let me know when you decide to come home."

"Yes…look I'd better go."

"Paula, we do need to talk eventually."

Paula's heart thumped. She didn't know if she wanted to hear what he had to say any more.

"Not now, Dan. They're waiting for me."

"I'll ring again soon. It is important."

"Yes, bye."

Paula stared at the screen a moment then slowly slipped the phone into her pocket.

"Was that Dan?" Diane was standing behind her with a tray of dirty glasses.

"Yes."

"How is he?"

"Fine." Paula averted her eyes under her mother's gaze.

"I love having you here but it's selfish of me. You must be missing each other." Diane tipped her head to one side and frowned. "Is everything all right?"

"Fine, Mum. Here, let me help you with that." Paula took the tray from her mother and followed her into the kitchen where they stacked the dishwasher together and began making coffee.

"I don't think your health has improved since you've come home. Why don't you go to the doctor while you're here?"

"Who needs a doctor?" Rex joined them in the kitchen. "Have you got any port stashed in here, Diane? That lot have polished off my last bottle."

Diane opened the pantry door. "There's one in here. I was just saying Paula is still looking pale, don't you think?"

"She's had pneumonia, Diane. Anyone would look pale." He winked at Paula while Diane stuck her head in the pantry. "You need something to do. You probably haven't given your brain a decent workout since you moved to South Australia."

"I have been doing freelance work, Dad."

"I've been working on something that I think will be a pleasant surprise for you."

Paula looked anxiously at her father. Not another surprise.

Diane turned back with a bottle in her hand and passed it to her husband. "Someone gave you this for your birthday. I don't know what it's like."

"It will be fine. Are you two coming back? I can't tell you any more about my little surprise, Paula, but I'm sure you'll be happy with the result." He went back to the lounge, whistling as he walked.

Paula remembered her father's last bombshell and looked at her mother in despair.

"Don't ask me, I don't know what he's up to," she said.

"He always interferes, Mum. I can't take any more of his meddling. That financial agreement he organised back at the farm was so embarrassing. I cast a look over it the other day. He wanted us to sign a document saying neither of us would lay claim to whatever finances and investments we had as individuals before we were married. How could he treat Dan and me so badly?"

"Darling, don't get upset. He thought he was helping."

"Well, he's not. Don't make coffee for me. It's getting late and I think I'll go to bed. Say goodnight to the others for me." Paula ignored the worried look on her mother's face and strode to her room. She was on an emotional roller-coaster and she didn't know which way to roll.

She lay in bed, awake, long after she'd heard her sisters leave and her parents go to bed. She was tired but she couldn't sleep. Reflected light from outside crept around the curtains. She'd got used to the total dark of night at the farm.

Dan's phone call had reminded her that she was really only on holiday. Sooner or later, she would have to go back to the farm. She didn't know if she could face it without clearing the air between them. Dan had said they needed to talk. But when it came down to it, Paula was afraid. Afraid of what he might say and fearful of how she would deal with it. Did she love him enough or had she been in love with a fairy tale?

In the early hours of the morning she finally fell asleep.

* * *

"What are you going to do today?"

Diane was fussing around in the kitchen while Paula picked at a late breakfast. After a restless night Paula had slept in and now she felt washed out.

"I don't know. Perhaps I'll go for a walk down to the bay." The Crawford house was only a few blocks away from the beach but Paula hadn't been there since she'd come home.

"I'll be out most of the day. I've got a hair appointment then a card afternoon at Marcia Hann's. I'm sure we could fit another one in, if you wanted to come."

"No thanks, Mum. I'll be fine." Paula forced a smile. "How about I cook dinner?"

"That'd be lovely, darling. There's all sorts in the fridge. Sorry to leave you."

"Don't worry about me, I'll be fine. You have a good day."

Paula waved her mother off and the phone rang in the hall behind her.

"Hello."

"Paula?" Dara's voice floated over the airwaves. "I'm glad I've got you. I've been trying your mobile number with no luck. Rowena gave me your parents' number as well."

Paula glanced around. "My phone's in the bedroom. I didn't hear it. How are you?"

"Wonderful. I wanted to let you know we've taken several bookings for the B & B and Chris has managed to transform the shop already and he's only been at it for a few days. We want to have an official opening but we want you to be here. Rowena wasn't sure when you were coming back and I can't reach Dan, he's never home. I hope you won't be away too long. He needs someone to make him stop and smell the roses." Dara's light laugh tinkled from the phone.

"Tell me about the shop, Dara. What's Chris done?"

"He's extended the counter into a large L shape with room for a food display case. We've rearranged the whole shop floor and set the furniture at different angles so it looks more like a home than a cafe. I can't wait for you to see it. When will you be back so we can organise the party?"

"I'm not sure, I'm only just starting to feel better." Paula picked up a pen and twiddled it in her fingers.

"Oh, you poor thing. That flu has knocked lots of people for six already this winter."

"Have you planned a menu?"

"Yes, but I'll need to buy crockery, glassware and cutlery. Most of my customers have taken their food away in the past. I'm not stocked for dining in."

"I'm sure I included that in the initial set-up costs."

"You did, but I haven't had a chance to get to the city and there's still so much to do here."

Paula thought of the contacts she had in Sydney. "Would you like me to look for you? I could send you some pictures and prices."

"Would you? Paula, that would be great. You know the kind of thing that would suit. And you know my budget." Once again Dara's laugh tinkled in Paula's ear.

"I'd love to. Give me a couple of days and I'll get back to you."

"I'd better go."

"Bye, Dara." Paula felt better than she had for weeks. Maybe her father was right; she did need something to exercise her brain. She picked up the pad from the side table and began to write.

★ ★ ★

By the end of the week her initial excitement at helping Dara had faded. She'd visited a couple of places she knew stocked the kind of equipment Dara needed but she couldn't shake the bouts of queasiness and lethargy that would sweep over her.

She'd tried to deny it but she was beginning to feel the same way she had after her breakup with Marco. She wasn't sleeping well and she had no appetite. Her nightly phone conversations with Dan were brief and unsatisfying and only left her feeling more miserable. Paula was desperate not to sink as low as she had in the past. She decided to take her mother's advice and visit the doctor.

Dr Belinda Markham had been their family doctor for as long as Paula could remember. She had a light and airy office a few streets away in an old house. The consulting room was more like a small living room with comfortable chairs and paintings on the wall instead of medical posters. The examination room was separate, through another door. Paula always felt it was like visiting her at home.

It was Belinda who had helped her through the dark days after Marco. Another doctor would have given her a script for antidepressants and sent her home but not Belinda. She preferred to try more natural approaches first and the meditation and relaxation techniques along with exercise had certainly worked for Paula back then.

Belinda welcomed Paula and listened carefully to her. She was well into her sixties and a few extra lines etched her face but her sharp gaze missed nothing. When Paula had finished she sat back in the soft leather chair and felt as if a weight had lifted from her shoulders.

Belinda studied her over the top of her purple-framed reading glasses for a moment before she spoke.

"I haven't met your husband but from what you've told me, he's not like Marco. You went through a tough time back then and I can understand your fear that this relationship may fail, but it's not the same. By the sound of it, Dan's communication skills could do with some improvement. In a strong relationship, that's usually a two-way street." Belinda took her glasses off and looked searchingly at Paula. "There isn't a pill I can give you for that."

Paula shifted in her seat but remained silent. Belinda picked up her glasses, replaced them on her nose and glanced at the computer screen where she'd entered some notes. "I'm more concerned with your physical symptoms. You've been unwell on and off for over a month now. I want to examine you and do some tests and we'll see what that reveals."

Paula followed Belinda into the examination room. She was sure there was nothing wrong with her body. The flu and pneumonia had long gone. Belinda was barking up the wrong tree this time.

CHAPTER

28

Paula's mobile rang for a long time. Dan waited anxiously listening to the tone echoing down the line and prayed that she would answer. He didn't want to use her parents' landline and run the risk of talking to anyone else until he had spoken to her. Then the rest of her family could tear him to shreds if they wanted. As long as he straightened things out with Paula, he didn't care.

She had been gone over two weeks. It was time she came home and they sorted things out between them.

"Hello." A smooth male voice answered. "This is Paula's phone, Marco speaking."

Dan hesitated. Marco? That was the name of Paula's old boyfriend.

"Hello? You've got Paula's phone," Marco repeated.

"I'd like to speak to Paula, please."

"May I say who's calling?"

"Dan." He paused for a moment. "I'm her husband."

"Just a moment." Marco didn't miss a beat and Dan heard the crackle as he covered the mouthpiece. Why would he be with Paula? Dan hadn't imagined there would be any major obstacles preventing his wife from coming home. Once he explained everything he felt sure she would understand what a fool he'd been and forgive him. If only he'd been honest with her, right from the start.

"Are you there, Dan?" Marco's oiled tones oozed to Dan's ear.

"Yes."

"She's not available at the moment. Can I take a message?"

Dan hadn't planned what he'd do if Paula didn't answer. At this time of the day he had hoped it would only be her or Diane at home. Perhaps Paula was there but she wouldn't take his call. Another male voice murmured in the background.

"Are you still there, Dan?" Marco asked. "Rex would like to speak with you."

Dan hung up the phone.

★ ★ ★

Paula walked up the path between beautifully manicured shrubs to her parents' front door then stopped. She'd noticed her father's car was in the drive. She didn't know how she was going to cope with the bombshell Belinda had just delivered and she didn't want to face him right now.

Rex opened the door immediately as if he'd been watching for her. "Good, you're home. I've got to get back to work. Your mother's over at Susan's, some crisis or other with Rupert. There's a visitor here to see you."

"Who is it?"

"I'm running late." Rex pushed past her. "Can you tell your mother I'll be late home tonight?"

"Dad?"

He gave her a mysterious smile and a wave, got into his car and backed down the drive.

"Damn," Paula muttered under her breath. She didn't want to see anyone. Who could it be?

She walked down the hall to the lounge room. A man stood with his back to her, looking out the huge picture window taking in the view out to the harbour. Paula froze in the doorway as he turned.

"Hello, Paula darling." Marco's smooth smile changed to a look of alarm as Paula slumped against the doorframe. He rushed to her side and took her arm. "I always knew I had the power to make women faint but I thought I'd lost my touch with you."

"I'm not going to faint, Marco." Paula pulled her arm from his grip. "I was surprised. You were the last person I expected to see."

"I'm here at your father's request." Marco stood back, now with the ruthless look that Paula had learned always lurked just beneath his smile.

"Whatever my father has cooked up with you, I don't want to know about it."

"I wouldn't exactly say I'm happy about it either but your father drives a hard bargain. Let's say he made me an offer I couldn't refuse."

"I don't want anything to do with it, whatever it is."

"I think you will." The smooth smile was back. He pulled an envelope from his jacket pocket and waved it at her. "I've recently sold the apartment that we so happily shared."

"Good for you." Paula lifted her chin and glared at him. "But if you've come here to gloat on the money you cheated me out of, forget it. I've long since gotten over it...and you."

"Darling, you are tense. I must say your farmer sounded a bit that way too."

Paula frowned. "You've spoken to Dan?"

"Only briefly. Your phone was ringing and ringing so I answered it."

Paula patted her pocket then remembered she'd gone off and left it on the charger.

"He didn't leave a message. Don't tell me all is not well on the land."

"My life is of no concern to you."

"Too true, my darling. You had your chance with me and you blew it." He threw up his hands, the envelope gripped tightly. "As I tried to tell you, your father has convinced me to share my profits. Although the apartment was mine, I guess I do owe you something for services rendered." He thrust the envelope at her. "Enjoy."

Paula didn't move until his footsteps faded and the front door closed. In the silence that followed she slowly opened the envelope. She blinked and looked again at the bank cheque she held in her trembling fingers. She knew the apartment had been a good investment but had never imagined she would see any money from it, certainly not a sum that large. She slumped down into a chair and closed her eyes. Two shocks in one day, she didn't know whether to laugh or cry.

★   ★   ★

Paula heard the distant knocking on the door and in her sleepy state thought it must be her father coming home. Then she heard it again, followed by the low murmur of her father's voice and the more anxious tones of her mother. She glanced at her bedside clock. It was nearly midnight. She'd gone to bed soon after dinner and she must have fallen into a deep sleep. She hadn't heard her father come home. Who would be calling at this hour?

There was more distant murmuring of voices, then her mother was tapping on her door. "Paula, are you awake? Dan's here."

Paula sat up and snapped on the lamp. "What's happened?"

Diane peered at her from the doorway. "Nothing, he's come to see you. Didn't you know he was flying in? What a lovely surprise!"

In the harsh light of the kitchen, Dan gave Paula a brief hug and for the sake of her watching parents she let him but she remained stiff in his arms and his kiss only brushed her cheek. Rex ushered his wife back to bed and left them alone. Paula turned her back on her mother's worried glances and looked at Dan. His hair was shorter but still tousled and he had a dark shadow of stubble around his chin. Her heart thumped at the sight of him. He was wearing the navy jumper her sisters had given him. It deepened the blue of his eyes which were now watching her guardedly.

There was an awkward silence then he stepped towards her, reaching out his hand. "Paula."

She took a tiny step back and turned away towards the bench where her mother kept her kettle. "Would you like a tea or coffee?"

"Coffee, please."

Paula kept her back to him but she could sense he hadn't moved. If she let him hold her again it would be her undoing.

Seeing him standing in her parents' kitchen had been a shock and her first reaction had been to want to throw herself into his arms. She longed for his kisses and his reassurance and ached for his body. She knew clearly in her mind that she loved him.

The jolt of Marco's visit had reminded her why she had ended that relationship. The love she and Dan had was different but there were too many hidden secrets between them, and now she had another. She didn't know how Dan would cope with the news Belinda had given her today. Paula was preparing herself for the fact that she may have to face the uncertain future alone.

They sat opposite each other at the small kitchen table. The last time they had sat here had been the day before their wedding. She recalled the excitement she felt that day, the anticipation of their future together, and now it had come to this. Paula took a sip of her tea and watched Dan realign the table runner.

She broke the silence. "How's Rowena?"

"Good, she sent you her love." He shifted the runner again.

"How's Bruce getting on?"

"Doing too much too soon according to Jane but he's okay." Dan shifted the little vase of flowers that sat in the middle of the runner.

"How's everything on the farm?"

"Okay, better if we had a decent rain. We've only had a bit."

Bloody hell, thought Paula, next he'll be telling me how many points, or was it mils, there had been.

"We've only had five mils since you left —"

Dan stopped as Paula clapped a hand over her mouth.

He frowned. "Are you feeling okay?"

"Dan, I'm sure you haven't come all this way to tell me the rainfall. It's late. Why have you come?" She knew she was being harsh but she was sick of talking in circles.

He looked at her as if she'd slapped him. "Bloody hell, Paula. I've come because I love you and I want you to come home with me. We can't sort out the differences between us if we're half a continent apart." He dragged his fingers through his hair. "I don't know how to start. There are things I should have told you before we were married. They didn't seem important then and I thought I could deal with them and they wouldn't matter to our relationship but Rowena has made me realise that's not fair."

He picked up his coffee cup and put it down again without drinking from it then he moved the runner again. Paula didn't speak. He'd come this far and she didn't want to stop him. Even if the truth was hard to bear she wanted to hear it rather than continue with the versions she had conjured up.

"I'm so sorry about Tarzan."

Paula bit her lip.

"It was an accident. I wouldn't intentionally hurt any creature, Paula."

Tears welled in her eyes. This was not the topic she'd expected him to start with.

"You must think I'm a monster —"

"I don't." She cut him off. "It was a shock and I wasn't well and… with everything else, it was the last straw."

"Tom's fixed the house fence and built a kennel. I've been visiting Tarzan every day. Rowena's fussing over him and he's made a good recovery but he misses you…like me."

Paula lowered her gaze. He had such an imploring look she couldn't bear it.

"I wanted you to know…before I explain about Katherine."

Paula held her breath. So this was it. At last he was going to tell her. She exhaled and looked directly into his eyes.

"Katherine and I were what you could call an item." Dan stood up and moved around the kitchen as he continued. "We were together for about eight months. Katherine is an all-or-nothing kind of girl. We were pretty full on." He glanced at Paula apologetically before he continued. "Her father had been our family solicitor. He and his wife had been through a messy divorce when Katherine was a teenager. He was a good man but he spoiled Katherine terribly."

Paula watched Dan but she didn't speak. He sat down at the table again.

"Some land came up for sale adjoining our property. We'd had some average years but it was good cropping country and I was keen to buy it. I didn't want to borrow all the money I knew it would go for. I've seen too many people struggle with huge bank debts. Katherine's father was a shrewd investor and he offered to go halves with me. I guess he thought Katherine and I were together so it was an investment in the family future."

Dan stood up and started to roam the room again. Paula would have preferred him to sit still but she didn't want to interrupt him now that he'd come this far.

"Katherine's dad died at about the time I was coming to my senses and realising Katherine was not the one for me. She was his only child and already helping him manage their firm so naturally he left everything to her, including his share of our new property."

Dan stopped opposite Paula, the table between them. "So you see I was bound to Katherine by a piece of land. Then I met you and that was all the more reason to sever my connection with her. I finally convinced her that there was no point in her owning a half share and I arranged to buy it back from her with interest. I already had the bank loan for my share. I wanted to cut all ties."

Paula stood up and the two of them stared at each other across the table. "So it's land that you are paying her for?"

"Yes, I know I should have told you right from the start. Apart from the fact that Katherine is involved, it wasn't fair to marry you without telling you about the huge debt I have to pay off. I've even thought of selling it."

"So you and Katherine don't have a child?"

"A what?" Dan stared at her in amazement. "No bloody way. What on earth made you think we would possibly have a child?"

Paula felt silly. "I don't know. Bits and pieces I'd heard, a combination of things..." She recalled the night of the party. "Something Katherine said."

Dan frowned. "Katherine is a nice enough person but she's been very spoiled. Her mother moved interstate and they don't get on all that well. Her father's death was a terrible blow to her, and then our split. I think she had some weird idea the land might bring me back to her. She probably did think of it as our baby."

Dan walked around the table and wrapped his arms around Paula and this time she responded. What an idiot she'd been. There was no child. It was a piece of land that Dan was paying off. Who cared about owing some money? They could work that out.

"I know I should have told you all this, right from the start. Rowena said I should have. She was worried about you feeling left out of the business but she agreed it wasn't fair to make you a part of a partnership that was carrying so much debt. When we went to Adelaide that weekend I was so happy. Wool prices were looking good and I'd decided to borrow more and pay Katherine out. Once that was done I was going to explain it all to you but she pulled out at the last minute and said she didn't want the lump sum. She wanted to continue with the payments. I was so angry with her."

Paula leaned her head against his warm chest. "Dan, I wish you'd told me."

"I know I should have. But the worst thing is, I decided to use some of the money to invest in more sheep with Ted Watson. Then Katherine changed her mind again but I couldn't pay her out."

"If I'm going to be your partner, Dan, we should discuss these things. I don't know much about farming but I understand business and money. I wish you had confided in me."

"So do I. We could be home right now, in our own place by the fire."

Paula melted against him as his hands began to roam over her. "I can't believe I was so stupid as to think you had a child."

Dan stopped, his face serious. "Children aren't a necessary part of a relationship. That's a complication I reckon we don't need. Just because the locals expect it, that's not a good reason to bring children into the world. Look at Dara and Chris, they don't have children and they're perfectly happy."

Paula's newly found joy ebbed away. Not only did he not have a child with Katherine but he didn't want children at all. She dropped her hands to her sides as Dan continued to speak. His hands remained lightly on her shoulders.

"That reminds me, Dara said to thank you for the information you sent. She's ordered what she needs and she wants to know when you're coming home so she can set a date for their official opening. I've got a return flight booked tomorrow. There might still be a seat for you if we ring now."

Paula stepped away from him. "I can't come home with you, Dan."

"I can't stay longer, I've got lamb marking booked."

"You'll have to go back alone." Paula was awash with misery again. "There are still things I have to sort out."

"Can't you do them from home?"

"No." Paula had been prepared to tell him her news but now she couldn't.

"Is it something to do with this Marco character?"

"No." Paula looked at the hurt in his eyes then turned away.

"What is it, then?"

"It's just…something I have to sort out here. Look, Dan, it's late. We can talk some more tomorrow."

"My flight is an early one. We could talk on the plane if we can get you a seat."

"I can't, Dan."

"Can't or won't?"

"Please, Dan."

"Haven't we had enough secrets?"

He was right but he'd made it quite clear he didn't want children. How could she tell him the doctor had told her that morning that she was pregnant? She moved away.

"I'm sleeping badly. I'll make up a bed for you in the other room."

"Don't bother. I'll get a taxi back to the airport. My flight leaves at six o'clock if you change your mind."

Paula watched helplessly as Dan walked out the door. She sat down again at the table and put her head in her hands. She was so stupid. Why didn't she just tell him? He'd come all this way, spent money he couldn't afford, to patch up their relationship and now she couldn't bring herself to be honest with him.

The problem was she hadn't come to terms with being pregnant herself. It hadn't been on the list of possibilities she had expected Belinda to give her when she'd returned to get the results of the tests.

Paula had been incredulous. "I take the pill, for goodness sake," she'd said.

"A low-dose pill," Belinda had explained. "That bout of diarrhoea could have been enough to stop your body absorbing the pill for a few days. Follow that up with the flu and pneumonia when you also missed a few pills."

"But won't all that have affected a baby? Aren't the early stages crucial?"

"It's too early to know anything except that you are pregnant. There are tests you can have later but plenty of women have conceived in far worse circumstances and delivered perfectly healthy babies."

Paula had left the doctor's rooms in a daze. She'd walked home instead of taking the bus, only to be confronted by Marco and his unexpected cheque. On top of all that, Dan had turned up, explained the truth about him and Katherine and then told Paula he didn't want children.

Paula turned out the lights and dragged herself back to bed. She was physically exhausted and emotionally drained. Eventually, she fell asleep but not before she had convinced herself she would probably miscarry the baby in the state she was in anyway.

★ ★ ★

She didn't wake up until long after Dan's plane had left.

Her mother was waiting for her when she went out to the kitchen. "Good morning, sleepy head. Would you like some breakfast?"

"Just tea and toast, thanks." Paula sat at the little table in the kitchen where only a few hours earlier she'd sat with Dan. She remembered her initial relief at his explanation about Katherine and then her devastation when she realised he didn't want children.

"Is Dan getting up? I could cook him something."

"He's not here, Mum." Paula looked miserably at her mother. "He's gone home."

Diane wrapped her arms around Paula as she began to cry.

"I knew something was wrong," she said. "What's happened?"

She sat Paula down and between sobs Paula tried to explain to her mother about Katherine and the land deal but it turned into a stumbling outpouring of people and events; Rowena, babies, two-way radios, long lonely days. Paula knew she wasn't making any sense. Her mother kept patting her back and making soothing noises until, finally, Paula got to the part about her own pregnancy.

"Darling, that's wonderful news. Surely Dan was thrilled as well."

Paula looked at her mother through her tears. "He doesn't know."

"Oh, Paula. Why on earth not?"

"He said he doesn't want children."

"Lots of people say that but when they have their own it's a different story."

Paula shook her head and looked sadly at her mother. "We've had lots of misunderstandings but he was quite clear he didn't want children."

"Why didn't you tell me why you were so miserable, when you first came home?"

"I knew you and Dad didn't want me to marry Dan."

"Paula! That is not true."

"You kept trying to put the wedding off —"

"That was only because of the short timeline. We managed it in the end."

"And Dad has given the impression I won't cope with country life and will come running home..." Paula stopped and put her hands to her face.

Diane looked at her and for once remained silent.

"He's been proven right, hasn't he?" Paula felt sick as the realisation hit her. "That's what I've done."

"Is it? I thought you came home to rest and meet your new nephew."

Paula looked miserably at her mother.

"Look, Paula. You are young. You've had a relationship that didn't work out. It was a tough time but you moved on. Dad and I don't want to see you hurt. Sometimes he goes a bit too far trying to make things right for you girls. Usually I can get him to see sense and let you work things out for yourselves but he can be so stubborn. I didn't know he was going to set up that financial agreement while we were at the farm. I found out after he'd done it. I tried to talk him out of it but he wouldn't listen. He loves you and he thought he was helping."

"Did you know about his deal with Marco?"

"No." Her mother's brow creased in alarm. "What's he done now?"

"I guess I should thank him. Marco's paid me a share from the sale of the apartment."

"So he should."

"But he wouldn't have if Dad hadn't stepped in."

"No, I guess not." Diane picked up Paula's hand. "Look, darling, the bottom line is you and Dan obviously do love each other. Marriage is a whole life of highs and lows but if you care for and nurture each other you'll overcome the low times and have the most wonderful high times." Diane ran her finger across Paula's face, wiping a tear from each cheek and smiled. "Go home, darling. Tell Dan about the baby. At least be honest with him and give him the chance to make his own decision. This child is half his. He doesn't strike me as the type to not care about his own flesh and blood."

"I've been so sick. What if there's something wrong with the baby?"

"Paula, darling, you always were a bit of a Henny Penny, worrying about things that may never happen. Whatever will be, will be." Diane put a finger under Paula's chin. "Now come on, clean yourself up. We've got to go and tell your sisters your exciting news and then we've got some serious shopping to do before you return to the outback."

Paula's spirits lifted for the first time in weeks but she couldn't help shaking her head at her mother's retreating back. Diane still entertained strange ideas about life on the farm.

Two days later, at Adelaide airport, Rowena was waiting to meet Paula when she got off the early flight from Sydney. Paula had decided she needed Rowena's help and had rung and asked her to come to the airport.

"I'm glad to see you back."

Rowena's warm smile and quick hug made Paula feel the welcome was genuine.

"Thanks for coming, Rowena."

"I couldn't resist." Rowena took Paula's cabin bag. "Did you bring all your bags back with you or is this a farewell visit?"

"I've got another bag but whether I stay will be up to Dan. Once he's heard what I have to say."

Rowena gave Paula a worried look. "What is it with you two? I thought he'd gone to Sydney to sort everything out. He's been like a bear with a sore head since he got back. He won't talk to me and he's even being short with poor Tom, who's been missing you nearly as much as Dan, I might add. Then I get a phone call from you asking me to meet you at the airport, but not to tell anyone you're here. What is going on?"

"I've got some things I want to go over with you and explain. Is there somewhere we can go where we won't be disturbed?" Paula could feel the nausea stirring in her stomach. She glanced at the bag carousel hoping hers would be among the first. "I think I'm going to need a cup of tea and a biscuit."

Rowena raised her eyebrows but didn't ask any more questions. "We can go to Austin's. He has an apartment near here and he's at work all day. We can have the place to ourselves."

Paula wondered if Rowena had told Dan about her relationship but she didn't ask. She was too busy willing the contents of her churning stomach to stay down.

A while later they sat by the front window of Austin's well-appointed apartment, overlooking the sea at Glenelg. The furniture was modern and new, so different to Rowena's house. There was a lovely big balcony but, although the day was sunny, there was a chilly wind blowing little white caps across the water and it was too cold to sit outside.

Once she'd sipped some tea and eaten a biscuit, Paula felt better. She put the butterfly feeling down to nerves. Rowena had remained silent but now the time had come for Paula to explain. She hoped Rowena would agree to help with her plan.

*   *   *

Dan bounced the dual cab through the potholes and watched the road ahead. He'd driven back and forth between his place and Bruce's so often over the years he could probably do it with his eyes shut. Tonight his eyes were open but his mind was far away.

Bruce and Jane had invited him over for tea and while he didn't really feel like talking he was sick of eating alone. Rowena had been in Adelaide for a few days. He was going to have to get used to that. He was amazed that she'd kept this Austin bloke a secret from him. She'd always been there for Dan. He would miss her but she deserved to live her own life.

There had been no call from Paula. He was tired of telling everyone she was still holidaying in Sydney. He had thought that he could explain everything and she'd understand and come home but there was still something troubling her. He'd gone over and over their conversation and he couldn't work it out. Her initial reaction to his confession about the land with Katherine had been delight, as he had expected, but then she had pulled away again.

It was weird to think Paula had thought he and Katherine had a child. Katherine was far too selfish to contemplate having children, he felt sure about that. He'd seen her disdainful reactions to babies.

He glanced sideways at the thick scrub along this patch of road. It was good to see it was recovering so well. It had been burned out by fire only a couple of summers ago. He wondered if he could be as resilient as the bush.

He had hoped that he and Paula would have children one day but whenever babies were mentioned she'd acted like a startled rabbit and made it obvious she didn't want them. When they'd talked in Sydney he'd done his best to reassure her it didn't matter to him but still something troubled her.

Dan slumped in the seat. Sooner or later he would have to face the truth. She wasn't coming back.

A kangaroo leapt from the side of the road and bounded in front of the dual cab. Dan swerved, then overcorrected. The vehicle slid and the back wheel slammed into the dirt bank on the edge of the road. He braced himself as the dual cab rolled. It seemed like it was happening in slow motion and he almost thought it would tip back but there was a slight drop on the other side of the bank. The front wheels were over the edge and the bounce from the back gave enough momentum to flip the vehicle right over.

Things inside were flung around and Dan managed to reach down and turn the key just before one of the pieces of pipe he'd left on the floor flew up and hit him on the side of his head as it passed.

★ ★ ★

Paula went through the house turning on lights. Rowena had dropped her off a bit later than expected. The traffic leaving the city had been very heavy and a couple of sets of roadworks had slowed them up even more. Dan wasn't home, so she had time to prepare herself. She wanted to make sure he would listen to what she had to say, with no distractions.

It was wonderful to be back. In spite of all that had happened, she had grown to love Wood Dell. The apartment with Marco was just a piece of real estate. This was her home. She wasn't prepared to give it up as easily as she had the apartment and she certainly wasn't prepared to give up on Dan without one last try.

Paula looked in every room. There was wood in the basket so she lit the fire to try to bring some warmth back to the house.

In the bedroom, Dan's clothes littered the floor and their bed wasn't made. She changed the sheets and took all the clothes out to the laundry. Tarzan's sleeping basket had been tucked in a corner with his bowls and toys packed inside. She couldn't wait to collect him from Rowena's tomorrow.

Out in the sleep-out she was surprised to see three of the walls had been lined with gyprock and in the corner was a desk with a new computer. A router was lit up beside it. She wriggled the mouse. The screen came to life and she clicked on a link to the internet which in turn opened on the screen. She searched for Google Maps and it loaded. The satellite dish must have been installed. She looked around the room, which was bare of any other furniture. A coat of paint, some rugs on the floor, some artwork on the wall and maybe a couch. It would be a perfect office. She hoped she would get the chance to use it.

Paula closed the door and went back to the kitchen and checked out what was in the fridge. She had eaten a snack on the way home with Rowena but she wanted something she could turn into a meal for Dan. While she put together a pasta carbonara, she kept listening for the dual cab. Her chest was tight with anticipation. She'd done what she could, now she wanted to talk to her husband and find out what their future was to be.

The evening stretched on. Dan didn't return. Paula couldn't think where to begin to look for him. She'd gone up to the sheds and they were all shut up. He wouldn't be at Rowena's, she would have sent him home. Paula looked at the two-way radio on the fridge but she couldn't bring herself to call him on that. Perhaps he was with Bruce.

Jane was excited to hear Paula's voice on the phone. "I'm glad you're home. I've missed you, but not as much as Dan. I bet he's pleased to have you home."

"That's why I'm ringing. Dan's not here." Paula tried not to sound anxious.

"Isn't he? He left here ages ago. I thought he was going straight home but I'll check with Bruce."

Paula hung on to the phone waiting nervously for Jane's response. She felt silly having to track down her own husband but she had to admit it was worry that had driven her to ring.

"Paula?" She could hear the concern in Bruce's voice. "Dan was going home from here. Are you sure he's not up at the sheds?"

"I've checked there."

"Have you tried calling him on the two-way?"

"No."

"Jane, give Dan a call on the two-way. He could be at Rowena's."

Paula relaxed. Why didn't she think of that? He could be working in the sheds there and Rowena hadn't seen him. "That's probably where he is, thanks Bruce."

She jumped as Jane's voice echoed into the kitchen from their own two-way on the fridge.

"Freeoh calling Woodie, are you on channel, Dan?"

There was no reply.

"Hang on a minute, Paula, don't hang up yet." She heard a clunk and then Bruce's voice boomed from the two-way.

"Dan, are you on channel, mate? It's Bruce, can you hear me?"

The two-way was silent for a moment then crackled into life.

"Rowena here, Bruce." The sharp response made Paula jump. "Dan should be home. Perhaps Paula's turned off the radio again."

"I've got Paula on the phone. He's not there. We thought he might be your way."

"No. Have you tried his mobile?"

Paula sighed as Bruce picked up the phone again.

"Did you hear that, Paula?"

"Yes, that's no good. The calls go straight to message bank."

"Are you still there, Bruce?" Rowena's voice called from the two-way.

Paula's head was starting to spin. She had the phone in one hand and the two-way barking at her from the fridge.

"Paula, hang up and use the radio, then we can all hear each other."

"Croft calling, Woodie, are you on channel Dan?" Rowena's voice continued.

"Bruce here, Rowena. Dan left here three hours ago. He didn't say anything about going anywhere else. I'm going to drive between here and his place to check the road."

Paula rested her head against the fridge for support. Could Dan have had an accident?

"Paula, are you there?" Bruce's loud call startled her.

"Yes, Bruce."

"He may have had car trouble. I'll be your way in a while, okay."

"Should you be driving?"

"No problem. Now don't worry. He's probably pulled over under a bush for a nap, the big lug."

"Bring him home for me." Paula joined in the joke. She knew Bruce was trying to be reassuring but her chest was tight with fear.

"Ted here, Bruce." The sound of another male voice startled Paula. "I'll come from my way just in case he's taken the other track for some reason. I'll meet up with you on Brown's Corner."

Paula hadn't imagined she'd ever be pleased to hear Ted's voice but right now she was grateful he'd joined the search.

"Thanks, Ted," she said, emotion swelling in her chest.

"Paula, I'll be there in a minute." Rowena's support was the last straw. Tears rolled down Paula's cheeks and panic overwhelmed her.

"Paula?"

"Yes, okay Rowena." She replaced the two-way and sat on a chair, waiting for them all to arrive. Then she stood up.

"Pull yourself together, girl," she muttered to the empty room. Dan had probably gone to visit someone else or even in to town, to the pub. It wasn't as if he was expecting her to be home.

By the time Rowena bustled into the kitchen, Paula had boiled the kettle and dug out a packet of biscuits. Rowena hadn't had time to speak before Ted's voice boomed from the two-way again.

"Bruce, I've found him. He's rolled the dual cab." Rowena grabbed Paula's hand and sat her down as they both listened. "He's on the edge of that patch of scrub, my side of Brown's Corner."

"Okay, Ted. I'll be there in five minutes."

The voices crackled around Paula's kitchen as if they were in a radio drama with no connection to her. She felt numb. Dan hadn't known about the baby and now his child wouldn't know its father.

"Rowena, are you on channel?"

Rowena hurried to pick up the two-way. "Rowena here, Ted."

"Did you get all that? I think he's okay but he's out to it and lost a bit of blood so you should call an ambulance. Can you direct them? I think we'd best leave him where he is till they get here."

"Leave it with me."

Rowena snapped the two-way back, looked at Paula and marched to the phone.

Paula could feel the churning in her stomach begin to rise. She took two deep breaths and another sip of tea, determined not to give in to her weak body. Dan was alive and that was all that mattered.

★ ★ ★

Bruce and Rowena sat either side of Paula in the hospital corridor while they waited for news of Dan.

"Just as well you came home tonight, Paula. We probably wouldn't have found him till the morning."

Paula smiled faintly at Bruce. Goodness knows how Dan would have been if he hadn't been found till the next day. The ambulance officers seemed to think he'd been hit on the head but miraculously the rest of him was okay. They took him to hospital for a thorough check over. Paula had been terrified when she'd seen the blood all over Dan's head but they'd reassured her it was just a gash that might need a few stitches.

"Hard to tell in the dark but the dual cab will probably be okay." Bruce filled their silence with conversation. "A few dents and scratches like Dan but once we get it back on its wheels, it will probably be fine."

"Thanks for everything, Bruce." Paula was pleased he was there.

"I hope you're not planning any more holidays for a while. He's been miserable since you left. Young Tom's been bearing the brunt of it." Bruce grinned. "Dan must have been able to hear us talking on the two-way but he wasn't with it enough to respond. While we waited for the ambulance he kept calling me 'Paula' and 'Sweet Pea', the great lug."

"Here's the doctor," Rowena said.

They all stood up as Lachlan Hunter approached. Paula hung on to Bruce's arm.

"How is he?" Rowena asked.

"Very lucky, I'd say. He's got cuts and bruises and he'll probably have a headache for a few days. He's had a knock to the side of his head, which needed a few stitches. He keeps trying to get up and see you, Paula. I suspect concussion but nothing more. He probably should stay here for twenty-four hours, but I guess we'll have difficulty getting him to agree. He comes from the local stock who think they are invincible." Lachlan looked sternly at Bruce then turned back to Paula. "You can go and see him now. It might reassure him. See if you can get him to stay the night."

Paula started forward then stopped, turned back to Bruce and hugged him. "Thank you." Then she shook Lachlan's hand. "And you."

"Between the Woodcrofts and the Freemans you've been keeping me in business." Lachlan gave a wry grin. "I wouldn't mind some time off for a few days so try to stay out of trouble." With a wave of his hand he set off down the corridor.

"I'd better get going too," Bruce said. "Jane will want to know he's okay. Tell Dan I'll see him at home."

"Yes, thanks for all you've done, Bruce," Rowena said. "You head off home. I'll wait and drive Paula." She turned to Paula. "You go in and see him first."

Dan's eyes were shut but they flew open as soon as Paula put her hand in his. He tried to sit up and Paula saw the pain flash across his face.

"Lay still, Dan." She looked around, worried the nurse who was checking the monitor attached to Dan's arm would send her away. "Lachlan says you've got to rest."

Dan looked at her. His lips twisted in a grimace. "It really is you, Sweet Pea."

"Yes, it's me." She bent down and kissed his forehead beside the plaster covering the gash that had required several stitches. A deep bruise darkened his cheek and dried blood congealed in his hair.

"I heard your voice on the two-way but I thought I must have been dreaming."

"I'm here, Dan." She patted his hand.

"To stay?"

"You shouldn't be talking now. Lachlan said you need to rest. You've had a nasty bang on the head."

"I've got a bit of a fuzzy head, that's all. I don't want to wake up and find out you've gone again."

"We'll talk about it tomorrow."

Dan looked at her in resignation. "You're not going back to Sydney?"

"I'll stay till you come home, then we'll talk." Paula watched as he closed his eyes. After a while his hand relaxed in hers.

Rowena came in and stood beside her. "Blasted fool," she said softly. "He was probably not driving carefully. Come on, we'd better get home."

Paula followed her out the door with a last look back at Dan. Like Paula, Rowena would have been terrified of losing the man who was her only family. She just had a funny way of showing it.

* * *

The next morning, Paula was preparing to go back to the hospital after sleeping late but she wasn't moving very fast. She heard a vehicle. She thought it was probably only Rowena so she didn't get up from the table where she'd been sipping a cup of tea.

They had both spoken very little on the way home last night but Rowena had promised to call back this morning with Tarzan.

Heavy footsteps thudded down the passage. Paula got to her feet. The kitchen door pushed open.

"Dan!"

He crossed the room in three strides and wrapped her in his arms.

"How did you get here?" she mumbled into his neck. It was soft and warm and smelled like antiseptic.

"Tom called in and I asked him to drive me. I was frightened I'd dreamed you were here."

"I'm here." She placed her hands on his shoulders and gently pushed him away. This was it. No more excuses. She was going to have to lay her cards on the table and see what his reaction would be. "Dan, I've got something to tell you."

He looked at her, his face set in the serious mask she had learned to expect. "And I'm not going to like it?"

"Please, Dan. Let me explain and then you can talk."

"Croft, calling Woodie. Are you there, Paula?" Rowena's voice barked into the room. Dan turned, walked across to the two-way and turned it off.

Paula sat back at the table. She took a sip of tea. The churning in her stomach was partly nerves, she knew, but it didn't stop the queasy feeling. She watched as Dan crossed back to where she sat. In the daylight she could see the bruising had extended down the side of his face and his hair was still crusted with dried blood. His eyes were bloodshot and the stubble on his jaw gave him a grey appearance. All in all he didn't look good.

"Please sit down," she said.

He sat opposite her, still watching her closely.

The phone began to ring. She glanced towards the dresser where it sat.

"Ignore it."

Paula took another sip of tea and then placed the cup in front of her and fiddled with the handle. The phone stopped and there was a moment of total silence.

She took a deep breath and broke it. "Dan, I know you don't want children —"

"I —" He cut in but she put her hand up to stop him.

"Dan, please. When I've finished, you can have your say." She had to get this out without him interrupting. Once she'd done that, he could make up his own mind. "I know we've never really discussed it properly and children are not something I'd thought would be a part of our lives just yet, but…I'm pregnant." At last she'd told him. She watched his face closely. "I know you said we can do without children but surely we can adjust. This is a shock for you. It was for me, too. I'd only just found out when you turned up in Sydney and then when you said you didn't want children, I didn't know what to do. I can't get rid of this child, Dan. It's a part of us and —"

Dan pushed his chair back with a rush that silenced her. He walked around the table and dragged another chair up beside her. He turned her round so their knees were touching and took her hands in his.

"Is it my turn?" He looked earnestly into her eyes.

She nodded.

"I thought you hated the idea of having children."

"Why?"

"Every time babies are mentioned you've bolted like a startled rabbit. The night of the party you made it quite clear you didn't want children and several times since then. I only said that stuff in Sydney to reassure you that I wouldn't pressure you to have children."

"So, you don't mind?" She looked at him carefully, watching for signs of pretence.

He leaned close to her, his face only a hand's length away from hers. "It's our baby, Sweet Pea. It's wonderful news. Is this the thing that you couldn't tell me in Sydney?"

"There's something else."

Dan watched her warily. "It's twins."

"No." Paula gave a nervous smile then tried to be serious again. She wasn't sure how he'd take the next bit. "While I was away, I came into a large sum of money that I've decided to invest."

Dan continued to watch her closely but he didn't speak.

"I asked Rowena to help me as she is a partner in the farm." Paula paused and took a sip of her tea as her stomach threatened to rebel again. Once it settled she went on. "I now own Katherine's share of Harvey's place."

"You what?" Dan looked at her in amazement. "How did you do that?"

"Rowena's very convincing. She helped Katherine to see that I was here to stay and a baby only cemented that. I bought the land for us. It belongs to all of us."

"Does your father know you've invested money in the land? It can be a fickle venture."

Paula straightened up. "I don't need my father's permission to spend my own money, Dan Woodcroft." She glared at him with a baleful look. "Or my husband's."

"Hey, little lady," he drawled, holding up his hands. "You won't get any arguments from me."

Paula stood, went to the dresser and retrieved the paperwork her father had left. She ripped it up. "From now on, we have to be honest with each other."

"So, can you tell me where this large sum of money came from? I'm not married to a bank robber, am I?"

Paula grinned and went back to the table . "No. I was owed some money from an investment I had with a previous..." She searched for the right word. "Partner."

"Marco?"

"Yes. Somehow, Dad managed to get him to give me my share from the sale of our apartment. Dad and Rowena have a bit in common when it comes to being persuasive."

Dan shook his head. "I can't believe I nearly lost you, over a few misunderstandings."

"Between us, we haven't done very well at communicating, have we?"

Dan grinned. "I don't know. We've obviously managed to communicate at some stage." His eyes twinkled and the dishevelled state of his head gave him a rakish look. He leaned forward and kissed her. His warm lips melted against hers

Tingles ran through her as Paula relaxed into his embrace. At last, there were no more secrets. She closed her eyes as his lips moved down her neck and then to her ear. How she'd missed his kisses, his touch, his —

"I hope it rains lots," he whispered.

She pulled away and studied him carefully. Perhaps the bang on the head was still affecting him.

Dan grinned and scooped her into his arms. "I think we're going to need it. I plan to be using that bath an awful lot."

Paula relaxed and smiled into those clear blue eyes. "Trust you to bring rain into the conversation, farm boy."

Dan leaned towards her as she caught a movement over his shoulder and screamed.

"Paula, what...?"

"Why do you keep doing that?" a voice grumbled.

Dan spun around with Paula still in his arms. "Uncle Gerald, you really should knock." He lowered Paula to the ground.

"I did knock." Uncle Gerald walked past them both and sat at the kitchen table. "It's looking a bit stormy out there. Any chance of a cuppa?"

"You've got some weird relatives," Paula hissed in Dan's ear.

"Uncle Gerald isn't really my uncle." Dan smiled at the old man. "He did a lot of work for my grandfather back in the day. He visits me regularly at the sheds." Dan lowered his voice. "Rowena didn't let him in the house very often. Once he'd heard we'd moved in here, I think he was keen to check the place out." He looked back at the old man. "Isn't that right, Uncle Gerald?"

"What's that, lad?"

Dan raised his voice. "You're just making sure Paula and I are looking after the place okay."

"Is that her name, Paula? I thought it was Orla."

There was a knock at the back door. Dan went to investigate while Paula put the kettle on.

"Tom's popped back, in case we need anything." Dan returned with Tom following.

Paula looked up from filling the kettle and Tom gave her his shy, crooked smile. She realised she'd missed him too.

"Hello, Tom."

"G'day, Paula." He shifted nervously from foot to foot. "Welcome home."

Paula put her arm through Dan's. Now that she had him back, she was determined to keep him close.

"Paula?" The back door banged. "Are you there?"

"Bloody hell," Dan muttered.

Rowena burst through the kitchen door carrying Tarzan then stopped when she saw Dan. "What are you doing out of hospital?"

"I didn't need to stay there. Tom gave me a ride home."

Rowena flicked a piece of hair from her eyes and looked at Paula. "I tried to call you on the two-way and the phone. I was worried when there was no answer." She put the squirming dog on the ground and he ran straight to Paula.

"Hello." Paula giggled as his tongue licked her cheek and he slid his nose down her neck.

Rowena turned her attention to the old man at the table. "You're up and about early, Uncle Gerald."

"Thought I might get a cup of tea here, at least," he muttered.

Rowena raised her eyebrows then looked back at Paula and Dan. "I hope you two have had a chance to talk...alone." She emphasised the last word.

"Yes." He brushed his lips over Paula's cheek. "Things are sorted."

She took in his ragged appearance and remembered how close they had been to losing each other.

"All sorted," she murmured back.

"No wonder you didn't hear the two-way, Paula," Rowena announced. "You've turned it off again. You really should leave it on, you know." She reached up and snapped the radio back on.

Dan winked at Paula.

"Did you put that kettle on, Orla?" Uncle Gerald asked. "It's taking a long time."

"Have you had much rain in town, Uncle Gerald?" Tom sat next to the old man who launched into a description of the latest weather report.

"Well, if the kettle's on, we may as well all have a cuppa." Rowena opened the pantry door. "I put some biscuits in here the other day. Have you eaten them yet, Dan?"

"Anyone home?" Bruce's voice called.

"Come in," Dan called then he bent closer to Paula. "Did we send out invitations?"

Bruce and Jane came into the already busy kitchen with the two boys.

"It's good to see your ugly mug up and about." Bruce clapped a hand on Dan's shoulder.

"Are you all right, Dan?" Jane asked. "I suppose you checked yourself out of the hospital."

"Hello." Rowena came out of the pantry with several packets of biscuits.

Andrew, who was wearing a Superman t-shirt today, tipped his bag of trucks onto the wooden floor with a clatter and Uncle Gerald remarked loudly about the lack of cups of tea.

Voices and noise filled the kitchen. Paula and Rowena filled cups and passed them around. No one noticed the grey day outside, until Paula called out.

"Listen."

Everyone stopped what they were doing, then they all heard it. Rain was falling on the tin roof. They watched out the window in silence for a moment and the rain fell more heavily.

"I told you there was a chance —"

"Of stormy weather," they all chorused with Uncle Gerald and then the room was filled with laughter and chattering voices.

Dan edged up beside Paula and put his arm around her. "So, little lady," he drawled. "Still think you can cope with life on the farm?"

Paula listened a moment to the heavy drum of the rain on the roof and the chatter of happy voices in their kitchen. Her stomach churned, once more reminding her of the baby they'd created. She grinned.

"Bring it on, farm boy."

ACKNOWLEDGEMENTS

The original version of this story was self-published back in 2004 when it had the title *Changing Channels* and the tag line 'From the city to the country – a rural romance.' It developed with the support of my then writing tutor, Marg McAllister, and the encouragement of the wonderful cyber CB writing group she began.

I am indebted to my first beta readers, Kathy Snodgrass, Mem Westbrook, Sue Barlow and Sue Hazel, and to my daughter Kelly who urged me to write 'her kind of book'.

My mother, Pat, was a wonderful example of dedication to family, community and rural life in general. She never got to read this book but I know she would have enjoyed it and been proud for me. My admiration also goes to the many country women I've met over the years who, along with my mum, have been an inspiration for my writing.

So many times I have been asked for this story since it went out of print. Many 'city girls' marry 'farm boys' and adapt to a totally different life. I hope I've done some justice to the changes they experience. Thank you to Margie Arnold who offers this story as a manual to new farm wives.

I am most grateful to the team at Harlequin for seeing its worth and helping me to bring it to a new and much wider audience over a decade later. The subject is still relevant today but many things have changed requiring extensive rewriting. I am very excited it will now be available to many more readers.

Thank you to my publisher Jo Mackay and my editor Annabel Blay for their foresight and talent in bringing out the best in this story. As always it's wonderful to work with you. Thanks also to the keen eye of proofer Kate James. To Romina Panetta and the design team, congratulations on another beautiful cover and to the whole team at Harlequin who bring my books to life, my heartfelt thanks – you're the best.

Thanks to Dr Georgie for assistance with things veterinary and to many farmer friends for their input. Of course I have been known to shift the truth a little in the name of a good story so, as always, any mistakes are my own.

I am lucky to have the continued support of friends and my family and my husband Daryl who is my rock. Thank you all for your love and support.

Finally to readers who have found my books and enjoyed them, you are the reason I write. Thanks for your encouraging messages and I look forward to bringing you more stories.

Turn over for a sneak peek!

Come Rain
or Shine

by

TRICIA
STRINGER

Available November 2017

mira

CHAPTER

1

Paula removed the protective hand she'd placed over the imperceptible bulge of her baby and lifted the magazine higher. The two women in the seats opposite had acknowledged her with quick smiles when they came in but now they had forgotten that she was sharing the doctor's waiting room with them and their conversation had turned personal.

"What will you do in the city?" one asked the other.

"I hope I can get an office job. I'm pretty rusty but I think I'll get something."

"What about Pete?"

"He's the one I'm worried about." Her voice wavered. "He's only ever known farming."

"You've had some help from the counsellor, haven't you?"

"Yes, but Pete is so hard to read. I'm on edge watching him all the time."

"Surely you don't think he'd...harm himself? Now that you've made the decision to leave, it must be a relief."

Paula couldn't help a quick glance over the top of her magazine. Pete's wife took the tissue offered by her friend. Tears rolled down her cheeks. She had a neat, tidy appearance and could have been about forty, but it was hard to tell. Her face was taut and she looked worn out.

"Yes and no. Pete still stews over it." The woman sobbed openly now. "He thinks we've failed."

Her friend put an arm around her. "You haven't failed, Sal. But if it doesn't rain, what can you do?"

Paula pressed herself into her chair, wishing she could disappear and give the women some privacy. Only last week the front page of the city paper had shown a family leaving their farm after years of drought. The report came from another part of the state and Dan had reassured her things weren't that bad here but the women she'd just overheard must live somewhere in the local district. Then there were the Watsons, their neighbours to the east. They'd recently gone through bad times, and she'd initially assumed that was because of Ted's mismanagement, but Dan had explained it was a combination of things out of Ted's control, market fluctuations and the weather being the main offenders.

"Paula?"

She jumped and the magazine slipped from her fingers.

"Sorry, I'm running a bit late today." Dr Hunter stood at the door, smiling at her.

Paula could feel the interest of the two women turn to her. Quickly she bent to pick up her magazine, then jumped to her feet. The room spun.

"Steady up." The doctor put his arm under hers.

Paula clapped her hand over her mouth. "I'm going to be sick."

★ ★ ★

At the sound of a vehicle Rowena gripped the edges of the kitchen bench and took a deep breath. She let it out slowly, switched on the kettle and glanced back into the sunny eating area where her small round table was set for two. Her gaze focused on the letter she'd left by her plate. It was the reason she'd asked her nephew Dan to call in for lunch. How she was going to break the news to him she still wasn't sure, but the worry of it had kept her awake half the night.

She moved through the arch into the little sunroom and sat down at the table, unable to resist the urge to pick the letter up and look at it again. Just when there was so much to look forward to, the past had come back to smack her in the face.

How she wished Austin was home instead of interstate. She would have been tempted to jump in the car and drive the couple of hours to Adelaide to talk things over with him. It was all too complicated for a phone call but she would talk to him once he was back.

Austin had become her rock and her confidant over the two years since she'd met him through a mutual friend. After so many years on her own, at first she'd resisted the idea of marrying him and moving to Adelaide but now that Dan was married and had someone to support him, Rowena had given in. She loved Austin and enjoyed sharing her life with him. No doubt some would think her foolish to marry at her time of life – she was approaching fifty-seven – but she wasn't one to dwell too much on what others thought.

Dan and Paula's wedding day flicked through her mind. Even though it had been a struggle for the new bride, fresh from the city, to adapt to country life, they seemed happy. Rowena hoped Paula would cope with the looming bombshell. Perhaps a country girl would understand the situation better but Dan had made his choice.

There was a clang as the garden gate closed and footsteps crunched along the path. Rowena hurried to take the sausage rolls from the oven and put them on the table beside the sandwiches. She wanted to give Dan a decent lunch. It was another of the things she did from time to time just to make sure they were eating properly. Paula wasn't fond of cooking.

Once again Rowena picked up the letter and unfolded it. She had to be strong. This wasn't Austin's problem, it was hers and it affected Dan and Paula and their unborn child. Dan's voice reached her as a low rumble from the back door. He must have the dog with him. She looked down at the letter again and brushed away the wisp of hair that fell forward over her face. How did life become so complicated?

*   *   *

"Everything's fine, Paula, and hopefully you won't have too much more nausea."

Paula gave the doctor a sheepish smile. She'd managed to make it to the toilet before she brought up her breakfast. "I thought I was over doing that."

"Nausea can come and go throughout pregnancy. Have you had a busy morning? You probably just stood up too quickly and the dizziness set you off. Your blood pressure is fine."

Paula slipped on her shoes. Lachlan Hunter appeared to be only a few years older than her. His youthful looks made it hard to tell but she didn't care how old he was. It was his confidence that reassured her.

He'd dealt very capably with Dan's Aunt Rowena when she'd had a bad bout of flu a few months ago. Anyone who could organise Rowena against her will was a miracle worker in Paula's eyes. When Paula had been hospitalised with the same virus, Lachlan had kept a close eye on her recovery. She had also seen his handiwork with their neighbour Bruce after his accident with the auger.

Then there was his patch-up job on Dan after he rolled his car. She gave an involuntary shiver when she recalled how easily she and her friend Jane, Bruce's wife, could have become widows. There was such a variety of things for a country GP to do and Paula had full confidence in Lachlan Hunter.

He looked at the computer screen on the desk in front of him. "Dr Markham has sent your notes from Sydney and with your recent ultrasound results we can be confident your March due date is correct."

Paula couldn't resist putting her hand on her stomach. Was she imagining a slight bulge there already, even though she was only twelve weeks along? She certainly couldn't stand to have anything tight around her middle. That was something that did make her feel sick.

"I've been a bit nervous. I was still taking the pill when I conceived. I've been worried it might have affected the baby."

"There's no need to worry. We'll send you for another ultrasound at twenty weeks but you're fit and healthy. No reason to think the baby is otherwise. How are you feeling in general? Apart from this morning, you said the nausea is easing."

"I thought I would have to start the day with a cup of tea and cracker biscuits forever." She gave the doctor a wry smile. "I still feel a bit queasy at times but this morning was the first time I've been sick in a while. Both my sisters were the same but they felt fine for the rest of their pregnancies."

"Country South Australia is a long way from your family in Sydney. How are you settling in?"

"Until I met Dan I'd never given farm life a thought but I'm very happy here." She smiled. "My sisters wonder what I do all day. They can't imagine how I keep busy without shops and movies and nightlife."

"I know what you mean."

She watched the doctor tap at the keyboard and wondered if there was a Mrs Hunter. "Are you from Sydney?" she asked.

"No. English father and Chinese mother who raised me in the leafy suburbs of Adelaide – a world away from here. I only came for a brief country experience a few years ago and I'm still here."

"I guess we're not that far from the city but I find the local community provides most things I need."

"There are some gaps, unfortunately." He turned to face her. "Like where you should give birth. You can book in at the regional hospital…"

"That's a long drive." Paula recalled the weekend she and Dan had spent in a tiny cabin at Wallaston, the seaside town that was the biggest in their region. It had taken well over an hour to get there. Between Paula's bouts of nausea and Dan's dozing in front of the football on television, it wasn't what you would call the romantic getaway as described in the caravan park brochure. So much had happened since their May wedding, they had both been glad of the opportunity to relax. Paula smiled at the recollection – the weekend hadn't been all nausea and sleeping.

Lachlan handed over some papers. "Or there's a choice of hospitals in Adelaide. Quite a few mothers from here choose one of them."

That was even further away. Paula took the pamphlets without even looking at them. "But you said everything's fine. I'm quite happy for you to deliver our baby here."

"Not an option, I'm afraid. The local hospital isn't able to do obstetrics and that suits me. Babies are unpredictable and I'm on call enough as it is. One of the downsides of living here is that you have to travel to have your baby."

Paula looked down quickly as tears brimmed in her eyes. She bit her lip. Where had they come from? "But how will I know…what if…?"

"You'll have plenty of time, especially with a first baby. But if you're worried you can always stay down in Adelaide for the last few weeks so you're closer to the hospital. Have you got someone you could stay with? Miss Woodcroft will be living there by then, won't she?"

"Well, yes…but…" Paula frowned. The thought of spending any longer than a day with Dan's aunt was not one she cared to entertain. Rowena Woodcroft was a woman used to doing things her way. Paula admired many of Rowena's qualities and had even come to like the woman who was both mother and father to Dan but, even so, she could only tolerate her in small doses.

"You discuss it with Dan." Lachlan walked her to the door. "You've got a bit of time but you should book in somewhere soon."

Paula was amazed; the excitement of her healthy pregnancy overshadowed by the idea of travelling away to have the baby. She thought of Jane on the neighbouring farm with her two little boys. They were both born before Dan and Paula had married but she had assumed they had been delivered at the local hospital. She'd have to talk to Jane about it. Maybe tonight there'd be a chance over dinner.

Deciding where to have her baby was forgotten once she was inside the supermarket propelling her trolley along the aisles. It was only September, the baby wasn't due till March and right now she had a dinner party to prepare.

Dan had been suggesting they invite Ted and Heather Watson over for a meal for some time. Now that Paula was feeling better she had finally given in but only with the proviso that they could also invite Bruce and Jane and her friends from town, Dara and Chris. Glancing from her list to the shelves, Paula cursed her insistence.

She was confident at cooking light meals but her lifestyle in Sydney had meant she'd eaten out a lot. Since marrying Dan, she'd had several cooking fiascos and their entertaining had been limited to casual 'everyone bring a plate' meals or barbecues. It was easy when the blokes cooked chops and sausages and the occasional piece of chicken, while the women all brought salads.

Dan had offered to do that tonight but Paula had been determined to have a proper sit-down meal, all provided by her. The Watsons on their own had been too awkward to contemplate and she'd insisted on inviting the others, but now that she had to cook for eight, she was worried she might have stretched her capabilities.

She picked through the potatoes trying to find several the same size and her thoughts turned to Heather Watson. With four children and a full-time job she was always on the run and Paula rarely saw her, while Ted was regularly at their farm helping Dan with the sheep. The two men had become partners in a new stud ram.

Dan got on well with Ted and even though Paula often found herself cringing at his crude remarks and insensitive comments she had grown to tolerate their neighbour. She wondered yet again how someone as gentle as Heather ended up with someone as boorish as Ted.

The supermarket was busy and around every corner she ran into someone she knew. It was hardly five months since she'd married Dan and moved to this rural community, yet she felt very comfortable most of the time. It was pleasant to have people smiling and calling you by name when you shopped instead of the dash and grab she used to do, or waiting for her Woolworths online delivery to arrive.

Paula consulted her list again. It was all very well to stop and chat but she still had lots to do and making sure she had everything on her list was very important. It was too far to pop back to the shop if she left off a vital ingredient.

Her mobile phone beeped. She read the brief message from Dan. He wanted her to collect something from the stock and station agent on her way home. That would mean a detour to the other side of town and she was already on a tight schedule. It was a nuisance but after the conversation she'd overheard in the doctor's waiting room it was strangely reassuring to get his message. She sighed. If only he'd thought of it earlier, she could have called in before her appointment.

She glanced at her watch. At least the chicken breasts wouldn't take a lot of preparation but the nibbles she'd planned were a bit of a fiddle and the dessert was only half made. She sent a brief 'OK' reply, shoved her phone and her shopping list in her bag and headed for the checkout.

★   ★   ★

talk about it

Let's talk about books.

Join the conversation:

 on facebook.com/harlequinaustralia

 on Twitter @harlequinaus

www.harlequinbooks.com.au

If you love reading and want to know about our
authors and titles, then let's talk about it.